TWISTING LEGACY

P. BRUNN-PERKINS

BookLocker

Paperback ISBN: 978-1-64438-309-4
Hardcover ISBN: 978-1-64438-315-5

Published by BookLocker.com, Inc., St. Petersburg, Florida.

Printed on acid-free paper.

The characters and events in this book are fictitious. Any similarity to real persons, living or dead, is coincidental and not intended by the author.

BookLocker.com, Inc.
2019

First Edition

Library of Congress Cataloging in Publication Data
BRUNN-PERKINS, P.
Twisting Legacy by P. Brunn-Perkins
FICTION / General| FICTION / Medical| FICTION / Psychological
Library of Congress Control Number: 2018913698

Disclaimer

Dedication

For Kimberly Brunn Russ, Jennifer Brunn Boger, and Ashley Brunn Dizney.

Thank you for making my life worthwhile and meaningful.

Acknowledgments

I am thankful for Bobby Christmas's adroit editing and for the crash course in writing I received at her hands; for Dave Carew and Cindy Solomon, editors, for patiently rescuing me at the last moment; for the folks at Booklocker.com (Angela Hoy, Ali and Justin Hibberts, and cover designer extraordinaire, Todd Engel); and for the following individuals for their support and encouragement: Carol Boston, Judy Dorphly, Ann Johnson, Christine Melchinger, Lanny Scholes, Art Taylor, and Ann Brown. It takes a community to publish a book.

Naples history buffs: The author acknowledges taking liberties for literary effect when describing Naples in the 1980s.

1948
Chapter 1 – St. Joseph's Orphanage, Tampa, Florida

The windshield wipers slapped out a rhythmic counterpoint to the moaning wind and the rumbling thunder. Isabella could not make out the details of the landscape through the fogged up windows of her car. In the face of the storm, the blur of buildings, road signs, houses, and trees formed a seamless union with the pewter sky and the flat horizon.

Isabella was close to her destination after driving for six nerve-racking hours. The pounding rain made the journey tedious; the hair-raising lightning and shifting wind made it dangerous. Fatigue tugged at her body and mind. Despite wanting to rest, she resisted to concentrate on the task ahead. Her objective, planned down to the last detail, left no room for failure.

The dark day was turning toward evening. Isabella was running out of daylight and time. Leaning forward in the driver's seat, she peered through the windshield at the morass of grayness ahead and searched for familiar objects to establish her bearings. After the long drive and the months of planning, she did not want to miss the left turn to the orphanage. If her memory was correct, it was on the far side of the canal.

Isabella, a native Floridian, was not a stranger to storms. She had often witnessed the devastating power of Mother Nature when her wrath was unleashed on mere mortals. That day, desperation forced her to venture into the angry storm. From experience, Isabella knew to be prepared for surprises, since no two storms were alike. With readiness in mind, she kept an eye on the battered palms swaying and bending back and forth in the fickle wind blowing from several directions at once.

Keeping her old yellow Buick on the road in the furious gale was a struggle. She swerved around fallen coconuts, dodged tree limbs and palm fronds, and avoided flooded areas for fear of hydroplaning. She hunched over the steering wheel to see through the windshield, wishing she could see more than the road in front of her.

A streak of jagged lightning split the black cloud above, reminding her that Mother Nature's temper was as hazardous as it was awesome. Even though Isabella enjoyed an occasional storm from the safety of her home, she thought it intimidating to be out in the thick of one. She told herself to stay calm and realized, with a twinge of regret, there would be no more storms on her horizon.

Several days before, she had accepted, without sorrow or fear, the impending end of her life. For the first time, she found herself detached from her death, an odd estrangement she supposed was a blessing. Nevertheless, taking her life by her own hand was not turning out to be as easy as she expected. She did not lack the courage; she worried God might not forgive her weakness. Perspiration dotted her brow. She hoped he would be merciful in his judgment. She had endured as long as she dared. Fearful of lessening her resolve, Isabella pushed thoughts of God from her mind. She reviewed her options, concluded the path she had chosen was sensible, and recommitted to following through with her plan. If she wanted her precious cargo delivered into safe hands, she needed to do it that day. She could not change her mind in the final moments, as she had on other occasions. Her worsening melancholy, memory, and coordination were constant reminders that procrastination was risky. She was terrified and relieved, terrified an unforeseen event might derail her plan and relieved the end was in sight. She was out of time.

Isabella had plotted the route and followed the weather for weeks, waiting for bad weather to carry out her plan. A stormy day, she reasoned, would obscure her actions and keep drivers and pedestrians at home. Aware she could ill afford to attract notice, she drove cautiously to avoid an accident or a breakdown. Camouflaged by the storm, Isabella's indistinctive car pushed forward on the gray road under the gray sky toward the gray horizon. She would succeed. Failure was not an option.

Through the gloom, Isabella spotted the gates of the orphanage ahead. They were open. "Thank you, God," she whispered, as her muscles relaxed and returned to her voluntary control.

Isabella had driven by the gates many times on those days when desperation nagged at her to find a practical solution to her predicament.

Although the gates were open each time, they were variables over which she had no control. If they were closed and locked, her plan would fail. To her relief, they stood wide open and welcoming like a warm embrace.

She stopped in front of the gates to consider the significance of the moment and at the same time, glanced around to see if anyone was watching. No cars or people were in view. With no one to intercede, she could proceed as intended. She drove through the gates and picked her way along the serpentine road toward the mission-style structure barely discernible in the distance. As she drew nearer, she was able to make out the edges of the building in the dim light. Perched on the shore of the Gulf of Mexico, the orphanage looked as if it were rising from the water like a breaching whale.

Isabella focused her attention on the road, keeping to the center to avoid the sandy washouts on either side. Gusts of wind threw torrents of rain at her windshield. Even with the wipers on high, the visibility was close to zero and the going slow. She braked with a delicate touch to avoid a large washout that had pulled rivers of sand across the gravel. Through the driver's side window, she took note of the canal beside the road. As she had anticipated, its swollen waters rushed toward the outlet into the agitated Gulf. The pieces of her plan were coming together.

Isabella wanted to ask God for help. Under the circumstances, she thought it wrong. Instead, she prayed to him for the protection of her daughter, for his understanding and mercy, and the forgiveness of her sins.

"I am not abandoning you, my dearest, Avalita. I do it out of love," she whispered to her sleeping baby.

Struck by the reality that the next few minutes would be the last shared with her daughter, a gut-wrenching sorrow seized her. She had prepared for their parting, but in that instant, she understood the disparity between intense sadness and grief. Although they sprang from the same well, grief felt sharper, deeper, and more final than the sadness with which she lived each day.

As she drove, she grieved for her precious baby and herself, assaulted by the thought she would not be able to mother her child as she grew up. Who would protect little Ava from harm and soothe her fears? She longed to tuck her darling child into bed with a bedtime story, kiss her boo-boos after a fall, and teach her about love, values, and morals, but fate had other plans for Isabella.

Fate had another plan for baby Ava as well. Someone else would send her off to her first dance, attend her wedding, and babysit for the grandchildren. Isabella chocked back a sob from the depths of her soul.

Tears pooled in her eyes, spilled over, and streamed down her cheeks. She batted the wetness away with angry swipes. She was tired of crying and trying to clear her mind and sick of her detestable twisted body. As she neared the end of the driveway, she recognized with stunning clarity that her life was also close to its end. A sense of calm replaced her former anger.

She steered the Buick to one side of the sprawling mission, shut off the headlights, and parked her car out of sight. Drawing a deep breath, she reached over the seat to adjust the card pinned to her baby's chest and to tuck back into place a loosened edge of the oilcloth wrapping her baby's basket. Next, she lowered the front windows and then the rear ones, tasks she had rehearsed in her mind a million times. The wind whipped the rain into her face. She accepted the stinging discomfort as punishment for having failed her baby.

A sudden spasticity seized her arms and legs, the involuntary contractions pulling her muscles into painful knots. Isabella, rigid and immobile, waited for her brain to release the captive muscles. When the spasms abated, she sprang into action, extricating the basket and her sleeping baby from the back seat. She clutched the precious bundle to her chest and struggled with her choreic limbs to move forward, one leg at a time. Oblivious to the pummeling rain and swirling wind, she trudged to the shelter of the arched mission entrance.

The alcove by the windowless doors—twice her height and as thick as two ordinary doors put together—was deep enough to be wind free and dry. While she caught her breath, she stared at the double doors. Sturdy enough to protect the orphans and their caretakers within, they were equipped with robust wrought iron handles and studded with round-headed nails similar to those found in castle gates. Isabella regarded the doors as her baby's gates to heaven and, quite possibly, hers to hell. She shuddered.

Isabella lowered the basket to the stone floor in front of the doors. Bending down, she loosened the oilcloth from around her baby's head for ventilation and then righted herself with difficulty. As she raised a shaky hand to the massive knocker, she spotted the door chimes. She depressed the button, hoping the storm would not drown out their call.

Turning away from the doors, she almost stumbled over her own feet. The message to walk was slow in getting from her brain to her legs. She took a moment to regroup and when she regained control, gave it another try. On the second attempt, her legs cooperated. With painstaking effort, she maneuvered her body around the side of the building to stand next to the stone wall beside her car. She could not leave until someone answered her summons.

In the gathering darkness, Isabella concentrated on the massive mission doors as her slight body swayed in the strong wind and hammering rain. She groped for the rosary nestled inside her pocket, slid it between her fingers, and prayed to God for strength and the protection of her baby. She ended her prayer with, "Most of all, God, thank you for letting me share in the first six months of my precious baby's life, a blessed gift."

Despite a bout of trembling, she kept her attention riveted on the imposing doors that were hard to see in the dim light. *Will they open?* She dropped her gaze to the basket. She yearned to see the face of her sweet baby one last time. She choked back a sob, shivered, and waited, vaguely conscious of the binding heaviness of her rain-soaked clothes.

She had not worked out a backup plan if no one responded to her summons. *How could I be so stupid?* The seconds passed in slow motion, and when no one opened the door, she labored to stave off her rising panic. With pounding heart, she corralled her energy to stay upright, when she felt her knees wobble. The task required the muscles she could control to work harder than usual to make up for those that ignored her bidding.

Afraid of losing her balance, she groped for a chink in the nearby stone wall. When she located a crevice, she worked her quivering fingers between the wet, mossy stones and held on for dear life, as a sudden attack of spasticity threatened to twist her legs out from under her.

Open the door, open the door, open the door. What is taking so long?

To keep her wits together, she focused her mind on the next step in her plan. Each person's death should matter to someone, she thought. Hers would matter to no one, a stark reality which further reinforced her determination. Since she was already half-dead, keeping the other half alive was pointless.

After what seemed like an eternity to Isabella, one of the heavy doors opened. A black-robed figure emerged. Isabella watched gentle hands reach for the basket and lift its cover. Assured of her baby's safety, she uttered a sob before turning away and staggering the several steps to her still-running car. She manipulated her twisted body into position behind the wheel, gunned the engine, and drove at high speed into the turbulent canal rushing to meet the Gulf. Her last words were "Thank you, God."

1980
Chapter 2 – Pelican View and the Office of Dr. Marquis, Naples, Florida

The morning, sunny and breezy, was a typical one for Naples, Florida. Ava Skinner took no notice. She was in a hurry to dress and escape from the Gulf Shore mansion she shared with her husband Langdon before he returned from his early-morning jog. By avoiding him, she would not have to explain she was keeping an appointment with their family physician. Until Dr. Marquist identified the cause of her unusual symptoms, Ava saw no point in worrying Langdon prematurely. The less he knew, the better.

Even though she was confident something was amiss and nervous about what Dr. Marquist might say, she comforted herself with the thought that she was only thirty-two years old. How grave could it be?

She selected a jacket from a closet in her dressing room and hurried across the expansive house to the kitchen where she found Rosa, the family's housekeeper, bent over the dishwasher unloading its contents.

"Good morning, Rosa." Ava smiled at the motherly Hispanic woman whose coal-black eyes missed little.

Rosa startled. "Oh, Miss Ava, it's you." Placing the bowl she was holding on the countertop, Rosa unfolded her body to its full stature, smoothed her apron with one hand, and smiled back at Ava. "Are you ready for breakfast?"

"No, thank you, Rosa, I am meeting a friend for breakfast." *A lie*, Ava thought to herself. "On second thought, Rosa," Ava said, "your coffee cake smells delicious. I'll take a small piece with me. I'll get it. Go on with what you were doing." She cut a thin slice of cake from the end of the loaf and cradled it in a napkin. "Langdon hasn't returned from his jog yet, has he?"

"No, Miss Ava."

"When he returns, please tell him where I'm going. I don't want him to worry. I won't be away long. Thank you, Rosa. I'll see you later."

Ava scurried from the kitchen through the south gallery to the front door, thinking how lucky she was to have such a loyal, competent, and sympathetic housekeeper.

While barreling across the courtyard and looking over her shoulder for Langdon at the same time, she bumped sideways into David. "Oh goodness, David, I am sorry. I wasn't watching where I was going." She greeted the family's faithful chauffeur with a warm smile.

"No, my fault, Miss Ava, I had my head in this car accessory catalog." He flipped it closed and tucked it under his arm.

"I guess we were both distracted," Ava said. "Are you going to the house to see Langdon?"

"That I am, Miss Ava. Buck's Rolls needs a new visor." David was referring to the 1955 Rolls Royce Silver Cloud belonging to Langdon's father,

William Buckminster Skinner, or Buck, as the townsfolk called him.

Ava was aware of the pride with which David tended to the Cloud. He kept it in tiptop shape, polished to a high shine, and ready to go at a moment's notice. With the elder Skinner battling a worsening kidney disease, however, it was a rare day when the Cloud left the barn.

"Langdon is out on his jog. He should be back soon," Ava said.

David stared at her handbag. "May I drive you somewhere, Miss Ava? What with your purse and all, you look like you're going out." His tone was hopeful.

"No, thank you, David, I'll take my car. I'm not going far."

"I'll back your car out then, Miss Ava. If you want to wait, I'll bring it around." His words were flat, unenthusiastic. He fiddled with the leather brim of his hat, rubbing it with his thumb and forefinger.

David's downhearted expression made her feel bad. She had no choice; she had to take her car. By driving herself, she would eliminate the possibility of Langdon's discovering her destination through David. Hiding anything from the man she loved and respected most in the world made her feel sneaky. She told herself it was for Langdon's own good. With Buck's health already a concern, she did not want to add to Langdon's burdens.

Ava put Langdon out of her mind to return to her conversation with David. "I'll walk to the carriage barn with you," she said to him. "It's such a beautiful morning." She hoped to cheer him up and get out of sight at the same time.

Ava was fond of David, a lanky Englishman who emigrated at the age of thirty. He was devoted to Buck. When Ava first met David, she found him hard to know. He seldom expressed his thoughts or feelings unless asked, and when addressed, his responses were always diplomatic. David preferred to straddle two sides of an issue than express a preference for one. Buck, a man of strong opinions, teased David, calling him a mugwump for his dithering. In turn, David replied having no opinion was better than having the wrong one. Over the years, their relationship had lost its employee-employer flavor. David was part of the family.

On the way to the carriage barn, David, in his clipped English, let slip a lament. "What with the older folks aging and the younger generation driving themselves, it won't be long before no one requires the services of a chauffeur," he clucked.

Ava was surprised to hear David offer an opinion, something he would do only if he thought an issue important. *He is worried about his job,* Ava thought. "David, you will have employment with us for as long as you want," she said. She patted his arm and smiled.

"Thank you, Miss Ava," he replied, "One does want to be useful, though." He ran his hand over the top of his graying brush cut.

"Yes, of course, you're right. If your services become impractical in the future, perhaps we can find something else you might prefer to do."

With Buck in a declining state, Ava understood David's anxiety over his future employment. She felt thoughtless for not recognizing his concerns sooner and reminded herself to follow up later on their conversation.

David backed her car from the carriage barn and opened the car door for her. She thanked him, settled herself behind the wheel, and drove away with a little wave.

On her way to the doctor's office, Ava's thoughts returned to David. Many service workers, like David, depended on the largesse—or the extravagance, as some countered—of the wealthy for employment. Tending to the needs and delights of the rich was a considerable business in Naples.

Ava often thought about the many workers who relied on her family for employment. The jobs Enterprises provided softened to a degree the unease her wealth provoked. Nonetheless, it bothered her to think David viewed her independence as a threat to his occupation. His observation was valid, however. Each time she drove herself, she endangered his livelihood.

Marquist's office, one of several professional workplaces in a rectangular, two-story building, was in downtown Old Naples, minutes from Ava's home. In short order, she was in his waiting room trying to make herself comfortable in a fake leather barrel-backed chair flanked by an end table stacked with magazines. Since there were only two other patients in the room, she did not think she would have a long wait.

Ava hoped Dr. Marquist would have a simple explanation for her unsettling symptoms, and then she could share her concerns with Langdon. Through seven years of marriage, they had never kept secrets from each other. Even under the stress of failing to have what they wanted most in the world, a baby, their marriage remained strong and their love passionate. They were true soul mates who respected, even cherished, each other's silly quirks and foibles. She could not imagine being happier and would not change a thing.

Twenty minutes later, Ava heard her name. She looked up to see a young nurse with fading acne scars and light brown hair, fastened by a clip at the nape of her neck, beckoning to her. Ava followed the young woman into an examining room. The nurse took Ava's vital signs and asked her to step onto the scale. As the nurse slid the weight across its metal bar, she remarked how rare it was to weigh an adult as light as one hundred pounds.

When her tasks were completed, the nurse showed Ava into Marquist's office, seated her in a chair, and left the room. A few minutes later, Dr. Marquist appeared. Portly and big-boned, he reminded Ava of a giant teddy bear. He was kind and comforting with gray-blue eyes that sparkled, especially after telling one of his own jokes, and he had a talent for not making his patients feel uncomfortable when they imposed on his time. In return, few patients, if any, complained about waiting a half hour or more to see him. They knew, when their turn came, Marquist would allow them the time they needed. An attentive listener, Marquist treated each patient as important, no matter how minor his or her afflictions. As he settled himself behind his desk across from her, Ava glanced with affection at the silver strands of his graying hair. She thought him a gift to the medical profession.

After a cordial conversation, Marquist asked about her symptoms. She described them as best she could.

Ava was surprised when he did not offer her an explanation as she had expected; instead, he asked for her family's medical history, a request she had not anticipated.

"Bill, you know I am an orphan. Can't you determine the diagnosis without a family history?" she asked.

"Yes, in time, however, a medical history might give us a trail to follow. An accurate diagnosis requires a measure of detective work sometimes."

"I don't think I understand your point. How is diagnosing an illness similar to detective work? I thought symptoms, physical findings, and test results would be enough to determine a diagnosis." Her facial muscles tensed.

Marquist crossed his legs and rocked his chair backward. "Ava, I want to find out the cause of your trouble without resorting to every test in the book," he said in his calming voice. "Yes, I could order a barrage of tests, but why go through all that, unless there is no alternative?"

"I don't know if the orphanage ever had a medical record for me," Ava replied. "St. Joseph's is a convent now and no longer in operation as a home for children. If you think it would be helpful ..." She trailed off, realizing she was thinking aloud. Ava doubted the sisters had retained records from as far back as 1948, the year of her birth. In those days, many mothers, after losing husbands in the war, were unable to care for their children and surrendered them for adoption. Orphanages were overflowing.

"The late nineteen forties and early fifties were secretive times," she said, meeting the doctor's gaze. "Years ago when I asked who my parents were, I was told the sisters didn't share the records of their charges with either the residents attaining majority age or parents wanting to adopt. Even if an authority agrees to release my record, rounding it up from the depths of a cloistered convent could be difficult, never mind finding within it useful information. My record might be lost altogether, if I even have one." She heaved a sigh. "Again, are you saying you must have a family history?" She scrunched an edge of her jacket between her fingers.

Marquist leaned forward in his chair, his bright blue eyes and composed demeanor reminding her of Sophie, the fat, good-natured cat at the orphanage. "No, Ava, a family medical history is not a must. Just the same, should you find one, it could provide helpful clues," he said. "Many diseases present with similar symptoms and test results, so figuring out a diagnosis can entail ruling out three or four other possibilities. I liken it to detective work because the process is similar to the methods used by police in solving crimes."

Ava wished Marquist would tell her what was on his short list of possibilities. Knowing he was a deliberative sort who would not be bullied or cajoled into disclosing information until he was ready, she refrained from asking. To press the issue was futile. She chewed her lip, and another layer of her patience peeled away.

Ava fidgeted in her seat and addressed the doctor. "Do you think I should visit St. Joseph's to see what I can find out, even though it is no longer an orphanage?" She knew his answer before he replied.

Chapter 3 – Pelican View, Naples, Florida

Several weeks after her appointment with Dr. Marquist, Ava set off on a bright sunny day to visit the orphanage in Tampa. Her objective was to find out what she could about her family, and visit her surrogate mother, Sister Teresa Claire.

Ava turned her car toward the ornate gates that opened onto Gulf Shore Drive and negotiated the long cobblestone driveway to the halfway point. She paused there to cast a loving glance back at her home, a graceful Mediterranean-revival mansion.

As breathtaking as the colorful gardens were against the backdrop of the blue Gulf waters, nothing tickled her fancy more than the whimsical four-tiered fountain decorated with cherubs. The cascading water in which they splashed sparkled in the sun as if it were liquid silver.

Buck and his wife, Millie, built the mansion and its outbuildings over a number of years, adding additions and new structures as the need arose. The Skinners named their home Pelican View because Millie loved the silly birds and rarely missed an opportunity to watch them at feeding time.

Langdon told Ava of the many meetings between his parents and the architect, Robert Meachum, before the 1955 construction began. "In those days, Meachum came to dinner at least several times a week," he explained. "I was ten and remember being dismissed after dinner to allow

27

the adults to get down to the business of poring over architectural plans and drawings. Meachum was a funny guy, wore a bow tie and had a sharp pencil behind his ear. The way he blinked his eyes and jerked his head reminded me of a falcon."

The history of the house fascinated Ava. She prodded Langdon for more details.

"When my parents and Meachum weren't discussing courtyards, balconies, or columns, they were throwing out words like parapets, pediments, grillwork, and arches. Most of the terms were unfamiliar to me," he said.

"I bet it was exciting to watch it go up," she said, a dreamy look on her face. "You were lucky to see it happen from beginning to end."

"I guess, but we were always under construction. Mother carped that Dad would keep building until he dropped dead. She said we could expect to live in mayhem forever.

"Each holiday when I returned home from boarding school, I discovered a new building had appeared in my absence. My parents built the main house first and then the carriage barn and house, the gatekeeper's cottage, the guesthouse, and the pool house. After that, Dad added onto each end of the main house. 'A room for every purpose' was his often-stated goal."

Ava remembered every detail of their conversation. She would never forget how Langdon had pulled her into his arms and teased her with his comment. "You can imagine my childhood, a very dusty one. It's a wonder I didn't die from clogged lungs."

"Poor baby," she responded in mock sympathy and laughed. "Poor little rich boy growing up in a mansion. It must have been horrible for you." As if soothing a troubled child, she stroked his sun-streaked hair back from his face.

"More, more," Langdon demanded. "Your sympathy is most enjoyable." He peered into her dark-brown eyes. "I swear, Ava, those studious eyes of yours can see deep into my soul."

He pulled her closer. "Ava, when you're born into money, you don't think of yourself as special, because you have no frame of reference. You don't realize the difference between rich and the poor until others point at you for being lucky or hate you for having money. I was pretty much a regular kid."

"You still are," she joked, poking him in the ribs, keeping the conversation light.

"You think?"

"A kid, yes, except you're anything but regular. In fact, in those ratty-tatty jeans, you could be mistaken for a beachcomber," she replied, feigning disapproval and scooping her long, chestnut-colored hair back from her face.

"Hey, I do my best investing in these jeans, thank you," he said. "These are my lucky pants." He stood, twirled, and feigned a ballerina's pose. "When I wear them, I pretend I'm outdoors instead of shuffling papers and fielding phone calls day in and day out in my stuffy old office."

"My, my, aren't we full of self-pity?" She smiled and wagged a finger at him. "Buck is lucky to have you, and I am, too." She pecked him on the cheek.

"Yeah, poor Dad, he would prefer to run the company and do the investing himself, if he could. I shouldn't complain about having to take over. So if I'm stuck in the office, I'll just have to experience my outdoor life through our four children, or was it six?" He grinned and with a mischievous look, grabbed her in a bear hug. "Want to squeeze in a little practice?"

Ava wriggled out of his grasp. "First Langdon Buckminster Skinner, I'll have you know an expert needs no practice, and secondly—"

"I know, you don't want your perfect figure ruined," he teased, giving her a lusty look and reaching for her again.

"You are very wrong, Papa Langdon. I can't wait to spend the next decade of my life resembling a joyous elephant." She knew Langdon was joking, but her longing for a child made her heart ache.

"Great, because I will direct, mold, and harangue each child into becoming an outdoorsman. Isn't that what fathers are for? Beachcomber-surfer is a good start. We could follow with an oil rig worker, a forester, and a rancher." He raised his eyebrows at her. "Hey, maybe a kid for each business?"

"What, four he-men or women?" she retorted. "Where's my ballerina?"

That particular conversation took place years earlier. As she dawdled in the driveway gazing at Pelican View and reminiscing, she felt an urgency to dig up her memories and hold them close for fear of forgetting them.

In her seven years as Mrs. Langdon Skinner, neither the nuptial glow she carried down the aisle nor the wide-eyed wonder she felt over her good fortune had diminished in the slightest. *I am incredibly happy,* she thought. *I don't want my life to change.*

Her most cherished memories were from the days when she met Langdon for the first time and afterward during his courting. Remembering his pursuit brought a smile to her face. Langdon's courting style was assertive and confident, not at all timid or reserved, as she had expected. His idea of getting her attention was to bombard her with his, and his passion for the chase so intense she laughingly referred to him as her stalker instead of her suitor.

Ava was twenty-five, and on a concert tour that included one performance in Naples, when she met Langdon at a pre-concert dinner party arranged by her teacher, Agnes Turner, and a benefactor, Margaret Spencer, a wrinkled patron of the arts and wife of a retired industrialist. The picturesque location was the rear loggia of the Spencer's Port Royal home.

Beneath an arched portico adjacent to an extensive lanai, damask-covered tables groaned under the weight of fine china, silver, and crystal. The tables, arranged to catch the February sunset, allowed guests to dine while viewing the pink and orange ribbons of light playing off the bay. In the center of each table was a lavish arrangement of colorful blossoms whose vividness complemented the tropical atmosphere intrinsic to Naples.

Twinkling lanterns directed guests to the several fountains, and flaming torches outlined the dock where the Spencers' yacht creaked against its moorings. No detail was left to chance. The grandeur dazzled Ava.

On that memorable evening, Ava freed herself during the cocktail hour to admire the impressive view and observe the people with whom she would be dining. She strolled around the grounds, taking in the beauty of the gardens and watching the elegant guests as they smiled, chatted, and glided with ease between groups.

She was alone in the garden allée, between the fountain and the pool, when Langdon came upon her. He introduced himself and engaged her in conversation, taking her by surprise with his flirtatious manner. She remembered his startling remark: "Decorum be damned. I offer no apologies for trying to charm the most beautiful woman here."

Although she was flattered, she gave his comment little serious consideration. She attributed his loosened tongue to the frivolity of the evening and the generous quantities of champagne passed by the uniformed waiters. After a brief conversation, she excused herself to mingle with the other guests.

When the dinner bell rang, she thought it a pleasant surprise to find Langdon seated on her right. "Hello again." She smiled down at him.

He rose to help her with her chair.

"What a coincidence," she said.

He winked at her. "Not true, I switched the place cards. Sometimes one has to take matters into one's own hands."

She laughed aloud at the recollection. No doubt about it, she thought, Langdon had an audacious streak. In time, Ava came to learn Langdon eschewed the niceties of proper etiquette, silly rules, or political trends if they rang hollow. He tended to poke fun—in a polite way—at self-promoting stuffed shirts that he considered arrogant. In a courteous manner, he popped their puffed-up facades with a careful blend of flattery and criticism, leaving them to wonder if they had been complimented or insulted. The narcissists, blinded by self-importance, were so eager to bask in Langdon's praise they took no notice of his criticism, but those who knew Langdon well understood the meaning of his comments.

Langdon's no-nonsense candor was an example of the boldness he manifested from time to time. Ava suspected he developed the quality in Beaumont Texas where he went to wildcat for oil, as soon as he graduated from college. His choice was a disappointment to Buck, who was frustrated his son had declined law school to work the oil rigs.

Langdon told her he spent many sleepless nights worrying about disregarding his father's wishes. Nevertheless, he said he was eager to put his newly-earned engineering degree into practice. The chance to work in Beaumont, where his grandfather had brought in the first Skinner well, was something he had wanted to do for years.

Grandpa Skinner's tales of wildcatters and oil companies, battling over land leases and purchase rights for the privilege of drilling the earth and bringing in big gushers, fascinated him as a boy. Ava understood his longing.

"I know it sounds silly, but I felt compelled to go as if a primeval urge had beckoned me to the wilds," he told her.

By the time Langdon got to Beaumont, the city had changed. It made no difference, he said, because retracing his grandfather's footsteps had grounded him. He compared it to a pilgrimage.

"My time in Texas was like a hajj, Ava, a spiritual trek back to my roots. When I returned home, I felt centered, as if I had regained my balance."

Ava paid careful attention to each detail of his story, happy he came away from his adventure with inner peace. She understood his desire to connect with the past. At the same time, she was envious. She yearned for a past, a history of any sort. Not a day went by without her wondering who her parents were and why they gave her away.

Rebuking herself for wasting time, Ava took a last look at her beautiful home, inhaled a deep breath, and drove through the iron gates of Pelican View. "Maybe I'll discover my roots at the convent," she said aloud as if the canopy of palms swaying above could compel it to happen.

Chapter 4 - Naples to Tampa, Florida

Exasperated with herself for wasting time dwelling on the past, Ava left behind the iron gates of Pelican View for St. Joseph's in Tampa. As she turned north onto Gulf Shore Drive, she felt a premonition of dread. If she succeeded in obtaining information about her family, would her life be the same? As much as she envied Langdon his family history, she had mixed emotions when it came to unearthing her own. Content in her ignorance, she had resigned herself years before to the foundling status conferred on her at the orphanage.

None of the children with whom Ava had lived at St. Joseph's knew anything more about their relatives than she did. Most of the residents inquired, some pressing the sisters harder than others—especially during adolescence when the development of a unique identity was important. In return, each child received the same homogenized response: "You are a special child of God who is your father, and his love will never fail you."

Ava found it difficult to be content with that explanation and harder still to suppress her longing to know something, anything, of the family that relinquished her. Each time she asked the sisters for information, the answer was the same. In the end, she accepted her ancestry as a mystery never to be solved.

How odd it felt then to be returning years later to the orphanage to ask the same old question: "Do you know anything about my family?" She had prepared herself for learning there was no historical record. If she did find one, however, her primary concerns were whether or not the information within her record would be helpful or hurtful and would she be able she cope with what she discovered?

There were moments when she thought it best to leave the truth buried because she presumed Marquist suspected a legacy from the grave, a familial disorder of some type. Why else would he send her on what would otherwise be a wild goose chase? Marquist was not alone in his suspicions. She had her own.

Since Marquist's unspoken conjecture of a tainted pedigree, a heightened sensitivity had taken hold of her senses. Her visual acuity had increased; her nose was more sensitive to smells, and her skin felt more sensations than usual. For example, she was aware of the weight of her clothes. Who notices that?

She believed there was a connection between her recent propensity to reminisce and the unusual keenness of her senses, but the exact nature of the link mystified her. She wondered if her subconscious mind was searching for earthly sensations and pleasant memories to store for safekeeping. She discounted the thought as ridiculous.

Ava snapped on her directional and turned right onto Fifth Avenue, the commercial center of downtown Naples. As soon as she made the turn, she realized her mistake. Unless she had business in the center of town, she went around it to avoid traffic. Her subconscious had decided for her.

She took her time driving the length of Fifth Avenue, delighting in such commonplace occurrences as children licking ice cream cones and sticky fingers in front of the ice cream parlor and the way the sun, streaming through the royal palms that lined the street, emphasized the architectural detail of a building.

Since her arrival as a bride seven years earlier, Naples had expanded several-fold with no end in sight. Existing facades were undergoing face-lifts, and new buildings were popping up everywhere. Boutiques selling trendy and high-fashion clothing had moved in between the banks and real estate offices, infusing Fifth Avenue with a shopper-friendly verve. A scattering of sidewalk cafés offered patrons outdoor dining under colorful table umbrellas. The sight evoked comparisons to Paris or the Riviera and contributed to Naples's resort-like atmosphere.

Under the towering palms, a mélange of potted plants and flowers in a riot of hot colors—flashy oranges, brilliant reds, sultry purples, perky pinks, and saucy yellows—brightened storefronts, sidewalks, and even alleys.

Burgeoning bougainvillea, in varying shades of purple and red, sprawled across trellises, climbed stucco walls, and twined around windows and doors. The unmistakable fragrance of jasmine drifted in on the fresh sea air blowing from the Gulf several blocks away.

Ava stopped her car at the pedestrian crosswalk and glanced at the sidewalk café on the corner. In a scene reminiscent of a nineteenth-century Montmartre painting, Neapolitans pored over their morning papers while enjoying their coffee and Danish. Despite the early morning hour, Fifth Avenue was astir with tourists strolling down the street, residents off to work or school, and dog owners exchanging greetings and looking on as their pets engaged in ceremonial sniffing and tail wagging.

The happy expressions on people's faces did not surprise her. What sane person would complain about waking up to a sunny day in a flower-filled town? Ava thought Naples was paradise.

At the end of Fifth Avenue, she turned left. The Tamiami Trail would take her north to Tampa and her meeting with Sister Teresa Claire.

Ava was grateful the diocesan had approved the use of a general telephone by any of the sisters. They were still denied the right to make calls, but at least they could answer the phone. Before the revised decree, Mother Superior was the sole sister granted the privilege of making and receiving calls. With the new installation, Ava was able to speak to Sister Teresa to arrange their meeting, instead of leaving a message on Mother Superior's answering machine. Although her conversation with the Sister Teresa was brief, the happiness in the sister's voice warmed Ava's heart.

Unwilling to ruin the moment during the phone call, Ava did not mention the overriding purpose for her trip. She would explain to Sister Teresa in person.

Although she looked forward to seeing Sister Teresa, Ava hoped her visit would eliminate from her mind the oppressive feeling of impending doom that consumed her. If she found her record and it revealed a familial disorder of a mild nature, the disturbing feeling might go away. The need to involve Sister Teresa was unfortunate, Ava thought, for the sister would be distressed when she learned the reason Ava wanted her record.

Sister Teresa Claire was a novice in her mid-twenties and assigned to the youngest residents when the Mother Superior discovered Ava on the mission doorstep. From that night forward, Sister Teresa assumed the role of Ava's surrogate mother. Like a caboose following an engine, Ava toddled behind Sister Teresa as she undertook her duties, a behavior that earned Ava the nickname, Choo-choo. Her earliest memory of the sister was when she read to the younger girls at bedtime, an event that incited a race for the coveted seat beside her.

Sister Teresa was the person to whom Ava had bonded. At the age of eight, Ava was obsessed with the notion of adoption. She saw other children placed with families and worried someone might take her away from the only mother she knew. When she shared her concern, Sister Teresa said, "Ava, you don't have to fret. Most of our adoptive parents want infants. We have few requests for older children, and even fewer for those of mixed race."

As relieved as Ava was to have a permanent home at St. Joseph's with her beloved Sister Teresa, an older and wiser Ava found the designation of mixed race troubling. With her long, straight, chestnut-colored hair, medium-toned complexion, and deep brown eyes, she thought she looked like everyone else. If she was a mixed-race child, what did that mean? The subject of mixed race and its many implications confused her.

In the fifth grade, she learned the racial categories—red, white, black, yellow—were no longer valid. The updated view declared race a social myth. Folks were encouraged to use the word *ethnicity* as the correct designation. Had Sister Teresa meant to say adoptive parents did not want children of mixed ethnicity? Did that include her?

Ava thought it upsetting that some people considered mixed children less desirable than others, and she detested being described by any label with that prefix. The designation made her feel as if she were a defective product needing repair or recall.

For years, Ava bore the unfriendly, mixed-child label as a secret shame and lacking the nerve to revisit the subject with Sister Teresa, stewed in her own ignorance. As the years went by, the burden became too heavy. Gathering her courage, she approached Sister Teresa for answers.

In response to Ava's question about her ethnicity or race, Sister Teresa told her, "Ava, God sees neither race nor ethnicity. I wish others would be as generous with their love."

Ava was unsatisfied with the sister's explanation, not an explanation at all, really, just a pronouncement about God. She wanted to understand what was wrong with mixed-race or mixed-ethnicity children. When she opened her mouth to ask, Sister Teresa cut her off as if reading her mind.

"You are a beautiful young girl, Ava, as anyone can see, and you are sensible, compassionate, and talented. One cannot have everything, you know. Be grateful to God for your blessings, and remember to thank him daily. He will give you the strength you require to face each adversity."

The sister's comment sidetracked Ava's train of thought. Her questions about race and ethnicity fell by the wayside, replaced by Sister Teresa's surprising description of her as beautiful. Ava was old enough to know boys thought her cute, but *beautiful* was a word with clout. Compassion, on the other hand, came easily to her. She assumed her work with abandoned and injured baby animals—rabbits, squirrels, birds, turtles, and chipmunks—was behind the assessment. The sister let Ava shelter her wounded menagerie in the back of the gardening shed, as long as she kept it clean and the animals fed and watered, until she returned them to the wild.

Ava reaped many hours of pleasure from her animal hospital, as she called it. The wild creatures, a substitute family, eased her yearning for a real family of her own. Sister Teresa understood and encouraged Ava's nurturing behavior, saying she had the makings of a compassionate nurse or doctor.

Of all the sister's compliments, the most meaningful one to Ava was the acknowledgment of her talent at the piano. More than anything in the world, even more than her animals and school, she loved the instrument.

She was a small child when she first heard Sister Mary Josephine play the piano at the school Christmas party, and she burned with eagerness to evoke its melodious sound herself by touching its keys.

One night after lights-out in the little girl's dormitory, she groped her way in the darkness to the other end of the building in search of the piano. She found the mahogany grand, majestic with its lid up, in the center of the music room. Outlined by the moonlight that filtered through the tall windows above, the piano appeared to possess a halo. The light around the piano reminded her of the pictures of the saints in the nursery, each with the same golden circle above their heads.

Awestruck, Ava moved closer to stare at the ivory and ebony keys. After a time, she sat on the edge of the bench. No longer able to restrain herself, she lifted a finger and struck a key and then another and another. She was so engrossed in listening to the tones of the keys and in understanding their relationship to each other that she forgot the scolding she could expect if the sisters discovered her out of bed. As she hummed the tune, "Twinkle, Twinkle Little Star," she used her right hand to match each tone to a white key. In no time, she played the entire tune. At first, she was satisfied, until she remembered Sister Mary Josephine played with two hands. Ava looked at her left hand; she had no idea what to do with it. Raising it to the piano, she picked at the keys and listened. Curious to hear how the notes from two hands sounded together, she added her right hand. At once she recognized some sounds clashed with others. If she struck a discordant note, the unpleasant vibration offended her ears. Bent over the keyboard absorbed in her task, Ava almost levitated at the sound of Sister Mary Josephine's voice.

"And she's only four."

"Yes, it's a miracle," Sister Teresa Claire agreed. She made the sign of the cross.

Ava anticipated an immediate reprimand for being out of bed. To her amazement, the sisters were smiling down at her. Confused, she hung her head and mumbled she was sorry. The astonished sisters patted her on the head and ushered her back to bed. Ava heard them whispering to each other as they walked away. They sounded excited.

From then on, Ava had unrestricted access to the piano. Sister Mary Josephine taught her until she was seven. At the end of second grade, Ava gave her first public performance in the school's annual fundraising event, and then something remarkable occurred.

Several days after the benefit, Mrs. Agnes Turner, a renowned instructor to some of the world's most famous pianists, called on Mother Superior. Mrs. Turner explained she had retired from her teaching career and moved to Tampa to be near her daughter and grandchildren. Bored, restless, and at loose ends, after several months of luxuriating beside the pool, Mrs. Turner said she would like to offer free instruction to the child who played in the school concert.

"Teaching Ava will give me something meaningful to do," Mrs. Turner explained as she flicked a lock of dyed, Day-Glo red hair back from her forehead. "Filling my days with hair appointments, massages, and bridge isn't especially satisfying. Besides, music has given me a lovely life. Bringing your gifted Ava along will allow me to give back for everything I've taken. I still have time to get right with God, don't you think?"

Dumbstruck by Mrs. Turner's flaming-red hair and rapid-fire verbiage devoid of censure or second thought, Mother Superior did not reply. As it turned out, her inability to respond made no difference for as Ava came to learn, when Mrs. Turner was on a tear, inserting a word was a daunting undertaking. After the meeting, Mother Superior clucked, "That woman's bright red hair could light up an entire city, but if her instruction is as brilliant, Ava will be blessed."

The flamboyant Mrs. Turner left a lasting impression on everyone. Difficult to ignore, Madame, a title she preferred, was a character of the most outrageous sort from her appearance to her blunt, not tactful, yet for the most part, correct opinions, and Ava loved her for it.

Such pleasant memories from such happy times. Ava wondered if her fear of dying was causing her to exaggerate the importance of her old memories and experiences.

As she sifted through the past, an expression she saw on a bumper sticker, "Reach out for life, or it will pass you by," came to mind. Her life had not passed her by, but she admitted she should have appreciated it more when she had the opportunity.

As Ava neared the convent, she asked herself if she had reached out to others often enough. Would an objective observer assess her life as having been purposeful and worthwhile? When it occurred to her she was thinking of her life in the past tense, she shivered.

The wail of a siren interrupted her reverie, and she returned her attention to the road. An ambulance with blaring siren sped by, its urgency reminding her of the fragility of life. She wondered if the passenger was young or old and if he or she would live or die. The live or die question was a familiar one, for she pondered it each day and again at night when it revisited her in nightmares.

Chapter 5 – Tampa, Florida

Lost in her memories, Ava's drive to St. Joseph's was a short one. She made the turn by the canal and traveled the gravel road toward the convent. In contrast to the ever-changing buildings in the downtown section of Old Naples, St. Joseph's was a relic from the past. The mission-style structure had endured decades without external alteration. She was pleased to see her childhood home, a glorious tribute to permanence, had not succumbed to the frenetic modernization going on elsewhere.

She parked her car under the clump of palms where, as a child, she had played tag and blind man's bluff with the other residents and the children who came to school for the day, returning to "real homes" afterward. The resident children envied the day students from real homes for having mothers and fathers. The day students were also the most popular, as if by association the resident children could reap the benefits of family life. Ava was not long in realizing a real family was an idealized concept constructed more of fantasy than reality.

Samuel, her favorite friend, opened her eyes one day when he came to school with a cheek so swollen he could not open his mouth or eat. He told the nuns he fell from his bike. He told Ava his father had hit him when he intervened to stop a beating of his mother. Over time, such sad slice-of-life stories of desertions, divorces, sickness, unemployment, violence, and even deaths in the idealized homes of the real families eroded Ava's envy.

The truth about real families freed her to develop a greater appreciation for her own lot in life and the sisters who cared for her. Compared to the lives of some of the children from real families, hers was peaceful, dependable, and secure.

Ava got out of her car and paused in the yard to listen to the playful squeals of children echoing through her mind. At the convent where life was simple and unchanged, the days of her childhood did not seem far away. In the shade of a stand of buttonwoods, she closed her eyes to recall without distraction the most exciting day of her life at St. Joseph's, the day she received the unforgettable letter from the dean of students at Julliard, the crème de la crème of music schools. Madame Turner, as solemn as a first pew of churchgoers and in front of Sisters Teresa Claire and Mary Josephine, handed Ava the letter. Overwhelmed by suspense, Ava opened it with trembling hands and a fluttering heart. The words *accept* and *scholarship* jumped at her from the page.

Speechless, she looked up to see three women waiting with bated breath and three pairs of eyes searching her face. When she recovered from her shock, she divulged the contents of the letter, and the four women lost all restraint. Such cheering, clapping, giggling, hugging, and dancing about had likely never occurred before on the campus of St. Joseph's. In the evening, the nuns gave her a party like none other, while a fervent Mother

Superior prayed for forgiveness from the bishop, should he get wind of the noisy and joyous celebration. Oh yes, the memory of cavorting nuns made the night one Ava would never forget.

Ava opened her eyes in time to see Sister Teresa, with outstretched arms and flying habit, hurtling across the parking lot. Moved by the love shining in the sister's velvet brown eyes, Ava reached out and embraced the surrogate mother who had shown her kindness and patience, soothed her tears, and offered her wise counsel. Seconds later, they broke the embrace and held each other at arm's length, searching for the familiar and the new. Except for deepening crow's feet, Ava thought Sister Teresa's cherubic face, soft eyes, and dancing dimples were as unchanged as the convent. When an expression of concern knitted her eyebrows together, Ava knew her distress was apparent.

"Oh, Ava Marie—Sister Teresa always called Ava by her full name, saying it reminded her of the Ave Maria—it's good to see you again. I've missed you." Her face aglow, she patted down her habit and restored her wimple to order.

"And I've missed you, too," Ava said. "Letters are fine, but seeing you in person is ever so much better." She hugged Sister Teresa as if for the last time.

Inside the convent, the nuns who remembered Ava gathered around her, as did several curious novices who came forward to meet the visiting celebrity. Blushing at the attention, Ava was happy being with the members of her surrogate family in her old home. For a brief time, her delight even caused her to forget the underlying reason for her visit.

When the fuss was over, Ava and Sister Teresa retired to a sunny corner of the refectory. Facing each other at a small table under the tall windows, they basked in each other's smiles, while Ava wrestled with how best to explain her quest. She rubbed her hands together, fidgeted in her seat, and wished there was another way to obtain the information she needed without causing her surrogate mother worry.

When Ava's anxiety reached crescendo proportions, she plunged ahead. "Sister Teresa, I confess another reason for my trip besides wanting to visit with you. I see you are not surprised. Am I so obvious?"

"After all these years, Ava Marie, I know most of your expressions. You're not good at hiding your feelings. Something is upsetting you. What can I do to alleviate your distress? I don't like to see you looking as somber as you do."

Urged on by Sister Teresa's smile and kind words, Ava said, "I'm not sure anyone can help me, Sister Teresa, not even you."

"Ava Marie, dear, the Lord reserves parables for himself. Would you please be more illustrative?" A teasing smile flickered across the sister's face.

The tactic was familiar to Ava. As a child when she was reluctant to confess a transgression, Sister Teresa used humor to prod her toward the truth. Despite the seriousness of the moment, Ava laughed softly. "I see your dry humor hasn't disappeared. I'm glad."

"As I've always said, God listens to happy faces as well as long ones, Ava Marie. I think you will feel better after you get what's troubling you out in the open. You must agree, or you wouldn't have come."

"You're correct, Sister Teresa, except I'm in need of information, not catharsis or forgiveness." *At least not yet,* Ava thought with a sharp twinge of guilt for her betrayal of Langdon. She sucked in a deep breath and let it out with a long sigh, the gravity of the task ahead visible in her long face.

"Oh? Go on," Sister Teresa said.

"Before I do—and forgive me for even mentioning it—you must agree not to share what I tell you with anyone, Langdon in particular."

Sister Teresa squirmed in her seat. "Why would you want me to make such a promise? You know any conversations of a personal nature are confidential. I can't weigh the wisdom of agreeing to your request without an understanding of what it is you want to keep between us."

Ava was stunned. "Are you saying you will not keep my confidence?"

"No, Ava Marie, I'm saying I will not keep a secret if it hurts another or prevents justice from extracting its due. For example—and this time it's your turn to forgive me—suppose you told me you killed another by accident, say a hit and run. In good conscience, I would not be able to keep information of that nature to myself. Do you see? I must understand what I'm promising to do and why before I agree. If what you want to share is harmless, I will keep your confidence, of course." She smiled, waited for her words to sink in, and then continued. "You know I have your happiness at heart. Trust me to judge if the information you seek should stay private." With a pleading look, the sister took Ava's hand.

Ava bristled. "I see," she said. "I understand your position. I don't want Langdon to know what I am about to tell you because if what I fear is true, it will upset him." She hung her head to hide the tears welling in her eyes. When she looked up, she saw her sadness mirrored in Sister Teresa's eyes.

"My dear, your anguish is a heavy load on my heart. It is unlike you to be so emotional. A dire circumstance must be at the bottom of your misery. Please tell me how I can help?"

"I'm sorry Sister Teresa. I can't without your promise." Ava bowed her head again.

"My darling child, as much as I want to see you restored to your usual optimistic and positive self, not even for you can I agree to keep a secret without understanding its importance."

Ava raised her head. The sister's concerned expression increased Ava's anguish.

"Let's approach the subject from another perspective," Sister Teresa said. "People can be stronger than you think. What do you want to keep from Langdon that he could not bear?"

"That's my dilemma," Ava responded, "I don't even know for sure what it is I think I know." She lowered her head into her hands, a picture of dejection. "I want to do the right thing; I just don't know what the right thing is." Her tears came in a rush too voluminous to impede, and when she turned her head to remove a tissue from her purse, she saw the sister struggling to keep her own composure from unraveling.

"Tell me, my dear, what is the onerous burden that's causing you such unhappiness? Let me share the load with you." With a mischievous smile playing around the corners of her mouth, the sister added, "I put away my gossip megaphone before you arrived."

For a moment, Ava forgot herself and laughed between her tears. Dabbing at her eyes, she said, "I am torn between sharing my problems and remaining silent. I don't have all the facts yet. I am going on supposition alone, a poor basis for causing you or Langdon distress."

Getting nowhere with extracting a promise from the sister to keep her secret from Langdon and having run out of sensible arguments and the energy required to devise new ones, Ava gave in. Irritated with herself for agreeing to confide in the sister without a promise of confidentiality, Ava searched for the appropriate words.

"Okay, Sister Teresa, you win. I've come to ask for your help with a critical matter. I do want to trust your judgment. It's just that I'm facing ... well ... a problematic situation, in truth, an extraordinary one. I pray you will not think me too dramatic when I tell you. I have a strong foreboding something terrible is wrong with me, and as silly as it sounds, I dread the future.

Sister Teresa turned her head to meet Ava's gaze. "It upsets me to see you forlorn. Why don't you start from the beginning, so I might understand and offer you a measure of comfort? I have learned appropriate action and prayer can resolve most problems and worries."

"I'm sorry, Sister Teresa. You must think me irrational. I'm talking in circles. I'll start at the beginning." Ava twisted her wedding ring. "I hope I won't sound hysterical or ridiculous to you," she said.

"Here's my problem. I have small tremors in my fingers, weakness in my extremities, and unexpected muscle contractions. Sometimes my arms and legs are unwilling to follow what my brain instructs them to do." She took a deep breath. "I can't get organized, either, a subjective change I can't prove. But there is a difference between how I was before and how I am now. I find it trying to process ideas in a sequence, which makes thinking ahead difficult, and I forget things like dates and times, even important events." Ava huffed a sigh of exasperation. "Am I making sense?"

"Have you been to a doctor?" Sister Teresa asked. Worry lines creased her forehead.

"Yes, and he's one of the reasons I'm here. He asked me for a family medical history. I reminded him of my orphan status and explained the sisters did not share the orphanage's family records, with either adult orphans or adoptive parents, when I was a resident. I told him the probability of finding information about my family was slim." As Ava spoke, she noticed a faraway look in the sister's eyes. Ava fell silent, reluctant to interrupt the sister's thoughts if she remembered something helpful.

"We closed the school more than ten years ago," Sister Teresa said. "We sent the records of our adopted children to the state agency."

"But I wasn't adopted," Ava interjected.

"Exactly," Sister Teresa said, "and it's why we have your record and those belonging to the other children who lived with us until they attained majority age."

"Oh, how wonderful," Ava said with relief, thankful her search would not entail rummaging through the dusty files of a departmental catacomb. Then it struck her, the full weight of what she might discover in her record. *Am I ready to know?* She twirled a strand of hair around her index finger.

"Is it a detailed report?" Ava asked. "Does it say who my parents were and why they gave me up? Does it contain a clue to my heritage? You once told me I was a mixed-race child, remember?" A million questions raced through her mind. She could not ask them fast enough.

"Ava Marie, it's distressing you remember my unfortunate comment made years ago. Give me a minute to think how best to explain myself. I am averse to making the same mistake twice and want to select my words with care."

"Take your time, Sister Teresa."

"Where to begin ... in the fifties, mixed-race was a term with several meanings," Sister Teresa explained. "Most thought it referred to a person of more than one race. Others interpreted it to mean a person of more than one ethnicity. For example, in the terminology of the day, folks considered the offspring of an African mother and a father from Europe, a mixed-race child, even when the parents were of the same race. The confusion between race and ethnicity caused the mislabeling of many children. It was a great shame.

"In my opinion, the term mixed-race is a misnomer," the sister continued, "a subjective term stemming from an unscientific concept. To confer such a label on anyone is wrong. A person may appear black yet have parents who look white, and of course, the reverse is true. I apologize for my former ignorance. I was repeating what I learned as a novice, before my awakening."

Ava bobbed her head. "Yes, I agree the designation is baseless. When a form requires a checkmark next to a racial classification, I resent it. I'm not sure what to write. If a blank asks for other, I write *human*. I can't understand why one's physical appearance should determine one's race anyway, especially since people of different races have intermarried from the beginning of time.

The sister smiled. "I see you have made your own observations, Ava Marie, and arrived at my exact opinion."

"Yes, I have," Ava acknowledged. "The real problem is race and ethnicity are often the targets of bigotry and ignorance, both dangerous weapons," Ava said.

"They are indeed," the sister acknowledged.

55

"I'm glad we've settled the issue," Ava said. "Let's get back to the subject at hand if you don't mind. Did you have something else you wanted to say?"

Sister Teresa seemed lost in her thoughts again. "Yes, I did. I wanted to say ... um, when you resided with us our children's records were the sole province of the Mother Superior. After the orphanage closed, the senior sisters were allowed to give former residents their records, if asked. But I digress. In thinking back to the stormy night when you arrived, I recall a long white envelope lying next to you in your basket. Maybe it will be in your record and contain information to put your mind at rest."

Or not, Ava thought with a little shiver, *it might be devastating.* For the sister's sake, Ava tried hard not to look as distraught as she felt.

"Ava, as I'm sure you know, I have no legal right to withhold information from you. I must ask, however, are you certain you want to proceed?"

"Yes, Sister Teresa, I am." Ava pulled a letter from her purse. "This will explain," she said and handed the letter to the sister. "It's from our family physician, Dr. Marquist."

Ava scooted to the edge of her chair.

Sister Teresa reached for her reading glasses, positioned them on the bridge of her nose, and opened the letter. When she finished reading it, she exhaled a noisy sigh and patted Ava's arm. "Let's see if your record offers any information useful to your doctor," the sister said. Collapsing her glasses, she tucked them into her habit and handed the refolded letter back to Ava. Together they rose to their feet in silence.

Before moving away from the table, Sister Teresa placed her hands atop Ava's shoulders. "My cherished child," she said, "I will ask again. Are you sure you want to know what your record may reveal, and are you prepared to deal with whatever you may discover?" She searched Ava's face.

Sister Teresa is looking for reassurance, Ava thought. She swallowed hard to dislodge the lump of fear forming in her throat. "Yes, I want to know what's in my record. I can't answer your second question. Is anyone ever prepared for bad news? I can only say I will try my best to deal with whatever fate has in store for me."

Sister Teresa tucked her arm through Ava's. "I'll help you as much as I can, and God is with you. Shall we do it together?"

She moved away from the table and with a pat to Ava's arm, took a step forward pulling Ava along.

The record room was at the far end of the convent in the same wing where the under-five girl's dormitory used to be. Ava marched beside Sister Teresa, feeling as if she had relinquished all control and thinking the envelope from her basket could change her life forever.

Oppressed by fear and self-doubt, Ava was disgusted with herself for being pessimistic and emotional, for neither attitude suited her temperament. She was not the type to exaggerate or indulge in negativity; she was a plodder, an optimist who refused to give up. Strong, determined, and happy, she had a fulfilling life. To have it shattered by a fatal illness defied logic.

Chapter 6 – The Office of Doctor Marquist, Naples, Florida

Ava, irritable and restless, was in Dr. Marquist's waiting room for the second time in several months. As she waited for the nurse to call her name, her thoughts drifted back to her trip to St. Joseph's. She recalled Sister Teresa's dimples and warm hugs, the rooms at the day school that had seemed larger to her as a child than they were, and the convent's old mahogany piano, her first instrument polished with love and maintained like a shrine by the sisters. Had the bishop allowed, Ava had no doubt Sister Mary Josephine would have lobbied for the installation of a sign that said, "Ava Marie played here."

Since her visit to St. Joseph's, Ava's new obsession was the letter in the white envelope Sister Teresa remembered seeing. After thirty-two years of longing for information about her family, Ava thought it incomprehensible that a letter from her mother, Isabella, was right under her nose. Finding the envelope sealed was equally astounding. Holding her breath, she ripped it open and removed the letter. When she read it, she learned how she came to be deposited on the doorstep of St. Joseph's. Her mother's letter also described several downright frightening events, the recounting of which awakened within her mind the unwelcome specter of death. Her fear of being its next victim overshadowed everything in her life.

In addition to the obsession over her mother's letter, Ava had developed a compulsion—a bizarre urge to explain her every action to herself as if she were a narrator speaking to an audience. Talking to herself was the same as having more than one voice in her head or speaking in an echo chamber.

While Ava was trying to make sense of her new behavior, another patient left the doctor's waiting room. Thinking she was next in line, Ava fought to keep her nerves under control. She shrugged her shoulders, squared them, and sat up straighter in her chair. She practiced deep breathing and tried to ignore her compulsion to explain her thoughts to herself.

Take a deep breath, exhale slowly, remain calm, seek serenity, and allow your body to release the weight of your worries, a voice in her head said. *Wait for the facts, avoid speculation, and be positive.* When the tenseness in her shoulders crept upward to her neck, she sighed. Meditation was not one of her talents or her only shortcoming.

In the two weeks that had elapsed since her visit to St. Joseph's, she was finding it difficult to control her emotions. One minute she was composed and optimistic, and the next, she was filed with a pernicious dread that gnawed at her nerves. Every so often, the mood swings occurred within the space of several hours, compounding the problem of maintaining her customary countenance in front of Langdon.

Isabella's letter had upended her life in many ways. "Why do you suppose Mother Superior didn't open the letter?" she asked Sister Teresa.

"My guess is because it was addressed to you with instructions to keep it sealed until you asked for it. Mother Superior's integrity prevented her from doing anything else. She wouldn't have minded not opening the letter for she preferred not to know our children's backgrounds. Mother Superior believed each child deserved to start life as an innocent untainted by familial baggage."

"I understand her desire to protect the children," Ava said, an edge of irritation rising to her voice, "still, I wonder how my life might have been different had I read my mother's letter."

"I've given some thought to why family information was withheld from our residents, staff, and adopting parents," Sister Teresa said. "I believe the intention was not to hide the identity of the parents, who relinquished their children, as many assumed. The purpose was to protect our children from judgment. I think Mother Superior was right. Our children started with a clean slate." She unclasped her hands and spread them across her lap.

"I suppose, or maybe someone in authority should have read the records before it was decided to disclose or withhold information."

"You may be correct," Sister Teresa said. "Other foundling homes may have had different procedures. At St. Joseph's, Mother Superior had the last word."

Rehashing her conversation with Sister Teresa did not erase from Ava's mind the reason she was waiting to see Dr. Marquist or shorten the wait. She glared with impatience at the closed door to the doctor's inner office as if it were a barricade to her very existence.

Once again, her mind wandered back to the letter in her file. Was it best she had not known about it? Would her life be different if she had read it years earlier? She could not say. Since she loved her life as it was, perhaps Mother Superior's decision was wise after all.

The nurse entered the room, and Ava, holding her breath in expectation, looked up from studying her fingernails. Would the nurse call her name? Her thumping heart refused to quiet; her palms were sweating.

"Mrs. Sullivan," the nurse announced. An elderly woman with a frail frame rose from her chair and with the aid of a cane, shuffled after the nurse.

From deep inside a silent scream rose to Ava's lips. *Take me, take me, take me,* she pleaded. The clock in her head registered each minute as an hour. The wait was interminable, and the longer she sat, the more anxious she became. Finding the suspense intolerable, she considered bolting from the office. She had already canceled two previous appointments with Dr. Marquist, however—stupid moves that had served no purpose other than to postpone the inevitable— and in all fairness, she could not stand him up again. She decided to stay put.

Ava knew fear was at the root of her stalling. Instead of dealing with it, she was retreating to the past, reliving it in her mind and clinging to memories. She found it hard to move forward when her intuition told her to expect a serious illness of some sort, maybe even a life-threatening one. The future seemed too ominous to face.

She took a deep breath to compose herself and then resumed picking apart her behavior and her feelings. Her most troubling concern was having to lie to Langdon. She was deceiving him at every turn, a nasty state of affairs that expanded as one lie gave rise to another, overwhelming her with guilt and remorse.

Ava crossed and uncrossed her legs, shifted in her seat, and crossed her legs again. Thinking about the future was hard. If fate handed her a fatal illness, she wanted to accept it with courage. At the same time, she had her limitations. Would she fall to pieces, embarrass herself and her family, lose her dignity?

She tried to imagine how she would react to a deadly disease. At first, she would be shocked, and then she would want to learn about her disorder, especially what to anticipate. In time, she might come to accept death as inevitable, although probably not before denial was unsustainable. She had to prepare for the worst, even though she prayed for the best.

After her brainstorming, Ava concluded there was no right or wrong way to deal with a catastrophic disease any more than there was a singular way to grieve. She gave herself permission to react without guilt because she had no idea what to expect. In the meantime, she would think of terminal illness in the abstract, not the concrete. A sensible approach, she thought, until a little voice inside her head asked if she was stalling again to avoid facing what the future might hold. She closed her eyes and sighed, tired of analyzing every thought, and tried not to think ahead.

In want of a distraction, Ava selected a magazine from an adjacent table. It was a good idea until her spastic fingers made turning the pages difficult. To have her fingers flying about, in spite of her effort to keep them still, was maddening. Embarrassed, she wondered if anyone had noticed her jerky movements. She stole a look through her lashes at the other patients. Nobody was paying attention to her. With no reason to feel self-conscious, she returned to her magazine, *Upscale*, a Naples publication about the rich and famous. When she came across the pictures of the previous month's benefit for children with cancer, she stopped to study them.

Ava, worried about twitching in front of the camera, had avoided the photographer at the event, unlike her best friend, Sunny Cavanaugh, who rarely missed an opportunity to publicize her pet charities. Looking like an advertisement for the citrus industry in an ugly, bright orange gown, Sunny preened for the press with her husband, Brock Starling, at her side.

Sunny's gown yelled "Look at me," though some might wonder why she wanted to attract attention. In spite of the best plastic surgery money could buy, Sunny's appearance, in kindest words, was unattractive. Nevertheless, her father's wealth had helped her land a suitable husband who followed her around at benefits like an imprinted chick.

Ava respected Sunny for shrugging off her looks as unimportant and developing instead the qualities that endeared her to those who knew her. The unchallenged queen of charitable causes in Naples, Sunny arranged benefits for deserving organizations and donated her money to fatten their coffers. Esteemed for her philanthropy, she garnered enormous respect. Without Sunny's kindheartedness, influence, and campaigns, the social season in Naples—devised to unload the pockets of the wealthy and entertain them at the same time—would be lackluster, and many charities would go under-funded.

Naples's affluent full- and part-time residents were unstinting with their charitable dollars, in part because there was plenty to go around and because fundraising provided a seasonal calendar of social events with meaningful underpinnings. The elite attended galas dressed in their jewels and finery, caught up with their friends, and had a good time without guilt because fundraising was a worthy endeavor.

The locals referred to the affluence in Naples as quiet money. Quiet or not, Ava's excessive wealth was a source of unease to her. She was not born into money, and in a lifetime, she could not have earned as a concert pianist what she was worth. Langdon had made her a wealthy woman.

As a newcomer to affluence, Ava still identified with the middle class. The first time she visited Naples, the sight of the elegant Mediterranean-style mansions fronting the Gulf of Mexico and the baronial manor houses in exclusive Port Royal, where residents moored their yachts within arm's reach, astounded her. She was curious about the luxurious estates and the people who owned them. In her wildest dreams, she never expected to join their ranks.

Even though many of the estate owners were in residence for only several weeks or months a year, Ava came to learn they employed an army of year-round service workers to maintain their homes and manicured grounds. In the high season, a steady stream of private planes flew owners, their friends, and families into Naples Airport. At season's end, owners and guests flew off to their other palatial homes and social engagements across the country and around the world.

The local newspapers and magazines, like the glossy one she was trying to read, documented the rounds of parties, galas, benefits, auctions, and art shows that distinguished the season in Naples.

When Ava could not translate the printed page into meaningful words and Sunny's orange nightmare swayed, as if it were alive, in front of her unfocused eyes, she closed the magazine and put it back on the table.

Consumed by anxiety, Ava was on the brink of panic. The cramp in her stomach refused to relax, and her throat, dry as a dessert, tightened when she thought about what the doctor might tell her. She wanted to shout at the nurse, "Let's get it over. Take me next!" Instead, she stared at her hands resting in her lap, concerned about learning, in a matter of minutes, that her life was heading toward a disaster.

Chapter 7 – The Office of Dr. Marquist, Naples, Florida

Still in Dr. Marquist's waiting room—*waiting ... waiting ... waiting*—and at the end of her wits, Ava thought she would turn to stone from inactivity if she were not called soon. She strained to relax the muscles quivering in her fingers, and then made a face at the oxymoron. *Straining to relax?* Feeling a step away from lunacy, Ava diverted her attention to a stain on the ceiling. As she stared at it, the discoloration took on a familiar shape. She squeezed her eyes shut. When she opened them, the skull and crossbones were gone.

The strange vision was puzzling. Was she losing her sanity? The thought had no sooner crossed her mind than a giggle slipped through her lips. Heads swiveled in her direction. A sheen of moisture formed on her forehead. Beyond horrified, Ava opened the magazine again and thrust her burning face between the pages.

Several minutes later, Ava withdrew her face from the magazine. No one was paying attention to her. She settled back in her chair and focused her thoughts on Langdon, thinking pleasant thoughts would help her relax. Her good intentions collapsed when she could think of nothing uplifting in the face of an uncertain future or in the terrible lies she was telling. She spent hours trying to justify them to her conscience.

Ava's head was spinning with questions. Would she be able to keep up the pretense with Langdon? Could she justify the erosion of the trust between them? The alternative was to tell him the truth, an option that turned her stomach. *Please, God, give me strength,* she prayed. In the same breath, she asked him to forgive her duplicity and begged him to awaken her from her nightmare.

"Mrs. Skinner," she heard a voice say from a great distance. Ava came to her senses, and when she looked up from her magazine, a stocky blonde in a white lab coat was hovering over her. The nurse held a clipboard folded against her chest.

"Mrs. Skinner, are you all right?" the nurse murmured.

The nurse's voice was so loud it made Ava wince. *How strange,* she thought. Surely the nurse would not shout at her. Absorbed in trying to understand the new turn of events, Ava did not reply.

The nurse hesitated and then tried again. "The doctor is ready to see you, Mrs. Skinner. Please follow me."

Ava mumbled, "Uh ... yes, thank you." The nurse stared at her. Mortified, Ava averted her face and rose from her seat, only to lose her footing and stumble. The nurse grasped Ava by the elbow to steady her and when she regained her balance, helped her to the doctor's office.

"The doctor will be with you in a minute," the nurse said, settling Ava into a chair across from Dr. Marquist's oversized mahogany desk. "He's finishing up a note on a previous patient." Ava did not respond. Her tongue, thick and leaden, would not move.

The nurse left the room, leaving the door ajar. With nothing to do, Ava studied the gold scrollwork border on the doctor's leather desktop. She recognized the design, the key motif, an ancient pattern used by the Greeks to decorate ornamental objects. Years ago on a trip to Delphi, Langdon had surprised her with a gold necklace in the same design. She examined the configuration at close range, thinking it looked like a maze of snakes joined end to end and bent at right angles. *Am I seeing things again?* She was pondering the meaning of her visions when the door swung wide. Dr. Marquist's stout frame filled the opening.

"Well, well, I see you found a slot in your busy schedule for your doctor," he joked. He rewarded Ava with a broad smile. "Twice jilted, I notice. I must be losing my charm."

At his mention of the broken appointments, Ava felt a prick of remorse. She returned Marquist's smile with a sheepish one.

"On the contrary, Bill, you improve with age."

"Like fine wine or old cheese, you mean." He chuckled. "Not the answer I was hoping for."

Dr. Marquist, at fifty-something, had not lost his charm or his jocular manner, Ava thought.

"To be serious, Ava," Marquist continued, "I hope nothing is wrong at home. It isn't like you to cancel appointments."

"Everything at home is status quo. Langdon is as healthy as a horse, and poor Buck is doing as well as can be expected. His kidney cancer is metastatic. After several rounds of chemotherapy, he was put on dialysis every other week. Last month it was changed to every week. Our biggest problem is controlling his pain. We know Buck will lose the battle, but he is clinging to life until Langdon is secure in running the family businesses. Buck is a courageous man. I think I would give up."

Buck's struggle reminded her of her own. Was she following in his footsteps? *Poor Langdon, he would lose the two people he loved most if*—she stopped herself mid-thought. Speculation was alarming.

When she returned to the moment, Dr. Marquist was looking at her with unusual frankness. She glanced at her fingers, wondering if they were twitching. They rested motionless in her lap. All was quiet on the spastic front.

Marquist ended the uneasy silence. "Ava, speaking of brave, did you have an opportunity to visit the orphanage for medical information?" He walked across the room to his desk, lowered himself into his extra-large leather chair, and peered at her over his glasses.

She raised her eyes to look at him and drew in a deep breath. "I guess I can't postpone the inevitable." She reached for her purse, her face solemn, and removing Isabella's letter from an inside compartment, handed it to him. "I found it in my record." She forced a stiff smile.

"Do you want me to read it?" he asked. He accepted the proffered letter.

"Yes, of course. I hope it will shed light on my situation. I can't judge. My mother, Isabella, wrote it. I've highlighted the pertinent items."

Marquist adjusted his glasses and unfolded the letter.

Ava was edgy. She picked at a cuticle while Marquist read, and then, unable to sit, rose from her chair and walked to the window. She stared unseeing at the street below, recalling the symptoms Isabella described in her letter. Ava thought they sounded like hers. Since she lacked the medical expertise to interpret the meaning or cause of Isabella's symptoms, she hoped Marquist would find the information useful.

In her letter, Isabella said she suspected she had the same illness as her father, Ava's grandfather. Ava did not doubt her mother, yet it struck her as odd that Isabella did not divulge the name of her illness. Why would she omit a detail so essential to the understanding of her story?

The information in Isabella's letter brought to a head Ava's other concerns. First, would Dr. Marquist be able to deduce Isabella's diagnosis from the symptoms she mentioned? Second, if her mother and grandfather suffered from the same disease, what was in store for her? Was it a genetic condition? Was she next? A wave of apprehension seized her. Did she want a diagnosis right then and there?

Ava's breathing grew labored. As her anxiety expanded, she felt her heart pounding in her chest. On spindly legs, she wove a path away from the window to the chair next to Dr. Marquist's desk and plopped into it. She felt warm and pulled at the collar of her blouse. Despite wanting answers to her many questions, she was unprepared to face the truth.

Marquist looked up from the letter. He refolded it with care, and as he handed it back to her, his eyes searched hers for a brief second. Ava wondered if he read her fear.

"A sad letter," Marquist said to her. "I can only imagine how you must have felt when you read it." He took a deep breath and continued. "Ava, I don't want you to jump to conclusions, and I won't either. I know you are expecting a diagnosis; however, it would be irresponsible of me to conjecture. I recommend further testing by a neurologist. I know an excellent one in Tampa, a Dr. Mark Osgood, unless you and Langdon have another preference. I could send you to Miami or even the Mayo Clinic, your decision."

Ava's pulse quickened at the mention of Langdon's name. "Please, do not tell Langdon," she said. "I haven't told him of my appointments with you, my trip back to St. Joseph's, or my symptoms."

Marquist's eyes grew wide. "Ava, you mustn't keep your medical problems to yourself, especially from Langdon." He rubbed his chin and paced. "You can't go through this alone. You have to tell him."

Ava raised her downcast eyes and looked at Marquist as if he had delivered a mortal wound. "I don't want Langdon to know yet. You must promise not to mention my visits or to hint in any way something is wrong with me. He has his hands full with Buck. I don't want to burden him further."

"Ava, I—"

She cut him off. "Bill, promise!"

"Okay, Ava, I promise. I must tell you, though, I think keeping your situation from Langdon is unwise." He sounded exasperated. "I implore you not to keep him in the dark. It's the wrong thing to do."

His concerned expression increased her terror. What was he not telling her?

"Bill, I know I sound ungrateful. I apologize. I appreciate what you're doing for me. I can't bear the thought of telling Langdon until I have additional information." She turned a stricken face to him. Her bottom lip quivered. "We don't even have a diagnosis. Why upset him for nothing? I'll tell him myself when it is appropriate. Please allow me to choose."

Marquist rose from his chair and walked around his desk to stand by her side. He bent down and took her small, cold hand into his large, warm one. "Ava, dear, I've known you since you first came to Naples, and I've known Langdon since he was a little boy. I was at your wedding, remember? You must believe me when I say I have your well-being at heart. Please tell Langdon." His expression was earnest, his tone pleading.

"I know you mean well, Bill, but I cannot concede the point." Her lips formed a firm line on her stern face. "I beg you to keep my situation between us and to let me decide when to tell Langdon."

"Okay, Ava," he sighed, "as you know, I'm not at liberty to reveal your health information without your permission, and I won't. I am your doctor, however, and it's my responsibility to advise you to change your mind."

She thought he looked sad. "I'm sorry, Bill, I can't. I wish I could be a more agreeable patient. I will tell Langdon when I think the time is right." She meant to sound apologetic yet not lacking in clarity or firmness.

"I understand," he said.

His half-hearted response told Ava he did not. How could he? Without loving Langdon as she did, he could not put himself in her place.

Marquist returned to his desk chair, sat down, and slumped, his sunny disposition in shambles.

"Thank you for understanding, Bill, and I apologize again for being difficult. Until we know more, I don't see the point of alarming Langdon. He has enough on his mind with Buck sliding downhill. And Bill, I need you. You're my sole confidant. Please don't be angry with me. I'm not as demanding and bossy as I sound." She hung her head. Tears rose to her eyes.

"Ava, you needn't apologize," Marquist said. "I'll keep your secret and be available any time you want to talk. Please consider my advice. Don't put off telling Langdon. He would want to know." He smiled at her then, blessing her with the endearing aura his patients thought magical.

Chapter 8 – Pelican View, Naples, Florida

Langdon arose at an early hour to jog along the beach, a three-mile run he tried to accomplish each morning. As he walked back to his Gulf Shore Drive mansion from the beach, he glanced at his watch. *Not bad for a thirty-five-year-old.* Pleased with his time, he was out of breath and in need of a long drink of water.

After showering and dressing, he took the shortcut to the kitchen across the mansion's outer courtyard. Along the way, he plucked out a leaf from the new infinity pool Buck installed several years earlier to replace the older one. Langdon ate a bowl of fresh fruit at Rosa's insistence, and after pouring himself a second cup of coffee, headed with cup in hand to his office.

The office, furnished in leather and mahogany and lined with floor–to-ceiling bookcases, was his, although he thought of it as Buck's. Langdon had not altered a thing, not even the ugly, stuffed alligator head with its shiny glass eyes that hovered over the desk from its position on the wall, greeting him each morning with open jaws and serious-looking teeth.

No sooner had he finished plowing through a pile of prospectuses and reviewing the family's investment portfolios, than Craig Stephenson arrived. Stephenson, the manager for Skinner Enterprises, had come to deliver his weekly report on the family-owned conglomerate. Founded several generations earlier, Skinner Enterprises had grown over the years to include a number of industries ranging from oil production, cyprus lumbering, and cattle ranching to agriculture, real estate, fishing, and hospitality.

Thirty minutes passed, and still, Stephenson droned on. Langdon was having trouble concentrating. He appreciated Stephenson's diligence, but his attention to minutiae was wearing. Langdon's left leg was asleep, he needed a stretch, and he wanted another cup of coffee. His inability to focus made Stephenson's update seem overlong.

Langdon attributed his restlessness to the altered atmosphere in his home. No longer predictable, comfortable, and nurturing, it was inconstant, worrisome, and confusing. He could not put his finger on the exact reason for his discomfort, but he felt as though he had stepped into someone else's shoes.

His day started off wrong as soon as he woke up. When he reached for Ava, as was his habit, he discovered she was not in their bed. Since he could not kiss her good morning, he had to be content with the fragrance on her pillow. Not the most earthshaking upset, he admitted, and yet similar off-putting incidents were cropping up more often than usual.

When he discovered he was alone, he dressed for his run in a hurry and set out to look for Ava. He spotted her rushing toward the front door. He crept up behind her, tapped her on the back, and said, "Good morning, Ava. Where are you off to so early?"

She jumped. "Oh, Langdon, you startled me," she said and laughed. "How silly of me. Good morning to you, too, my darling. Are you off for your run? Have you eaten breakfast? Rosa baked the most delicious coffee cake. I have some in my napkin." She lifted the napkin to show him and then turned her face upward for a morning kiss.

Before Langdon could answer, she smiled at him, and turning away, opened the door. "I'll be home for lunch. Bye, sweetheart."

In a flash, Ava was down the wide stairs through the arch and halfway across the courtyard. Not until she turned the corner by the carriage barn did Langdon realize she had not answered his question. *Where was Ava going?* No matter, he thought, he would find out when she returned.

Langdon redirected his attention to Stephenson who was wading into a new subject, the demographics of developing housing for the migrant workers on their several farms in Immokalee. Langdon cracked his knuckles and drummed his fingers on one knee. His mind was wandering. He was not absorbing the facts.

"Craig, would you mind if we cut it short?" Langdon asked. I'm a bit off and could use a little air. I apologize." He stood to stretch his sinewy limbs. "Could we reconvene either later or in the morning?"

Stephenson pushed back from the desk and collapsed his hefty report into a compact pile. "Sure, Langdon," he answered, a note of concern in his voice, "the rest can wait until you feel well.

How does tomorrow morning sound, give you a little more time to fight off whatever it is?"

"Sounds great. Tomorrow it is then, same time if that works for you, and Craig, thanks for understanding, buddy."

Stephenson gathered his briefcase and papers together. Langdon walked with him to the door. In the foyer, Stephenson said, "By the way, how's Buck doing?"

Stephenson, who had been with the company since Langdon was a boy, was Buck's right-hand man. As illness eroded Buck's ability to fulfill his former role, Langdon had turned to Stephenson for guidance. The general manager was bringing him along, teaching him the ropes of the family businesses. As Langdon applied himself to the task, he leaned heavily on Stephenson for guidance.

"Buck's the same, Craig. He's on dialysis once a week and holding his own. Controlling his pain is a day-to-day thing. Despite his ordeal, he's no more cranky and cantankerous than usual. No doubt he'll want me to repeat every word of your report. It's hard for him to relinquish the reins."

"Well, you can't blame him." Stephenson grinned. "He always was inclined to grab the bull by the horns, you know, like the time he wrestled alligators out of the back ponds because the workers refused to pick produce and look over their shoulders at the same time. The gator wrestling was one messy job, I can tell you. When the show was over, all you could see was the whites of Buck's eyes. The rest was covered with mud, but the gators got the worst of it, by golly. Your father always was one to take matters into his own hands, alright."

Langdon smiled. He had heard the story many times. "Yes, Buck's shoes will be hard to fill," he said without reservation. "I'm just not ready to think about his not being around."

Stephenson gave him a hearty clap on the back. "Langdon, you are your father's son. Don't worry. You are capable of carrying the torch forward, so to speak."

"Thank you, Craig. My head is above water only because you keep me from drowning. By the way, if I haven't thanked you for your patience before, please know I am appreciative. I realize I've been distracted and not the best student."

"Heck, Langdon, you have a lot on your plate these days. Besides, it isn't as if Skinner Enterprises is some mom-and-pop operation. It's a complicated network of businesses, each different from the other. Trust me, I know better than anyone it takes time to get the nuances under your belt."

"Again, I thank you, Craig. I'll do my homework and be ready for you in the morning with a razor-sharp mind."

"I don't doubt it, Langdon."

The two men shook hands and Stephenson left.

Alone, at last, Langdon was grateful for the reprieve. He had more important things on his mind than business, in particular, Ava. She was acting peculiar, leaving the house earlier than usual and often in a dither. When he reached for her in the middle of the night, her side of the bed was empty. On four occasions, he had discovered her sitting motionless in the dark and staring off into space, once by the pool and the arbor, and twice on the lanai that stretched toward the Gulf. The first time she disappeared from their bed, his frantic search took him to the garden. He found her sitting under the arbor by the reflecting pool and looking off into the night, a blank expression on her face.

Alarmed, he said, "Good God, Ava, why are you outside in the middle of the night?"

"Oh, Langdon, I'm just enjoying the moment," she whispered. She gave him an angelic smile before reverting to her trance-like state.

Worried, irritated, and sleepy, Langdon wanted nothing more than to return to bed without further conversation. He placed his arm around Ava's shoulders and guided her in silence to their bed. She did not protest. It seemed to him Ava was more asleep than awake. He wondered if she were sleepwalking. He would ask her about her nocturnal travels in the morning.

At breakfast the following morning, Langdon said, "Ava, you've been wandering around at night. Is there a reason for your nighttime forays?"

Ava shoved a strand of long hair behind an ear and folded her napkin as she formulated her response. "Really, Langdon, haven't you noticed how beautiful our property is by the light of a full moon?" she replied. Her soft voice had a testy edge to it.

"Of course, I've noticed, Ava. You haven't answered my question."

Ava pushed her breakfast aside and stood. She smiled at him. "I have to brush my teeth and get going, darling. Please excuse me."

Before Langdon could protest, she walked away. Her unresponsiveness irked him, and she had made light of his concern by changing the subject. He would not run after her for an explanation, though.

After reflecting on Ava's fresh-air outings for several weeks, Langdon concluded she was sleepwalking. On subsequent occasions, when he discovered her missing from their bed, he withheld his questions, after finding her, and led her back to their bedroom in silence. Ava's jaunts around the property at night were a constant worry to him.

Another troubling issue was the absence of music in their home. Ava used to go to the piano after breakfast each morning and again after dinner. A few weeks earlier, she stopped playing altogether. Even Buck commented on the quiet, thinking it was out of deference to him and his condition. Langdon assured him he was not the reason.

Langdon remembered to bring up the piano at lunch one afternoon. "Ava, I miss hearing you play," he remarked.

Her face was blank at first, and then she smiled at him and said, "Thank you, darling. The piano needs tuning."

"Why didn't you tell me? I'll call the piano tuner," Langdon said.

"Don't rush. I sprained my finger, too."

"Gosh, how did you do that? Which one?"

Ava hesitated. "This one," she said and pointed to her left little finger. "I have no idea how I did it."

Langdon noticed she avoided his eyes. "You should see George or someone in his orthopedic group."

"I suppose," she said.

"You don't act worried. Don't you want it to mend correctly?" Langdon asked.

"Oh, it's a simple sprain, Langdon," she said. "Please don't concern yourself. If you'll excuse me, I have a tennis match in an hour and must get ready."

She rose and left the room without saying anything more, leaving Langdon to wonder why they were not communicating as they should. Her nonchalance about her finger was puzzling, and the excuse she gave him was lame. She was careful with her hands. What had changed?

Ava's several recent shopping sprees also mystified him. She was not a big shopper, and the in-season galas and parties that required new outfits were months away. Adding to the mystery was the lack of packages from the stores or receipts for her purchases around the house.

After one of Ava's shopping trips, she came home late in the afternoon looking more tired than usual, and when she did not share her new selections with him, his suspicions were aroused.

At dinner, Langdon said, "Are we having a fashion show after dessert, Ava? You know I enjoy seeing you in your new outfits."

"I didn't find anything to my liking, even though I scoured the stores," she said with a sheepish smile.

"No kidding, isn't that unusual for you?" He was skeptical.

"I've gained a few pounds," she mumbled. "I decided to wait until I lose them before buying anything new."

Langdon noticed her bowed head. *Avoiding my eyes again*, he thought.

Ava's early-morning departures, trance-like episodes, luncheon cancellations, and late night meanderings were out of character for her and upsetting to him. He asked her more times than he could remember if she was under the weather or troubled. Her response was to change the subject, claiming she was fine, or offer a plausible excuse. Her behavior made him uneasy.

To top it off, his preoccupation with Ava was undercutting his ability to concentrate on business. Short of interrogating her, a loathsome tactic, he had no idea what to do. His only recourse was to wait for Ava to confide in him.

Buck's discomfort also preyed on Langdon's mind, even though Juanita, the practical nurse he hired in response to Buck's desire to be cared for at home, took splendid care of him. Juanita, who resided in quarters adjoining Buck's, was as congenial as she was medically astute. She and Buck enjoyed each other's company, a bonus for which he was grateful. He could not have asked for a better arrangement.

Thinking of Buck reminded him of the day Dr. Gallo, a six-foot-tall man with long thin fingers and a boot-camp haircut, delivered the shocking news: Buck's right kidney tumor was malignant and the largest one he had ever excised. The stunned silence that followed Gallo's announcement and the exchange of staggered looks between those huddled around Buck's bed was seared into Langdon's memory. The possibility of metastases, although on everyone's mind, went unmentioned.

The bad news shook Langdon to the core. He felt lightheaded and groped for a chair. Ava turned pale. Buck stared at the ceiling, his lower jaw set in stoic resignation.

Unable to bear the oppressive silence, Langdon ripped it open. "The backaches Buck's had the last few months were caused by the tumor?"

"Probably," Gallo answered.

"I knew it," Langdon growled, shaking his head. He should have forced Buck to see a doctor. Langdon had suggested it several times, but Buck, the old mule, insisted he had only thrown out his back. He said over-the-counter painkillers, anti-inflammatory drugs, and massage therapy would heal it fast enough. Although Langdon could not have known his father was harboring a growing malignancy, he felt responsible for allowing Buck's stern no-doctors dictum to stand as law. *I should have put my foot down.*

On second thought, telling Buck what to do was a laughable concept. Langdon snorted. No one, except his mother, Millie, possessed that talent. In her hands, Buck was putty. Langdon missed his mother. He took comfort in knowing Millie's sudden heart attack three years earlier had saved her from a slow and painful death like the one Buck was facing.

Not only did Millie handle Buck with an ease no one else could mimic, but she was also an accomplished woman in her day. She devoted her energies to the Collier County Cancer Center by bringing in top-notch oncologists, raising money for the center's refurbishment, and organizing the financial support needed to educate the community on the importance of early detection. Langdon thought it ironic Buck's cancer went unnoticed until it was too late to cure. All the modern improvements his mother had worked so hard to put into place would not save his father.

Several rounds of chemotherapy had arrested Buck's metastatic renal carcinoma, at least for a time. Although some of his tumors were shrinking, others were not, and his kidney function had declined to the point of requiring dialysis. Even though the oncologist spoke with optimism in front of Buck, Langdon read between the lines, understanding that his father's existence was tenuous, at best.

Life can change in an instant, Langdon thought. Four years earlier, he had a wife, two healthy parents, and everything to look forward to. With the distance Ava had put between them, the death of one parent, and the terminal illness of the other, Langdon felt alone for the first time in his life.

Chapter 9 – Parking Garage, Naples, Florida

Ava stumbled through the doorway of Dr. Marquist's office in a stupor of despair. At the elevator, she stabbed the down button with such violence, her finger went numb for a few seconds. Alone in the hallway, she waited for the car to descend, hoping it would be empty. She was incapable of being polite to anyone.

At ground level, Ava fled the medical building and dashed across the street to the two-level garage and her parked car. A sensation of nausea rose in the back of her throat. After two hard swallows, it disappeared. She chalked it up to an empty stomach. To be on time for her early appointment, she had skipped breakfast, except for the piece of Rosa's coffee cake that she took to taste on the way to Marquist's office.

When Ava found her car, she fumbled through her purse for the car keys. Her head felt three times its normal size, the back of her eye sockets burned, her skin was clammy, and she was frantic to get into her car to collect herself. After searching every compartment of her purse, she came up empty-handed, no car keys. Had she lost them? Would she have to return to the doctor's office to look for them? Exasperated at the thought, Ava squatted and turning her purse upside down, dumped its contents onto the pavement: lipstick, tissues, change purse, wallet, pen, checkbook, a couple of old receipts, and a case for her sunglasses. Still no car keys.

Trembling with frustration, she chased a lipstick that rolled behind a tire. Nothing was going right, Ava thought, a sob catching in the back of her throat. She scrambled out from under her car, and as she rose to her feet, the pocket of her jacket brushed against the back door with a ding. She remembered where she had put her keys.

Furious with herself, she fought to stave off tears. Out of breath and distraught beyond endurance, Ava unlocked her car, jerked open the door, and slammed her body down in the seat behind the wheel. She was fed up with restraining the mountain of pent-up emotion that sat on her chest like a heavy weight. She pounded her fists on the steering wheel and burst into tears. Her self-control was in shreds.

Slumped in her seat like a rag doll, she let her tears skid unchecked down her cheeks, each one representing an erosion of the resolve she had mustered to be strong. Drop by drop her strength to fight dripped away. The war had just begun, and she was already defeated.

As her tears flowed, despair numbed her brain, transporting her to an anesthetized plane of darkness. Time passed. When her sobs throttled back to little shudders, her rational mind returned. She had no understanding of what was happening to her or why frustration was her constant companion.

Ava wanted to shout a long, loud, ugly scream. Why? She had never uttered a scream in her life. Maybe she *was* losing her mind. She was not always in charge of her extremities. Could she lose control over her mind, too? The ideation seemed melodramatic, even to her, yet an unknown illness was letting her body do what it wanted, not what she wanted. Was her illness allowing her mind to do the same thing? In a tantrum of anger, she threw her purse as hard as she could to the floor of her car. *What is happening to me?*

Grabbing the car keys from her lap, she jammed one into the ignition and started her car. Preoccupied with sorting the debris that cluttered her mind, she neglected to back out of the parking space. Instead, she sat in her idling car absorbed in her thoughts.

What would she do? Keeping her appointment with Marquis had required every ounce of her courage, and in spite of her effort, she was no closer to learning the cause of her symptoms than before she saw him. In place of a diagnosis, she had yet another doctor's appointment, with a neurologist, no less. The delay, the new referral, and the suspense intensified her suspicion that her life was hanging by a thread.

The lack of a diagnosis also meant she would have to continue deceiving Langdon. More lies and more guilt, she thought. Langdon deserved better. Ava's misery was further compounded by the tension growing between them. She was sure Langdon felt it too because he had asked her why she was acting so distant—remote was the word he used, even though Ava was sure he meant cold, a less palatable and harsher judgment that weighed on her heart.

Ava released a long sigh. Until she had answers to her questions, she could not make decisions or share her issues with Langdon, who already had Buck's illness and Skinner Enterprises on his mind. The anxiety on Langdon's face stabbed at her conscience. The only thing she could do to help him was to act cheerful and bright when he was around. Despite her effort, Ava sensed Langdon's confusion. Her subterfuge made her feel unclean.

Opening a sweaty hand, Ava glared at the appointment card crumpled in her palm. A death warrant, she thought, a free pass to see Doctor Death, lucky her. "Maybe not," a tiny voice called out to her through the doomsday din rattling in her brain. "Maybe not, maybe not, maybe not," it echoed.

Ava identified the voice. Hope was reaching out to her with its message not to give up, the same hope those who faced certain death clung to until the end. The inability of hope to prevent death begged the question: Why bother to hope? The expression, "hope against hope," meant to her it was hopeless to hope.

Ava thought the expression nonsensical. All the same, if she were to hope, she would hope not to have the same illness as her mother and grandfather. From Isabella's description, Ava could not imagine any disease more monstrous or sad. Since Ava had no idea if her symptoms—

trembling, spasticity, forgetfulness—were the same as Isabella's or her grandfather's and Dr. Marquist said it was common for several disorders to share some of the same features, maybe either her symptoms or the cause of her symptoms were different from theirs. Was hope giving her some wiggle room?

"That's right," the voice of hope intoned, growing more insistent with each repetition. "Hope until you have all the facts, or until you have a reason not to."

She wanted to believe there was room for hope. If nothing else, it might keep her from going to pieces until she saw the neurologist in two weeks.

The steady breeze blowing through the garage made her feel chilly in the wake of her heated meltdown. She pulled her jacket closer, closed her car window, and returned to thinking about hope and miracles. Ava was of the opinion people believed in miracles because it was easier than facing the truth, a form of self-indulgence she viewed as human weakness. Finding herself in need of a miracle, however, she was having second thoughts. Tossing her hair back from her face, a stab at bravado, Ava decided to let hope have its way. She was human, after all.

Ava turned her thoughts back to Langdon. He had noticed her uncharacteristic behavior and was asking questions. Keeping her wits and her secret would require an extra measure of diligence. One slip and her house of lies could tumble down. She racked her brain for a failsafe smokescreen that would hide the source of her anguish—her symptoms—from Langdon. Could she devise one?

After pondering the issue, a passage in Isabella's letter gave her an idea. Removing it from her purse, Ava searched it for the part that might buy her time, while she decided what to do. If she could fashion a workable plan around the information in Isabella's letter then she would be out from under Langdon's observant eye.

Chapter 10 – Parking Garage, Naples, Florida

Still in the parking garage next to Marquist's office, Ava took her mother's letter from her purse. She wanted to look for the particular part that had struck a chord the first time she read it.

My darling Avalita, I write my letter to you with a heavy heart, but I must because I want you to know how much you are loved and adored. You are my little princess, my shining star, and the part of my life that stands above all else as meaningful. Let me start from the beginning.

I was born in Maracaibo, Venezuela, in 1918, the sole child of Alejandro Prada Perez and Mariana Quinones Prada. My name is Isabella. Even though I had no brothers or sisters, I was not lonely as a child. We celebrated Christmas, other holidays, and family events with our small extended family, my father's younger brother, Ramon, his wife Angeles, and their two sons, Joaquin and Miguel. We lived in Lagunillas, a small town on the shore of Lake Maracaibo, Venezuela, in a wooden house elevated on stilts.

There it was, the reference to her relatives. If she were creative, perhaps she could keep Langdon at bay by constructing a strategy around them. She dug into her purse and pulled out a tissue, wiped the tears from her face, and blew her nose. With the beginnings of a plan taking shape in her mind, she felt less helpless. She took a deep breath and released it slowly. Holding Isabella's letter to her chest, she thought it more precious than anything, except Langdon. Although nothing more than several sheets of paper, the letter was her sole connection to her family. "My family," she murmured, the words bittersweet to her ears. Ava had read Isabella's letter, rich in detail, many times. With each reading, she discovered a new tidbit to savor. At that moment, Isabella's penmanship caught Ava's eye. The graceful flair of Isabella's flowing cursive was artistic. The discovery was not a surprise to Ava for like her, Isabella had played the piano, an endeavor through which she expressed her creativity musically. The passion she and Isabella shared for the instrument was the only proof Ava needed to know, without a doubt, that Isabella was her biological mother.

Picking up the cherished letter, Ava continued to read.

Our descendants came from Spain, and my father and mother were born in Venezuela. Papa was a dock manager for Royal Dutch Shell, one the many companies that drilled for oil under the waters of Lake Maracaibo. Mama worked in the offices of the same company. Although our lifestyle was modest, we were rich compared to those around us, most workers for one of the oil companies. Conditions were inadequate for the families who lived in the stilt houses and for the unmarried men who slept in wooden barracks.

What I remember most about our town, Lagunillas, was its strange appearance. Despite a semi-arid climate, the vegetation by the shore should have been lush and green; instead, slippery oil from the leaking wells discolored everything. Greenish-black palms bent low under the weight of it, and an oil slick rested like a gargantuan black parachute on the surface of the water. Under the sunny skies, life by the lake was in perpetual mourning.

Ava closed her eyes and tried to visualize the landscape. Against the blue sky, it must have looked like a silhouette even in daylight. Depressing, she concluded, and read on.

The oil, Mama's sworn enemy, coated the men's boots, our shoes and clothes, and the sides of our houses. An ever-present oily residue covered everything, even the paths that wound between the buildings and down to the docks. We were careful about wiping our feet and taking off our shoes, but we tracked oil into the house anyway. Mama was forever cleaning stains off our grass mats and wood floors and muttering that the oil was a black plague. Sometimes we found thick, sticky blobs of it in our hair, even after a shower. Mama rubbed the oil out with lard, and then we washed our hair with rainwater collected for cooking and drinking. No one dared to drink the water piped into our houses.

Papa complained nonstop about the frequent oil fires, spills, and well blowouts. He said a tragedy would occur one day, and then the oil companies would pay attention to the safety of their workers. Sure enough, in 1928, when I was ten years old, most of Lagunillas burned to the ground. The fire started when a spark ignited oil spilled from a leaking drill. Fed by the oil-covered wooden docks, stilt houses, and barracks, the conflagration leaped from structure to structure. We were in Maracaibo on our monthly shopping trip when the fire ravaged our town. We thanked God for sparing us the panic and death endured by others, but our house and belongings were ashes.

How devastating for them, Ava thought. Imagine leaving your home intact and returning to find it a charred pile. Isabella and her parents had survived the disaster, however, unlike many in their community. Sharing their relief and sadness, Ava turned the page.

In the disaster's aftermath, the oil company denied responsibility for the blaze, a denouement that embittered the workers. Their resentment grew. Papa said another incident, no matter how minor, would cause the workers to explode. Distraught over the destruction of our town, and with the blackened countryside as a reminder, Papa vowed never to work for an oil company again. Several months after the fire, we immigrated to Miami.

When you own nothing, it is easy to move. We stayed with a distant relative in Miami until Papa secured a job in the Valente Cigar factory across the state in Ybor, a northeastern section of Tampa, and then we moved again.

Our life in Ybor, a city of 16,000 people, was exciting and very different from the way we lived in Lagunillas. Many of our friends and neighbors were recent immigrants either searching for work or already employed in the factories of one of several cigar companies in the area. Papa's friend, Hernandez, helped us join a social club, El Centro Español, after Papa proved our Spanish heritage. We made many new friends there and attended dances, picnics, and parties. The men had an excellent baseball team, and the women met at the club to socialize and plan various functions.

I went to a school built for the children of factory workers, most of whom were Cuban, Spanish, and Italian immigrants. In addition to the expected lessons, I learned to play the piano at school. Father Mendez allowed me to practice my pieces on the piano in our church. When I was fourteen, the manager of the social club to which we belonged asked me to play for the afternoon Sunday socials. He put a jar on the piano for tips and told me to keep the money from it.

For five years, even during the Depression, our life was idyllic, compared to what it was in Lagunillas. When I was fifteen, however, our world as we knew it crumbled.

The day after his fortieth birthday, Papa experienced strange muscle contractions. He clenched and relaxed his jaw repeatedly, even when he was asleep, and the muscles in his face jumped and twitched. One day Papa refused to go to work saying the stares of his coworkers embarrassed him. Not long after, he would not leave the house at all.

Papa, once a gentle man, became someone we didn't know. He was irritable, quick to anger, prone to verbal outbursts of gibberish, and challenging to be around. Mama and I were frightened and begged him to see a doctor. He said we were the crazy ones. When he was agitated, he shouted things like, "You think I'm a head case, don't you? Maybe you should see a doctor." We learned not to argue with him because he was illogical. We lived in a state of extreme tension waiting for the next outburst.

After several years of disturbing behavior, Papa withdrew. He stopped speaking, and his body jerked with strange writhing movements. He stayed in bed because it was difficult for him to walk. Papa refused to eat or to let us feed him, and he wasted away before us. His eyes seemed to be begging us to let him die, or maybe it was our imagination.

Mama moved us closer to Tampa to be near St. Michael's, a new hospital that had just opened. One day when she went to inquire into resources for Papa, she returned with a new, better-paying job and an appointment with a neurologist for Papa. Unlike the previous time, Papa was too sick to object. When the doctor told us we could do *nothing for Papa, except provide for his comfort, we knew he was dying.*

One by one, Papa's last days dragged on. He became harder to manage. We had to watch him every minute. Mama was exhausted, her sunny smile buried in fatigue. Balancing our schedules around his care was not easy. Somehow, we managed. I finished high school with the support of my teachers, who allowed me to do my classwork at home in the afternoons. The altered schedule meant I could look after Papa until Mama got home.

After I graduated from high school, I worked in the evenings during the week when Mama was home to watch Papa. I earned money by playing the piano at hotels and restaurants in the area. I played for church functions, such as baptisms and weddings, on Saturdays and for the church services on Sundays. We spent most of our waking moments either caring for Papa or working. Papa's illness, though not his fault, made us captives.

Each time Ava read that part of Isabella's letter, her heart beat faster. Did she have what her grandfather had? If she did, would Langdon feel like a hostage? Would he grow to resent her, maybe even hate her? *Please God*, she begged, *don't let the same thing happen to me.*

Ava stopped reading to steel herself before continuing. When she felt she could handle her emotions, she returned to Isabella's letter.

It was a sad day when an ambulance came to pick up Papa because he never came back home.

He died at the young age of forty-six in 1939. We accepted his death as a blessing because his suffering was over. The person who died was not our beloved Papa anyway. Our Papa, the one we loved, had died several years earlier. His soul left long before his body followed.

Ava asked herself which was worse, not knowing your father, or losing the father you knew and loved as Isabella had. Even though Ava lived with a strong sense of incompleteness, she had never experienced the loss of a loved one. She inhaled a deep breath and released it with a heavy sigh. Perhaps she was the more fortunate.

Mama and I had our lives back after Papa died. For several years, we had not seen a movie, gone to a social at our club, or visited a friend. At twenty-one, I was eager to discover what life had to offer. My debut came at an unfortunate time, however, because 1939 was a year of unrest and worry.

The Depression had diminished the demand for cigars, and the declining revenues forced industry cutbacks and the closing of several factories. Many of the men in our old neighborhood were out of jobs and searching for new ones. Some of our friends were forced to move away to secure employment. The smaller hotels and better restaurants also felt the economic pinch and to survive, eliminated luxuries. Live music was the first to go.

For several months, I was unable to secure a paying position as a pianist. Papa's old friend, Hernandez, interceded to help me find interim employment in his sister's flower shop. Inez, Hernandez's sister, told me I had a knack for creating floral arrangements, and although I was grateful to have an income again, I longed to have a job playing the piano.

One day a woman came into our shop and overheard me talking to Inez about the shortage of piano-playing jobs. The woman suggested I inquire at the Belleview-Biltmore Hotel in Belleair, a small town near Clearwater. I knew the hotel, an elegant, sprawling resort on the Gulf of Mexico, from the newspaper. Located across the bay from Tampa, the resort was famous for dispensing hospitality to an impressive list of clients. European royalty, heads of state, movie stars, and famous athletes were a few of its more notable guests.

I thought the idea worth pursuing. I reasoned the hotel's extraordinary guests would expect entertainment, and unlike the smaller hotels in Tampa, the Biltmore's management would not have to tighten its purse strings. The town of Belleair was too distant for a daily commute from Tampa, however. I would have to move to work there, and then Mama would be alone.

Despite these issues, I decided to present myself at the hotel and worry later about where to live. I knew it was a long shot, still I had to try.

Ava stopped reading to reflect on the similarities between her mother and herself—both pianists, imagine that—and then, she realized her car was still idling in the garage. She chided herself for daydreaming again, but since she was calmer and the tremors in her hands had stopped, perhaps staying in the garage until she was collected was the right thing to do. Caught up in Isabella's letter, she decided to finish reading it on a sunny bench in Cambier Park.

Chapter 11 – Cambier Park, Naples, Florida

After she parked her car, Ava found an empty bench near the fountain in Cambier Park, one of her favorite public places. The mid-morning sun had cleared the stratified clouds typical of September mornings from the sky, and the breeze on her skin felt as if a thousand feathers were stroking her. She surveyed her surroundings—the green lawns, the fountain, the band shell, and the Har-Tru courts of the Cambier Tennis Center— and wished she could turn back the hands of time. If given a second chance, she would never again overlook the contentment of sitting on a park bench.

Ava felt a kinship with Cambier Park, the centerpiece of downtown Naples. The thirteen-acre park, dedicated in 1948, the year of her birth, had as quirky a beginning as she did. Back then the townsfolk, who campaigned for the park's construction, named the project Make Naples a Better Place to Live.

Buck once referred to the park as a pass-the-hat trick. When Ava asked him to elaborate, he said town officials had petitioned the IRS to classify the project as a political subdivision, an unusual request. When the desired designation was approved, fundraising for the park proceeded in earnest, even by passing the hat at public events.

The people of Naples appreciated the value of a deduction come tax time, the affluent donors in particular, and were generous in their giving. In the end, the people got their park and donors, their tax deductions—a victory for everyone. Ava needed an innovative idea, one with a win-win outcome like the financing of the park, to buy time with Langdon. She had to come up with a plan that would reassure him and achieve her goal at the same time. The problem was, she would have to lie again. So what? she thought. She had told so many lies it was too late to worry about one more.

Besides, most of what she would say was true, except for the part she omitted. Lying by omission was not as bad as outright lying, Ava told herself. If she could figure out the details, her plan might work.

Although Ava pretended to herself that her idea was clever like the pass-the-hat trick, in moments of guilt, she admitted it was no more than a well-intended lie. She wondered if she were capable of pulling off such an elaborate scheme. Any one of many hazards could trip her up. As she pressed her mother's letter to her heart, Ava wished she could summon Isabella for guidance.

Torn with self-doubt, Ava looked to her mother's letter for comfort. Packed with details Ava read it in layers: first the gist, then the particulars, and last, the minutiae of the particulars. She opened the letter and resumed where she had left off in the parking garage.

Before I describe my day at the Belleview-Biltmore, I must digress to tell you about Hernandez, Papa's dear friend. During Papa's illness, Hernandez demonstrated his kindness and compassion by helping Mama and me at every turn. If a doorknob was loose, he fixed it. If Mama or I needed a ride, Hernandez drove us. He always brought bags of groceries when he stopped by to visit Papa. Hernandez never overlooked an opportunity to tell us a joke or make us smile. He was a sturdy anchor. We leaned on him as if he were the head of the household. Hernandez gave us his best and asked for nothing in return.

A year after Papa's death, I was not surprised when Hernandez asked if I would mind his taking my mother on a date, providing she accepted his invitation. I was delighted. Mama devoted six lonely years to Papa and his illness. It was time for her to live a little.

When I went to the Belleview-Biltmore for the first time, the developing relationship between Mama and Hernandez was in the back of my mind. I was aware Mama needed my help to meet the rent on our apartment; however, I was certain Hernandez would take care of her if I moved. The idea of living near the hotel was feasible; the likelihood of my landing a job was tantamount to finding a needle in a haystack.

She's adventurous, Ava thought.

Hernandez gave me his old car when he bought a new one, and I drove it for the first time to the

Biltmore, crossing Tampa Bay on the Davis Causeway, a five-year-old span that shortened the northern land route by thirty miles. I had never driven across a bridge before, and afraid to look away from the road, I missed the beautiful scenery. To crunch a lifetime into a short story (my handwriting is beginning to deteriorate ...

When Ava compared Isabella's penmanship in the last paragraph to the previous one, the difference was apparent. No longer elegant and free-flowing, her handwriting was cramped and difficult to read. Individual letters, pointed and jagged, suggested poor motor coordination. Before Ava resumed reading, she told herself to look for changes in her own handwriting.

To my surprise, I secured a job at the Biltmore. The regular pianist was ill, and until she either returned or resigned, a stand-in position was available. An employee behind the reservation desk told me the woman's illness was terminal.

The stand-in position was only temporary as far as the management was concerned, and it paid the same as part-time work. Even though I needed a full-time job to meet my expenses, I reasoned that by taking the stand-in position, I would be next in line for the permanent job should the poor woman not return. In the meantime, I could supplement my income at the flower shop.

As I was waiting to meet the manager and weighing my options, I learned there was an opening for a part-time assistant in the gardening division. I thought it ironic the position entailed creating flower arrangements for the interior of the hotel and for special events from time to time and tending the potted plants outside. I was less confident in my ability to arrange flowers than I was in my skill at the piano. Despite my misgivings, I told the manager I would take both jobs if he wanted to offer them to me. I hoped he would find my suggestion appealing. Two part-time jobs earned the same as one full-time position, and I would not have to drive back and forth between the flower shop and the hotel.

I must have dangled the right carrot because after I demonstrated my aptitude on the grand piano in the dining room, the manager asked me to follow him to a cubicle off the kitchen, where cut flowers soaked in buckets of water. He instructed me to create an arrangement and then left. I selected several appropriate containers from the shelf above the counter, and did the best I could with the flowers. When the manager returned, he gave my arrangements a cursory glance. I thought he hated them. I was steeling myself for disappointment when he smiled and said both jobs were mine. I felt as if I might faint from shock. I was excited to tell Mama.

Forgetting her problems for a moment to enjoy Isabella's success, Ava looked up from her letter and into the eyes of a small child standing before her bench. The little girl had on white sandals and a bright colored sundress. A bow in her ponytailed blonde hair matched the material of her dress. A snub nose and round blue eyes complemented her ice cream mustache. She clutched a chocolate ice cream cone in a pudgy fist and stared at Ava as the forgotten ice cream dribbled onto the grass below. "Hi," Ava said. She smiled at the child. "Where's your mommy?"

The little girl pawed the grass with the scuffed toe of her sandal. "Over there." She pointed to a woman reading a magazine on a nearby bench. "You have pretty hair," the child blurted.

"Thank you. You do, too."

The child scooted away, the bow in her hair bouncing as she ran. Ava looked after her with a pang of longing. She wanted a child of her own more than anything in the world. With a wistful expression, Ava turned to look at the playground. She surveyed the parents and children gathered around the slide and swings and wondered if they were grateful for their blessings or if having children was something they took for granted.

Thirty-two years old and childless after trying to become pregnant for years, Ava's biological clock ticked louder with each passing day. She told Langdon, "At the rate we are progressing, we'll be the oldest parents at the PTA meetings when we have a child or two and the ones with the biggest smiles." The joke, often repeated between them, served to dispel the anxiety of their childlessness, a subject they avoided confronting head-on.

After several fruitless years of leaving procreation to chance, Langdon and Ava consulted a fertility expert. The doctor found no abnormalities and sent them home with advice to relax. A pregnancy would happen in good time, he said.

Ignoring the doctor's advice, Ava took her temperature each day at the same time for an entire year. At the tiniest increase above normal, she beckoned Langdon to their bed. Twice that year, she missed her period. She and Langdon were delirious with joy until both occasions turned out to be false alarms. The disappointments were crushing. When they grew tired of having their lovemaking relegated to a medical procedure, they resolved not to dwell on having children.

Ava's menstrual cycles were anything but predictable. Missed periods were typical for her. In fact, she had skipped the previous month, or maybe it was two months ago? On second thought, maybe last month she only spotted after having no period the month before. Who knew? She preferred not to dwell on her failure to conceive. Past disappointments had taught her not to raise the flag of victory over one or two missed periods. She had adopted a wait-and-see attitude.

In spite of her best intentions not to think about having children, Ava ached for a child. She and Langdon could not refrain from talking about the characteristics their children might have—her musical talent or Langdon's skill at building things—as if it were only a matter of time before children arrived. They did not discuss what they would do if they failed to have children, superstitious the mere act of entertaining another option might curse them forever with deprivation. Ava looked away from the playground, feeling traitorous for ruminating on having no children. She and Langdon had agreed to put having babies out of their minds.

She returned to Isabella's letter, smiling in anticipation of the uplifting part to come.

The time I spent working at the Biltmore and the several years that followed were the happiest days of my life.

Ava noticed Isabella's handwriting was normal again and wondered if she had rested between sections.

As it happened, the Biltmore offered individual rooms on the third floor of the east wing to employees, and with Mama's blessing, I moved at once. My room with an attached bath was spacious. To me it was luxurious. I did not need a kitchen; I ate my meals at the hotel for a small compensation deducted from my paycheck. Living at the hotel was thrilling. I felt like a princess, a fitting comparison because many of the hotel guests were royal or related to nobility.

Mama called me once a week. Each time, she asked, "What are you doing?" I answered, "Consorting with princes," and then we laughed.

I was not asked to mingle with the guests—nor was I cautioned not to—but it did not take me long to realize the importance of improving my knowledge of the world. The guests who stayed at the hotel were sophisticated, and I did not want to be embarrassed by ignorance.

I enrolled in an English class for adults at the local high school, and I learned a great deal by listening and watching at the hotel. I observed the demeanor of our guests, overheard their conversations, took careful note of the way they interacted with each other, and studied their stylish clothes. I was a voracious reader, and with the help of the extensive hotel library, my knowledge of the world expanded.

Once a week, I visited Mama. Each time she asked me for news about our hotel guests. My second job as the flower arranger gave me access to the kitchen, the nerve center of hotel gossip, so I was privy to all the stories that circulated. Mama called me The Informer and begged me to tell her everything I had overheard.

The goings-on at the hotel captivated her like a soap opera, and for a time, she took a keen interest in the clothes worn by the hotel's guests. As if I were a witness to a murder, Mama grilled me about the women's gowns. She wanted to know the details: the fabrics, the styles, the lengths. Every time I changed the subject, Mama returned to it. I would groan, "Mama, not the gowns again."

One day on my weekly visit, Mama greeted me at the door with an unusual effusiveness. My feet were not even over the threshold when she held up three beautiful gowns. "I sew them for you," she said, "to play your piano in." I was so touched I cried.

Ava rose from the bench to stretch the kinks from her back. She smoothed her skirt front and looked at her watch—thirty minutes to kill before she was expected at Sunny's to work on the fundraiser for the Children's Cancer Center. Sunny's group of supporters was gearing up for the annual benefit held during the high season. Ava, conscripted by Sunny, who never took no for an answer, did not mind. The Children's Center was a worthy cause.

The cooperative relationship between the seasonal and year-round residents of Naples was no mystery to Ava. The full-time residents laid the groundwork for the charitable events held during high season from December through March, and when the seasonal residents arrived, they did their part by donating items for auction, hosting parties, functioning as guest or celebrity speakers, and providing the necessary glitz and dollars to ensure the success of each benefit. The symbiotic association between the part-timers and year-rounders was a profitable one for the recipient charities.

Ava refolded her mother's letter and slipped it back into her purse. Lost in thought, she walked from the park to Fifth Avenue under the bright azure sky scraped of clouds. When she reached Fifth, as the locals referred to the avenue, the bustling activity on the street immediately engaged her attention. Ava smiled at a cluster of grinning tourists posing for pictures in front of the dolphin fountain and jumped at the clang of a delivery truck door sliding shut. An elderly couple nodded to her as she walked by, and on a bench, two businessmen, looking limp in their summer suits, said good morning. She heard the hum of air-conditioners and the noise of traffic and smelled the contrasting aromas of coffee, jasmine, and frying fish that filled the air. A winding line of children, holding hands and led by a young teacher with a pinched expression, crossed the street in front of her.

Ava shut out the distractions to think about the uncanny similarities between her mother and herself. Both reared in humble surroundings, they were good students and professional pianists. Each had rubbed elbows with affluence at the same age. Disadvantages had not kept them from building successful lives. Ava believed resiliency was the characteristic that allowed them to survive and excel.

As she stepped off the curb to cross the street, it occurred to her, on second thought, that the word *survive* did not really fit either of them. Even so, Ava liked to think if her mother were alive, they would enjoy a close relationship like the one Isabella shared with her beloved Mama, a bond Ava envied.

Absorbed in her thoughts, Ava strolled along until she found herself in front of the ice cream parlor. When she recalled the little girl in the park and the cone gripped in her hand, she surmised the power of suggestion had guided her steps. She ordered a double scoop of orange sherbet in a sugar cone.

When Ava stepped back outside, the mica in the sidewalk made it shine as if it were sprinkled with crushed diamonds. Even with sunglasses on, Ava's eyes watered at the brilliance and required a few seconds to adjust to the glare.

As Ava stood on the sidewalk relishing her sherbet, she caught a glimpse of herself in a store window. The casement, protected from the sun by a blue-and-white-striped awning affixed to a bougainvillea-covered wall, tempted Ava to step up for a closer look.

Did she resemble her mother? Given the many things she and Isabella had in common, it would not surprise her. Ava wished Isabella had enclosed a picture of herself in her letter. Was Isabella's hair darker or lighter than her own and which parent gave her a heart-shaped face and round eyes. Was Isabella petite, too? Which did she like best, ice cream or sherbet? Who was her favorite composer? Ava's mind was dizzy with questions. She felt sad that she would never know the answers.

Leaving Fifth Avenue behind, Ava retraced her steps to Cambier Park and her car. Distracted by her thoughts, she came close to colliding in the crosswalk with an elderly gentleman in a seersucker suit. Embarrassed, she apologized for her clumsiness. As she walked on, she thought about Sister Teresa's advice to be thankful for what she already knew of her mother. *I am grateful,* she confirmed to herself. For thirty-two years, she had worried about being an unwanted baby, an inconvenience left over from an irresponsible evening of lust or worse. Isabella's letter had answered her question. The profound discovery that she was wanted, loved, and not resented soothed her soul like a beautiful piece of music. Tiny half-moons of gratitude slipped down her cheeks.

Using the napkin wrapped around her cone, Ava blotted the tears from her face. When a cold blob of sherbet dripped onto her hand, she glanced at her cone. Instead of the mounded delight of minutes before, her ice cream was a mess of trickling goop. The sun had taken its toll. With a lash of her tongue, Ava rescued a chunk of sherbet on its way down the side of her cone. She was in a race with the sidewalk for the treat, one battle she was determined not to lose.

Chapter 12 – The Cavanaugh Estate, Naples, Florida

Ava was breathless, late, and apologetic when she arrived at the Cavanaugh Estate. Sunny, always a gracious hostess, welcomed Ava at the door and after an exchange of air kisses, led her outside to join their friends. The year-rounders, Cindy, Amelia, Elena, and Mary Beth, were exchanging pleasantries and gossip around a glass-topped table, protected from the hot sun by a striped canvas awning.

Ava greeted her friends and seated herself next to Mary Beth, who was regaling the group with tales of her mother-in-law's recent visit. Ava loved Mary Beth's stories. They were witty, embellished with a scattering of the right details, and injected with a dose of no-nonsense humor.

Mary Beth resumed her anecdote. "As I was saying, when Charles asked his mother if she wanted dessert, she said, 'Absolutely. I firmly believe in seizing the moment. Think of those women on the Titanic who waved away the dessert cart.'" Everyone laughed.

The chatter of her friends on the lanai grew distant as Ava's mind drifted. Her gaze lingered on the water in the swimming pool, the color bringing back a memory of the sapphire-colored silk gown she wore to her opening performance at Lincoln Center. When she took her bows onstage, the dress had sparkled under the spotlights like the pool water in the sunlight.

Ava turned to admire the adjacent gardens—clipped, weeded, and edged to perfection. She inhaled deeply, appreciating the smells of wet soil, fragrant flowers, and sea air. The water applied to the vegetation in the early morning was evaporating in the warm sun, releasing invisible wisps of steam that caressed her skin in the shifting breeze. Beyond the pool, the quiet bay was a sheet of platinum-blue cellophane, its surface undisturbed, except for an occasional ripple.

Even the clowns of the avian world, the pelicans, were immobile. Dressed in their tan and white summer suits, they crouched in silence on the dock near the Cavanaugh's moored yacht. With shoulders gathered into geriatric hunches, comical beaks tucked into over-sized chests, and webbed feet planted wide, as if a huge gust of wind might topple them, they reminded Ava of little old men.

Morning siesta, she thought and smiled. Pelicans made her laugh, in particular, the brown ones. They had an amusing and not the least bit graceful way of fishing, unlike gulls or cormorants. Brown pelicans were daredevil dive-bombers. They lined up their tidbits from high above and fell out of the sky at breakneck speeds, crashing headfirst into the water, snaring their prey, and by a miracle, keeping their necks intact.

Over her shoulder, Ava saw Sunny, grinning her toothy smile, step from the kitchen out to the lanai. She carried a tray of refreshments.

"Maid's day off," Sunny announced. She bent her tall, big-boned frame to put the tray on the table.

Ava studied Sunny's kind face. Sprinkled with freckles that peeked through her concealer, Sunny's pale complexion was unusual for someone living in the Sunshine State. Crow's feet, deep for her age, etched the skin at the outer edges of her small, pale-blue eyes. Her longish nose ended abruptly in a bob, the likes of which only an inept surgeon's scalpel could deliver. The narrowness of her brow, eyes, and nose was disproportionate to the lower portion of her face, which flared into a square prognathous jaw. A cleft chin and a mere slash of lips completed the picture. *Paul Bunyan and Lassie combined,* Ava thought, in an instant regretting her unflattering judgment. To be fair, she acknowledged Sunny's teeth, evenly aligned and brilliant white, were the envy of all.

Ava admired Sunny. She had more gumption than anyone Ava knew. Sunny was an ugly duckling, and yet she was happy and well adjusted. Ava thought Sunny's childhood could not have been easy. Children must have taunted her at school. Despite the challenges, Sunny emerged from her childhood with an exceptional combination of spirit, determination, and backbone, qualities she maximized to rise above the small-minded shallowness of others.

Sunny had plenty of friends, and since Ava had come to know her, Sunny even seemed attractive in her own way. People were drawn to her, and not for her money. Plenty of folks in Naples had money. Sunny garnered admiration because she treated each person as special, and she had an aptitude for bringing diverse factions together in pursuit of a common goal, a valuable quality when it came to fundraising. Sunny viewed a donor's smallest contribution, whether time, money, or energy, as a great gift. She brought out the best in people, ferreting out their useful qualities and talents, sometimes to the surprise of the individuals themselves, and her expertise at organizing was legendary. Sunny's endowment came from her heart, and like an intoxicating drug, she made people feel good. Ava thought Sunny an addiction.

After passing around the iced tea, the women broke into groups to discuss their respective topics. Sunny and Elena, the financial wizards, itemized and prioritized the needs of the center, estimated the dollars required to meet them, and set the monetary goal. Amelia, Cindy, Mary Beth, and Ava brainstormed various fundraising formats such as auctions, speakers, dinner parties and banquets, walkathons and races, regattas, balls, garden tours, open houses, and children's activities.

The women discussed appropriate themes for the weeklong festival and its grand finale, a sumptuous banquet and formal ball, aimed at unloading the pockets of the wealthy. The group decided to call the event the Naples Arts-Wave, a title that would accommodate cultural pursuits like music, dance, architecture, literature, art, food, theater, and gardening along with beach and water activities. The events would be open to the residents of Naples, seasonal visitors, and children in particular. The point was to have fun while raising money for a deserving cause. When the sun reached its noontime peak, the philanthropic ladies scheduled their next committee meeting and rose from the table, all but Ava who stayed behind at Sunny's request. As Sunny dispensed with her hostess duties, Ava waited on the lanai, wondering why she was asked to remain.

She did not have to wait long. As soon as the last guest departed, Sunny came right to the point. "Ava, is something troubling you? If it's none of my business, tell me."

"Wow, Sunny, why would you ask?" Ava stood and forcing a posture of nonchalance, meandered from the lanai to the towering spiral staircase in the center of the foyer.

"It's hard to put my finger on," Sunny said. "You didn't seem as enthusiastic as usual."

To avoid Sunny's intense stare, Ava raised her eyes to a tapestry hanging on the wall above Sunny's head. "I'm worried about Buck, that's all." She hoped Sunny would go on to another subject.

"Oh dear, has he taken a turn for the worse?" Concern spread across Sunny's face like honey on a warm biscuit.

"Nothing specific, he's the same," Ava said. The fingers of her right hand chose that moment to contract into a rigid claw. Oh no, she thought. She told a lie, and her punishment was a claw instead of a long nose like Pinocchio's. Worried about her other hand joining the insurrection, Ava turned her back to Sunny, placed her purse on the foyer table, and jammed both hands into it. "Goodness, what did I do with my sunglasses?" she muttered, rummaging through her purse. *Oh dear, God, not in front of Sunny.*

To distract Sunny from the claw-hand battle raging inside the depths of her purse, Ava kept the conversation going. "I wish I could do more for poor Buck and Langdon." Bent over the table with her nose in her purse, she mumbled, "Chronic illness is difficult for everyone involved."

Stop it, stop it, stop it, Ava commanded her brain. She willed it to relax her fingers, thinking of the metamorphosis of Dr. Jekyll into Mr. Hyde. *Please, this cannot be happening.* Ava's mind splintered then, and her thoughts and Sunny's words melded together in disconnected fragments. Ava found it hard to follow their conversation.

"They're on your head," Sunny said.

"What?"

"Your glasses, they're on your head."

"Oh, so they are." Turning her head toward Sunny, Ava offered a guilty smile, and then as if to avoid discovery, her strange talon reverted to an ordinary hand. Ava exhaled a sigh of relief and withdrew both hands from her purse, too distracted to notice a card that fluttered from it to the floor.

"I'll tell Buck you asked about him," Ava said, her face flushed, "and thank you for your concern." She forced another smile, turned, and started for the door, desperate to escape before she morphed into Bird Woman again.

As Ava sped toward the door, Sunny called after her, "Does Buck have visitors? Dad and I would like to see him. Buck and Dad have been good friends for a long time. We don't want to impose, though. We understand you have your hands full."

Words, words, words, Ava found them hard to decipher when they came at her all at once. She did make out Sunny's comment about having her hands full, however. *If Sunny only knew,* Ava thought, *or does she?* Sucking in a deep breath, she rubbed the hand that had come close to betraying her. Had she succeeded in hiding it?

Having one's hands full is an expression, you idiot, don't read into it.

"Oh, Sunny, you wouldn't be ... an imposition," Ava said, her hesitation making her sound inhospitable. She had tossed the words over her shoulder like an afterthought. Ava's face grew warm with shame. She was hedging instead of leaping at the opportunity to arrange visitors for Buck. Escaping before Bird Woman returned was her only concern, and under the circumstances, a distant response was the best she had to offer.

Fear was choking her, she thought, making her crazy and self-centered. Preoccupied with her problems and angry over the mystery of her symptoms, she could think of no one but herself, never mind feel all warm and fuzzy about arranging visitors for Buck.

Wait, did I admit to being angry? Yes, God help her, she was angry, angry, angry! Compounding her misery, the dull headache that had nibbled at her brain all day became a full-blown skull-banger accompanied by waves of nausea. *This is no time for polite chitchat or Sunny's interest in Buck's health.* Desperate for fresh air, Ava had to get out of Sunny's house.

"Well, I'll call first, maybe next week ..." Sunny's words died away as if she were waiting for encouragement.

Ava had none to offer. Escaping from Sunny's house was her only thought. She darted across the black-and-white marble floor of the three-story foyer past the Doric columns, immense crystal chandelier, and matching wall sconces to the door.

Sunny loped ahead of Ava with long strides, swung the front door wide, and shot Ava a quizzical look. Ava's heart skipped a beat. Sunny was insightful. Did she know something was wrong? To avoid Sunny's perceptive eye, Ava lowered her head. She would not explain her behavior.

Ava bolted to her car without a parting good-bye or even a thank you. Gasping for breath, she yanked the door open, got in behind the wheel, and started the engine. As she negotiated the circular driveway to the extension that curled away from the Cavanaugh's opulent beaux-arts estate, she came close to running over the gardener on her way past the massive gates.

Frightened by the close call and overwhelmed by emotion, Ava pulled her car to the side of the road three blocks down Rum Runner Lane, stopped, and gave in to body-racking sobs.

Her tears took her elsewhere for a time, back to her days at the orphanage where life was uncomplicated and dependable. She recalled the little girls' dormitory and the security she felt in her child-sized bed. She remembered the conversations in the schoolyard about real families. In her mind, she heard the sisters at their evening prayers and Sister Teresa Claire reading bedtime stories.

The harder Ava cried, the faster her mind conjured up events and images like a series of movie previews. Snippets of the past came at her with dizzying speed. She remembered the red shoes she wore when she played in her first school concert, the currents in the water that flowed in the old canal next to the school, and the sound of the wind bending the palms in the play yard on stormy nights. Her school friend Samuel's swollen cheek stood out in her mind. Next, she recalled Madam Turner's bright red hair that looked as if it should glow in the dark, and the disappointment she felt, when she realized it did not. She heard an audience clapping at Carnegie Hall and saw herself on stage waiting for the conductor to raise his baton.

She stopped sobbing long enough to puzzle over the vivid and detailed flashback. What did it mean? Confused, she began to weep again, and the parade of memories resumed. Time passed, and her tears stopped. She was all cried out.

Reentering the present, Ava looked at her watch. Her thoughts were a bit fuzzy, but her dreadful nausea had passed. As she considered her crying jag, the second of the day, she shook her head, appalled at her tearful behavior. She reflected on her self-centeredness at Sunny's, the headache and nausea, her tears and spasms, and the strange parade of past events. Her jaunt back to an earlier time was realistic and detailed. She was at a loss to explain the experience until her insight kicked in.

"Damn," she swore and crossed herself for forgiveness. She knew what the flashback represented: a need to feel safe like she had at the orphanage. With her security threatened in the present, her mind, seeking balance, had retreated to the past.

Chapter 13 – The Naples Pier, Naples, Florida

On her way home from Sunny's, Ava parked her car at the end of 12th Avenue South to call Langdon. Her emotional upheaval by the roadside had wasted thirty minutes and caused her to be late for her lunch with him. She would apologize and ask him to wait another twenty minutes before beginning. She did not think he would mind, and she would have time to walk to the Naples Pier and let the Gulf breeze work its magic on her puffy face.

Rosa answered. "He went to the farm, Miss Ava," she said, her Spanish accent evident, despite her mastery of English. "He told me to tell you he waited as long as he could."

"Thank you, Rosa. The meeting at the Cavanaugh's ran later than I expected. I'll be home soon."

Ava did not ask if Langdon was upset. Why cause the staff discomfort by calling attention to the awkwardness that had arisen between Langdon and her?

Until Rosa mentioned the farm, Ava had forgotten her commitment after lunch. She and Langdon were supposed to meet Ray Velez, the architect hired to design the housing for their seasonal workers at the farm. Upon reflection, she remembered Langdon's cautioning her the previous evening not to be late for lunch and their meeting. Even with his reminder, she forgot.

The missed appointment was an example of her inability to keep dates and times organized. If she had too many things to remember, her brain shut down like a blown circuit. She wrote her engagements in an appointment book, which she forgot to look at most of the time, and she had even neglected to tell Marquist about her disorganization. She shrugged off the oversight. As preoccupied as she was with worry, memory lapses were understandable, and for all she knew, her forgetfulness was unrelated to her twitching and spasms.

No matter the cause of her inability to remember, Ava was heartsick over the person she was becoming. She hated herself, and before long, Langdon would hate her, too. The thought was unbearable.

She decided a walk down the pier would help her sort things out. As she negotiated its weathered planks, she gulped the healing sea air and wrestled with contriving a believable excuse for missing lunch and the appointment with Ray Velez.

She could not tell Langdon she forgot, even if it was the truth. Her forgetfulness was a subject she avoided discussing with him because if she was unable to explain it to herself, how would he understand? *I will have to lie again.* Until her symptoms had a name and her illness a prognosis, the torment caused by her lies would continue.

Time was marching on as Ava waited for answers. Several months had elapsed since she started twitching. Dr. Marquist had required two appointments before he referred her to a neurologist. She did not blame him for the delay. The fault was hers for stalling at least a month before making her first appointment. Getting herself to St. Joseph's ate up another couple of weeks; she could not bring herself to pick up the phone and make the arrangements. Fearing she would have no record, or she would learn something hurtful, such as her mother was a prostitute or her father a rapist, she procrastinated. After that, she made and canceled two appointments with Marquist because she was terrified of what he might say. Mired in dread, Ava had delayed and delayed, waiting for a miracle. She had no one but herself to blame for the time she had frittered away.

After failing to pretend otherwise, she acknowledged the many things that had escaped her mind in the last month or two were more than ordinary slippage. It was unlike her to forget an appointment as significant as the one with Ray Velez, especially since the suggestion to build housing on the Skinner farms for the migrant workers and day laborers was an idea that came to her one night over dinner.

That evening, Buck, Craig Stephenson, and Langdon were grumbling about the cumbersome process of obtaining laborers for the farms. When her curiosity got the best of her, she encouraged them to elaborate.

"The main issues are transportation and worker turnover," Langdon said.

"Why, what's the problem?" Ava prompted.

"The way the current system operates, Ava, is laborers looking for a day of work queue up at designated points in Naples, where trucks from the farms meet them," Langdon said. "Then contractors hired by the growers or overseers from the farms work their way down the line of laborers from beginning to end. They select the number of men they need until every job is filled or no one is left standing."

Buck nodded. "Yep, and most of the time the men looking for work outnumber the need," he said.

"Selecting the workers sounds easy enough," Ava said. "Then what?"

"After filling the quota, the trucks transport the workers to the farms in Immokalee. At the end of the day, the same trucks return the workers to the pick-up spot in Naples," Langdon explained.

"It's been that way for a couple of decades," Stephenson said.

"Yes, and that's the problem." Langdon shook his head.

"Why?" Ava asked. "Have I missed the point?"

"The time spent transporting workers is part of the problem," Langdon said. "The workers and overseers spend more than two hours on the road each day, wasted hours which could be better spent elsewhere."

"I see." Ava nodded.

Langdon continued, "The second issue is the magnitude of worker turnover. Growers are forced to select their laborers from the front of the line, which means we end up with a different workforce from day-to-day, and then we have to instruct the laborers before the day's work can begin, a time-consuming and costly practice. We have to do it, though, because farms differ in their standards and methods, workers vary in efficiency, and produce requires handling specific to type. Picking tomatoes is not like picking citrus."

"More complicated than I thought," Ava said.

Buck raised his head to look at her across the table. "That's not the only problem. We have to pick workers from the front of the line. That means we don't know who we're getting. Men who excel in their abilities can be standing behind those who don't come close to getting the job done with any efficiency. With the system as it is, we can't select the better workers first or avoid those who are slow or lazy. It's a darn shame."

"Frustrating, too, I imagine," Ava said. "I agree with you, Dad. The way it's done now doesn't make sense."

"Dad's right," Langdon added, "and as far as I'm concerned, Ava, that's not the worst part. From one day to the next, workers might find themselves on different farms, a circumstance that makes it impossible for them to perfect specific skill sets. If capable workers go unnoticed and unrewarded, they have no incentive to continue working hard or to improve. That's the real crime."

"I have no doubt it would discourage me," Ava agreed.

She understood why each man believed the system was broken and detrimental to workers and growers. As the men continued to air their grievances, Ava was quiet. She considered the hardships migrant workers endured as they moved from place to place and farm to farm, when crops of vegetables, nuts, fruit, cotton, and sugar cane were ripe for harvesting.

Unable to afford decent housing, the workers and their families set up transitory camps in the poorest neighborhoods or rented by the week or month from neglectful landlords. To earn enough money to bring their families to the States or to improve the lives of the family members with whom they lived, the laborers worked long, hard hours. Ava was sympathetic to their needs, and it made her angry to see them mistreated or exploited.

Ava was a college student at Julliard when activist Caesar Chavez brought the plight of the migrant worker to the nation's attention in the late 1960s and early 1970s. She supported the cause and followed the progress of the movement as best she could. In the years that followed, a few conscientious growers took Chavez's suggestions to heart. Nonetheless, Ava saw room for improvement. Many farm workers were still underpaid, overworked, and without representation. They labored in high temperatures and suffered exposure to dangerous pesticides and poor sanitation in the fields.

Ava was proud of the way Skinner Enterprises treated its workers. Over the years, Buck and Langdon had fired several overbearing overseers for mistreating workers or for being neglectful. She thought Skinner Enterprises could do better, however. As she listened to the issues over dinner, it occurred to her that creating housing for the workers on the Skinner farms in Immokalee would eliminate many of the systemic problems plaguing the men. Closer to her heart, it would raise the workers' standard of living and at the same time, empty the pockets of exploitive landlords.

Ava thought her idea, although motivated by compassion, had practical value as well. She waited for the first lull in the conversation to broach the subject.

"Langdon, perhaps we might eliminate the turnover problem and keep our workers on our farms by building housing for them. With little or no turnover, we could train our workers to be more efficient. Wouldn't that increase our production and our profit margin?" She looked around the table for reactions.

For a long moment, no one said anything. Ava blushed.

"Genius," Langdon declared. "Over time, the cost of construction would be repaid. Better yet, the daily hassle of obtaining and transporting workers long distances would be a thing of the past."

"Glory be," Buck said. He slapped his thigh. "You got yourself a smart cookie there, Langdon." He smiled at Ava with a twinkle in his eye.

Langdon embraced her idea, and they hired Ray to design The Village. Excited about the venture and eager to see the progress made, Ava accompanied Langdon to the farms when he met with Ray. The project was hers as much as it was Langdon's, and yet she had forgotten their meeting.

Halfway down the length of the Naples pier, Ava sat on a bench and stared at the horizon where the waters of the Gulf met the sky. The scene was a monochromatic vision in blue, except for the few boats bobbing up and down on the silken surface of the water and the many varieties of seabirds busying themselves diving, flying, or floating on the air currents.

On an ordinary day, the scene rejuvenated her spirit. That day her need for repair was too great. She did not require a diagnosis to know she was a victim of an unknown enemy that made her twitch, turn into Bird Woman, forget important things, and be a lousy friend, wife, and daughter-in-law. She had become the kind of person she most disliked, a self-centered one. Her list of woes was long and at the top was helplessness.

Unwilling to devote one second more to her sad situation and longing for the support of someone who understood her misery, she withdrew Isabella's letter from her purse, opened it, and began reading.

The next five years were full of drastic changes. I think of them as my "becoming period." The job at the Biltmore opened doors for me by providing opportunities I would not have had if left to my own devices. I took full advantage of each one to become more educated and self-confident. As my knowledge increased, I grew more curious about the world around me. I woke up each morning feeling as if I were on the verge of discovery. I thought of myself as a caterpillar becoming a butterfly.

One afternoon at the Biltmore, I was playing the piano in the library during high tea when a middle-aged couple and a younger man settled themselves on the sofa nearest the piano. The young man, who looked as if he were close to my age, was quite handsome and attentive, and he glanced my way several times. I thought he was a musician or an ardent music lover. Before he left the library, he came over to me at the piano, introduced himself as John Phillips, and said he hoped to hear me play again. I was flattered and a bit excited. His comment hinted he might return in the future.

Because there is no room for the many details that followed, I will describe the salient parts. John Phillips is your father. After courting me for a year, John asked if I would marry him. I said yes, and we were married at the Biltmore in 1941. John was an extraordinary man—smart, kind, thoughtful, and funny. I adored him. Like me, he was an only child. John's parents, your grandparents, Margaret and Wade Phillips, who had moved to Florida from Connecticut, welcomed me into their family with open arms.

After our marriage, I wanted to continue working at the Biltmore until we were ready to have children, and since John was a junior partner in his father's large accounting firm in Tampa, we rented a small bungalow halfway between our places of employment. We were delirious with happiness in our little cottage for several months, and then the Japanese bombed Pearl Harbor. The event changed everything.

In 1942, John enlisted in the army. Selected to attend Officer's Candidate School in Miami Beach, he would not go to the front to fight right away, a stroke of luck. We were grateful beyond measure. With the assistance of John's parents, I found and rented a small apartment near the base to be with John when he was free. To keep busy, I supplemented our income by playing the piano in Miami hotels and nearby churches.

After John graduated from Officer's Candidate School, Second Lieutenant Phillips (so dashing in his uniform) elected to serve his country as a fighter pilot. The Army Air Corps assigned him to the San Antonio Aviation Cadet Center at Kelly Field in Texas.

I wanted to go with him, but rentals in the area were scarce. Military wives packed the hotels, motels, and boarding houses, and some even rented garages in desperation. The lack of housing prevented me from joining John. I decided to move in with Mama until he completed cadet school.

After flight school, John had several days of leave before he reported to his next station. We used the time to see Mama and Hernandez marry in our old church in Ybor, and then we surprised them with a reception at the social club we belonged to before Papa's illness. I was happy for Mama.

John distinguished himself at the Aviation Cadet Center, and when he graduated, the army promoted him to flight instructor. Once again, he avoided combat. We refrained from bringing his good luck to anyone's attention for fear it was an error that might be put to rights.

Ordered to a new facility right in Naples, John taught flying at an airport built to train fighter pilots, bomber crews, and gunners. I prayed for new students to keep coming until the war was over. God heard my prayers. When the war ended in 1945, we were still in Naples.

Ava stopped reading, folded the letter, and put it away. Her hands were shaking again, and she felt jittery. Rising from the bench, she decided a bit more exercise might help to quiet her twitching muscles. As she headed for the end of the broad pier jutting out over the waters of the Gulf, she picked her way with care, not wanting to catch her heel in the cracks between the boards. She was thinking about her parents when an intense sensation of déjà vu swept over her. The hair on her arms stood erect. Ava knew then without any doubt that Isabella, frightened, alone, and pregnant had walked the same pier thirty-two years earlier.

Even though Ava had resolved to think positively, she could not keep from fretting over the lack of progress in getting to the bottom of her symptoms. While matters were running on and on,

137

she and Langdon were drifting apart, a repercussion she had not foreseen in her earnest desire to protect him. Instead of safeguarding their relationship as she intended, her love for him was destroying it.

Chapter 14 – Immokalee Farm No. 1, Naples, Florida

Langdon reached to the floor of the Mercedes and pulled up his briefcase. He placed it on the empty back seat, opened it, and extracted the blueprints of the buildings Ray Velez had designed for the farm workers. Langdon, thinking he could use the forty-five minute trip to the farm to review Ray's changes, had asked David to drive; however, Langdon was finding it impossible to concentrate. Despite his good intentions, he was unable to shake Ava's erratic behavior or her conspicuous absence at lunch from his mind.

Defeated by his inability to focus on business, and with the blueprints resting unrolled in his lap, Langdon stared at the back of David's graying head, and then at the flat, sprawling countryside streaming by the window.

The Mercedes made its way east on Immokalee, turned north to bend around the lower fringe of Corkscrew Swamp, and headed due east again. Lost in thought, Langdon was oblivious to the vast wilderness rushing by. Swamps, scrub bushes, cedar hammocks, cabbage palms, saw palmettos, pines, and wildflowers were little more to him than a greenish-gray impression. Only the occasional blight of human habitation—a ramshackle building or dilapidated mobile home—attracted his notice.

Unlike other parts of Collier County, the land around Immokalee was sparsely populated and untamed, except for a few areas cleared for agriculture and cattle ranching. South of Immokalee near Sunniland, Grandpa Skinner, wildcatting for oil, brought in several wells in the mid-1940s. When Langdon was a boy, Grandpa Skinner kept him spellbound with stories from those exciting days.

Not long after the discovery of the Sunni-Felda oil field in the 1960s, Buck followed suit with two wells in the same area. Both continued to produce. South of Sunniland, near the Big Cypress Swamp, Skinner Enterprises owned a sizable cypress-lumbering concern.

Usually Langdon rode through the stretch of wilderness with a sense of family pride, but on that day, his concerns about Ava took precedence over the Skinners' business successes.

Langdon was tired, irritable, and finding it hard to rally after a restless night of waking each hour to determine if Ava was in or out of bed. Her strange behavior perplexed him, and her walks around the property at night alarmed him.

Cracking his knuckles, Langdon told himself to get back to business and to put Ava and his worries about her out of his mind. He needed to divert his energy to The Village, a challenge he found invigorating and one that satisfied his aspiration to give back to his community.

Like Ava, Langdon thought Chavez's depictions of the lives of migrant workers compelling. At the time, he was fresh out of college and in Texas, miles away from the farms in Naples. Issues happening back home were not part of his day-to-day reality. Not until Buck's illness thrust him front and center into the spotlight of the family's businesses did he give much thought to improving conditions for the workers. Ava's idea to build housing for them was the perfect solution to both the daily hassle of obtaining farm hands and the problems faced by workers looking for safe, affordable accommodations for themselves and their families.

Langdon also had a selfish reason for wanting the project to work. As the heir to Skinner Enterprises, he had several generations of big shoes to fill, a mind-boggling challenge he hoped to meet successfully. By completing The Village, he would not only be contributing to his community, but also leaving his own footprint on the company.

Ava's idea to build housing for their laborers was the seed from which his vision for an entire village had grown. If what he imagined came to pass, the result would be a legacy to hand down to the next generation of Skinners. As he explained to Buck when he detailed the benefits to be reaped from the project—leaving out the part about his legacy—the positive publicity would enhance their corporate image and serve as an example to other growers.

When he and Ava examined the project in earnest, Ava's idea to build housing for the workers grew from a simple undertaking into an ambitious plan. They both recognized the workers, who lived on the farms, could not travel to Naples for every necessity. They would require a few basic amenities nearby, at the very least, a grocery store. Ava asked where the workers' children would go to school and how would the workers and their families get to a hospital without transportation? Maybe there should be a medical clinic. Before long, they were in over their heads.

Not wanting to scrap the idea, Langdon enlisted the help of a local developer skilled in putting communities together from infrastructure to finished product. He and the developer were working to prepare a proposal to put before the city council. Meanwhile, Langdon was talking up the project with the other growers in the area, hoping to generate both interest and revenue, and Ava was doing her part by encouraging her friends to mention the subject to their wealthy husbands.

Their plan was taking shape, and yet after the many hours spent together on the project and Ava's expressed desire to participate, she was a no-show for lunch and their meeting with Velez. He shook his head, mystified.

He was not either unobservant or stupid. He knew something serious was troubling Ava. Since she would not confide in him, he had come right out and asked her, "What's going on with you? You are not yourself these days, Ava." Her response was to look right through him as if he was not there. Did she avoid meeting his eyes for fear of his reading a secret in hers?

"Oh, Langdon, you do exaggerate," she teased. "All this concern because I've forgotten a few things."

"No, Ava, it's more than that, and you know it. I can't understand why you're pretending everything's fine. It's not. What's wrong?"

When Langdon reflected on their conversation, he acknowledged the sincere concern he had meant to convey had sounded impatient and demanding. "Damn it," he swore under his breath.

When he thought about Ava's avoidance and her mysterious silence, his gut churned with anxiety. Their once-satisfying relationship was deteriorating, and he was powerless to fix it, as long as Ava insisted on being secretive. She made him feel extraneous to their marriage, and even more damaging, impotent.

Every time he asked Ava to tell him what was troubling her, she avoided his questions with a tactical maneuver of some kind. Langdon was becoming desperate just to hear Ava agree that something was wrong, never mind find out what it was. Running out of ideas for gaining her confidence, Langdon brought up the piano again, hoping to make his point.

"There's a good example of what's changed," he said.

"What do you mean?" Ava asked.

"You don't play anymore."

Ava gave him a wounded look. "Langdon, I told you I sprained my finger. It's not quite right yet."

"Oh, come on, Ava, how long does it take a little finger sprain to heal?"

She was so calm and he so upset that it irked him. In hindsight, he knew it was a dumb thing to say. He had scoffed at her. His mother was right when she told him, "Langdon, you catch more flies with honey than you do with vinegar." His comment, made in the heat of the moment, was a knee-jerk expression of his frustration. Ava's blasé attitude, pretending everything was normal, had belittled his concern.

Langdon meant the comment about the piano as an example of how things had changed. To him, Ava's avoidance of the piano was a concrete example of something gone very wrong. As soon as his words tumbled out, he regretted them. His remark was intended as an observation; instead, it sounded like an accusation. In his eagerness to repair his and Ava's broken relationship, he had tripped over his own feet.

As if that incident were not unsettling enough, Ava had either forgotten their lunch date and their meeting afterward with Velez, or she was no longer interested in participating. *Maybe she had something better to do,* Langdon's inner voice whispered. He pushed the unwanted thought from his mind. He would not think that about her.

Had he failed to communicate to Ava his sincere desire to have her work with him on the project? He thought he had made himself clear by asking if she was available to meet with Velez. She said she was and expressed her excitement. After that, they talked about how the idea for The Village sprang from her comment at dinner and agreed it would be fun to work together on the project.

As Langdon was mulling over these events, he recalled Ava's saying to him earlier in the morning, on her way out, that she would see him at lunch. If she did not forget their meeting, then what had kept her from it? She had not even bothered to call. It was unlike Ava to be thoughtless. Where was she going at such an early hour, he wondered. Was her unresponsiveness to his question deliberate? "Damn," he said again, annoyed with himself for questioning everything.

As attentive as a sea captain to changes in the weather, David monitored the moods of his passengers. He peered at Langdon in the rearview mirror. "Did you say something, sir?"

"Yes, well no ... I mean, yes," Langdon answered, "I said damn. I was thinking out loud. Sorry."

"Is there something I can assist you with, sir?"

"No, David, thanks. Looks like I forgot something. It can wait." For Pete's sake, he thought, now he was lying to the help. He clenched his jaw.

"If you say so, sir."

David's reply made it clear to Langdon that his explanation was lame. "David," Langdon said, "how many times have I asked you not to call me sir? I have known you since I was a little boy, and the title does not fit comfortably."

"Sorry, sir, I mean, bad habit, sorry."

Embarrassed by his apparent inability to converse in a civil manner, Langdon sighed like a man with many burdens and unrolled the blueprints Velez had submitted. Ava's craziness had spilled over into his business life. He could not let their marital issues distract him from the bigger picture. Before his meeting with Velez, he needed to clear his mind of Ava and focus on the project.

A cursory glance at the blueprints revealed Ray had made the changes they discussed. Langdon was not surprised. He had come to expect a high degree of excellence from Ray, who had proved to be worth his weight in gold from the first day of their association. Articulate, astute, creative, and diligent, Ray was passionate about The Village, and for a good reason. During his interview—one of five Langdon and Ava conducted together, after narrowing the field of candidates—they learned Ray came from a family of six, and his parents were migrant workers.

He and Ava set out to hire an architect and came away with the prize. No one understood better than Ray the obstacles battled by migrant workers and their families when it came to finding decent housing, health care, and education for their children or how hard it was to look for work without a car. Ray was familiar with the impact on workers of dangerous working conditions and long days of labor in the sweltering heat without rest and water.

When he was a child, Ray watched, wide-eyed and frightened, as a cruel overseer brutalized his father. Ray's family endured the sting of discrimination, the hollowness of hunger, and the humiliation of squalid living conditions. As a result, Ray had more insight into the needs of the day laborers and migrant workers—often the same thing—than anyone Langdon knew. Ray's willingness to express those needs, without evincing rancor or recrimination for the hard life he had endured, was not only admirable but also valuable to Langdon.

Langdon pondered how rare it was for a man to overcome such a difficult childhood to excel as Ray had. His success, achieved by hard work and without the advantage of shortcuts or unearned opportunities, meant he owed no man for the person he had become. Ray had earned the right to boast, but Langdon found him as modest and unassuming about his accomplishments as he was intelligent.

Langdon was learning about Ray in bits and pieces because Ray did not talk much about himself. When they discussed migrant workers, now and then Ray would share a story—without mentioning the part he played—to exemplify a point or a concern. Langdon had become adept at discerning, from Ray's stories, the events that were his experiences, and it was from those fragments of information that Landon was gaining an understanding of who Ray was.

To Langdon's delight, Ray brought another asset to the table, a thorough knowledge of the demands and constraints on big agriculture, and the narrow line between expense and income walked by growers. Ray understood the many nuances affecting production—chief among them climate and disease—and how a single bad year of either could set a farm back several years before it returned to profitability. He had a good grip on the economics of farming, from planting to distribution, and the broader view driven by supply and demand, futures, and market trading. Without a doubt, Ray was brilliant. Langdon was in awe of the man's intellect. Ray's enthusiastic support for Langdon's vision of The Village pleased Langdon, and even though their backgrounds were dissimilar, he and Ray got along well. Langdon sensed they were on the verge of forming a firm friendship. He looked forward to their meetings.

When the Mercedes pulled up in front of the farm office, a remodeled tobacco shed, Langdon saw Ray, dressed in jeans, waving from the porch. As Langdon walked toward him, Ray rolled up the sleeves of his red and white pinstriped dress shirt and greeted Langdon with an ear-to-ear smile radiating from his clean-shaven face.

Langdon offered Ray a firm handshake. "Hi, Ray," he said, smiling.

"Good morning to you, Langdon. Where's your better half?"

Good question. "Ava must have mixed up appointments." He hated lying.

"It happens," Ray said. "An accident bollixing up Tamiami held me up. I made up the time on the flats, though."

When they turned to go inside the building, Langdon noticed Ray was favoring one leg. "What'd you do to your leg, Ray? Please tell me it's more exciting than tripping over the dog."

"Almost as mundane. I think I pulled a calf muscle or something playing squash."

"I didn't know you were a squash player. There aren't many courts around. Where do you play?"

"At the Y in Fort Myers."

"That's a hike if you're in a rush." Langdon carried the rolls of blueprints over to his desk and plunked them down.

"It is, but beggars can't be choosers." Ray shrugged.

"How long have you been playing?" Langdon asked. He put his briefcase down on the desk chair.

"Since my prep school days. Taft had a great team and six courts. I also played at Berkeley and Harvard, when I could fit it in. Not on a team, though. Too busy. You play?"

Langdon was doing the math. Ray was four years older.

"As a matter of fact, I do, and I was on Choate's team," Langdon said. "I missed you by one year. If you hadn't graduated from Taft, before I went to Choate, we would have faced each other as rivals." He laughed.

"No kidding. Who would've thought two Connecticut prep school squash players would find each other in Naples? We should play sometime," Ray said.

"I can do better than that. How about this weekend, if your leg is ready for action and you have some free time?"

"Okay, you're on. First, we have to check court availability, and then get ready to be crushed." Ray's eyes twinkled challenge.

"Spoken like a pompous Taftie," Langdon parried. "Pick a time and be prepared for defeat."

"I'll call the courts," Ray said.

"No, you don't have to. We have one."

Ray's deep brown eyes snapped open wide. "You do?"

"Yep, one of your job perks."

"No kidding, really?"

Langdon was enjoying Ray's reaction. "Buck learned to play during his stint in the military, and since he wasn't fond of playing tennis in the summer heat, he put one in on the backside of the carriage barn, figuring an air-conditioned squash court would be a great alternative." Langdon chuckled.

"Wow."

"Name your time," Langdon prodded.

"Wow again," Ray said. "How about nine, or is that too early?"

"Nope, perfect. It'll give me time to do a few bench presses, jog the beach, and ride my bike twenty miles first," Langdon boasted, trying to keep a straight face.

Ray groaned." Braggadocios Choatee."

Langdon gave Ray a playful slap on the back.

As the men turned their attention to business, Langdon considered how full of surprises his new friend and business partner had turned out to be. Ray was the diversion Langdon needed to take his mind off Ava.

Chapter 15 – Pelican View, Naples, Florida

Full of remorse, Ava left the pier. She had disappointed Langdon again. What would she say to him when she went home? Even if he did not mention her absence at lunch, the ache behind his eyes, injured and pleading, would remind her of his misery. She avoided him as much as possible, fearing she might weaken and tell him everything. At times, she thought the medicine of avoidance worse than any possible illness she might have.

Ava returned to her car and examined her face in the rearview mirror. To her relief, the Gulf breeze had soothed away the swelling and puffiness left by her episodes of crying. Wanting to look refreshed when Langdon returned, Ava decided to go home and take a nap.

At Pelican View, Ava found Rosa in the kitchen baking. The smell of cornbread filled the air with a tantalizing sweetness. After her earlier nausea, she decided against having a piece. She did not want to set off the queasiness again.

"Oh, Miss Ava, I'm happy you're home. Mr. Langdon was worried," Rosa said. She set the cornbread on top of the stove and pulled off her oven mitts.

Ava's heart picked up its pace at the mention of Langdon's name, a guilty reminder she had forgotten their appointment. "Sunny's meetings always run overtime." Ava smiled and hoped Rosa did not notice the color rising to her cheeks. *I am a terrible liar.*

"I'm a little tired, Rosa. I think I'll take a short nap before Langdon comes home."

Wiping an errant wisp of raven black hair back from her face, Rosa clucked in sympathy. "Would you like some lunch first, Miss Ava? I saved yours."

"No, thank you, Rosa. My appetite is a bit off, too, for some reason."

When Ava turned to leave the kitchen, she sensed Rosa assessing her. Was her distress apparent to everyone in the household? She felt like an infection spreading from person to person.

Rosa called after her. "Should I tell Mr. Langdon not to wake you, Miss Ava?"

Ava turned back around. "No, it's okay if he does," she said. "I think a catnap will do the trick. I want to see how Buck is doing, first, though."

When Ava poked her head into Buck's room, Juanita looked up from her magazine and raising an index finger to her pursed lips, indicated Buck was sleeping. Ava smiled, nodded, and with a little wave, returned Buck's door to its previous position.

In her bedroom, Ava stretched out on the canopied bed and stared at the ceiling through the gossamer folds of fabric. She closed her eyes and begged for sleep, any past time to help the hours and days go by faster. The wait for another doctor's appointment was discouraging, and the distance she had put between herself and Langdon preyed on her conscience. After twenty minutes, Ava gave up the notion of sleeping to finish Isabella's letter instead. She sat up in bed, gathered a light blanket around her shoulders—Langdon kept the air conditioner too low for her taste—plumped up the pillows, and opened Isabella's letter to the last pages. They were the saddest ones for her and Isabella, and the relationship they might have enjoyed, had it not been stolen from them. With a sorrowful sigh, Ava considered how her mother had struggled to achieve her dreams, only to have her life end in despair. Ava picked up the pages of Isabella's letter and read.

Several weeks have passed since I wrote the previous paragraphs, and as I read back through the pages, I realize I have laid out the facts of my life without expressing any emotion. When you read my letter, I pray it doesn't sound cold.

Writing to you, my dearest Ava, has been an arduous journey because my emotions have been on a roller coaster the entire time. Putting my life on paper has made me relive it, in a sense. I have re-experienced the joy, sadness, surprise, relief, gratitude, and worry that I felt at the time. I am sorry for having done a poor job of conveying those feelings to you. Despite my ineptitude, writing to you has brought me great relief, for I have confirmed to myself what I must do. I no longer have any doubts, a significant gift.

To begin again where I left off, when the war ended, your father...

How strange the words your father sounded to Ava. She hesitated for a moment and then continued.

...your father was released from the service without being posted overseas. For us, it was a blessing. For the families of the men who never returned, it was a hard time. The war years had taken their toll on everyone, even those who had no sons or husbands in the service, like Hernandez and Mama. They moved to Atlanta to work in a munitions factory, Mama in the office and Hernandez as a production manager. People contributed what they could.

After his discharge from the Army Air Corps, John went back to his father's firm in Tampa for a short time, and several months later, he opened an office in Naples. The population had burgeoned during the war, because of the nearby airbase, and when the war was over, people stayed. John was excited about having his own office in Naples. At last, he had the autonomy he craved. We were thrilled to stay in Naples, as we preferred its neighborly size to the larger and more impersonal city of Tampa. When we bought our first house two blocks from the beach, it was a happy day.

Our version of heaven was short-lived, however, destroyed by the death of John's father from a cataclysmic heart attack. John's mother's grief sent her into a tailspin. She was a constant worry to us.

When time passed, and she did not improve, we thought it best to move her in with us. At least we could keep a closer eye on her, and John was able to enjoy a weekend at home for a change, instead of driving round trips between Naples and Tampa to check on her. We understood she was severely depressed, but having her underfoot was a strain. Rising above her despondency was hard.

Now my hand is shaking because I must tell you about another sad thing. One rainy day in August 1947, John and his mother were on their way to Margaret's doctor when a truck, skidding out of control, crossed the median, slammed into John's car, and crushed it beyond recognition. Both John and Margaret died at the scene.

You can imagine my shock. After John's death, Mama came down from Atlanta to stay with me. My recollection of that time is vague. Lost in grief, I wanted to die, too. Mama did not want to leave when her vacation time was up. I worried, if she did not return to Atlanta, she would lose her job. By pretending I had to get back to work and on with my life, I convinced her to go home.

To be truthful, I was not myself. I was in survival mode, going through the motions of getting through each day. I struggled to keep to an ordinary routine. Without John, I was a lifeless cardboard cutout searching for a reason to go on.

Three weeks after Mama went back to Atlanta, I discovered I was pregnant with you. My heart came to life. John had left part of himself behind, a baby I could hold and love. In the midst of the darkness, I had a reason to live. I threw myself into doing everything right for my pregnancy—eating the right foods, getting lots of sleep, and taking long walks. I bought the stores out of baby clothes. You were the most wanted baby in the whole world.

Mama and Hernandez came down to Naples for your birth. They brought a bottle of champagne to the hospital, and we toasted and toasted, happy to have something delightful to celebrate and to chase away the sadness. Afterward, Hernandez returned to Atlanta, and Mama stayed on to help me. You were such an easy baby. In three days, you slept through the night. Mama didn't have to stay long.

When I held you, I thought about John, who I missed every minute of the day. You gave me a reason to go on with my life. I had just turned away from the dark days of grief and was moving toward the sunlight again when the symptoms of the illness that would end my life appeared.

You were a little more than two weeks old. I was Papa all over again. He had left behind a terrible legacy, a death sentence for me. When my doctor confirmed my fears, I began to plan for your future.

John was gone. John's parents were gone. There were no aunties or uncles to step in. Mama and Hernandez had settled in Atlanta. I did not want to burden them with my illness, not after what poor Mama had been through with Papa. I kept the horrible secret to myself and prayed to God to show me the way.

You were growing by leaps and bounds. As your development progressed, so did my illness, a situation that created problems for both of us. I thought my life had reached rock bottom when

Mama suffered a stroke that left her in a vegetative state. She was in a coma, hooked up to machines, and dying. I took you to Atlanta to see her one last time and say good-bye. She died while we were there. I was holding her hand. With Mama's passing, we were alone in the world. You were four months old.

I went home knowing what I must do. I do not think it safe for me to care for you much longer. You deserve to have a full, happy life with a family that loves you and gives you what I cannot. Everyone I care for is dead. There is no one to help.

Each passing day brings a new hurdle, worry, or malfunctioning body part. It has taken several months to write to you because my poor coordination and inability to remember things make writing a letter difficult. I fret about not hearing you cry and the possibility of dropping you if I begin to shake. At the present time, I can do what I must, but I also know my condition can change at any time. I am on a hopeless course. Death will take me before I can rear you.

Aside from the predicament of having no one to turn to, I may be physically or mentally incapable of delivering you to loving hands, if I delay. To keep you beyond your infancy is a risk to your safety and quick adoption. People want to adopt infants more than older children.

I have come to terms with what I must do. I hope you will find it in your heart to forgive me. Even though I have failed you, God will not. I am not taking my own life. I am delivering myself to God a

*little sooner, for he has already called me. I love
you, Ava Marie, my darling, sweet baby.*
                              Your loving mother, Isabella

Ava reached for a tissue, blotted her cheeks,
and wiped her eyes. *Isabella's death was so
damned unfair.* She crossed herself for swearing
and as her resentment peaked, buried her face in
the pillow and cried. She did not require a
neurologist to tell her what she already knew: she
had the same illness as her mother and
grandfather. The only reason to keep the
appointment was to learn the name of the disease
and find out if there was a cure.

Once again, Ava wondered why Isabella had
not mentioned the name of her illness. Ava
doubted it was an oversight. She was certain
Isabella had a reason. What was it? The
puzzlement taunted her.

Rising from the bed, Ava folded her treasure
and took it to her closet, where she selected a
shoebox from the highest shelf. She buried her
treasure out of sight, under the tissue paper that
wrapped the shoes. Until she made a decision, she
could not risk a chance discovery.

Chapter 16 – Office of Dr. Osgood, Tampa, Florida

Looking prim with her legs crossed at the ankles, Ava sat in a chair next to Dr. Mark Osgood's desk doing her best to appear composed, even though she was an emotional wreck. Seconds before, Osgood had greeted her with a warm handshake and a genuine smile, a promising beginning, she thought.

The neurologist, a trim man Ava thought to be in his late forties, was dressed in a white lab coat weighed down by an assembly of implements: a rubber-headed mallet, a stethoscope, a notebook, several pens, what looked like a folded electrocardiogram strip, and another instrument she could not identify.

After a cordial exchange of words, the doctor fell silent to study her records. As he pored over them, Ava took a second look at him. His skin was fair but tan, and his athletic physique suggested a favorite sport or regular visits to the gym. Ava thought she liked him. She would wait to assess his bedside manner before deciding.

Osgood looked up from the pages of Ava's record. "Dr. Marquist's report is detailed and helpful, in particular, the history he's noted on your mother and grandfather," Osgood said, "and his exam was thorough, so there is no reason to duplicate it. I would like to check your eyes and reflexes, however, if I may. I see your blood work is in order, too. Have you experienced any new symptoms since your visit to Dr. Marquist?"

Ava nodded. "I forgot to tell Bill, uh ... Dr. Marquist about my trouble getting organized. I forget dates and times. I write engagements in my appointment book and then forget to look at it. My mind is a sieve. I have also been having bouts of nausea, and my emotions are all over the place, if you know what I mean. One minute I'm as calm as can be, under the circumstances, and the next I'm tearful."

Osgood nodded. "Forgetfulness is important to note, Ava. Let me know if it worsens. Can you recall when you experience nausea? I mean the time of day?"

"In the morning for the most part," she replied, puzzled by what difference the time of day made.

"I see." Osgood's voice was vanilla, giving nothing away. He stood, walked to the door, and summoned a young nurse scurrying down the hall. "Marlene, would you assist Mrs. Skinner in obtaining a urine specimen, please?"

He turned back to face Ava. "Would you mind? I know you gave a sample at Dr. Marquist's office. I want a more recent one."

"No, I don't mind," Ava said. She rose to her feet, pondering the significance of the doctor's request, and followed the nurse.

When her task was completed, Ava turned the sample over to the nurse and returned to the examining room, grateful to find it vacant. Feeling tense and short on patience, she welcomed the moment to collect herself.

A few minutes later, Osgood addressed her from the doorway of the examining room. "Ava, we've figured out one issue." His face was somber as he crossed the room and settled himself in his desk chair.

Ava held her breath.

"You are pregnant," Osgood said. "I can't tell how far along. I had a quick consultation with Dr. Friedlander down the hall, an excellent OB-GYN. Since you've come such a long way, he has agreed to see you after we finish. He'll determine how many weeks along you are. We should have that information as soon as possible."

At the stunning news, Ava froze, her body becoming as rigid as a broomstick and her mind grinding to a halt. For several seconds, she was silent, fighting to pull herself together.

When she was able to gather her words, she stammered, "I ... really? Pregnant?"

"Yes, it explains your nausea and in part, the mood swings," he said. He sat down in a chair across from Ava's.

Osgood's smile was gone. His serious expression frightened her. Ava thought, *something is wrong.* She could not bring herself to ask. Her feelings in turmoil, she stared straight ahead, looking at nothing, saying nothing, vaguely aware Osgood was watching her and waiting for her to respond. She could not form the words she needed; her tongue, as heavy as stone, would not move.

Osgood maintained his silence until Ava was able to raise her head to look at him.

"In most cases, morning sickness goes away during the second trimester," he said.

Was he throwing her a bone? Offering her something positive to anticipate?

"You ... you ... said my pregnancy was responsible for only some of my symptoms," Ava faltered. "And the rest of them ... is there a name for what's causing the tremors, the spasticity, the forgetfulness?"

"Let's do an exam first," Osgood said, "and then I will answer your questions. You needn't undress." The doctor got up from his chair and patted the examining table.

Osgood had postponed her inquiries. Had her whispered questions given away her reluctance to know the truth? When Ava, searching for an answer, raised her eyes to Osgood's, he looked back at her with compassion.

Feeling as if she were moving in slow motion, Ava kicked off her shoes, climbed up on the examining table—covered with paper that crinkled beneath her like breakfast cereal—and stretched out.

Osgood removed the rubber-headed mallet from his pocket. He used the rubber end to tap her knees and ankles and the cold, pointed end to drag across the soles of her feet. Next, he peered into her eyes with the instrument she had been unable to identify. Osgood asked her to walk across the room and back, to touch her nose, to raise her arms above her head, to catch a soft rubber ball, and to balance first on one foot and then the other.

When Ava returned to the examining table, Osgood questioned her about her hearing, vision, sense of smell and touch, and her memory. The entire exam took less than fifteen minutes. Afterward, Ava eased herself off the table, amid more paper crackling, and returned to her chair.

Osgood sat in the chair facing hers. He took her hands in his and was poised to say something when Ava's right hand stole the show. As if it knew the doctor was paying attention, it trembled. In short order, the tremble became a spastic twitch, and then the muscles of her hand drew themselves into a tight contraction. Her claw was showing off. Osgood watched with a solemn face and unwavering eyes.

"Try to open your fingers, Ava," he said.

"I can't," she said. "My brain has no control over what's happening to my hand."

"Try again, please. Close your eyes and think 'Open, open, open.'"

Ava followed Osgood's instruction. After a few seconds, she opened her eyes and looked down at her right hand. Her Bird Woman talon was still there.

"Do those contractions occur in both hands?" Osgood asked. "How many times a day, would you say?"

"Yes, both hands, although mostly my right," Ava said. "I haven't counted. Maybe three or four times a day. The twitching is more frequent than the contraction." She cast her eyes downward as if shamed by her contorted appendage.

Doctor and patient sat together staring at Ava's dysfunctional hand for little more than half a minute until Ava's muscles released her Bird Woman claw.

Osgood drew in a deep breath. "Ava," he said, "do you want to know what's causing these?" He gestured at her hand.

He was bringing her back to reality, she thought. "Yes, of course, I do, except I'm frightened," she said. She had blurted out the admission, never mentioned before to anyone, as if she and Osgood had shared an intimate moment while staring at her claw and being forthcoming with him as a result was normal.

"Ava, you strike me as a sensible, intelligent, and strong woman. We can't avoid talking about why you came. I know you want to learn the cause of your symptoms," Osgood said,

"Thank you, doctor," Ava replied, "except in the last few months, I haven't been either sensible or strong. I'm terrified. You read my mother's letter. I know I have what she and my grandfather had, and we both know how they ended up. Will I be next?" Lowering her head, she brushed away a single tear.

"Ava, you can't think that way," Osgood said, offering her a tissue. Scientific breakthroughs are daily occurrences. People who once died of one thing or another, no longer do. I see patients who out-perform expectations and reach new milestones every day. You must be positive."

Ava heard his words, a jumble of sentences and sounds she could not put into a comprehensible order. She nodded as if she understood. Emotion filled her like a balloon; she could feel the pressure of it pushing against her ears and eyes, filling up her throat, crowding out her thoughts, her feelings, her perceptions. Soon she would pop and explode emotion everywhere.

Like a man walking into a fire determined to be brave, Osgood drew himself up and plunged forward. "Ava, you have Huntington's disease. Do you know what it is?"

"No, not really, I've heard the name. It must be a neurological condition, or I wouldn't be here. What is Huntington's disease?" Alarm enlarged her pupils. Ava closed her eyes to concentrate on Osgood's words.

"In a nutshell, Huntington's disease is an inherited illness that affects the nervous system. Most of the time, it strikes people in mid-life. We suspect a gene causes it. We treat HD with various medications as the patient's condition warrants.

"It will be important for you to get plenty of exercise and sleep and to eat nutritious meals. You should keep track, if you can, of your twitching and spasms. Note the number of times a day they occur. It will help me determine the progression of the disease. I will want to see you at least once a month and maybe more often, as needed. If anything troubles you, call me. I want you to come back in two weeks with a family member—preferably your husband. HD requires teamwork to manage." The gaze from his blue eyes lingered on her face.

As if his words had nothing to do with her, Ava crawled inward, deep into the cave of herself, and with her eyes closed, sat motionless in the chair. The room was quiet, except for the ticking of the clock on the wall. Ava opened her eyes to look at it, an old-fashioned timepiece like the one in Millie and Buck's bedroom, *Biedermeier,* she thought. She watched the black wooden pendulum swing back and forth in the highly polished maple and mahogany case, its sound and repetitive motion soothing, hypnotic.

A sense of tranquility washed over her bringing with it a peacefulness that smoothed away the ruts and pits of her fear and anxiety. From a distance, she heard her name. Someone was calling her. She did not want to answer, to leave her cocoon of tranquility.

"Ava, Ava, what are you feeling?"

She blinked and turned in the direction of the sound. Osgood stood above her, rubbing his chin and studying her face.

"Nothing, I don't feel anything," she mumbled. She had trouble forming the words. Her lips were rubber.

"Ava, it's not unexpected," Osgood said. "You've experienced a terrible shock and numbness is an understandable reaction. May I get you a glass of water? Do you want to lie down?"

"No, thank you. I guess I am ..." Her whispered words floated away into the air.

Osgood sat back down in the chair across from her. His gaze sought hers. "Ava, why don't you stay here in my office until you feel collected, and then visit Dr. Friedlander down the hall about your pregnancy. I will see you are not disturbed. After you finish with Friedlander, come back to my office. My nurse will provide you with a packet of information to take home. Read the enclosures when you are up to it. You will have many questions. Write them down as they crop up until we meet again in two weeks. Friedlander and I will consult after your visit to him. When I see you again, we'll talk about what comes next. Is that agreeable?"

"Yes," she heard herself say. "Thank you, doctor."

When Ava left the medical building, loaded down with appointments and brochures on Huntington's disease and pregnancy, the sun was nearing the western horizon. She was glad she had the foresight to book a room at the Royal Breezes Hotel; she was in no condition to drive home. After she checked in, she wanted nothing more than to sleep, a deep, shut-out-the-world, healing kind of sleep before she had to face the brutal reality of her new life.

As Ava opened the door to her hotel suite, she remembered she had to call Langdon. He would want to know she had reached the convent. She told him she was visiting Sister Teresa, a good alibi since Langdon would never phone the convent, for fear of interrupting the sisters at an inopportune time. Despite wanting to assure him of her safety, she hated to lie to him.

Ava glanced at her watch. If she could depend on her unreliable memory for a change, Langdon was in a meeting with town officials about the Immokalee project. She could avoid him altogether by leaving a message and letting Rosa pass on her lie. Ava knew her solution was cowardly. *It can't be helped,* she told herself. She needed time to regain her self-control before facing Langdon.

Chapter 17 – Royal Breezes Hotel, Tampa, Florida

Three hours after Ava checked into the Royal Breezes Hotel and Resort, she awoke from a fitful sleep to find herself in unfamiliar surroundings. The bedroom in her hotel suite was dark, except for the ambient light of Tampa that filtered through the sheer curtains at the window. As she cleared the remnants of sleep from her mind, her stomach growled a reminder that it was empty. Overcome with worry, she had forgotten to eat, even though both Osgood and Friedlander had advised her to follow a healthy diet. Reaching for the bedside lamp, she turned it on, and then, full awareness stormed her consciousness like a powerful brain freeze, bringing with it the mind-numbing discoveries of the day. Dear God, she was pregnant, and she had Huntington's disease, a double blow.

Ava thought it beyond belief that her body was dying at the same time it was bringing a new life into the world. She could acknowledge the facts of her situation; responding to them was another matter. She was separated from the full weight of her dilemma, emotionless, and observing from the sidelines.

She likened her detachment to being in limbo or having an out-of-body experience. Both the Huntington's and her pregnancy demanded action. She had decisions to make and a strategy to devise, and yet she was not motivated. She supposed it would take time to recover her emotions; she was in no hurry.

She looked at her watch, eight in the evening. No wonder her neglected stomach was demanding attention. She picked up the phone and pressed three for room service.

When she returned the phone to its base, she happened to glance at the entry table in the small foyer where she had dropped her purse. Next to it was the pile of information from the doctors' offices about Huntington's and pregnancy. She regarded the brochures with a dispassionate eye. After months of waiting for an answer, she felt no urgency to examine them. Denial had replaced frustration as her new companion.

Thirty minutes later, a soft knock on the door announced the arrival of room service. Ava directed the placement of her meal, tipped the young eager-to-please waiter, and sat down to appease her hunger. Halfway through her meal, the pamphlets fell into her line of vision again. She decided she might as well read as she ate. She would have plenty of time to absorb the material and consider her options on the drive home in the morning. *Options*, she countered. *What options?* She picked up the first pamphlet.

> *Huntington's disease (HD) is a fatal hereditary disease that destroys the neurons of the brain controlling movement, intellect, and emotions. Jerky, uncontrollable movements of*

*the limbs, trunk, and face (chorea);
progressive loss of mental abilities;
and the development of psychiatric
problems characterize the course of
Huntington's. There is a fifty percent
chance that each child born to an HD
parent will acquire the disease.*

Oh goody, she thought. A bitter taste rose to
her mouth. *I have so much to look forward to. I will
become a writhing, jerking, raving lunatic with a
slowly disintegrating brain, the perfect wife.* She
put down her fork—her appetite had vanished—
and moved to the sofa.

As Ava read more about HD, she unraveled the
mystery of Isabella's omitted diagnosis. From the
beginning, Ava believed Isabella was too thorough
to overlook such an important piece of information
in her letter. After reading the pamphlet on HD,
Ava understood why the diagnosis was not
mentioned. When Isabella wrote her letter, she
most likely knew what Ava had just learned: not
every child of an HD carrier acquires the disease.
Isabella withheld the name of her illness to spare
her child needless worry if she were HD-free or if
she were not, to allow her child to have a normal
life for years before HD surfaced.

Ava asked herself if she had known from a
young age that HD was inevitable, how would she
have lived her life, with zest or fear? Without
question, Isabella had asked herself the same
thing. Ava thought she had made the right
decision.

With the mystery of the omitted diagnosis solved, Ava swallowed hard against her awakening emotions and picked up the pamphlet from her lap.

Huntington's disease appears most commonly in middle age. Infrequently it can develop in younger and older people. The course of the disorder progresses without remission over ten to twenty-five years. Eventually, patients decline to the point that they are unable to care for themselves.

Ava felt cheated by the age parameter. She was thirty-two. *Why didn't the darned illness wait until I was at least fifty before surfacing?* The ghastliness of existing as a non-human being for ten or more years before dying was beyond her understanding.

She thought back to her conversation with Osgood. The poor man had done his best to offer her a shred of hope. He had shared with her his excitement over a scientific undertaking called the US-Venezuela Huntington's Disease Collaborative Research Project.

"An American doctor named Nancy Wexler, inspired by the work of a Venezuelan doctor, organized a project to study the members of several large interrelated families," he said. "Those families are of particular interest because there is a high incidence of Huntington's among them. The research in Venezuela began last year, and I expect a breakthrough any day."

"I'm sorry, Dr. Osgood, I don't understand your point," Ava said. Her tone was impatient. "Besides having a parent and grandparents who were born in Venezuela, how does Wexler's work apply to me?"

"Oh, don't be sorry," Osgood said. "I'm not explaining myself well. I'll start over." He folded his hands into a tent and leaned his chin on them. "Researchers can better understand how a disease is inherited or transmitted if they have a large pool of related individuals to study. The scientists in Venezuela are looking for a gene or genetic markers." He stopped to take a breath and then smiled at her. "What I'm trying to say, Ava, is we are making progress. The Venezuelan project is a good example."

Listless, Ava sat before her plate thinking about Osgood's pep talk. She wanted to be as optimistic as he was. The sad fact was: a cure, discovered in a decade or several years, was too late for her. One by one, her brain cells were turning to useless gray matter.

Ava recalled Sister Teresa's admonition. "Ava, no matter how terrible your plight, someone else is worse off. Don't waste time on self-pity. Pray for them." Ava was hard put to think of anything more devastating or cruel than Huntington's, however.

As if rehearsing the name of a new acquaintance, Ava said the word Huntington's aloud several times, trying to make it fit, trying to make it real. With a deep sigh, she reached for another brochure on the treatment of Huntington's.

There is no cure for Huntington's disease. Treatment focuses on reducing symptoms, preventing complications, and providing support and assistance to the patient and those close to him or her.

In other words, treatment was little more than life-support, as far as Ava could judge. With death inevitable, it made no sense to her to waste time, energy, and resources on prolonging its arrival. She sneered at the pretty butterfly that decorated the page. An absurd choice for a brochure about death, she thought. It brought to mind the expression, "Butterflies are free." She wondered if the designers of the pamphlet knew Huntington's trapped its victims in their bodies.

The section "Medications and Huntington's Disease" screamed insanity. Among the array of drugs were antipsychotics to control hallucinations, delusions, and violent outbursts; antidepressants to counteract depression and obsessive-compulsive behavior; tranquilizers to reduce anxiety and jerking or writhing movements; and mood stabilizers for mania and bipolar disorder. How lucky she was to have the entire psychiatric spectrum of mental illness to anticipate. Ava felt sick to her stomach.

She skipped to another part of the packet, "The Health and Well-Being of the Caregiver." Beneath the title was a bulleted list of what caretakers and family members could expect: sleep deprivation, poor dietary habits, lack of exercise, and neglect of their own healthcare needs. Depression was common, as was the increased use of tobacco, alcohol, and other drugs. Meant to warn the family members who cared for HD patients not to overlook their own health and personal needs, the section alerted her to the hell Langdon would endure on her behalf.

Ava pictured the look on Langdon's face when she told him of her illness, the initial shock he would experience, the sadness he would feel, the helplessness that would turn to anger and resentment, the worry and exhaustion she would see in his eyes as her illness progressed, and the grief they would share.

The road ahead seemed too hard to bear. Ava could not imagine telling Langdon what she had learned. She would *not* tell him. She would rather die alone than watch him break into pieces little by little over years and years. One lost life was enough. She would not be responsible for destroying Langdon's as well.

And what about her baby, their baby, the gift they wanted most in the whole world? Dear God, what would she tell him about the baby? She could not go home and say, "Guess what, Langdon, I have Huntington's, and oh yes, I'm pregnant. By the way, I won't be around to mother our baby. I'll be off in psycho-land jerking and twisting and requiring help in the bathroom. No problem. You can manage Buck and me and the baby at the same time, can't you? Wait, there's a bonus. After you slog your way through that swamp of wretchedness, you might have an opportunity to do it over again with our son or daughter, if she or he inherits my HD.

My dearest God, she moaned from the deepest reaches of her soul. How much could one person be asked to endure? Her tears flowed unrestrained then, as reality penetrated her intellect. She cried for herself and her unborn child and her beloved Langdon, as she grappled with what her future would bring. The concepts of cognitive decline, psychosis, lunacy, and dementia circled in her mind like vultures over carrion.

Chapter 18 – Pelican View, Naples, Florida

After a long trip from Tampa, the Ava who drove through the gates of Pelican View was different from the one who had consulted a neurologist a day earlier. In the last twenty-four hours, a spiritual journey with an outcome she could share with no one had changed her. Her self-exploration had dragged her through the depths of sadness, indecision, and grief. In the end, she acknowledged a future that included HD.

Her acceptance came after a restless night of dozing between bouts of jarring emotion, the dizzying episodes sweeping her away to foreign planes of perception and layers of awareness beyond any she had experienced. With her heart ripped to shreds and her mind terrified, she begged to die.

When she awoke to find her wish denied, the boiling emotions of the previous night had weakened to a simmer. As if to fill the void, reason returned to her in small increments, followed by an eerie calmness and incredible clarity. The experience was transforming. When the sun's early-morning tendrils spread across the horizon, she was released into a peaceful sleep. She awoke at noon with a precise understanding of what she had to do.

As Ava drove up the driveway to the front entrance of Pelican View, she swept aside thoughts of the previous evening. She turned off the ignition, and out of the corner of her eye, spotted Langdon and Ray, dressed for squash, leaving the carriage barn. From their uproarious laughter, it was apparent they had shared a joke or some other amusing tidbit.

When Langdon looked up and saw her car, his happy expression turned serious, as if seeing her had annihilated his pleasure. His reaction evoked within her a pang of sorrow which she countered by thinking he would soon be rid of her and her tiresome moods.

Langdon broke away from Ray and charged up to Ava's car. Flinging open the door, he said, "Hi honey. Welcome back. I missed you." His greeting was warm and delivered with a smile.

"I missed you, too," she said. She balanced on tiptoe to accept Langdon's kiss. She smiled up at him and then turned to Ray. "Hi, Ray. You guys have a good game of squash?"

"Game? More like a fight to the death. Langdon wouldn't give up," Ray said and grinned. "We missed you at dinner, Ava. Cathy said she would catch up with you during the week."

"Oh?" Ava had no idea what Ray was talking about.

"We were invited for dinner, honey," Langdon explained.

"I ... oh gosh, I must've mixed up my dates," Ava stammered. "Gee Ray, I am very sorry. I'll call Cathy. Please accept my apologies."

"Don't worry about it. We missed you, that's all. Gotta go. Thanks for the game, Langdon. Ava,

I'll see you soon." Ray kissed her on the cheek, turned, and walked to his car.

Ava and Langdon stood in the driveway until Ray drove away.

"He's a great guy," Langdon proclaimed, as Ray's car disappeared around the turn, "and a good friend. The Village was worth the effort just to meet Ray and Cathy."

"Langdon, I'm embarrassed," Ava mumbled, ashamed to raise her eyes to meet his. "I didn't realize we had a dinner date with Ray and Cathy."

"We talked about it, honey, remember? You said you were going to wear your lady-in-red dress." With his head cocked to one side like a parrot and his eyes conveying concern, he looked at her with a quizzical expression.

"I sort of remember now that you mention it. I guess I didn't realize it was last evening; otherwise, I wouldn't have stayed over at the convent." She blinked at the lie and chastised herself for forgetting another commitment.

"That's okay, honey. I knew you had forgotten when you left the message saying you were spending the night with Sister Teresa. I had a little time to alert Cathy. She understood."

Ava's heart fluttered. Thank goodness, he did not call the convent and learn she was not there.

"I'll call Cathy in the morning. I'm fond of her and Ray. You know I wouldn't disappoint them on purpose. Like you, I enjoy their company, and Ray's work on The Village is invaluable." Her tone was beseeching, her expression contrite. *Lord knows, I honestly did forget.*

"Ava, you don't have to convince me. Let's forget it and move on. How was your visit with Sister Teresa?"

"I have a lot to tell you. Why don't we have cocktails in the garden? Let's say in about fifteen minutes on our favorite bench. We'll have privacy there, and I'll explain everything. I want to get out of these clothes and into a pair of shorts. I'm sticky," she said.

"It's a deal. I'll put your car away. No, David is coming. He'll do it. I'll get the drinks and meet you in the garden."

The note of cheerfulness in Langdon's voice made what she was about to tell him more difficult. Having no other solution in mind, she had to plow ahead. Langdon could not know her ultimate goal, for he would attempt to thwart it. If she had to ruin his life, she was determined to do it in the least painful way. The solution she had devised would accomplish everything she wanted. What Langdon did not know could not hurt him.

Minutes later, Ava and Langdon sat on the bench under their ancient banyan tree, a symbol of eternal life to some and to others, a resting place for God. Langdon handed her a cocktail. For several moments, they sat together in silence, paying homage to the enormous reddish-orange fireball as it slid into the Gulf, coloring the surf a psychedelic pink.

Langdon broke the silence. "Guess what I learned from Cathy and Ray?"

Glad to have a few more minutes to put her thoughts together before she presented her proposal to Langdon, Ava responded, "What?"

"They are adopting a child," Langdon said.

Ava was speechless.

"Honey, did you hear what I said? They've already hired an adoption attorney, a guy named Feingold from Miami."

Ava looked sideways at Langdon and smiled. "Wow, that's incredible," she said, wanting to remember the attorney's name. "Langdon, would you excuse me for a moment?" Without waiting for his reply, she left abruptly, walked to the house as fast as she could, wrote down the attorney's name, and stuffed the piece of paper in her pocket. When she returned to Langdon, she said, "Sorry, bathroom call."

"Oh," he said, looking discombobulated, "well anyway, Cathy confided she couldn't have another child, and she and Ray want Elizabeth to have a sister or a brother. Ray said they'd examined all the issues and were comfortable with their decision to adopt." Langdon raised his glass to his lips.

"I bet they're excited," Ava said. She managed a smile. "I'm happy for them."

"Me, too," Langdon said. "We'll talk about Ray and Cathy later. First I want to hear about your visit with Sister Teresa."

Ava took a second to remember the words she had rehearsed. Inhaling a deep breath, she forged ahead. "Langdon, I learned something astonishing at St. Joseph's." She took his hand and squeezed it hard to lock away the memory of its warmth.

"I'm all ears." He leaned toward her.

"The sisters are sorting old records, clearing away those of the orphans once in their care," Ava said. "An unopened envelope with my name on it fell from a file when it was transferred into a carton. Sister Teresa gave it to me. Inside the envelope was a letter from my birth mother." She took a deep breath and braced herself for what was to come.

"No kidding," Langdon said. "What'd it say?" He studied her round eyes.

Ava sensed Langdon wanted to read her mind, to judge beforehand if the news he would hear was good or bad. She hesitated before answering, thinking through the first part of her plan.

"Isabella—my mother's name was Isabella Prada Phillips—was quite an amazing woman, as it turns out. Her letter answered a question I've had since I was a child."

"Which was?"

"If she loved me, and she did, Langdon. She gave me up because she believed I would have a better life. Her husband, my father, died right after the war, and before I was born. My father's family was dead, and my mother's mother succumbed to a stroke soon after I was born. My mother was sick, alone, and dying. She had no alternative."

"Sick? Dying of what?" Langdon asked. He narrowed his eyebrows.

"I don't know. The letter didn't say." She would keep to herself her assumption that HD drove Isabella to her death.

"After the war, it was not uncommon for a mother to give up a child," Langdon said. "Many people had to make hard decisions, and women who were alone faced some tough ones. Jobs weren't easy to come by, even for healthy people, and if she was sick, well ..." As his voice drifted away, he held her hand in a tight grip. Ava sensed his empathy.

"I know, and I don't blame her. I think she was right to give me up. I've had a wonderful life."

He squeezed her hand, looked at her, and smiled. "And we have many more splendid years ahead of us."

She realized he had corrected her use of the past tense. "Of course we do," she responded with a thin smile, warning herself to be more careful.

"If giving you up was the right thing to do, then the letter is good news, isn't it?" He looked to her for confirmation.

"Yes, yes it is," she said, searching for the right words with which to open the next subject and fiddling with a leaf from a nearby hibiscus bush.

"What else did the letter say?" Langdon's face reflected wary anticipation.

"Langdon," she said in measured words, "do you remember when you told me about tracing your grandfather's footsteps in Texas and how the experience helped center you? You referred to it as a spiritual trek and likened it to a hajj, an apt description, I thought."

"Yes, I remember. That trek was something I needed to do, despite Buck's objections, and I don't regret it. Why? What do my Texas days have to do with anything?" Chewing his lip, Langdon sat up straighter and took a sip of his cocktail.

Ava's heart flip-flopped. She considered her words and decided to be straightforward. "Langdon, I want to go to Venezuela to trace my roots and find any members of my family that may be alive." She held her breath and waited for his reaction.

"Sure, we could get away for a week or two depending on Buck's condition," he said with no detectable enthusiasm. "I haven't been to Venezuela. That's big oil country and right up my alley." He cracked his knuckles.

Ava drew herself up and collected her courage. "Thank you for offering to go with me, Langdon. Would you mind if I went alone?" Taking his hand she stroked it, hoping to mollify him.

A painful silence followed. Langdon looked stunned. Ava felt small, infinitesimal.

With his face averted, Langdon rose from the bench and paced the garden walk. After a moment, he said, "I think I'll get another drink. I'll be right back." He walked away before she could respond.

Langdon's terse tone had conveyed his thoughts. She had prepared herself for a strained reaction, but with the moment at hand, she was in doubt about how to proceed. She wanted Langdon's blessing, not his disapproval. As Ava gazed at the fading pink, red, and orange streaks hanging over the horizon, she searched for the best words to use to dismantle the roadblock Langdon had erected. Minutes later, he returned carrying two fresh drinks. He handed her one and joined her on the bench. She thanked him, set the second drink aside, and pretended to sip from the first. She eyed the dribbles on the walkway where she had poured most of it out. She was heeding Friedlander's warning about alcohol and pregnancy.

The cries of the gulls on the shore were loud in the profound silence. Tension, thick with suspense, hung between them like an invisible partition.

Langdon ran his fingers through the front of his hair and slugged down a large gulp of his vodka tonic.

She waited, her breath coming in shallow inspirations.

"Ava, forgive me," Langdon began, "because I'm going to be blunt. Is there another man in our little picture?"

"Oh dear God, Langdon, of course not! Why would you think such a thing?" Her face registered unadulterated shock. She shook her head at him and studied his face. He seemed somewhat reassured by her response. Had he really thought she was having an affair?

"Ava, you haven't been yourself for several months. Now you want to run off alone to Venezuela, a country you've never been to. You must admit, it's more than a little odd." The firm grip on his glass turned his knuckles white.

"Langdon, look at me." She reached up and took his face between her hands. "I love you more than anything or anyone in the world," she said. "You are everything to me." Cupping his face in her hands, she pulled him down to her and kissed him with gentleness, hoping to convince him of her sincerity.

An idea occurred to her then, and she pulled away from him. "Langdon, why don't you come down for the first week, while I get acclimated? You'll be able to see for yourself where I am, and we can have a little vacation together. What do you think?"

"I could get away, maybe, if you tell me why you want to go to Venezuela alone." He wrung his hands. "That's the part I find confusing. And how long do you plan to be away from us? And when did you decide you wanted to go?"

Be strong, she told herself as his barrage of questions flew at her. *Do not back down.* "Whoa, Langdon, a dozen questions at once. Which one do you want me to answer first?"

"How 'bout the first one?"

"Which was?" She did not remember it.

"Why do you want to go alone to Venezuela?"

Ava sucked in her breath. "The reason I want to go is similar to your reason for going to Texas, the only parallel I can draw to help you understand. All my life I have wanted a family. I have no one who shares my history, no siblings, no living parents. The lack of a connection to the past makes me feel hollow inside. I thought our children would fill the emptiness." Her statement was accurate as it was, however, if she wanted to convince Langdon she had no ulterior motive, she would have to stretch the truth in the rest of her explanation. She forced herself to continue, wincing at having to lie. "Isabella's letter suggests I may have relatives in Venezuela, maybe Maracaibo or a town nearby," Ava said. "I want to find them, get to know them, and learn how my parents lived before they came to our country. It will take time. I can't do it in one or two weeks."

"How long do you think you'll be gone then?" he asked.

"Oh, Langdon, I don't know. As long as it takes is an honest answer. Please understand. I have wondered about my family for years. When I was at the orphanage, everyone around me speculated about living in a real family. If I find my relatives, maybe I can learn through them what my own family was like. Don't you see? It's a gift, Langdon. Please be happy for me."

Langdon put down his drink and turned to face her. "I'm trying to understand. From your explanation, I can see going to Venezuela is important to you. I'll try to come to terms with your desire to go. I am happy for you, and I apologize for sounding selfish. I was thinking about how much I'll miss you, dang it. I didn't sleep very well last night with you away." He gave her a half-hearted smile.

"I'll miss you, too." She raised Langdon's hand to her lips and kissed it. "I want to go with your blessing, my darling, and your understanding. Think about coming with me and staying for a week or two. What do you think?"

Langdon heaved a sigh. "As much as I would love to go with you, my responsibilities for Buck, The Village, and Enterprises make it difficult to leave. I'm running on all eight cylinders." He hung his head and shrugged.

"I know, darling," Ava soothed. "You're saddled with far too much, and I've added to your worries. For that, I'm sorry. I admit the timing is lousy. The problem is, my mother would be in her sixties if she were alive. Some of her relatives may already be dead. I can't afford to wait until you clear your plate, and I doubt your life will ever be uncomplicated. That's not a complaint, my darling; it's a fact. You love to burn the candle at both ends. It's your nature. Everyone should aspire to be as productive as you are. It's a quality I adore."

How good it felt to be honest, she thought. She meant every word.

Chapter 19 – La Chinita International Airport and Hotel del Lago, Maracaibo, Venezuela

The first lights of the evening were on in Maracaibo as Ava's connecting flight from Caracas entered the incoming flight pattern over La Chinita International Airport. From her window seat, she surveyed the landscape in the gathering dusk, taking in the sprawling suburbs and the tall skyscrapers. Even though Maracaibo was the second-largest city in Venezuela, from the air it appeared more extensive and modern than she expected.

As the plane banked into the left turn of the traffic pattern, leveled off, and descended toward the approach runway, Ava could see many oil rigs poking through the surface of Lake Maracaibo, each a miniature Eiffel Tower with a twinkling light on its peak. As Langdon had said, Maracaibo was oil country.

The plane came to a stop adjacent to the terminal. Ava and the other passengers deplaned and negotiated the metal steps of the portable staircase to the tarmac. Inside the passenger terminal, Ava found her way to the baggage area, collected her suitcase, and lugged it over to Customs.

The Customs line was short. A sleepy-eyed official thumbed through her documents, handed them back to her, and waved her through the turnstile. With no luggage handlers in sight, Ava wrestled her suitcase to the exit zone, pushing and pulling it and stopping in between to catch her breath. After one final push, she drew herself up and scanned the area for the driver the Miami travel agent had arranged. Unable to find a man holding a card with the name Skinner written on it, Ava remembered she had used her maiden name, Phillips, the same name she had given the adoption attorney, Eric Feingold. Before leaving Naples, she had arranged to meet him during her layover in Miami. Ava came away from their meeting convinced God had granted her wish by delivering the miracle for which she had prayed.

Ava searched the exit area again. She spotted a man holding a handwritten sign with Phillips spelled out in red capital letters. He was a slight man with brown eyes and dark brown wavy hair combed back from his forehead. She guessed he was in his late twenties. In addition to a broad smile, he wore a pair of khaki-colored pants and a loose-fitting, hip-length white cotton shirt, worn over his pants instead of tucked in. She assumed the style was a concession to the heat.

She walked over to the young man, stood in front of him, and smiled.

He returned the smile. *"¿Señora Phillips?"*

"Sí, soy Señora Phillips," she acknowledged. *"¿Cómo se llama?"*

"Carlos," he answered, bobbing his head in a half bow. He shook her hand. *"¿Se habla Español?"*

"*Un poco,*" she responded. She felt like a first-year Spanish student.

"*Muy bien, Señora Phillips.* I speak a little English. You are American, *¿sí?*"

"*Sí, vivo en el estado del Florida.*"

"*Florida está muy bonita, ¿sí?* Florida is pretty, yes?"

"*Sí,*" Ava agreed. She felt silly stumbling over the words in her schoolgirl Spanish. "I am sorry to speak your language so poorly."

"No worries, Senora Phillips. My wife, she speak good English. She teach me a little." He grinned and gestured with a grand sweep of his arm to a car at the curb. "You go to the Hotel del Lago, yes?"

"Yes, thank you, Carlos." Ava gaped at the 1957 Chevrolet Bel Air sedan displayed at the curb. As Carlos stowed her luggage, she scanned the taxi's dented and dinged exterior, eyeing the precarious, red front bumper, once chrome, fastened on with wire and the left headlight taped in place. The contraption looked unsafe. She thought the boxy car had been blue at one time, but because a rainbow of paint colors covered the rusted areas, she could not be sure. In her estimation, Carlos's amazing piece of rolling workmanship, held together by sheer optimism and maracucho ingenuity, was an obvious source of pride to him.

The lights of the airport faded as Ava and Carlos traveled through the suburbs from west to east toward the city business center that rested on the shore of Lake Maracaibo. Carved out of the northern portion of the Venezuelan coastline, Maracaibo, a teardrop-shaped lake, was one of a handful of ancient lakes formed 5 million years earlier, according to what she had read.

The residents of Maracaibo called their city *La Tierra del Sol Amada,* the land loved by the sun. Ava understood the reference to the sun, for temperatures in the semi-arid climate did not rise or fall much above or below the seventy-to-ninety-degree Fahrenheit range. When packing for her trip, Ava had selected clothing for a hot, dry climate, glad humidity would not be an issue. She had neglected to factor in the lake effect.

Lake Maracaibo, the largest in South America, produced plenty of humidity. The thickness of the moisture-laden air made each ordinary movement a conscious exertion. Her dress was sticking to her legs, her makeup was melting, and her hair clung around her neck like a fur collar. She would wear her hair up the next day and see about buying some lighter clothing. If she found her cousins and moved to Lagunillas, native clothing would help her blend in.

Thirty minutes later, Carlos's taxi rumbled to a stop under the porte-cochere of the Hotel del Lago. In an instant, three bellhops swooped in to unload Ava's luggage. Inside the hotel, a dwarfish, obsequious hotel manager welcomed her and ushered her to her room. While he waddled around the suite like a penguin pointing out each commonplace amenity—the telephone, the TV, even the room-service menu—Ava's luggage was delivered. Before she could tip the bellhop, he was gone. When Ava turned around, the penguin man was throwing open the double doors of the gigantic wardrobe for her inspection. When his flourishes abated, Ava thanked him and saw him to the door. She closed the door behind him, threw the deadbolt, and affixed the chain.

She experienced a moment of unease as she sank to the sofa in weariness. The empty room reminded her that she was alone, without Langdon, and doubt flickered across her mind. Was she doing the right thing? As if to answer her question, the fingers of her right hand trembled the tiniest bit. To keep from thinking about Langdon, she forced herself to unpack. Dwelling on what used to be was a luxury she could not afford. She was in Venezuela, and for better or worse, it was her new and final home.

The following morning, Ava slept a little later than usual, ate breakfast in her room, and took a leisurely shower. After the third cup of decaf coffee, enjoyed on the small porch off her room, she dressed for her eleven o'clock appointment with Carlos. The day before, when she mentioned shopping for clothes to him, he volunteered his services, claiming he knew where *las damas especiales*, special ladies, shopped for *ropas*, clothing.

Carlos was at the hotel right on schedule. He greeted her with his engaging smile as if she alone could make his day. As it had turned out, Carlos was a useful discovery, something the Miami travel agent must have known when she suggested him. What the agent could not have known, however, was Carlos's worth to her was not his skillful driving or even his ability to speak English. Ava admired and needed Carlos's sociability, an asset she hoped would serve her purpose in the future. The day before, she had witnessed how Carlos, blessed with a gregarious nature, dealt with people. They remembered him because his genuine, friendly manner put them at ease. Ava hoped Carlos could call upon his many friends and acquaintances to help her locate her grandfather's younger brother, Ramon Prada Perez, and his two sons, Joaquin and Miguel.

During the drive to the shopping area, Ava thought about how to broach the subject of searching for her family. Carlos gave her a timely opening when he asked if she was in Maracaibo for a vacation. She told him she was moving to Lagunillas in several days to search for her relatives.

His surprise was reflected in the rearview mirror. "*¿Tienes usted familia aquí?*"

"I hope I have family here, Carlos," she replied. *"El hermano de mi abuelo."* She hesitated over the Spanish words, wondering if she had put them in the right order.

"Ah, the brother of your grandfather," he nodded. *"¿Como se llama?"*

"His name is Ramon Prada Perez."

"He live in Lagunillas?

"No lo sé. He used to live there. He has two sons, Miguel and Ramon."

"You look for the sons, *¿si?*"

"Yes," she said.

"*Entiendo, señora.* I can help you maybe. *Mi abuela viviós en Lagunillas tambien.* My grandmother, she live in Lagunillas. Now she live in Cabimas. I visit to her one time a month."

"I do need help, Carlos. Thank you. *Es muy importante.*"

"No worries, *señora.* It is important, and I help you."

Carlos drove her to several clothing stores in the center of the shopping district and waited for her between purchases. After Ava bought three sleeveless cotton shifts, two brightly patterned skirts and blouses, and a pair of sandals, she returned to Carlos's rolling death trap and declared in faltering Spanish that she was finished shopping.

After planning to meet in the afternoon to see some of the highlights of Maracaibo, Carlos dropped her off at the hotel for *una siesta,* as he put it.

Several hours later, refreshed by her siesta, a dip in the pool, and a small fruit salad, Ava found Carlos in front of the hotel. He was engrossed in a conversation with the taciturn doorman. The portly greeter, oblivious to the traffic jam that Carlos's colorful Chevy—left in the no-parking zone—was creating for other vehicles trying to pull in to the entrance, appeared stiff and reserved. When Carlos whispered something in his ear, the doorman's upper torso shook, at first only a little, and then as the smile on his face grew wide, his shoulders bounced up and down in outright mirth. Without a doubt, Carlos had a way with people, Ava thought. He seemed to know everyone.

The doorman, recognizing Ava as she approached, gathered his composure, stifled a grin with one hand, acknowledged her with a bob of his head, and nudged Carlos.

Carlos looked over his shoulder. When he saw her, he turned back to the doorman and giving his friend a departing handshake, centered his full attention on her.

"*¿Ah, señora,* your siesta, it is good?" He smiled at her as if she were the center of his world.

"*Sí, Carlos, muy buena, gracias.*" As Ava climbed into the car, she noticed a fresh towel laid across the plastic covering on the back seat. She thought the idea sensible given the high humidity and lack of air conditioning in the taxi.

"Where we go, *señora?*"

"You decide, Carlos. *¿Entiende usted?*"

"*Sí, Señora* Phillips, I understand," he acknowledged. "I show you our city." His face expressed unmistakable pride.

Chapter 20 – Pelican View, Naples, Florida

Langdon ushered Stephenson to the door after his weekly discourse on the status of Skinner Enterprises. Grateful to have one chore out of the way, he returned to his office to call John Blaine, his investment advisor. Langdon wanted to increase Enterprises' position in a small, natural gas exploration company. A convergence of factors had ripened the company for takeover.

When his business with Blaine was concluded, Langdon terminated the conversation on the pretext of having another appointment. Blaine, an astute advisor, was also a big talker, and Langdon was in no mood for convivial chitchat.

Drained of energy, he plodded to the kitchen in want of a vigorous kick-start. He filled his mug with coffee, his third since lunch, and carried it through the gallery to Buck's rooms. He was curious about the success of Buck's and Juanita's walk through the gardens.

The door to Buck's suite of rooms was ajar. Langdon peered around it. His once-strapping father, thin and pale, was stretched out on the bed fully dressed, except for his shoes.

Although Buck looked peaceful in his sleep, Langdon's heart ached at the sight of his father's fragile condition. Plastic bottles of pills, a cup with a straw, and a pitcher of water cluttered the nightstand next to his bed. Juanita, Buck's nurse and sentry, was asleep in the chair across from his bed, her arms folded under her ample breasts. Langdon stood for a time inside the doorway watching his father's chest rise and fall and listening to Juanita's light snoring. *What a pair!* he thought. Sometimes he wasn't sure who was taking care of whom, although, in truth, Buck needed less medical care than he did the age-appropriate companionship Juanita provided.

On any other day, Langdon would think the scene humorous—a sleeping nurse and patient—but he was overwhelmed by the sight of his once-robust father reduced to frailty. Neither father nor son had expected life to turn out as it had. Millie left Buck earlier than anticipated, and Ava—he shook his head. He was not ready to explore her unspoken reasons for leaving.

The phone rang, and Rosa answered. Several minutes passed before Langdon heard her footsteps echoing on the marble floor of the south inner courtyard. Surmising the call was for him, he went to meet her. Years earlier, he had suggested the installation of an intercom. Buck had decried the idea. Walking from room to room and one end of the house to another was his idea of exercise.

Rosa rounded the bend of the gallery. "Mister Langdon, you might want to take this call," she said. Her palm covered the phone in her hand. "It's Mrs. Cavanaugh. She asked for Miss Ava, and I didn't know what to say. I asked if she wanted to speak to you." She handed Langdon the phone and hurried off. Langdon assumed Mariana, the newest addition to the cleaning staff, was the reason for Rosa's haste. Rosa told him she did not trust Mariana out of her sight. "She has *mal de ojo*, evil eye like a gypsy," Rosa announced. As a precaution, she insisted on locking up the silver.

"Sunny, hi," Langdon said. He put the phone to his ear.

"Hi, Langdon, have I caught Rosa at a bad moment? She sounded a bit flustered. Is everything all right over there?"

"Yes, we're fine. Rosa doesn't trust the newest member of the cleaning staff, so she's in a tizzy, and Ava is away for a couple of days." He groaned. *Why did he bring up Ava?*

"I suspected she had a reason for missing our meeting. My first thought was Buck," Sunny said.

"Ava missed a meeting?" Langdon asked. "I'm sorry she didn't call you. I'm sure it slipped her mind, what with packing to go away and all." *Oh great, why did I say that?* He had not intended to provoke Sunny's curiosity.

"Where did she go? Some place fun, I hope." Sunny's voice dripped with interest.

Only Sunny would have the nerve to be so direct, he thought. He had known Sunny for years, and even with—or maybe because of—Sunny's propensity not to mince words, he was fond of her. "Uh, actually, Sunny, Ava went to Venezuela, Maracaibo, to be exact." *Sunny is being nosy.*

"Really, Maracaibo?"

"Yes," he growled. By offering no elaboration, he hoped to cut the conversation short.

Sunny paid his brusqueness no mind. "When can I expect Ava back? She's on the Events Committee and an essential contributor. We depend on her."

When indeed, Langdon thought to himself before responding. "Listen, Sunny, I have a client waiting for me. Mind if we discuss this another time? I hate to keep him waiting." Having told his second white lie in an hour, he felt miserable over his deception and irritated at Ava for making it necessary.

"I understand. One more thing before you go. May Dad and I stop by to visit Buck? Dad misses Buck at the club. He was the best bridge player in their group."

"Sure, Sunny, Buck would love it. When do you want to come?" Langdon wiped his hand across his brow, relieved the subject of Ava was dropped.

"This afternoon?"

"Tomorrow would be better," he answered. Before Sunny's visit, Langdon wanted to talk to Ava to get their stories straight. "How about three o'clock?"

"We'll be there. Thanks, Langdon, see you then. Bye."

Langdon walked to the kitchen to return the handset to its base. *Superb invention, the cordless phone,* he thought, looking at it with approval. The phone reminded him of Ava and the distance between them, however, and his admiration was replaced by an ache so strong it came close to buckling his knees.

Langdon was not coping well with Ava's absence. Her hurried departure left him no time to adjust to the idea. One minute she was acting strange, the next she was gone. He could not shake the unsettling premonition that her trip entailed more than tracing her roots and locating her family. The thought that he had missed something important nagged at him, and the emotional distance that had weaseled its way between Ava and him fed his uncertainties.

He hated himself for wondering if Ava had an ulterior motive for her trip. *She would not*—he could not bear to finish his thought. He would set aside his unwarranted suspicions and call her after dinner. He wanted to know what he should say to their friends about her trip, and how Ava expected him to explain that she wanted to go alone. That entreaty still stuck in his craw.

Langdon kept to himself Ava's desire to visit Maracaibo unaccompanied. If people knew, they would have a field day. His private life would be discussed over cocktails at the club as if it belonged to everyone, an abhorrent invasion he would find intolerable. As if he were preparing for the worst, Langdon imagined how he would react if all of Naples were gossiping about his and Ava's marriage, a rumination that increased his sense of rejection. He could see himself in the uncomfortable position of having to explain Ava's absence at every turn, a situation that would provoke his anxiety and fuel his resentment.

For those reasons and because the tenor of his last conversation with Ava was brittle, Langdon was unwilling to stick his neck out by expressing how much he missed and loved her. The next time he called, anything intimate said between them would have to come from Ava first.

Only his closest circle, Ray, Cathy, Sunny, and his immediate household, were aware of Ava's trip to South America, but they had no idea Ava wanted to go alone. He was too embarrassed to share that piece of information. The day before, he told Cathy about Ava's trip because Cathy called to invite Ava to lunch, and he mentioned her absence to Ray during a conversation about The Village.

A few days away Langdon could understand, but Ava's trip had no foreseeable end. He was an idiot for caving in to her demands without insisting on a few of his own. At the very least, he should have negotiated a deadline.

He glanced at his watch. He had to stop feeling sorry for himself and change his clothes before Ray arrived to play squash. Langdon welcomed their games. For a time, he would not think about Ava.

When Ray arrived, the two men got down to the business of beating each other up on the court. After three ferocious sets and a down-to-the-wire tiebreaker, Langdon hoisted the victory flag. The exercise was palliative.

Ray shook Langdon's hand. "You're hot today, my friend. Did you take an extra vitamin pill at breakfast?" He grinned and slapped Langdon on the back.

"I was thinking the same about you. It took me forever to hang those two points together in the tiebreaker." Langdon was breathless from his exertion. "Anyway wasn't it my turn to win for a change?"

"Consider it your last," Ray said, "and if I have anything to say about it, there won't be another." He puffed out his chest to look fierce.

"You wish." Langdon loved their sparring.

The men toweled off, put away the racquets and balls, and returned the thermostat to its pre-play position. Langdon followed Ray out the door, and together they walked through the west garden toward the house.

"Ray, before you take off, can you stay for something to drink? Cathy isn't home from the hospital yet, is she?"

"No, she's doing a nine to five, filling in at the employee health center, and Elizabeth is at a friend's house. I'd love a beer. I'm done for the day and done in for the day, thanks to you. I've earned it." He smiled at Langdon.

The two friends eased their exhausted bodies into lounge chairs on the lanai. For a time, they fell silent to enjoy the quiet Gulf and observe the few people basking in the last rays of the afternoon sun. The tranquility was relaxing until an earsplitting screech put an end to it.

Ray jumped. "What the devil was that?"

Langdon laughed. "The peacock in the south garden. You know, the area with the high hedges and the little pond."

"I didn't see a peacock when you took me on tour."

"He must have been lying out-of-sight in the condominium."

"Condominium?"

"Yeah, it's what we call the peafowl pen," Langdon said. "Mother designed it. She was enamored with the birds. You didn't notice it, because it's hidden behind the pergola. It's more like a small castle than a peafowl pen, though. Mom got carried away. The more Buck groused about the birds—he hates their shrill squawks—the larger she built the pen. We used to have eight birds. We've whittled them down to two, a male and a female. We keep them out of deference to Mom. They are over thirty years old."

"Wow, I knew parrots had long lives. I didn't realize peacocks did."

"In fact, they can live as long as fifty years." Langdon took a long swig of his beer.

"And they don't fly?"

"Oh, they can fly, just not for long distances."

"Then what keeps them in the garden? I didn't notice any fencing."

"If you keep them contained as chicks, they settle into their surroundings. When you release them, if they have food and water and are safe from predators, they have no reason to move on."

"Fascinating," Ray said. "Aren't you a man of surprises? First a squash court and now peafowl." He chuckled.

"What about you?" Langdon replied. "Adopting a child is a colossal surprise. Are you comfortable with all the issues that adoption entails? I'm asking because Ava and I have wanted a child for seven years. When Ava didn't get pregnant, we went through the usual testing, and the doctor told us there were no abnormalities. No pregnancies, either."

"Are you and Ava thinking about adopting a child?"

"Speaking for myself, I haven't given up on having a baby the usual way, and I think we've avoided the subject of adoption for fear we'll jinx ourselves. You know, be careful what you wish, and all."

"Understandable," Ray said. "You have time. In our case, we knew Cathy couldn't have any more children after Elizabeth without multiple surgeries, large expenditures of money, and the inevitable disappointments along the way. Infertility treatment is expensive, and there is no guarantee of success. A few years back, we started thinking about the alternative, adoption. We're more than ready; we are excited."

"Will you explain to me how the process works? I mean, I've heard about adoption agencies, adoption attorneys, and open and closed adoptions. What's the difference between them, and if I'm not being too nosy, which are you using?" Langdon handed Ray a napkin and shoved a bowl of nuts in his direction.

Ray swallowed a gulp of beer before answering. "We engaged an attorney instead of going with open adoption, and I'll tell you why. As I understand it, there are several types of open adoptions. One kind involves hiring a surrogate mother whose expenses you pay until the baby is born. Another, adopting a child who has been relinquished by the birth mother, is more common. In any case, open adoption had several sticking points we found troublesome."

Ray blotted his mouth with a napkin and helped himself to a handful of nuts.

Langdon waited for him to continue.

"In open adoptions," Ray said, "biological mothers can request information about the adoptive parents. They can also ask to share in the child's life with scheduled visits. The exact terms are worked out by the biological mother, the adopting family, and the agency."

"Visits? That's surprising. Something I didn't know," Langdon said.

"We didn't either, and we weren't comfortable with having a forced relationship with the biological mother, an arrangement Cathy said would make her feel more like a foster mother than the real one. The other option, to entrust a surrogate to abide by all the proper precautions while carrying our baby, was a little scary."

"Yeah," Langdon said with a nod of his head, "I don't know if that would sit right with me either."

"We chose a closed adoption and after speaking to parents who had used him, retained the attorney I mentioned the other night, Feingold. In a closed adoption, the birth mother gives up her rights to the child after a short waiting period. Our names are put on the birth certificate, and we're not obligated to have any contact with the mother. A closed adoption seems cleaner to us."

"I see what you mean," Langdon said. "Let's go back to surrogate-related adoptions for a second. Isn't a surrogate implanted with a fertilized egg from the biological parents?"

"Yes, except it's more complicated. While you're correct that the use of a surrogate involves the implantation of a fertilized ovum, the origin of the genetic material varies. It can come from both parents or only one parent, as when either the husband or the wife is infertile. In the case of infertility, a friend, relative, or anonymous donor provides the required genetic material." Ray raised a finger to indicate he wasn't finished with his explanation and took a quick swallow of beer.

"I mention genetic material," Ray continued, "because Cathy asked if it was important to me for our child to be half mine, in which case I would contribute my sperm. I answered her question with my own. Did it matter to her? She said loving a child had nothing to do with biology. Besides, she wasn't enamored with taking hormones to ready her ovaries for harvesting and implantation, part of the in-vitro process. She reminded me of the time-consuming and expensive nature of hormone therapy and the emotional devastation that can follow a failed procedure."

Langdon thought about his and Ava's failures. "Yeah, I get it."

"Cathy's question got me thinking, though," Ray said. "Did I want to provide half the genetic material to fertilize a donated ovum? Cathy's sister offered hers, for example, a tempting idea until I thought about the reverse: How would I feel if the baby's genes were half Cathy's and someone else's? I think I would feel left out. When I put myself in Cathy's place, I thought it best not to have a larger biological stake in the child than she did. You know, keep the playing field level. Anyway, Langdon, when a child is put in our arms, we will love it like we would any child that was ours."

Langdon tried to hide his skepticism.

"I know it's hard to believe," Ray continued. "What I'm trying to say is a shared bloodline doesn't matter much when it comes to children. I think nature planned it that way. Understanding what I mean is easier if you already have a child. For instance, if we were given the wrong baby in the hospital, we would love it as much as we do Elizabeth. You love what you get."

Langdon took a moment to consider Ray's comments before leaving the subject of surrogacy. "And you're satisfied the attorney you've retained won't take your money and run or try to palm off a child with disabilities or the genes of a sociopath?"

"We are. If you think about it, no child is born with a guarantee. Any child can develop a disability along the way. Parents can't expect more from an adopted child than a biological one."

Langdon nodded. "You're right. I was spouting off before thinking it through. Of course, there is no guarantee. Even biological parents can't know in advance how their children will turn out until the deed is done."

"My Aunt Maria would agree," Ray said. "She swears the black sheep of our family is hers, even though she wants to disown him every other year. She says she regrets not having the milkman's child instead." Ray chuckled.

"That's funny," Langdon said, "Milkman or not, someone must screen the babies, wouldn't you think? I mean, Feingold wouldn't allow you to adopt an unhealthy baby, would he? I can't imagine adopting a sick child and then losing it to an illness. How shattering."

"No kidding," Ray said. "Babies slated for adoption are tested for the same things other newborns are. Again, adopted kids come with no guarantee above and beyond non-adopted ones and vice versa. Same treatment for all."

"They don't come with an instruction manual either," Langdon added.

They both smiled at every parent's lament.

"And you can't exchange or return them," Ray said, joining in.

"Kidding aside, Ava and I are happy for you and Cathy. I will love being his or her favorite uncle." With a playful smile, Langdon said, "I can do tutus or choo-choos. I'm a flexible guy."

Ray exploded with laughter. Gulping between guffaws, he said, "Sorry, I was visualizing your knobby knees in a tutu." He whooped some more.

Langdon waited for Ray to catch his breath before he continued. "How long will you and Cathy have to wait? Does the attorney have tons of people who want babies, or what? Does he put you on a waiting list?" He was not comfortable talking about children as if they were commodities.

"I know what you're thinking. I agree it's a little weird, but we'll do whatever is required to have another child to love."

Langdon steadied an elbow on one knee and rested his chin in the palm of his hand. "I'm not disparaging the process. Adopting a child is admirable. Ava tells me the children in her orphanage envied the 'children from real homes,' as they referred to kids who lived with families. I think it's too bad she wasn't adopted."

Ray shook his head. "And look what those prospective parents missed: a five-foot package with beauty, brains, and talent. Their loss," he affirmed. "Someone was looking at the wrong criteria."

"Criteria?"

"Yes, criteria. Feingold asked for our preferences on characteristics like hair and eye color, sex, and age of the child we wanted. He also wanted to know if the race, ethnicity, or religion of the biological parents mattered to us. He'd try to find a child that matched our expectations within reason, he said. The fewer the requirements, the quicker it is to find one. The timing is anyone's guess. When Feingold calls, we go to Miami. We have the right to see the child first. If we reject him or her—although I can't imagine doing such a thing—the baby goes to someone else, and we wait anew."

"Do you suppose anyone would have the unmitigated gall to turn down a child? Imagine handing a baby back and saying he or she wasn't cute enough or didn't have the right hair color." Langdon groaned. "How awful." "No kidding. Feingold said it had happened to him once in his entire career. He told Cathy and me that some wannabe prima donna refused two infants. Not very classy, if you ask me." "And then what? Feingold found her another?" Langdon croaked, aghast at the thought. "God help the child she adopted in the end." He rammed his fingers through his hair.

"No, Feingold told her she didn't have the qualities he was looking for in a potential mother and refused to work with her. He threw her out of the office as she was screaming 'lawsuit.'"

"Good thing," Langdon said. "What a relief. So you think Feingold has integrity?"

"I do. When we met, I asked him why he had chosen to deal with adoptions. He told me he was an adoptee. I did a little investigating before we went to Miami to be on the safe side. I didn't want Cathy to be crushed with disappointment if the guy turned out to be a crock or a cheat."

"Good for you," Langdon said.

"You would have done the same, am I right?"

"You are," Langdon said without hesitation. "Lots of pitfalls to think about."

"Isn't that the truth. We've done extensive research, so I'm hoping we'll avoid surprises."

Ray rose from his chair. "Uncle Langdon," he teased, "I have to get going. Cathy should be home soon. Thanks for the beer and the conversation." He walked to the door and then turned. "Langdon, you and Ava are at the top of our list for godparents."

"Thank you for the honor," Langdon said. "We accept." He stood, deepened his voice an octave and rasped, "Godfather Langdon suits me, don't you think? Maybe I should change my name to Vito or Vincenzo. Dye my hair, grow it a little longer, pack some heat?" He grinned.

"I think we like you as you are," Ray said. "A blond godfather works for me." He made a face and laughed.

Chapter 21 – Hotel del Lago, Maracaibo, Venezuela, and Road Trip to Cabimas, Venezuela

When Ava awoke to the desk clerk's wake-up call, she was bleary-eyed and lethargic. If she had not agreed to visit Carlos's grandmother in Cabimas, she could stay in bed. Ava toyed with the idea of canceling by leaving a message with the doorman—the one with whom Carlos was conversing the day before—but when she imagined Carlos's disappointment, the notion seemed selfish. Aside from wanting to do the right thing by not offending him, she would not think of asking for his assistance in locating her relatives unless she honored her commitment to him.

Ava dragged her bone-weary body to the shower, hoping to surmount her listlessness. She had not had a restful night; tortuous dreams and an unrelenting longing for Langdon had fractured her fitful sleep. When she reached for him during the night, the emptiness of her bed startled her awake. She was alone. Between bad dreams, she was out of bed pacing in the dark, disturbed by the many details of the plan she had yet to work out.

One of those details, her excuse for being in South America—finding her great uncle's offspring—would not satisfy Langdon for long. By getting out of town, she had concealed her illness and pregnancy, but as the days grew into months, Langdon would ask her why she was still there.

She had to fashion a plausible reason for staying in Venezuela until her baby was born. Then she would be free—*an ironic choice of words*—to carry out the remainder of her plan. For the next few months, she needed a plausible explanation to keep Langdon content, or he might pay her a visit.

Ava had no doubt Langdon would be disinclined to travel as long as Buck was alive, but who knew how many more months Buck had left? Tears rose to her eyes when she thought of not being at Buck's bedside to comfort him in the end. He had no idea she had said her final goodbye to him before she left, and he would never understand her desertion. Wiping away her tears, Ava told herself she could do nothing more for poor Buck, and if she continued to dwell on him or any other anxiety-provoking subject, her baby might be affected negatively.

Drowning in sorrow, Ava thought it would be easier to die than deal with her situation. More than ever, she understood Isabella's choice. Unlike her mother, however, she had a baby to bring into the world. In the meantime, if she wanted to avoid an immobilizing depression, she had to be resourceful. She had no defensive weapons in her arsenal.

Osgood had mumbled an apology for not offering her an antidepressant. "In most cases an antidepressant is helpful," he said, "although I understand your objections to taking one during your pregnancy and your concern that the medication could cause a negative consequence to the fetus. I respect you for taking the tough road for the sake of your baby. On the other hand, if you want to terminate the pregnancy—"

The look on her face stopped him in mid-sentence.

The obstetrician agreed with the neurologist. He also cautioned her not to take any medication during her pregnancy, unless prescribed by a physician.

As Ava saw it, the burden of her sanity was up to her. With no surefire antidote to madness at her disposal, the best way to help herself was to keep busy. Her trip to Cabimas to meet Carlos's grandmother was her antidepressant for the day.

Rejuvenated after her shower and in a hurry, Ava tossed on one of the loose-fitting shifts she had purchased the day before and styled her hair up off her neck. With a light breakfast in mind, she sought out the dining room.

Seated by herself next to the window, she rejected the caffeine-laced *café con leche,* which she adored, in favor of a healthy glass of orange juice. She bolted down a piece of smoked ham and a corn muffin filled with guava paste, she guessed. She was in the fifth month of her pregnancy, and as forecasted, her terrible morning nausea had disappeared.

Grateful food was no longer her enemy, she finished her breakfast, settled the bill, and hurried outside to meet Carlos.

Carlos greeted her with the dramatic flair offered to a visiting dignitary. His bright eyes sparkled, and his broad smile engaged her attention, but not to the extent that she failed to notice he was eyeing her native clothing.

"You wear the new dress, ¿sí?" he said and nodded his head. "*Muy* beautiful, *señora*."

"*Gracias*, Carlos," she said, thankful her complexion was not fair when the blood rushed to her cheeks. She wondered if Carlos could tell she was pregnant, although aside from a thicker waistline and the slightest enlargement of her breasts, her appearance was much the same.

To avoid the effort of conversation during the hour-long ride to Cabimas, Ava hid behind a Maracaibo newspaper, delivered to her room each morning. From the window, she examined the countryside and followed their route on a map she picked up from the concierge. According to the directions, the quickest way to get to Cabimas, the second-largest city in the state of Zulia, was to cross Lake Maracaibo using the General Rafael Urdaneta Bridge and then to turn south on coastal Highway 3.

She was interested in seeing the eight-and-a-half kilometer span, the longest concrete bridge in the world. Named after the general who led Maracaibo's patriots against the supporters of the Spanish monarchy, a tourist pamphlet said the bridge took five years to build and opened in 1962. The patriots won the skirmish and their freedom on July 24, 1823. In addition to being an impressive structure, the bridge was a symbol of pride to the people of Maracaibo. When it came into view, Ava could sense Carlos's excitement over sharing the wondrous structure with an American tourist.

"*¿Es magnífico, sí?*" Carlos said.

Ava heard the excitement in his voice. "*Muy magnífico,*" she agreed.

As they crossed the long span, Ava recalled her mother's letter and the comment in it about driving across the Davis Causeway, missing the beautiful scenery for fear of taking her eyes from the road. If her mother were with her now, Ava thought, the stunning view unfolding below would fill Isabella with pride.

In that very moment, Ava sensed Isabella's nearness for the second time. The impression was even stronger than it had been on the pier in Naples. Convinced the feeling was not her imagination, Ava embraced it as real. She was not alone on her journey. Isabella understood her anguish.

In thinking about her mother, Ava wondered if some HD offspring viewed the parents from whom they inherited their disease with anger or bitterness. Despite the lethal HD gene passed to her, she harbored no resentment toward her mother. As a matter of fact, Ava felt a kinship with Isabella for who else, Ava thought, could truly understand her distress?

Ava wondered if her feelings toward her mother were the norm for HD offspring or if her desperation to know about her family had made her all accepting. Had her neediness blunted her true feelings? Would she even know if her behavior was abnormal? Was her brain disintegrating already?

Ava spent a great deal of time worrying about being normal. She knew the cells of her brain that controlled her ability to move, think, and feel were deteriorating. The thought chilled her to the bone. Was it any wonder she felt compelled to measure her responses against a paradigm of normalcy? Did others with HD do the same?

She might have learned the answers to some of her questions had she investigated the support group Osgood recommended. She would have attended one meeting, at least, but by the time Osgood mentioned it, she had already purchased her plane ticket to Maracaibo.

On her second visit to Osgood, Ava told him she was going away. When he asked if her husband was going with her, she had to scramble for a suitable answer.

In hindsight, she should have lied to put an end to the discussion. Instead, she told Osgood the truth, worried about the possibility of Marquist mentioning the referral to Langdon at a chance meeting and the long shot that Langdon might follow up with an inquiry.

"No, my husband doesn't know about my illness or the pregnancy," she said. "I'm waiting for the right moment to tell him."

Osgood stared at her as if she had already lost her mind.

"Ava, I advise you in the strongest terms to bring your husband up to speed at once," he lectured. "If you want to have your baby, you cannot ignore your situation." His tone was starchy.

"I understand," she mumbled. "I only want a little more time. You and I know everything will change when Langdon finds out. I want to preserve our relationship as it is for as long as possible. I'm taking a little trip to clear my mind. I won't be gone long," she lied. She hoped her explanation would produce the result she wanted: Osgood's collusion in covering her tracks.

"Ava, I am sympathetic, and I do want to be supportive. In my best medical judgment, however, it's wrong to exclude your husband. You and your baby will need help soon." His electric blue eyes bored into hers. She imagined they were pleading with her to be reasonable.

"Doctor, I'm asking you to keep my medical information between us. It's my right, isn't it?" She knew she sounded overbearing, but she would be a screaming shrew to keep Langdon uninformed if need be. Determined to have her way, she stared back at Osgood with a look of defiance.

Osgood shifted his gaze to the floor. When he raised his eyes, she was stony-faced.

His posture sagged. "Yes, it's your right, Ava," he muttered.

When she thought of that exchange, she felt awful. Osgood had been kind and compassionate, and she had responded with a verbal slap across his face. In her zeal to protect Langdon, she was hurting everyone around her, a burdensome backlash that caused her to feel mean-spirited and nasty.

Carlos's dilapidated taxi left the bridge and turned onto Highway 3, the only road south to Cabimas that skirted the perimeter of the lake. Pursuing a distraction from her worries, Ava peered out the window.

In every direction, ubiquitous oil rigs reached for the sky from the waters of the lake, their arbitrary placement forcing passenger ferries and cargo-laden boats to weave between and around them. Along the edge of the lake, one-story structures with metal roofs turned rusty by the humid climate rested on stilts and extended out over the water. A maze of boardwalks connected the shacks and provided access from the land. She thought the hovels were small warehouses until Carlos explained that the people who lived in them were called *the water people.* She did not believe human beings could live in such squalor.

Like the rigs, every industry in view was associated with oil. Oil tankers floated on the water and oil refineries marred the land. The refineries—huge engineering nightmares of jumbled piping that bent outward, curved inward, and coiled upward toward the sky—stood out against the flat landscape like abstract art sculptures. Behind the refineries, acres of silver cylindrical tanks filled with liquid gold reflected the sun's rays with eye-stabbing brilliance.

Farther south, the landscape was flat and uninteresting. The countryside, brown in the dry season, was devoid of flowers and forests. Scrubby bushes, grasses, and weeds competed for survival in the semi-arid climate and sandy soil. In the distance, a meager stand of deciduous trees clung to wizened leaves. The lush palms Ava expected were scarce, as were the birds perched high in their drooping fronds. Ava lost the view of the water when Highway 3 curled inland. The scenery, monotonous in its homogeny, continued unchanged, except for several herds of grazing cattle and a sign for a passion fruit farm. She was fighting boredom when small neighborhoods appeared along the eastern side of the highway. Carlos referred to the clumps of houses squatting on the sun-scorched land as *barrios*.

The first town, Santa Rita, reminded Ava of an American frontier town. The commercial buildings, one-storied for the most part, were painted in vibrant colors and grouped side by side along the main thoroughfare. Behind the buildings, small square dwellings resembling military bunkers hunkered down on the dry earth. Winding dirt roads connected the houses to the main street.

The scenery was not inspiring. Between Maracaibo and Cabimas, each *barrio* looked the same to her, and the dry landscape offered little in the way of interest. She was restless and prickly when Carlos announced their arrival on the outskirts of Cabimas.

Chapter 22 – Hotel del Lago and Prada Home, Maracaibo, Venezuela

As Ava predicted, Carlos was indispensable. Her trip to Cabimas several weeks earlier to meet his grandmother produced useful information.

Señora Ortiz knew the Prada family. Before the Lagunillas fire mentioned in Isabella's letter, *Señora* Ortiz's brother and Isabella's cousin, the son of Ramon Prada, worked for the same oil company. After the great fire in 1928, *Señora Ortiz* moved to Cabimas with her family and the Pradas to Maracaibo. She did not know if Miguel had married or had children, he was a small boy when the family moved. She knew nothing of Miguel's older brother, Joaquin. Since their relocation, *Señora Ortiz* had not seen the family. She suggested tracing them through the birth, death, marriage, or baptismal records maintained by the Catholic church, the primary guardians of such statistics in Maracaibo. Ava grasped at the straw.

With Carlos's competent assistance, Ava scoured the ledgers of six churches in Maracaibo, working her way back through their records. In the seventh church, an old set of documents produced the listing of a marriage between a Miguel Prada, Jr. and a woman named Mariela Velasquez Ortega. Ava could not tell from the entry if the family lived in the general vicinity of the church or if they had moved away. The notation verified the family's affiliation with the church, however, a sign she was on the right track. When Ava located a newer set of church records, she struck gold. She found the couple's first address in a list of marriages, and a second address noted three years later. She was ecstatic.

Carlos, who had grown up in Maracaibo, knew every inch of the city. He looked at the address and nodded his head. "No worries, *señora*, I find it for you."

On the trail like a bloodhound, Carlos was true to his word. He found the house, a small-whitewashed structure on a lot sprinkled with scraggly vegetation. A knock on the door brought a stout, middle-aged woman to the front stoop. Yes, the Pradas used to live there, she said, her smile showing discolored teeth. They had to relinquish their house for financial reasons. The husband was seriously ill. Yes, she knew where they went. She wrote down the address and gave it to Carlos. As he translated, the woman said she was sorry for the young couple.

Carlos drove to the vicinity of the new address. When the road ended before he found the house, he mopped his brow with a handkerchief, brought the taxi to a stop, and pointed to a jumble of shacks ahead. They would have to walk to the house. He looked to Ava for further instruction.

Dumbstruck by the sight of the improvised, barely habitable shacks piled one atop the other to avoid wasting an inch of land, Ava hesitated. Was wading into such a foul area sensible? The extreme poverty was shocking.

Carlos suggested, "I park car. We walk, ¿sí?" Noting her uneasy demeanor, he added, "Poor people not bad people. We be okay. No worries, señora."

She replied yes to Carlos's proposal to walk. What else could she do? She did not want him to think her spoiled and unsympathetic. As she and Carlos picked their way between the shacks, the thought crossed her mind that she was smart to hide her money in her bra. Without her purse, she was less of a target. Her idea to wear closed shoes in place of sandals was also a good choice. Her feet were protected from the trash that littered the narrow dirt and sand paths.

The foul-smelling odors emanating from the open sewers and the trash piled high behind the shacks made it hard to breathe. To avoid the stench, Ava inhaled through her mouth instead of her nose and worried about exposing her unborn child to dangerous germs.

Despite the oppressive heat and sickening odors, Ava and Carlos persevered. After knocking on several doors and following more than one erroneous lead, they found the home of Miguel and Mariela. Little more than a wooden shack with a corrugated metal roof, the structure was not much bigger than the peafowl condominium at Pelican View. *Unfit for human beings*, Ava thought.

Carlos knocked on the rickety door fastened in place by rusty hinges. Ava held her breath in nervous anticipation. After Carlos knocked, waited, and then knocked again with no response, Ava's eagerness turned to disappointment. She was ready to give up and go home when the flimsy door creaked open. A pair of eyes assessed her through the narrow crack. She must have passed inspection because the door opened wide to reveal a petite young woman with shoulder-length brown hair, round doe eyes, and a perplexed expression on her pretty face.

Carlos and the young woman exchanged words. Ava stood to one side, trying to look friendly and wishing she could understand what they were saying. An eternity seemed to pass before Carlos broke into an ear-to-ear grin, and with a little bow, affirmed the woman was Mariela, the wife of Ava's cousin Miguel. Ava suppressed her excitement as Carlos explained to Mariela who the American woman at his side was.

The astonished look on Mariela's face was memorable. With a shy smile, she extended her hand to Ava.

Ava smiled in return and shook Mariela's hand. Mariela turned to Carlos, said several words, and then whirled around and disappeared into her house. Ava, left on the stoop, was puzzled.

Carlos explained. "She want to make house nice for you. We wait. Her *esposo*, husband, *está muy enfermo* ... sick, she say."

Ava had second thoughts about intruding into the privacy of the young couple. The sound of furniture moving on the other side of the door caused her further discomfort. She wrung her hands, thinking it was ill-advised to show up without notice.

"Carlos, please tell Mariela we can come back another time, and apologize for our blunder," Ava said. She turned to leave.

Carlos detained her with a light touch on her arm. "Señora, we wait. It is polite, no?"

Ava turned back toward the door, amused by Carlos's tactful way of directing her without seeming to—another of his diplomatic talents. Under the blazing sun, Ava and Carlos waited on the doorstep for Mariela to return.

They did not wait long. Several minutes later, the door opened, and Mariela, looking scrubbed and wearing a fresh dress, invited them inside. Her hair, brushed back from her face, was fastened with a strand of ribbon.

Inside the one-room shack, it was dark, except for a splotch of light across the floor from a single window. When Ava's and Carlos's eyes adjusted to the dimness, furnishings came into focus. A faded, green-chenille bedspread affixed to the ceiling sectioned off a third of the room. Carlos told Ava it was Miguel's area. To the left of the door, two scarred wooden chairs and a tattered, upholstered lounger formed a semicircle. Across from the chairs, a fifties-style Formica-and-chrome table leaned against the wall, its spindly legs teetering under the weight of pots, pans, and a two-burner hotplate. The only other appliance was a loud, hard-to-ignore compact refrigerator. Beside a tall wooden cupboard that Ava assumed held dishes and food, a frayed, dangerous-looking cable snaked through a hole in the wall. It connected the several appliances and a lamp on a TV table to an electrical source. At the back of the room, a second rusty TV table flanked a tightly made cot. A battered wooden trunk rested on the floor at the bottom of the bed, and an old oversized wardrobe loomed over everything. "Austere" was the word that came to Ava's mind. The interior was neat and uncluttered.

Mariela offered Carlos and Ava a chair. As Ava lowered herself into hers, she was flabbergasted to discover the rainbow-colored rug beneath her feet covered a dirt floor. She did not see a toilet, sink, or shower.

Chapter 23 – Pelican View and Naples Town Hall, Naples, Florida

Flushed with excitement, Langdon hurried home to check on Rosa's preparations for the small dinner party he was giving to celebrate Buck's seventieth birthday. Twenty minutes earlier, he had delivered his updated proposal for The Village to the Collier County Development Agency. When the commissioners applauded his ideas and commended him for his foresight, he was surprised.

As the meeting continued and the subject turned to old business, Langdon understood the reason for his warm reception. The commissioners were in the process of formulating an economic development plan for the entire area of Immokalee, a bit of information that was news to him. His timing could not have been better. The Village was the first project selected for construction.

After the meeting, a commissioner said, "Langdon, we are looking for consultants on the Immokalee project who understand the potential of the area and the needs of growers and workers. Are you interested?"

Langdon accepted the position. He returned to Pelican view feeling happier than he had in a long time until Ava's absence put a damper on his enthusiasm. He wished she were there to share his elation. Although only a month had passed since her hurried departure, it seemed longer to him. He talked to her by phone, as often as he could. The lousy connection between the two countries made a phone call challenging. Ava wrote every day, usually a paragraph or two, bundling the pages together to mail once a week. Langdon appreciated her effort to stay in touch, but her words did not make up for her absence.

Ava told him she had located a relative on her mother's side, a cousin, Miguel Prada Vargas Jr., and his wife, Mariela. Even though Langdon understood Ava's desire to find her relatives, her last brainstorm—to remain in Maracaibo to help Mariela with her ill husband until Mariela's baby was born—was another story. The extension of time was hard to accept. He thought Ava's priorities were backward. Her responsibility was not to help Mariela and Miguel at the expense of her obligations at home.

He felt cast aside like an old junker, and his willingness to go along with Ava's cockamamie plan made him a pushover. What choice did he have? As long as the birth of Mariela's baby was a foreseeable deadline, he would leave thing alone and hope for the best. Maybe Ava would come to her senses before then. Until she returned, he was plenty busy with The Village, Skinner Enterprises, and Buck, even though he thought them poor substitutes for Ava.

The spat he and Ava had the previous week about her decision to stay on in Maracaibo was fresh in his mind. When Ava told him what she planned to do, his reaction was less than encouraging. He refrained from expressing his disappointment to her in words, relying instead on the cold tone of his voice to get across his message. Their conversation had ended on a sour note. A brief vacation was one thing, an extended stay for months was altogether different. Ava's absence was starting to feel like desertion.

He offered to send a large sum of money to Miguel and Mariela, thinking it would enable them to hire help. Langdon's motive was to eliminate Ava's reason for staying longer and bring her home sooner.

Ava responded, "Thank you, Langdon. The idea is a good one, except Mariela is too proud to accept charity."

He replied with heavy with sarcasm, "Really? They were willing to accept your offer to help with Miguel. Sounds like charity to me."

He regretted the rude remark; the words came tumbling out before he had the good sense to think them through. He believed goodness was the motivation for Ava's offer to help Mariela, yet he had lashed out at her, his impolite comment stemming from the aching emptiness with which he struggled every day.

Ava accepted his remark in silence. Since then, neither of them had picked up the phone. The stalemate was anxiety-provoking, but what was a man to do? He could not bring himself to roll over without a whimper.

When Buck asked him when Ava was coming home, Langdon tried to put a good face on it. He told Buck that Ava was like a visiting saint to her relatives who were desperately poor. The husband,

Miguel, had a terminal illness, and his wife, Mariela, was pregnant and having a difficult time.

Langdon told Cathy and Ray the same thing. He would repeat the story to Sunny when she came for dinner. Langdon asked her to arrive before the other guests; he thought it best to explain the reason for Ava's absence to her in person. He did not want Sunny to assume he and Ava were having marital discord, which they were, except not to the extent the local gossip mavens would have it if he failed to counteract their wild imaginations. By telling Sunny why Ava was in Maracaibo, Langdon hoped Sunny would help nip gossip in the bud.

Chapter 24 – Hotel del Lago and The Prada Home, Maracaibo, Venezuela

Ava shook her head to clear the vestiges of sleep from her mind. When she gathered her bearings, she remembered she was in her bed at the Hotel del Lago. With a groan, she pulled the bed sheet over her head and turned away from the blade of early morning sunlight that pierced the center seam of the heavy curtains. Saturated with despair, she longed to stay in bed. She was on a downward spiral.

An ever-present, seductive shadow of depression beckoned her to come into the darkness. She yearned to follow, to close her tired eyes and resolve the conflict between her and HD forever. In the vast emptiness of her bed, she thought about Langdon, the turmoil he must be experiencing, and the unhappiness she had caused. She hated herself. With a deep sigh, she buried her head in the pillow and sobbed.

Between episodes of crying, Ava pulled a second pillow over her face. She considered suffocation. How long would it take? The suicidal ideation was typical for her. She battled the desire to end her life several times a day, especially at night, when Langdon's absence reminded her of the misery she was causing him.

A sharp rap at the door by the room-service waiter jolted her back to reality. She pulled herself together, threw on a robe, and accepted her breakfast. Too lazy to search her purse for smaller change, she gave the waiter a hefty tip. After he left, she sat before her plate staring at her food, until she remembered she had promised Mariela an early start. She glanced at her watch. She would have to hurry, or Mariela would miss the bus and her appointment.

Mariela's employer, the owner of a dress shop, expected an entire bridal party for a morning fitting, and Mariela, the seamstress she counted on most, was supposed to welcome them. For the past two days, Mariela had talked of little else, excited by the prospect of earning enough money to buy Miguel's medicine for a month.

Ava found Mariela's positive attitude and never-ending cheerfulness mystifying. Forced to relinquish her former job as a nurse at the San Jacinto Hospital to become Miguel's full-time caretaker, Mariela altered, repaired, and sewed new clothes for several of the downtown dress stores. Except for fittings and deliveries, she could work from home and care for Miguel at the same time. On that particular morning, however, Mariela needed to be at the store early.

Ava, sincere in her desire to help, offered to stay with Miguel during Mariela's absence, even though she found Miguel's writhing, spastic movements, and verbal outbursts downright frightening. She was thankful Mariela's mother, who did not work on Saturdays, would be on hand to help. On those rare occasions when Mariela was away, two people were required to manage Miguel, a stocky man who was a welder before his illness.

Undaunted by her small stature, Mariela was the only person who could deal with Miguel single-handedly. She had a sixth sense when it came to understanding his garbled words and spastic gestures.

Ava viewed her eye-opening acquaintance with Mariela as a blessing. In her lifetime, Ava had known good people—there were plenty in the convent—but Mariela, who eschewed the trappings of religion, except for a small crucifix pinned above Miguel's cot, was goodness itself. The woman was a wonder, a paragon of strength, an exemplary human being.

Until Ava arrived to lend a hand, Mariela took care of Miguel by herself, day in and day out, except for the occasional help of a friend or family member. Hers was a solo journey borne with equanimity and immense patience, despite losing her home, her previous full-time job, and any hope for the future with her terminally-ill husband. Poverty-stricken Mariela, who lived in a one-room shack in an alley, had surrendered everything in the name of love. Sainthood awaited Mariela. She was the yardstick against which Ava measured her own fortitude. By any calculation, she fell short.

After watching Mariela care for her husband, Ava learned that both tolerance and endurance were required to look after someone with HD. Miguel's tantrums, verbal abuse, thrashing, and food spitting could stretch even the most patient person to the breaking point. If Mariela experienced anger or frustration, however, she hid it behind a serene countenance.

A few days earlier, in the midst of an episode of prolonged writhing and garbled shouting, Miguel swung his arms wide, as if lashing out at Mariela. Frightened for her, Ava jumped up to help. Mariela, a picture of calmness, waved Ava away and stood her ground until Miguel was soothed and stroked back to stillness.

After Miguel was settled, Mariela returned to her sewing as if the incident was nothing out of the ordinary. Ava assumed she had failed in hiding her expression of concern because Mariella said a phrase in Spanish that Ava understood to mean "It's the disease talking, not Miguel." At that moment, Ava realized Mariela could be calm and caring with Miguel because she separated the man she loved from his illness-driven behavior.

With an eye on the time and wishing she did not feel like a dishrag, Ava dressed in a hurry and hustled to the porte-cochere outside the lobby to meet Carlos, whose cab blocked traffic, as usual, in his commandeered no-parking space. Ava quickened her step. She would not cause Mariela to be late. Mariela needed the money and Miguel his medicine.

During the drive to Miguel and Mariela's, Ava thought about the extreme poverty in Maracaibo and the inadequate medical care available to the terminally ill. If Miguel were in a hospital, Mariela could concentrate on being the breadwinner. In reality, Mariela was stretched to the limit caring for Miguel and at the same time, trying to earn an income sufficient to meet their needs, a double cruelty.

The lack of proper sanitation and fresh water also bothered Ava. How could anyone care for an ill person without either?

The day before, she asked Carlos, *"¿Dónde está el baño de Mariela?"*

"Ah, you ask for place of bathroom of Mariela, no?" he affirmed.

"Yes."

"Mariela y Miguel no tiene bathroom *en la casa.* No bathroom in house. *Usan el baño del casero* ... um ... how you say, landlord?"

"The landlord's bathroom," Ava repeated. *Dear God, they use the landlord's bathroom.* *"¿Es verdad?"*

"Si, it is true," Carlos said.

"¿Dónde está la casa del casero?" she asked. She hoped the landlord's house was nearby.

"Está en frente."

"The landlord's house is in front of Miguel and Mariela's house," Ava said aloud. She was shocked. The idea of sharing a toilet with a neighbor was inconceivable to her.

"Si, no es bueno."

"Not good" is an understatement, she thought. *"¿Carlos, y agua para lavar? ¿Donde esta?*

"You ask where water for wash, *señora?"*

"Si," Carlos.

"No en la casa ... um, not in house. *Muchas familias utilizan el mismo agua de la pipa."*

Ava consulted the Spanish-English dictionary she carried with her for a translation of the word *pipa.* Of course, *pipa* is pipe, she thought. Many families use water from the same pipe. "*Entiendo,* Carlos."

Ava wondered about the drinking water. Did it also come from the *pipa*? "*¿Carlos, por favor, y agua para beber*? *¿De la pipa también?*

"No. *El agua de la pipa viene del lago.* The water of the pipe is of the lake. No good drink water of lake," he replied, screwing up his nose and pretending to spit. "*Hay mucho aceite en el agua.*"

She opened her dictionary again. *Oh, aceite is oil in English. Water for washing comes from the lake and to the pipe. The lake water is not good for drinking, because it's polluted with oil.*

"*Gracias,* Carlos, *entiendo,*" she said.

"*Bueno, señora.*"

Not long after Carlos's explanation, Ava verified his claim. She accompanied Mariela to a rusted water conduit across the alley, and when Ava filled her jug from the pipe, her nose itched and her eyes watered.

The message was clear. Several days later, Ava and Carlos took four cases of bottled water to Mariela. Convincing her to accept it took some doing, however. Ava insisted the water was a gift from one cousin to another, and finally, Mariela hugged her in a fierce grip and with tears in her eyes, accepted it. "*Para Miguel, gracias,*" she said.

Ava's thoughts bounced from one issue to another as Carlos's pride and joy traveled north to the San Jacinto sector of the city on the western shore of Lake Maracaibo. As Ava shifted her attention from the window to her purse, she happened to look down at her right hand. With morbid fascination, she watched the small twitch of a few muscles grow into a sustained contraction that involved every muscle in her hand. Her Bird Woman claw was back, reminding her again of Dr. Jekyll, who jerked and twisted his way into the new form of Mr. Hyde. The association brought to mind her future and how she would change into an inhuman being like Hyde, Miguel, and her grandfather. Her transformation was only a matter of time. Her heart picked up its pace.

Ava did not find it easy to visit Mariela and Miguel. Watching Miguel suffer through the terminal stage of HD offered her a preview of her own frightening future. She would be helpless and insane like Miguel. The thought set her teeth on edge.

Despite her fear, Ava could not watch Mariela's battle without jumping into the fray. Ava was no saint; she thought that contributing her time and energy was the morally correct thing to do. Besides, helping her cousins served as penance for the newest lie she told Langdon: that Mariela was pregnant. Ava unconsciously patted her own belly.

Ava had given plenty of thought to purchasing a proper house for Mariela and hiring a caretaker for Miguel. After the bottled-water incident, Ava recognized her offer would be rejected as charity, and she did not want to insult her cousins by appearing to disapprove of the way they lived or the care Mariela took of Miguel. Instead, Ava volunteered to help the young couple by staying with Miguel when Mariela was away, an offer Ava thought Mariela would accept as the kind of assistance a family member might offer. Ava was no fool. Not for one second did she view her actions as altruistic. She was saving herself from fixating on her own situation. If she did not lend a hand to her cousins, what would she do in Maracaibo, where she knew no one? Her baby was due in March, and it was only November. Ava thought helping Mariela was healthier than isolating herself for four months in a hotel room. Being alone with nothing to do could drive her into depression and threaten the health of her baby. Ava viewed Mariela's need as a blessing.

Chapter 25 – Pelican View, Naples, FL

Thanksgiving was over and Christmas a thing of the past. January was nearing an end. Ava was still in Maracaibo. Langdon lived in his own private hell. He was angry with himself for being a spineless, gutless chump and for clinging to the beguiling memory of a relationship that no longer existed. He felt lonely, desolate, and abandoned. His infrequent conversations with Ava, little more than an agony of meaningless drivel, meant to fill the emptiness left by what they should talk about but avoided, had become strained.

Ava's letters were full of small talk about the poor people of Maracaibo and long-suffering Mariela. He was on the verge of hating Ava's relatives. Worse, more than once he found himself wishing for the speedy demise of Miguel. Having no patience for martyrs, he was disgusted when he realized he was one, a long-suffering, deserted husband forced into martyrdom by Ava and her relatives.

To a man of action like Langdon, helplessness was unbearable, and one day when he and Sunny were in the garden during Scotty's visit to Buck, Langdon said to Sunny, "What do you think I should do next?"

"About what?"

"About Ava and me?"

"What do you want to do?" Sunny asked.

"I want to bring her home. Should I confront her, stop receiving her phone calls, file for a legal separation, what?" His dilemma was that none of the obvious options accomplished what he wanted: to have Ava back, his marriage restored, and his reason for living returned. "I thought you wanted her to come home," Sunny said. "Those actions will drive her further away. Is that what you want?"

"No, I guess I'd be cutting off my nose to spite my face, yet there would be a certain measure of satisfaction in ending my limbo, for better or worse," Langdon said. His face red with frustration, he clenched his fists and banged them together. "For the first time in my adult life, I'm stymied by indecision. I go about my business every day as if nothing has changed. I'm stuck in the muck, if you will. The rug has been pulled out from under me, and I don't know what to do about it."

Sunny heard the frustration in Langdon's voice. "I know you prefer action to inaction, Langdon, but the ball's in Ava's court," Sunny said. "Let me ask you something. When Ava comes home, will your relationship be the same as when she left?"

As Langdon was thinking about his answer, Scotty interrupted to announce the end of his visit with Buck, and the Cavanaughs' left Pelican View, promising to return in the near future.

Langdon walked back to the garden to mull over Sunny's last question: When Ava comes home will your relationship be the same as when she left?

His honest answer was he did not know. After giving the subject considerable thought, he doubted the ease with which he and Ava were open and vulnerable to each other before her departure could be recaptured when she returned. By ignoring their matrimonial promises of honesty and trust and cloaking their feelings in propriety for so long, they may have damaged their relationship beyond repair. He had no faith it could be set to rights.

Langdon felt as if he were treading water. On the one hand, he wanted to confront Ava and demand a earlier deadline to her Maracaibo adventure than the birth of Mariela's baby, and on the other, he realized such a demand would require him to act if Ava ignored him. Since he did not want to back himself into a corner, he decided to leave things alone.

He would hold on until March, the month Mariela's baby was due. When Ava came home, he would find out if his feelings were the same as before she decided to play Mother Teresa in Maracaibo.

He admitted he was bitter. He had no wife to share his bed and no companion to fill his lonely days. He had socially isolated himself, tired of making excuses for Ava every time someone asked where she was, and why she was still away.

Sunny had commented on his avoidance of events at the yacht club and his refusal to accept dinner invitations.

"Are you going to grow a beard, too, like a real hermit?" Sunny teased.

"That would be funny, Sunny," Langdon said, "except I know you mean I should socialize more. The truth is, I would rather refuse an invitation to a dinner party than expose myself to gossip. I don't want every busybody in town nosing into my business."

"Do you really think the gossip is that bad?" Sunny asked.

"Are you kidding? At the height of the season, it's impossible to hide from it. Ava's and my absence at the usual balls and social functions is as glaring as a red flag."

"Has anyone asked where Ava is?"

"Oh yes, and even though I don't go to the events, I donate to every cause. It doesn't matter. People call on the pretext of missing us. Nice on the face of it, but they always ask about Ava. I find it irksome fielding questions about her time after time." He scowled.

Sunny smiled at him. "Yes, I can see that would be annoying, but you can't lock yourself away. As time goes by, the tongues will wag less."

"I doubt it," Langdon said. "I went to the club by myself for a function once, and that was enough for me. Ava's absence garnered so much attention I could almost hear the tongues flapping," he snorted.

He did not tell Sunny every brazen woman in town had solicited his attention. Apparently, the word had gotten around about Ava's absence. The gossip, the unwanted notice, and the flirtatious looks thrown his way made him feel like a target. Hunted by the gossip mavens and haunted by his memories of Ava and the life they had shared, Langdon preferred to stay home.

Other than the staff, Stephenson, and Buck, Langdon saw only those who came to Pelican View by invitation. He could count them on fewer than five fingers: Cathy, Ray, Sunny, and Scotty, his intimate group of supporters.

Since Ava's departure, Sunny's and Scotty's weekly visits were the only good things that had happened at Pelican View in months. Langdon considered them a godsend. When Scotty was around, the strain of illness left Buck's face for a time, and the vaudeville-like interaction between the long-time friends amused Langdon. The two old goats cracked hackneyed jokes, threw friendly barbs at each other, reminisced about ancient adventures, and told stale stories as if hearing them for the first time.

When Langdon stood outside Buck's sitting room and listened to Scotty and Buck carrying on, Langdon felt his burdens grow lighter. In particular, he enjoyed hearing Buck guffaw again. Scotty's company was better for Buck than any pill in his medicine cabinet. After each visit, Langdon was positive Buck had improved mentally and physically. The old twinkle was back in his eye, and the sharpness had returned to his tongue.

Even though Buck's mood perked up during Scotty's visits, after a day or two, Buck would slip back into his usual melancholy, a gloominess Langdon noticed for the first time after Ava left. Her absence had altered not only Buck's mood, but also the relationship between father and son. Before Ava's departure, the Skinner men's shared love for her was an unspoken bond between them. In her absence, their sadness, although also shared, was a wedge between them. Neither man could admit his sense of loss to the other. Buck stopped short of saying, "I guess I'll never see her again," but Langdon read the sorrow in his eyes. They avoided talking about Ava.

Sunny's and Scotty's visits came at a good time for the Skinner men, who were in need of pleasant distractions. Langdon encouraged Sunny to bring along her husband—a man Langdon considered a fortune hunter—because he thought it polite to extend the invitation.

"Thank you for being considerate," Sunny said to him, "but Brock is rarely home. He travels a lot."

Sunny's cheerful façade did not fool Langdon. He sensed her underlying loneliness. No one understood better than he.

On the days when Sunny drove Scotty over to Pelican View, the younger folks left the old geezers to kibitz and moved to the lanai or garden to enjoy a drink and share a conversation out of earshot. In Ava's absence, Langdon had grown close to Sunny. He made no attempt to hide his anguish from her, and he could share his feelings without prevarication, the primary weapon he used elsewhere to staunch the flow of gossip. Since Sunny could see through his customary defenses, Langdon had come to realize hiding behind them was pointless. In Sunny's company, Langdon could be himself.

Langdon needed a willing ear, and Sunny, who was neither judgmental nor biased, was a compassionate listener. Her neutral position allowed him to talk about his feelings and worries, and she provided a woman's viewpoint. Sunny insisted he was doing the right thing by giving Ava the slack she needed.

Sunny had made several cryptic comments to him about Ava's trip to Maracaibo. The first was that things are not always what they seem, and the second was that sometimes it was necessary to look beneath the surface for a deeper meaning.

Langdon was unsure how Sunny meant for him to apply her philosophy to his situation, but her advice to wait and see how events unraveled was encouraging.

Langdon, disgusted with himself for being indecisive, found Sunny's approval of his inaction heartening. She made his lack of initiative appear wise, no small boost to his bruised ego. He needed Sunny's friendship as much as Buck needed Scotty's. The Cavanaughs were good for what ailed the Skinner men.

Chapter 26 – Ritz Carlton Hotel and Miami-Dade Hospital, Miami, Florida

Ava walked away from the Maracaibo prenatal clinic flooded with relief. Her pregnancy was near an end. The doctor told her to leave Venezuela within the month if she wanted her child to be born in the United States. The sooner, the better, he said.

Ava followed his advice. After ensuring the orderliness of her documents, she bid Mariela a tearful goodbye, saying she was going home to have her baby, and flew instead to Miami.

Feingold, Ava's attorney, met her outside the gate at the airport.

He greeted her with a smile. "Hi, Ava, how was your trip? You're looking well."

"Thank you, Eric." *No one looks good at the full-term mark*, she thought. "The trip was uneventful." She was finding it hard to make polite conversation.

"Let's go retrieve your luggage, shall we? I'll do the heavy lifting."

On the way to the luggage carousels, Ava rearranged reality. She imagined a different scene: a grinning Langdon meeting his pregnant wife and unborn child. She blinked hard to hold back tears.

Feingold handled her luggage and the cab. In the hotel lobby, he suggested, "Ava, why don't you sit over there for a moment while I check you in?" He pointed to a chair.

Thankful to get off her feet, Ava sank into the lounge chair and realized too late that sitting down in it was easier than getting out would be.

When his business at the reservation desk was completed, Feingold walked over to her. Looking down at her, he smiled and offered her his arm. "May I help you up?" His perceptive behavior told Ava he was accustomed to dealing with pregnant women.

After Ava was settled in her room, Feingold asked, "Can I do anything more for you before I go?"

"No, thank you, Eric, I'm fine. You've been very considerate," Ava said.

At the door, Feingold turned to face her. "I'll be back in the morning to check on you. You haven't seen the last of me." He smiled again and handed her his business card. "In the meantime, if you need anything, please call day or night. Promise?"

"I promise," she answered. After Feingold left, Ava breathed a sigh of relief, thankful her claw did not reveal itself.

Glad to be back in the States with the end in sight, Ava kicked the shoes from her swollen feet, settled on the sofa, and paused to review the pieces of her plan. Her worry that Feingold would discover she was married had turned out to be needless. From the beginning, she had taken several precautions to avoid entangling the Skinner name in the adoption transactions.

First, she told Feingold she was unmarried. Second, she signed the preliminary adoption papers with the name Phillips because her legal documents were still in her maiden name. She had not changed them to her married name thinking it silly. While she did not object to being called Mrs. Skinner, she would always be Ava Phillips. As far as she was concerned, Mrs. Ava Skinner was a designation, a title, not her name.

Feingold had examined her papers line by line, and since he did not ask to see them again, she assumed he was satisfied. She rubbed the soreness from her feet, thinking she could cross one more hurdle off her list. After months of suspense, her plan was working out.

When Feingold returned to the hotel the following morning, he brought along the legal papers to transfer her baby to the adopting parents. He also gave her the name of a doctor to see. Ava signed the documents and excusing herself with a headache, put an end to their meeting. The less time spent with Feingold, the better. A claw-hand attack in front of him would raise unwanted questions.

Ava had not mentioned her HD to Feingold for fear the adoption process would come to a screeching halt, and she had gone to some trouble to keep him from knowing about it. The first time they met, she tossed a scarf over her shoulder like a shawl to hide her twitching. Each time after that, she covered her right arm with something—a cape, a shawl, a coat worn over her shoulders. As it happened, the concealment was unnecessary. Her Bird Woman claw had minded its manners every time.

Huntington's made having a baby more complicated than usual, Ava thought, especially if adoption was planned. She felt it necessary to substantiate her health at every turn. To eliminate any suspicions Feingold might harbor about her health, she gave him the reports of her monthly and weekly visits to the understaffed prenatal clinic in Maracaibo, where overworked nurses and doctors had not noticed her tremors. As an extra precaution before turning her records over to Feingold, she used a Spanish-English dictionary to look up every word that could describe HD: tremor, tremble, shake, quake, seizure, convulsion, twitch, contraction, and writhe. As far as she could tell, nothing in the doctors' notes mentioned HD, and since they were written in Spanish, the language difference provided an extra layer of protection. Ava doubted Feingold would go to the trouble of having them translated.

On her third day in Miami, Ava visited the obstetrician. She hid her twitching with the same scarf she had worn before, and during the physical exam, kept her arms under the sheet that covered her.

After the examination, Dr. Gulliver said, "Ava, you have a narrow pelvis. Your robust baby might have a hard time traversing the birth canal if it continues to grow, and since it is mature enough to be delivered a week or two before your due date, I suggest an induction."

"An induction?" She was mystified.

"Yes. We give you medicine to start your labor. If we wait for you to go into spontaneous labor, the baby might be too large to deliver, except by C-section."

"As long as there is no danger to the baby, an induction is fine with me," she said.

She left the doctor's office knowing her pregnancy would be over in two days. March 7 is a good date for a birthday, she thought. Supposing the delivery went as expected, she would be back in Maracaibo by March 15, with no responsibility to anyone.

Forty-eight hours later, Ava was in labor at the Miami-Dade hospital. The room to which she was assigned, used for both labor and delivery, was uninteresting. Diamond-patterned curtains hung from the single window. Beneath it sat two upholstered chairs separated by a table on which rested a vase of fresh flowers. Ava assumed they were from Feingold. The only lighting came from an overhead fixture whose harsh illumination caused her eyes to tear.

Ava closed her eyes against the glare and when her pelvic contractions became strong, reminded herself that she was not a mother-to-be. She was a surrogate for the family who would rear the child after it was born. Her duty was to produce a perfectly formed, healthy baby, nothing more. Her detachment was complete.

Between contractions, Ava thought about Mariela and Carlos. After so many months of depending on them for her sanity, it was hard to leave them behind.

Carlos would miss the additional income she had provided. On the day Ava left for Miami, she waited until she and Carlos were at the airport to thank him for his service and his friendship. Telling him it was time to replace his rolling death trap—except in kinder words—she gave him enough money to buy a new one. She handed it to him in a sealed envelope, winked, turned, and walked away.

Mariela's gift was a small house with indoor plumbing near the university-hospital complex. Ava purchased it with the savings banked from her concert days. She instructed the real estate agent and attorney to deliver the reassigned deed on the day after her departure from Maracaibo. The happy thought that Mariela and Miguel were enjoying their new home brought a smile to her lips. She no longer had to think of them living in a peafowl pen.

Langdon was the one loose end left dangling from the plan Ava had conceived with scrupulous care. She could not compensate him for the HD that had stolen her away. She could only hope that Langdon, once freed of her, would pick up the pieces of his life and go forward to discover the happiness and peace he deserved.

As her labor intensified, Ava focused her mind and heart on Langdon, the love of her life, with feelings of overwhelming tenderness. Between the strong, sustained contractions initiated by the Pitocin coursing through her veins and deep breathing to relax, she thought only of him. She remembered his smile, the hitch in his walk when he ambled down the beach, his silly jokes, the way his neck arched when he bent over the books at his desk, the coordination of his athletic body, the hardness of his muscles, how safe she felt wrapped in his arms, his tingling kisses, and their lovemaking.

Bringing every ounce of emotional energy to bear on loving Langdon from afar, Ava delivered a healthy, wailing infant, sex unknown. The baby she would not see and could not hold was Langdon's child. He would never know. Her simple signature gave the precious little life to someone else.

Chapter 27 – The Cavanaugh Estate, Naples, Florida

Sunny Cavanaugh was not a woman to watch from the sidelines. She was of a mind that action spoke louder than words. Her tendency to take the initiative when others shied away from it was a characteristic instilled in her by her mother, Virginia, who, despite having severe multiple sclerosis at a young age, had been a fighter to the end. Years after Virginia's death, Sunny could still hear her mother whispering in her ear, "Sunny, as long as I can draw a breath, I will not give up. Every moment God grants me on this earth is precious."

Sunny had her mother's carrot-red hair and steadfast optimism, and she had no doubt Ava would return to Naples at some point. As time passed and Ava was still in Maracaibo, however, Sunny found it hard to sit back and watch while Langdon pined for Ava and tried to understand why a distant cousin had relegated him to second place.

Sunny, believing Langdon and Ava could resolve their issues if they discussed them face to face, urged Langdon to action, but he said again that he was averse to leaving Buck during the last months of his life. Sunny knew Buck's advancing illness was part of the problem. The other part was Langdon's stubbornness and male pride which, when brought to the fore by what he considered Ava's abandonment, had paralyzed him. The positive side to his inertia was he had not made a preemptive move toward a legal separation. Sunny thought it was better for him to stagnate than to react in anger.

Langdon summed up his indecision for her. "Sunny, I would go to Venezuela, confront Ava, and get my questions answered if it were not for Buck. What if he died during my absence? I might blame Ava forever. That wouldn't help us." He stopped pacing the lanai long enough to shake his head from side to side.

Sunny, understood Langdon's reluctance to leave Buck. Nevertheless, she hated to see Langdon stand idly by while his marriage disintegrated. Sunny thought if she could find a way to break the impasse between Ava and Langdon, they could heal their marriage.

As Sunny mulled over the last few times she and Ava were together, Sunny recalled the card she found on the floor in the foyer where Ava was rummaging through her purse. Intent on cleaning up after the meeting, Sunny had not bothered to examine the card, putting it instead in the foyer table drawer for safekeeping. Since Ava left for Maracaibo before Sunny could return it, she thought she would give it to Langdon.

Pulling open the drawer, Sunny found the card, a commonplace appointment card with a doctor's name and address on the front. She thought it strange Ava would go all the way to Tampa to see a neurologist. As Sunny studied the card, a memory from her past, the content of which she could not recall, slipped around in her mind. She wondered what it was she was trying to remember.

Even though Sunny busied herself by attending to her correspondence, her thoughts kept returning to Ava's card and the memory she could not bring to mind. She sat at her desk drumming the top with her fingers. She told herself, if she could stop fretting about it, the answer would come.

Sunny's patience was thinning. Thinking if she called the number on the card the action might nudge her memory, she picked up the phone and then hesitated. What should she say? How would she explain the reason for her call? She eyed the phone. Should she? In the end, the anxiety created by her waffling compelled her to call. She would make up a story as she went along.

The phone rang several times before a recorded voice answered. The message offered Sunny a lengthy menu of options. She selected seven for Dr. Osgood's nurse. When the nurse came on the line, Sunny drew in a deep breath to reinforce her courage.

"Good afternoon," Sunny said. "I'm calling for a friend of mine, Ava, Ava Skinner."

"Oh, yes, Mrs. Skinner. Dr. Osgood will be relieved she's back from her trip. He was worried about her."

"Yes, we were, too." Sunny heard her heart pounding in her ears.

"Now that she's back, she needs another appointment. Dr. Osgood wants to see her."

"Yes, I can imagine."

"Let's see. What's good for Mrs. Skinner? Mornings or afternoons?"

Sunny's mind raced. Did she dare continue the charade? Why not? She could always call later and cancel the appointment. "Afternoons, please."

"Hmm, oh dear, this week is already booked on HD day."

"HD day?"

"Yes, he only sees HD patients on Thursdays. What does a week from Thursday look like for her?"

"Fine," Sunny said. *What is HD?*

"Okay, then, a week from Thursday at two o'clock. Will that work for her?"

"It will, thank you."

Sunny slammed down the phone. Even for her, the call was audacious. She felt guilty for prying into Ava's affairs, and the call had not helped her determine the connection between Ava's card and the childhood memory she wanted to recapture. Be that as it may, since she had already overstepped her bounds, Sunny thought she may as well find out what HD was. She went to her father's study to look for the thick book that had served as the family's medical reference for several decades.

When she spotted its green and gold cover, worn thin with use, she pulled it from the shelf, sank into her father's beloved leather chair—the one her mother called "the embarrassment"—and turned to the index. She ran her finger down the H list of diseases, and there it was, Huntington's disease, Huntington's chorea, HD, Saint Vitus's dance. She turned to the page referenced.

Huntington's disease, chorea, or disorder HD, is a neurodegenerative disorder that affects muscle coordination and leads to cognitive decline and eventual dementia. Typically, it becomes noticeable in middle age. HD is the most common cause of abnormal involuntary writhing movements called chorea.

Sunny's heart thudded and her throat tightened as she moved her eyes down the page.

Huntington's disease can begin at any age, from infancy to old age. It most commonly affects people in adulthood from thirty-five to forty-four years of age. The earliest symptoms are a general lack of coordination and an unsteady gait. As the disease advances, uncoordinated, jerky body movements become more apparent, mental abilities decline, and behavioral and psychiatric problems manifest themselves.

"Oh my God, oh my God, oh my God," Sunny repeated. Goosebumps prickled her skin and tears spilled onto the page.

Life expectancy is ten to twenty years after symptoms begin. Death usually results from complications such as pneumonia, heart disease, or injuries from falls. A genetic link is suspected, but the exact mode of transmission remains unclear. Patients in the final stages of the disease require full-time care. Symptoms can be managed with a wide array of medications, but at the current time, there is no cure.

Stunned, Sunny slammed the book shut. As she endeavored to come to terms with what she had learned, she traced the years of stains on the worn armrest of her father's chair with her index finger and listened to the century old grandfather clock ticking off each agonizing second with the sweep of its pendulum. Was HD the reason Ava took off to Maracaibo? Sunny crushed the medical tome to her chest as if to squeeze the life out of it for divulging the sickening information. She asked herself, what next?

Sunny had no doubt Ava was unwilling to confide in Langdon, but why go to Maracaibo? Was her search for relatives a hoax, an elaborate ruse to hide her illness? What was she doing in Maracaibo, and why, if she were not planning to return, would she keep writing to Langdon? Much of Ava's behavior was cryptic. Perhaps she could not find the words to tell Langdon about her HD. Maybe she left to give herself time to decide what to do. Did Ava hope Langdon would grow tired of waiting for her and give up or stop loving her? Had she wanted him to take legal steps to end their marriage? Sunny could not put the pieces together.

A bird screeched in the garden. The pool circulator shut off. The bar icemaker rumbled and spat out a fresh batch of cubes. Wind chimes tinkled in the breeze. In the distance, a leaf blower growled. The aromatic sweetness of honeysuckle wafted through the open window by her chair. An airplane droned overhead. Through it all, Sunny, as stiff as a soldier and oblivious to her surroundings, scrambled to put into perspective what she had just learned.

When she was able to gather her thoughts together, she wondered how best to deal with what she had discovered. Poor Ava and Langdon, she thought, swiping at the wet streaks on her cheeks with a tissue. Sunny found it hard to accept that two good people would have their lives destroyed by HD, an undeserved tragedy.

Sunny thought back to Ava's hasty departure, an act that left a million questions in its wake. What did Ava hope to gain by leaving and where did she expect to go, when as her illness progressed, she would need help? Sunny imagined herself in Ava's shoes, and then struck by a dreadful thought, she moaned, "Oh, my God, what if—" The terrible answer was unthinkable. Chilled by her speculation, Sunny shivered in the heat.

And then it came to her, the memory that had eluded her for hours. When she was eleven, she found a doctor's appointment card on her mother's dresser similar to the one Ava dropped on the floor. When Sunny asked her mother why she was seeing a doctor, her mother told her she had multiple sclerosis.

Furious that she was not informed, Sunny felt excluded; she was resentful. She gave no thought to her mother's or father's feelings or how the years of chronic illness, yet to come, would affect them in the future. Full of self-pity, she blamed her mother for being secretive and in defiance, proclaimed she did not need protection.

As Sunny matured, she understood her parents' caution and recognized her own selfishness. The incident was not without merit, however, for she managed to extract several positive observations from her experience. She learned the hard way not to leap to conclusions before she had the facts, and that appearances alone did not tell the whole story. She had not forgotten those lessons. She would refrain from judging Ava's motives until she knew the full story.

In thinking about Ava, her mother, Virginia, and chronic illness, Sunny recalled a comment made by her mother. "I can give up and sit around like a pathetic creature, or I can fight. I choose to fight, and I know you and your father will help me." The remark had a significant impact on Sunny's perspective.

Sunny knew better than most the challenges ahead for Langdon and Ava. Their lives would be turned upside down. Ava had to be in turmoil already, and when Langdon found out—Sunny needed a deep breath.

When Sunny envisioned Langdon's reaction to learning of Ava's fatal illness, she felt ill. At first, he would be shocked, and then when he remembered how angry he was over Ava's leaving him, he would hate himself. Next, he would search for a cure, desperate to forestall the disease. Unable to find a remedy, he would experience disappointment and discouragement. As the days and years wore on, he would reach a certain level of acceptance, but it would come buried in profound sadness. The course of events was predictable with cases of terminal or chronic illness. Sunny was intimate with the progression of emotions, for she had lived through the cycle with her mother.

HD was manageable, though. She had to make Ava see the possibilities. *If Mom were alive she would help,* Sunny thought. Virginia, the realist, would not offer false hope, but she would have the right words to help Ava wring out from her situation every reason to live, no matter how insignificant, until the sum was greater than its parts. If Virginia could hold on to her life, Ava could, too. Sunny remembered the day her mother told her, "I don't count the days until I die, Sunny, I make each day I live count." Keeping to Virginia's philosophy, mother and daughter embraced as a precious gift each day they had together.

Never in her life had Sunny felt a more vital call to action, and following in her mother's footsteps, she would find a way to show Ava and

Langdon that each day they shared was a blessing.

When Scotty arrived home several hours later, he found Sunny in his favorite chair with an expression on her face as long as a grieving widow's. Sunny suspected her father knew she was working through a problem, and she expected him to pry, in the fashion of good fathers before him. He did not disappoint her.

"Hi, honey, whatcha doing? Solving the problems of the world?" Scotty asked. He walked over to her with a smile on his face and bent to plant a light kiss on her forehead.

"Yeah, Daddy, something like that. How was your match?"

"I didn't exactly tear up the course, but I took a couple of bucks from Howard, much to my satisfaction. Excuse me while I gloat. He's such a puffed-up ninny. That's not news to you, though, is it?"

"No, Daddy, I agree. Howard is unjustifiably pompous." She rose from Scotty's chair and moved toward the study door. "And everything's fine with me. Thanks for caring. Would you like a martini? I could use one."

"Love one. Thanks." His gaze followed her to the other side of the room.

On the way to the bar, Sunny began to formulate a plan. She had several issues to iron out, none of which were insurmountable, but she admitted to herself, anything could go wrong. *Not if I can help it,* she vowed, her prominent jaw locked as if to reinforce her determination. After she plopped olives into the martinis, she carried one to her father. As she handed it to him, she said, "I'll be right back, Daddy, to hear about your game. I have a phone call to make first."

"Sure, honey. Thanks," Scotty said. He took the drink from her hand.

Sunny returned to the bar, swallowed an extra-large gulp of her martini, picked up the phone, and dialed Langdon. She needed Ava's address.

Chapter 28 – Hotel del Lago, Maracaibo, Venezuela

Sunny stepped from the plane at the Maracaibo airport, into the atmosphere of a sauna. The humid and heavy air, undisturbed by the slightest breeze, clung to everything like an invisible blanket, increasing the difficulty of performing even simple activities like breathing.

Sunny followed the other passengers down the steps of the portable staircase and across the tarmac to the baggage area. After a brief wait, a tractor-like contraption, pulling a cart piled high with luggage, arrived. She located her suitcase at once, the one with green shamrocks affixed to the handle.

She hauled her luggage over to Customs, where a red-faced official examined her passport and the contents of her suitcase. She stopped to wipe the moisture from her brow and then blazed a path through the riotous baggage area littered with wheelchairs, luggage carts, and strollers and abuzz with the noise of incoming and outgoing passengers, shrieking babies, quarreling children, and scolding parents. Wishing she had earplugs, she found the cab line outside the terminal. Grateful to find her hearing intact, she wondered why no one had thought about soundproofing the building.

Sunny offered a written address to the first cabbie who pulled up to the curb, and after seeing her luggage stowed, settled into the back seat of the taxi. As the beat-up vehicle lurched forward, she turned her face toward the side window to examine the sights. She was so preoccupied with what lay ahead—surprising Ava—that she was unable to appreciate the scenery.

As the cab drew nearer to the Hotel del Lago, Sunny fought to overcome her jitters. Self-doubt, a concept alien to her, gnawed at her confidence. A daunting question flashed in her mind like a yellow caution light: Was she doing the right thing?

Meddling in the affairs of others was risky business. Sunny was levelheaded enough to realize her actions might destroy her friendship with Langdon and Ava. She told herself if good came from her interference, then it would be worth it. If not, at least she had tried. And anyway, the compelling feeling that she was in Maracaibo as part of a higher plan was stronger than her reluctance to intercede.

Still, she could not ignore the bothersome thought that butting into the Skinners' business might make a bad situation worse. What would she do then? She would have to live with the consequences of her actions, and could she? She took a tissue from her purse and blotted away the moisture on her upper lip.

Despite her misgivings, Sunny expected to do less harm than good. What else would justify her presence in a foreign country where she was choking on exhaust fumes and fighting a queasy stomach, riled up by the bumps and jolts of a neglected road, in a car sporting fifteen-year-old shocks? She hoped she had not made too many assumptions about her ability to sidetrack a possible disaster.

Sunny had one confidant in her escapade, Scotty. After three back-to-back martinis—she suspected Scotty had oiled her up on purpose—she had given in to his incessant probing and shared with him her discovery of Ava's HD. She was glad Scotty's detective work had paid off; sharing her load made it lighter. As inscrutable as a Buddhist monk, Scotty could be trusted to keep their secret, even though he had deemed it necessary to warn her about "messing in the business of others," a quaint expression, she thought. Sunny knew Scotty had sensed her resolve because he stifled his usual doom-and-gloom forecast, and in the end, agreed something should be done. He was just not convinced it should be his daughter doing it.

Sunny and Scotty discussed the pros and cons of telling Langdon about Ava's HD. They decided to wait for more information. The acquisition of additional facts would require hearing from Ava herself, and since Ava was not going to come to her, Sunny decided to go to Maracaibo.

In front of the Hotel del Lago, Sunny tipped the cab driver while a bellhop collected her luggage. As she approached the reservation desk, her knees trembled. The moment of reckoning had arrived.

"Good afternoon," she greeted the reservation manager, a middle-aged woman in navy blue and layers of makeup. "Do you speak English?"

"Yes, *señora.* How can I help you?"

"I am looking for a friend, a Mrs. Skinner."

"I see, one minute please," the woman replied, turning her back and opening a thick ledger.

While Sunny waited for the receptionist to thumb through the guestbook, she fiddled with the emerald ring Scotty had given her on her eighteenth birthday, along with a tale of blarney about Irish luck and leprechauns. As the minutes wore on, she felt a sense of urgency. Had Ava used another name, a possibility Sunny had not considered?

The manager turned away from the ledger to face Sunny.

"We have no Mrs. Skinner, *señora.* I am sorry."

Sunny frowned, hoping she had not traveled to Maracaibo for nothing. She offered the manager a strained smile. "My friend sends her letters from this address. She must be registered here."

"Maybe she has another name?"

Yes, Sunny thought, but what name would she use? "Maybe Langdon, L-a-n-g-d-o-n," she spelled for the woman.

Another minute or two passed while the manager consulted the ledger a second time.

She shook her head. "I am very sorry, *señora.*"

"Wait, please ... How about Ava? A-v-a? It's her first name."

The woman's face lit up like a grinning jack-o-lantern. "Ah," she sighed. "¿*Señora* Ava, the American from Florida, no?"

"Yes!" Sunny wanted to lunge across the counter and hug the manager. "May I call her room?"

The manager leaned toward her, a look of concern on her face. She whispered, "*Si, señora,* you can try. It is one *cero* four. She no answer the door for two, maybe three days."

An alarm clanged in Sunny's brain; panic was on her threshold. "Really? Maybe she is sick."

"It could be," the manager said with a nod. "She was *embarazadas y entonces nada.*" She shrugged.

"¿*Embarazadas?*" Sunny asked.

"*Si, embarazadas.* Um, how you say, big with child." The manager ran the flat of her hand in front of her abdomen in a semi-circle.

"Pregnant?" Sunny nearly shouted.

"*Si, pero no está embarazadas ahora, y no bambino,*" the manager explained, lapsing into Spanish in her excitement.

"I don't understand, *señora.*"

The manager hesitated. Sunny thought she was weighing the consequences of revealing Ava's personal information. With lowered head, the manager said, "She no have baby *aquí,*" she pointed again to her belly, "*y* no baby in room." Sorrow clouded her eyes.

Putting Ava's puzzle together as the receptionist was speaking, Sunny had a shocking thought. If she was right, the implications were staggering. Ava was hiding a pregnancy from Langdon, the reason for her long absence. HD was believed to be a genetic disease. Did the baby also have HD? Was that why it was gone? According to what Sunny had read, there was no prenatal test for HD so Ava could not have known if the baby carried the suspect gene. Okay, Sunny thought, then why on earth would Ava hide her pregnancy? Where was the baby? Had she harmed it? No, not Ava!

"I am very worried," Sunny said. She turned to face the manager and placed her hands over her heart to indicate distress. "Can you open Ava's door for me?" She pantomimed unlocking a door. "She might be sick." To drive home her point, Sunny put both hands together as if she were praying.

Before the woman answered, she hesitated again. Sunny imagined the manager was deciding if the situation warranted opening a guest's door without permission.

As Sunny was thinking about what to do next, the manager drew herself up abruptly, turned to the board that hung on the wall behind her, and removed a key. "We go," she instructed. "Come." Leaving her post, she set a rapid pace across the lobby.

The hallway next to Ava's room opened onto a courtyard of potted plants and an asymmetrical pool. Sunny was in such a tizzy her mind registered only green and turquoise and the smell of chlorine. Her anxiety made it hard to breathe.

The manager stopped before Ava's door and rapped once, twice, and then three times. "*Señora Ava. ¿Está aquí?*"

In the silence that followed, Sunny and the manager exchanged anxious glances.

"*Señora Ava. ¡Abra la puerta, por favor!*"

"Ava, it's Sunny. I've come for a visit. Please open the door." She chewed on her lip and looked at the receptionist again.

Without further delay, the manager opened the door, and both women entered the suite. The shades, drawn against the daylight, made it difficult to discern anything other than vague outlines. As their eyes adjusted to the darkness, they discovered an empty living room. Hurrying into the adjoining bedroom, the women found Ava in her bed.

For a fleeting instant, Sunny experienced extraordinary relief—Ava was sleeping—but when the full impact of the scene in front of her pierced her senses, fear paralyzed her. As she eyed the empty container of pills overturned on the bedside table, her throat constricted, and she froze, until a surge of adrenaline forced her to act.

"Ava, Ava, wake up!" Sunny rasped. She grasped Ava by the shoulders and shook her. Ava's head bounced on the pillows as if held to her torso by a string. She was unresponsive.

"Oh my God," Sunny stammered. She looked to the manager for help.

"*La policía y una ambulancia,*" the woman said and bolted from the room.

Sunny felt for a pulse. She thought she detected a faint beat, although she could not be sure. She lifted Ava's eyelid. A glassy eye devoid of life looked back at her.

Her own eyes bright with alarm, Sunny put her ear against Ava's heart and ordered it to beat. "Please, God, don't let her die," Sunny begged, and started cardiac resuscitation as best she could.

Chapter 29 – San Jacinto Hospital and Hotel del Lago, Maracaibo, Venezuela

Jarred awake from a light sleep at the San Jacinto Hospital by the clatter of a hospital breakfast cart wheeling by, Sunny yawned, stretched, and cursed the idiots who invented carts, intended for quiet places, with metal wheels instead of rubber ones. She was irritable after spending a restless night in the visitor's lounge trying to sleep on a rattan love seat designed for a contortionist.

Not for one minute did she agree that the windowless room, no bigger than a closet and furnished in bargain-basement style, was a lounge. A holding cell was a more apt designation.

Two broken-down love seats positioned across from each other, a banged-up square coffee table boasting water rings, a floor lamp with a tattered, yellowed shade, and a prehistoric TV on a table resembling a crate did not make for an appealing space, in her book. No wonder she had been the sole denizen for—she looked at her watch—about twelve hours. Nothing except the gravest of circumstances would warrant the lounge's use.

Sunny massaged the kinks in her back, wincing as a burning sensation slithered from between her shoulder blades to the base of her neck. Thinking the doll-sized furniture surrounding her deserved the ax, she rolled her head in a circle to loosen her tight neck muscles.

Without a doubt, hospital policy did not consider comfort for visitors a high priority. Never had she regretted being a tall woman more than she did on that particular morning, and the lack of amenities did little to improve her mood. She was desperate for a toothbrush, a drink of water, and a change of clothes. Despite her discomfort, she decided to stay put until someone told her Ava was awake and able to converse.

In the middle of the night, Sunny learned Ava would recover. The puffy-eyed doctor who delivered the news credited her with saving Ava's life and shook her hand.

Sunny brushed off her effort as the easy part of what she was in Maracaibo to do. The hard work was still ahead. The time would come when she would have to look into Ava's eyes and explain. Sunny had given plenty of thought to how she would defend her actions. Confessing she faked a call to Osgood's office did not seem the best way to begin her explanation, however.

While she was wrenching her back overnight on the loveseat in the cheesy lounge, Sunny came up with several justifications for her nosy behavior, but she admitted the explanations were lame. She would deal with the issue by avoidance if the subject of her discovery of Ava's HD came up. Sunny also considered how to ask Ava about her pregnancy. Did she have a baby, and if so, where was it? Ava's pregnancy was an unexpected circumstance for which Sunny was unprepared, and it put a new spin on things. Sunny had grappled all night long with the many questions she wanted to ask Ava, and she also imagined what Ava might ask in return. In the light of day, she recognized that her overnight thrashings had only deprived her of sleep, for she was no further along in deciding how to approach Ava and what to ask than the day before. Sunny shook her head. *What a mess.*

When Sunny learned Ava was alive, Sunny's first thought was to return to her hotel and sleep in an actual bed. Then she thought about her plan to break the news about Ava to Langdon, and she discarded the idea. She needed to stay at the hospital, until six o'clock Florida time, to call her father, an early riser.

Several hours later, Sunny set off the find a public telephone. The task of locating one before most of the world was awake proved challenging. She was ready to give up when a doctor wandering the halls in scrubs pointed her in the right direction. The phone, an antiquated piece of equipment in an old-fashioned booth, was outside the hospital entrance. Unable to figure out the proper coin required for a dial tone and with no one around to ask, Sunny felt stupid and gave up.

Several hours earlier, a doctor said he would notify her when Ava could converse. Sunny was still waiting to hear from him. Thinking she might have missed the doctor during her phone expedition, she sought out the charge nurse on Ava's unit to inquire.

The nurse smiled and patted Sunny's arm sympathetically. "She sleeps," the nurse said, referring to Ava.

Thinking it pointless to wait at the hospital for Ava to wake up, Sunny asked to be called at the hotel when Ava could talk. Sunny found the telephone number for the Hotel del Lago on the itinerary the travel agent had prepared for her and left it with Ava's nurse.

Impatient to return to the hotel, Sunny rode the creaky hospital elevator to the main floor to get a taxi. The lobby was deserted. Disappointed by the absence of cabs outside, she was ready to turn away, when one pulled up and discharged two passengers. *Lucky,* she thought, charging out to engage the driver.

At the hotel, Sunny looked for the receptionist she met the previous day. The night clerk, a slight, balding man, said Estella would not be in until nine o'clock. Sunny asked about the suitcase she had abandoned at the front desk in her urgency to see Ava off to the hospital. The clerk nodded and led her to a storage closet.

The clerk asked, *"¿Cómo está Señora Ava?"*

Sunny wondered if everyone at the hotel called Ava by her first name. *"Asi así, gracias,"* Sunny replied, repeating a phrase meaning so-so that Dominga, her housekeeper, was fond of using.

Sunny checked in, reserved a room for Langdon, and followed the night clerk down the hall to her room. The clerk deposited her suitcase inside the door of her suite with a little bow. Thrilled by the sight of a real bed, Sunny tipped the clerk, who returned to his duties, and then hung the *no-molestar* sign on the doorknob.

Collapsing her weary body into a nearby chair, she telephoned her father. Already afoot, Scotty answered on the second ring. Sunny gave him a shortened version of events, leaving out Ava's pregnancy. She thought it best to keep that private until Langdon had absorbed the facts and determined the face he wanted to present to the world.

Sunny asked Scotty to deliver a message to Langdon in person. "Dad, tell him I am in Maracaibo, and ask him to come as soon as possible. Don't go into detail, and don't tell him we know about Ava's HD. Act as if you are as ignorant of the facts as he is. Ask Langdon to call me at the hotel to let me know his arrival time. I'll take it from there." She gave Scotty the telephone number of the hotel and her room number. "And Dad, please ask Langdon to leave a message if I'm out. Tell him I will meet him at the hotel. Thanks, Dad. I'll call you later."

Uncomfortable with revealing Ava's situation to Langdon over the phone, Sunny did not intend to take his call. Until she and Langdon were in the same room, she would not dream of telling him anything about Ava. If Langdon could not reach her, Sunny was confident he would feel an urgency to join her in Maracaibo. He would trust that she wanted him there for an important reason.

No matter how gently Sunny broke the news to Langdon about Ava, he would be distraught. Sunny feared he might do something desperate. One friend in trouble was bad enough, she thought. When Langdon arrived, she would help him absorb the shock as best she could. First, she needed to talk to Ava.

Reeling from exhaustion and nerves, Sunny shucked her clothes beside the bed, stepped over the jumbled pile on the floor, and fell between the sheets. While her tired body relaxed in relief, her mind fretted over Langdon's reaction to Ava's attempt to end her life. *How in the world do you tell a man that his wife, the love of his life, wanted to die?* She could think of no appropriate words with which to explain the unspeakable.

She also had a few loose ends to tie up. Before she could help Langdon, she had to find out what happened to the baby Ava had carried. Sunny knew the task ahead would be difficult, especially when Ava realized her suicide plan had failed. She would be angry, reticent, and uncooperative. Sunny could only hope she would get the answers she needed before she had to face Landon.

Sunny had read that most attempted suicides were distress calls made by people who thought their options were limited. They did want not to die as much as they wanted their misery to go away. Because Ava had removed herself from anyone who might have come to her rescue, Sunny's instincts told her that HD or pregnancy, or both, had driven Ava to suicide. Hers was not a cry for help; she intended to die.

And yet, Sunny acknowledged, without knowing Ava's full story, jumping to conclusions was foolhardy. There was the remote possibility of an accidental overdose, especially if Ava wanted to rid herself of severe depression, and for someone coming to grips with HD and its ominous symptoms, depression would not be unusual. Then too, there was post-partum depression, Sunny reasoned. In the midst of her worries, Sunny sensed the tiniest bit of hope: depression was treatable.

Sunny calculated it would take Langdon several hours to get to Miami from Naples and another three hours or more to reach Maracaibo, assuming he was lucky enough to get on the first direct flight. More than likely, he would have a layover in Caracas. Adding time to pack and travel to the airport and the hotel, she calculated Langdon would arrive, at the earliest, in eight hours. She would have time to sleep undisturbed for several hours, take a shower, dress, and return to the hospital to talk to Ava before his arrival. The thought was Sunny's last before drifting off to sleep.

1999
Chapter 30 – Pelican View, Naples, Florida

Before she rang the bell, Sunny scanned the vast courtyard of Pelican View. The gracious home had witnessed its share of tragedy in the last eighteen years, she thought. During Buck's and Ava's long illnesses and deaths, the beautiful mansion and its meticulous grounds had been a refuge for Langdon. He lived within its walls in isolation, except for Rosa. *Poor Langdon,* Sunny thought, picturing her friend's face. Still a handsome one, it reflected the toll grief had taken—each furrow, line, and wrinkle a testament to years of worry, sleepless nights, sorrow, and frustration.

The gene for HD was identified in 1993, the same year of Ava's death. Sunny thought it was too bad the discovery did not occur when Ava was lucid enough to celebrate the victory. After Ava's death, Langdon continued to long for a cure. Sunny attempted to console him by reminding him that before Ava's mind was taken away, she was pleased to see Huntington's receiving the attention it deserved, at long last.

Sunny attributed a large part of the public's awakening, at least in southwestern Florida, to Ava. Her willingness to share her experience at fundraisers and informational meetings brought HD to the forefront of people's minds and hearts and prompted an infusion of money to fund research.

From Sunny's perspective, it took courage for Ava to stand or sit in front of people while she jerked and writhed and stuttered out her message. As the disease progressed, she sometimes forgot her speech altogether. During Ava's appearances, Langdon exhibited unbounded anguish, and on several occasions, he struggled to hold back tears. Sunny recalled a comment he made to her one night before a fundraiser.

"I have no alternative but to respect Ava's right to make her own decisions, when it comes to standing in front of an audience. If I tried to talk her out of it, she would think me paternalistic and be offended."

At another event, Langdon asked, "Sunny, do you think Ava is competent to make an informed decision about speaking in front of an audience?" With a look of distress, he went on to say, "I feel disloyal questioning her mental state, as though I'm betraying her." Except for those two occasions, Langdon kept his torment to himself and let Ava do what she insisted on doing.

Sunny rang the door chimes. As she waited for Rosa to answer her summons, she reflected on the hard times Ava and Langdon had suffered. Fate had denied them bright, happy lives and a house full of children.

At times Sunny thought the twists and turns in life were little more than a confluence of chance events, like winning or losing a jackpot with a spin of the roulette wheel or a toss at the crap table.

Why else would good people have to endure such terrible suffering?

As Sunny waited for Rosa to navigate her way across the sprawling house from the kitchen, it occurred to her Langdon would have to look for another housekeeper before long. She calculated Rosa must be at or beyond seventy.

The warm February day had cooled down from its earlier high of eighty degrees, and the sun hung low in the sky. The stately palms, bordering the driveway, cast late afternoon shadows across the courtyard, their striped pattern prompting Sunny to think of prison bars. The analogy was appropriate, for Pelican View was little more than a prison for Langdon.

As Sunny thought about all Langdon had endured, her mind wandered back to 1983, three years after Ava's diagnosis. On that evening, Langdon, jubilant with news about a team of scientists who had located a genetic marker for HD on chromosome four, had telephoned to share the good news. In a voice bursting with hope, he explained the significance of the finding to her.

"Sunny, this is amazing progress. Soon there will be a test for Huntington's even before people have symptoms. Isolating the exact gene can't be far behind, and after that, well ..."

He did not complete his thought. Sunny read his mind. Langdon thought a cure for Huntington's might allow him and Ava to resume their previous life. He wanted back the simple things they had taken for granted, such as the sound of Ava's piano music filling the house or a walk together on the beach at sunset. Sunny understood Langdon's longing. As Virginia's illness progressed and she became housebound, Sunny remembered wishing for one more chance to enjoy shopping with her mother or dining out, without canes or motorized chairs or watching Virginia struggle to hold her head up or keep her eyes open. She knew what Langdon hoped for every day; oh yes, she knew.

Her mother's illness taught her the importance of living in the moment with joy and gratitude because no matter how big or small the occurrence, that particular moment could never be recaptured.

On the evening of Langdon's call, Sunny rejoiced with him over the progress, pretending hope for his sake. She kept to herself words that would have cautioned him not to be overconfident in his optimism. She knew the hope he was feeling was only one emotion of many he would experience as Ava's Huntington's worsened, for the tragic aura of chronic illness was predictable. The response began with fear, progressed to hope, floundered in frustration, smarted with defeat, and at the end, culminated in acceptance. She had dealt with every emotion during her mother's lifetime. The discovery of a marker for a gene, even though a significant breakthrough, was only one step in the right direction. Experience had taught her that cures were oblivious to the timelines of the afflicted.

Sunny's prediction was on the mark. Ten more years went by before the Huntington's Disease Collaborative Research Group discovered the HD gene itself. The invaluable cooperation of families from the Maracaibo area made the painstaking research possible. The discovery came too late to benefit Ava. She was already thirteen years into her suffering.

Several months after the discovery, Sunny was at Pelican View to help Langdon with a project for the HD center, when Ava's nurse burst onto the lanai. "Mr. Skinner, you'd better come immediately," she said.

From the look on the nurse's face, Sunny surmised Ava was nearing the end. Langdon rushed to her side, and Sunny went home, after leaving a message with Rosa for Langdon to call if he needed her.

The following morning, Langdon telephoned. In a choked voice, he said, "Sunny, Ava died. Pneumonia closed down her lungs. My angel has gone to heaven."

Yes, Sunny thought as she waited at the door of Pelican view, Langdon had endured the weight of his burdens, but he had not thrived. During Ava's illness, he had withdrawn from his beloved community and friends, working from home on his businesses and causes and limiting his social circle to her, Cathy and Ray Velez, and the Velez children. They were the only visitors to Pelican View other than Craig Stephenson, who had retired from his service to Skinner Enterprises.

Langdon made one exception to his self-imposed isolation. He attended the significant events in the lives of the Velez children, Elizabeth and Mike. Langdon was present for first Holy Communions and ballet recitals, baseball and soccer games, pet parades, school Christmas pageants, birthdays, and graduations. If a function was meaningful to the children, he went. He even dragged her along from time to time. Sunny did not mind. Her life was not so full of excitement that she had no time to spare.

Langdon rarely failed to mention to her how blessed he was to have Elizabeth and Mike Velez in his life, acknowledging they eased the ache of being childless. Sunny knew he cherished his role as Mike's godfather, viewing himself as a favorite uncle, advisor, and friend.

Sunny thought the ease with which Langdon developed a rapport with children remarkable. She was not a parenting expert, but over the years, she had witnessed Langdon's many encounters with the youngsters who grew up with Elizabeth and Mike. In her opinion, Langdon would have been an exemplary father, an observation that made the memory of Ava's stillborn child more poignant.

Sunny knew Ava had not wanted Langdon to know about her pregnancy because when she was in the hospital in Maracaibo, she extracted a promise from Sunny not to tell him. Since the child was stillborn, Sunny saw no reason to upset Langdon further and kept the secret to herself. Langdon was comfortable with the notion that untreated depression associated with Ava's HD was behind her decision to end her life. He did not suspect what Ava had told her: She was depressed over her baby's death.

Sunny's lengthy wait on the doorstep ended when Langdon instead of Rosa opened the door. "Hi, Sunny, come in," Langdon greeted her. You're prompt as usual." He ushered her into the great hall. "Good to see you, and thanks for coming." He hugged her. "I couldn't live through another anniversary of Ava's death alone. I know she's been gone six years, Sunny. To me, it seems as though it were yesterday."

Sizing up Langdon's expression as both reflective and gloomy, Sunny smiled at him. "Should I scold you for dwelling?" She shook a schoolmarm finger at him.

"It wouldn't be the first time." He sighed. "Yes, I know I live or dwell, if you will, in the past. It's a failing."

"Where's Rosa?" Sunny asked, turning her face in the direction of the kitchen. "Why did you answer the door?" God forbid something had happened to Rosa, too.

"Poor Rosa. Her hearing is getting worse, I'm afraid," Langdon answered with a shake of his head. "She must not have heard the bell. After a while, it occurred to me she had left you standing in the courtyard. Sorry."

"No matter, it gave me a little time to reflect." Sunny smiled up at him. "The Gulf looks beautiful this time of day, Langdon. I hope you pause to enjoy it each evening."

"I love that about you, Sunny. You look for the good, even in times of sadness. It's an enviable gift."

"No, it isn't a gift, Langdon. A gift is something given to you. The ability to focus on the good things, the simple things, is a learned behavior, a skill. In a way, it's a form of escapism. It's as easy to dwell—yes, my favorite word—on the good stuff as it is to wallow in the bad. I prefer to feel cheerful rather than miserable. It's that simple."

Langdon nodded. "Easy for you to say and do. I find it more complex. Despite my teasing, I do listen to your words of wisdom, and I don't mean that sarcastically. You are the reason we will not remember Ava's death this evening; instead, we will celebrate her life."

"Good man," Sunny responded and kissed him on the cheek. "I think I prefer the new you."

Langdon poured two iced teas, and they walked out to the small garden next to the pool. If it were not for the utter lack of mutual attraction, the timing and the evening were perfect for the start of a romance between two people who had been through so much together. As the sun slipped closer to its watery berth amid streamers of pink and yellow, Langdon and Sunny toasted their firm and long-lasting friendship as though they were brother and sister.

After the toast, Sunny put her drink down. She glanced toward the lanai and pool. "When is everyone expected?" she asked. She assumed the guest list began and ended with Cathy and Ray. "Have I come too early?"

"Cathy, Ray, and the kids will be along soon. I wanted a minute to speak with you alone first."

"Oh, about what?" She was intrigued.

Not one to share his feelings about the Maracaibo days with ease, not even with Sunny, Langdon searched for the correct words. "To thank you for what you did for Ava and me. I haven't expressed my appreciation formally, and it's overdue. I should have done it sooner, but you know how hard it is for me to think back to Maracaibo. Dredging up those old memories makes me feel sad."

"Thank you, Langdon," Sunny said, touched by his comments. "I wish I could've been more helpful. Besides, you've thanked me in your own way many times."

"You deserve it. You're the reason Ava didn't die in Maracaibo. Your bravery gave us three more years together before her illness made it difficult for us to live a normal life." He gazed at the Gulf, his face a scrapbook of memories.

"The other good thing that came from those additional years was the foundation, don't you think? It meant a lot to Ava," Sunny said. She wanted to keep the conversation positive.

"You're right. The foundation was everything to Ava. We were lucky to have the resources and connections to establish it and to care for her at the same time. I can't imagine how the average family deals with the challenges of Huntington's— all those years of medications, physical therapy, and constant oversight. It's emotionally and financially draining."

"Yes," Sunny said. "I agree. HD is an astronomical burden. The worst part is its propensity to strike its victims at such a young age. The illness robs people of their vitality, their productive years, and their lives. I am hard-pressed to think of a more devastating waste." She twisted a hibiscus flower from a nearby bush and tucked it behind her ear.

Langdon rubbed his chin. "By the way, Sunny, after all these years, it's hard to believe, but I still don't know how you happened to be in Maracaibo." He leaned toward her. "Surely you didn't go there for a vacation. Did Ava contact you?"

"No, Langdon. The truth is Ava dropped a card on the floor at my house. When I saw it, I picked it up and put it in a drawer, intending to return it to her. I didn't remember it again until Ava was in Maracaibo. The card was for an appointment with a neurologist. I snooped," she confessed, "called the number, and quite by accident, the nurse told me the weekly HD clinic was booked. Had she not made that mistake, I wouldn't have known."

"Did Ava know you knew? Wasn't she curious about your sudden appearance?"

"No, I didn't tell her what I discovered. I said I was there because I missed her, needed a break from Naples to think, and came to help her with Mariela and Miguel. She bought it. I guess my do-gooder reputation stood me in good stead."

"Then how did she think you found out about her HD?"

"When she came out of her drug-induced state in the hospital, she was angry to be alive, a typical reaction when suicide is thwarted. She shrieked that she had Huntington's and didn't want to spend the rest of her life being a freak and a burden to you. 'A freak without a mind,' she said."

"How awful for you, Sunny. I am sorry."

Langdon closed his eyes and hung his head.

"Don't be sorry. I expected as much and wasn't shocked by Ava's reaction. I knew I'd stepped into a maelstrom. I thought it was necessary at the time."

"She was pretty calm by the time I arrived."

"Yes, seeing you and knowing you wanted her, in spite of what she'd done, made the difference, I suspect. The thought of living and dying by herself with HD had to be frightening. Under those circumstances, suicide made sense to her," Sunny continued. "I suspect depression colored her decisions. Don't you think once she started taking the anti-depressants, she appreciated having a second chance?" Sunny looked at Langdon's face for affirmation.

"I do." Langdon nodded. "I also think your suggestion to start the foundation to help others with Huntington's was her saving grace. Establishing it kept her from feeling useless."

"That was my mother talking," Sunny said. "Mother used to say she owned her multiple sclerosis: it didn't own her."

"She was right," Langdon said and to express his gratitude, reached across the distance between their benches and squeezed Sunny's hand.

Sunny rolled and unrolled the edge of her napkin. "Langdon, I have a question, if you don't mind. Were you able to decipher what Ava was trying to tell you near the end?"

Langdon shook his head. "Nope, I didn't. The words were garbled, something like *fein ah abie.*" He rubbed the back of his neck. "It sounded as if she were speaking a foreign language. She repeated the phrase over and over, clutching my arm as if she wanted to break it or pulling at my clothes. I am certain she was desperate to communicate something. My inability to understand what she wanted was frustrating. To this day, I wonder about it."

The doorbell chimed on the lanai, cutting their conversation in the garden short. "Excuse me, Sunny, I have to answer the door," Langdon said. He rose to his feet. "Rosa won't hear it. I'll meet you on the lanai." He turned on his heel and headed for the front door.

A few minutes passed before he joined Sunny on the lanai with Cathy, Ray, and their children, Elizabeth and Mike, in tow. Behind them was a fifth person, a tall, redheaded man who Sunny did not know.

Chapter 31 – Pelican View, Naples, Florida

The guests on the lanai of Pelican View took a moment to appreciate the colorful display provided by the sun as it descended below the western horizon. Langdon welcomed his guests and then, turning to Elizabeth, said "Why don't you introduce your friend to Sunny first? I can tell her curiosity is getting the best of her." He winked.

"Sure, Uncle Langdon." Elizabeth took the tall, redheaded young man by the hand and led him over to Sunny. "Anthony, I would like you to meet my aunt, Sunny Cavanaugh. Aunt Sunny, meet Anthony, my fiancé." Tossing her shoulder-length hair back from her face, Elizabeth flashed her engagement ring at Sunny.

Sunny shook Anthony's hand. "I must say, Elizabeth, you've found yourself a good-looking fellow by anyone's standards. No one told me you had a serious beau." She kissed Elizabeth on the cheek, said her ring was stunning, and smiled at Anthony, whose better-than-six-foot height made him as tall as Langdon.

"Anthony proposed before we came over, Aunt Sunny; the reason we are a little late, Uncle Langdon," Elizabeth said, turning to face him. "I apologize." She whirled back around and with a squeal of delight, hugged Sunny.

"You didn't hear about Anthony, Aunt Sunny, because I kept him a secret for more than a year. I didn't see the point of putting him through Dad's cross-examination until we were sure of our plans."

"No, my fault," Ray spoke up. "I mean, we were late because I was grilling Anthony," he said with a conspiratorial wink at the young man. "He came to us like a gentleman, to ask for our permission and blessing before proposing to Elizabeth. I put him through the wringer."

"He passed the interrogation with flying colors, though, didn't he, Dad?" Elizabeth boasted.

"He did indeed, Elizabeth," Ray said, nodding. "Anthony's a lucky man."

Smiling at her father, Elizabeth linked her arm through Anthony's and tugged him closer to Langdon. "Anthony, I want you to meet my Uncle Langdon. After Dad, he's the most important man in my life, aren't you, Uncle Langdon?"

"I sure want to think so, but aren't you too young to get married, Missy?" he teased.

Anthony laughed, shook Langdon's hand, and looked at his bride-to-be. "*Missy*, huh? You didn't tell me you had a nickname, Elizabeth. I think it fits you."

Elizabeth made a face. "I'm already an old lady at twenty-three, Uncle Langdon," she said.

"And law school?" He feigned a fatherly sternness.

"Oh, we're not getting married until next year. I'll graduate before our wedding."

"I suppose it's okay then." With a big grin, Langdon clapped Anthony on the back, as if he had won a first-place trophy.

"Uncle Langdon," Elizabeth said, "may I show Anthony the gardens?"

"Go right ahead, Missy." As the young couple stepped off the lanai Langdon looked after them with a wistful expression. The engagement talk brought back the memory of telling Buck he wanted to marry Ava. Before Buck conveyed his pleasure, he made Langdon nervous with his many questions about Ava. Langdon flinched. He was becoming his old man.

Dear God, how he missed Ava. He wished she were celebrating Elizabeth's happy moment with him. The hitch in his chest felt deep and long and hurtful, and his eyes grew watery. He would never stop missing her.

HD had been a twenty-four-hour challenge. Langdon had experienced moments of frustration, irritation, helplessness, grief, sorrow, and anger—not at Ava, at their situation. Despite the negatives, caring for Ava had filled his days with purpose. Everything he did was for her or them. Since Ava's death, his life was little more than a bottomless pit of time to fill with to-do lists and meaningless busywork. He had lost his way.

Langdon often questioned the sanity of spending the years he had left repeating the same stale routine. Without goals or expectations for the future, he was not living; he was existing. When he woke up in the morning, he wanted to be more than an old fool thrilled to find himself breathing. He wanted to look forward to something, to feel alive, to be needed.

Langdon had enough insight to realize he was floundering. He needed an anchor, something or someone to infuse his flat, dull life with substance and purpose. The problem was figuring out how to find what he needed without extracting more energy than he had to give.

The intensity of his melancholy scared him at times. When he felt low, he thought how easy it would be to leave the world. He would not turn back for a second glance. He had no reason to stay on God's earth, nothing to look forward to, no children to live for, and no burning passion, animate or inanimate, about which he cared. Unable to find a meaningful reason to drag through one more day, he sometimes imagined himself clinging to a log watching the flotsam of his shattered life drift by. He believed the current would rip him from safety in time.

"Uncle Langdon, are you all right?"

Mike's voice was calling him from far away. A second passed while Langdon regained his senses. "Sure, Mike," Langdon replied, his voice hoarse. He cleared his throat and, remembering his duties as the host, pasted a smile on his face. He turned to look at his godson.

"What do you think of Anthony, Mike? I mean man-to-man, no holding back."

"He seems like a good guy, at least as far as I can tell." Mike folded his gangly eighteen-year-old frame into a lounge chair across from Langdon. "Elizabeth kept him under wraps. She brought him home last year during her winter break from school. When we heard nothing more about him, we assumed he was just another discarded boyfriend. You know how girls are." He rolled his eyes upward. "The good news is, Anthony says he plays squash. You and Dad should get him on the court to see what he's got."

"Great idea, Mike. You come, too. If he can beat you, I guess we'll let him marry Elizabeth. What do you think?"

Mike said, "I think I have nothing to say about it. The day Elizabeth listens to me will be one to remember." At the mention of his sister's name, the newly engaged couple returned to the lanai from the gardens. Mike cast an affectionate glance in Elizabeth's direction and then screwed up his face. "Who understands women anyway?"

Langdon thought it was ideal the two siblings were close. In his estimation, Cathy's and Ray's devotion to intelligent parenting had paid off. A large part of their success stemmed from giving their children unconditional love coupled with knowing when to put the skids on and when to slack off. He felt fortunate to have Elizabeth and Mike in his life.

Elizabeth had distinguished herself in law school as a leader, and Mike, a high school senior, spoke with eagerness about following in his father's footsteps at Harvard. Mike was also a leader but, unlike Elizabeth, who organized and delegated, Mike led by example, rolling up his sleeves and getting down to work. Langdon understood the man Mike the boy would become. Their natures were similar.

Langdon thought Mike's interest in studying public administration and city planning in college a good fit, given the many years he had watched The Village grow from a sketch on his dad's drawing board into a vibrant community. Curious about his selection, Langdon asked Mike one day why he had chosen that major.

"I like the idea of making something useful out of nothing, of converting wasteland into a thoughtfully planned community," Mike said. "It's similar to slow-motion photography, Uncle Langdon. Think of watching a bud unfold into a beautiful flower, one petal at a time."

Mike was a do-it-yourself type of guy. He followed his parents' example by contributing his time and energy to The Village, volunteering his band for fundraisers, neighborhood picnics, block parties, and farmers' market days. In his sophomore year, he organized the younger boys of The Village into a soccer team that was tearing up the local competition. Langdon was proud to call Mike his godson. By any measure, the Velez children were exceptional.

Langdon tried not to be envious, and in the real sense of the word, he was not. Still, the Velez youngsters provoked within him an acute awareness of having no children of his own. His mind told him that his childlessness was a blessing because there were no descendants to pass on the HD gene, but to his heart, it felt like a curse.

When Langdon was around Mike and Elizabeth, he imagined what his own children might have looked like or grown up to be, and his memories of his and Ava's jokes about ballerinas and oil rig workers haunted him. With no children to fill his home, the absence of noisy squabbling and joyful squeals made the silence at Pelican View downright oppressive. As if he had not experienced enough grief, he found himself mourning children he did not have.

Chapter 32 – Pelican View, Naples, Florida

The phone jolted Langdon awake at three in the morning. Ray was calling.

"Langdon, forgive me for waking you in the middle of the night. Cathy thought you might be able to help." Ray's voice quavered. "Cops took Mike down to police headquarters, and Cathy went with him."

"Good God, for what?"

"For questioning. Betty's daughter was raped."

"Natalie? For Christ's sake, the cops are crazy if they think Mike is responsible. There isn't a better kid on the face of the earth." Langdon gasped for breath.

"We know that, but the police didn't take my word for it," Ray said.

"Why would they even think he's involved?" Langdon asked.

"Because after you and I left the office, Betty stayed to finish up some office work, and Mike knew Natalie was being dropped off by a friend, so he stayed as well. He has a crush on her."

"And," Langdon prodded, "so what?"

"Natalie didn't get to the office, that's what, and her girlfriend didn't answer the phone when Betty called her house. Betty, thinking there must have been a miscommunication, went home to wait. She asked Mike to stay at the office in case Natalie showed up there."

Langdon rammed his hair back from his forehead. "When Betty went home, did she find Natalie?"

"No, according to Mike, Natalie wasn't home when Betty got there. She didn't find a note either."

"How did Mike know that?"

"Mike said Betty called the office from her house to see if Natalie had turned up. When Mike told Betty no, she said not to wait, to go on home. She told Mike she would call Natalie's girlfriend again. The girlfriend was the one who was supposed to have dropped Natalie off." Ray was breathing hard.

"Did Mike go home?"

"Yes. According to the police, Natalie was dropped off at the stoplight before the corner, not in front of the office. She cut through the rear parking lot to come in the back door, and that's when someone attacked her. The police think the rapist dragged her from the lot into the alley behind the Crazy Monkey. I guess it was some time before the police were called. Cops think she blacked out."

"Then the police think Mike raped Natalie after Betty left the office?" Langdon asked.

"That's my understanding," Ray said. "I'm not sure of the exact timeline. Since the police are looking at Mike, they must think he was in the vicinity at the time of the rape. Maybe he was, but he was in the office, not the alley." Ray's voice broke. For a second, the connection sounded muffled, as if Ray had put a hand over the phone.

Langdon imagined Ray struggling to gather his composure. "Ray, Ray," Langdon said. "Are you there? Listen, does Mike have an attorney?"

The weighty silence at the other end of the phone was upsetting. Langdon, fighting to keep his feelings in check, envisioned the emotions his friend was experiencing. It occurred to him that instead of having a nightmare in his sleep, he had awakened to one.

Ray cleared his throat and mumbled, "That's why I'm calling. Do you know a good defense attorney we can call at this time of night? Cathy went with Mike to the station because I didn't want him questioned alone without an attorney. You know how cops can trip you up. I'm sick to death about poor Natalie and Betty. Until I can clear Mike, though, I can't help them."

"Sure, I'll call Everett. Do you know Jim Everett? He's a first-rate attorney. Why don't you drive over to my house while I call him? We'll go to the police station together. Jim will meet us there." Langdon did not want Ray to drive in his emotional state. Langdon's own hands shook. "You can fill me in on the details on the way."

"Thanks, Langdon. See you in ten minutes."

Langdon scrambled into jeans, a shirt, and sandals and then phoned Jim Everett.

After Langdon explained Mike's situation to Everett, the attorney said, "I'll be there in ten minutes. I'll call ahead to ask the police not to question Mike further until I arrive. The department will honor my wishes as a courtesy. We have a good working relationship."

As soon as Langdon hung up, the doorbell rang. He opened the door to find Ray pacing the courtyard with untied shoelaces and his shirt partially tucked into his pants. His grave face and red-rimmed eyes conveyed his intense distress. Tousled into curls, his hair needed combing. Ray had dressed in a hurry. Langdon understood.

The two men climbed into Langdon's Mercedes and sped away.

"Who found Natalie?" Langdon asked.

"I heard the police say when they talked to Mike that Natalie must have dragged herself to the small house behind the parking lot. The people who live there called the police, and they, in turn, called Betty."

"My God, sweet little Natalie. She'll be traumatized for life. Have you spoken to Betty?"

"No, we've had our hands full. The cops showed up several minutes after two."

"Why are the police looking at Mike?"

"I'm guessing Betty told them Mike stayed behind to wait for Natalie."

"Betty wouldn't think Mike did it," Langdon said. His tone was fierce. "She knows him too well."

"I agree, Langdon, but frankly, if Elizabeth were raped and beaten up, I'd be looking at everyone, no matter how nice I thought they were. Think about the nice con artists, psychopaths, and serial killers who can charm a snake out of its skin."

"Scary," Langdon admitted. "Well, we know Mike didn't do it, and the cops will, too, in short order. The problem with the cops looking in the wrong direction, though, is they aren't looking in the right one if you know what I mean. Meanwhile, the creep is getting away."

"Believe me, I've made myself crazy thinking the same thing. Mike's crush on Natalie doesn't help either. I hope the police won't leap to conclusions. Mike hasn't even asked her out. We've talked about her, and Betty is aware of his interest. I pray she doesn't mention it to the police." Ray rocked back and forth in his seat.

For a moment the friends were silent, preoccupied with their thoughts. The Mercedes hurtled through the darkness, a lone car on the hushed streets of Naples. At each intersection, the stoplights, guiding invisible traffic, turned red or green automatically, a frustration to Langdon who was striving to make time. The city, a silhouette of square and rectangular structures in the silvery moonlight, resembled a deserted movie set. Tourists and residents alike were asleep in their hotels or homes. Except for a raccoon rummaging through a trash receptacle, only Langdon and Ray were not in their beds.

Langdon broke the heavy silence. "What about other suspects. Are there any?"

"I don't know, and I have no idea when the rape took place either. Natalie could have been attacked an hour before Mike left the office or even after he left the office. The cops didn't say. In fact, they didn't say much of anything."

"Will Natalie be okay? I mean physically."

"The police wouldn't give us details. I gathered from their conversation with each other Natalie's in the hospital."

"If she could identify the rapist, Mike wouldn't be a suspect."

"I've thought about that also. I agree. Natalie either gave the cops a partial description loosely fitting Mike, or she didn't see the rapist's face."

"Makes sense. If Natalie didn't see the rapist's face," Langdon said, "then anyone in the area is a suspect and fair game for questioning."

"Yes, and that means the two of us as well. We left separately and a few minutes before Betty and Mike."

"True." Langdon's stomach lurched. "I hate the implication."

A suffocating hush ensued as the men contemplated the significance of being possible suspects.

"Ray," Langdon asked, "did the police question you?"

"No."

"Do you suppose they will?"

"Probably."

Langdon craved fresh air. He opened the windows and welcomed the blast of wind as it ripped through the car. Thinking aloud, he said, "Can the police can estimate the time of rape like they can the time of death." Verbalizing his thoughts to Ray as they arose confirmed his reality. He was not dreaming or hallucinating.

"I doubt it."

"I know sperm can live inside a woman's vagina for up to five days," Langdon said, "a piece of trivia I picked up when Ava and I were trying to get pregnant. Outside the body, I have no idea. Do you?"

"No," Ray mumbled. "We don't even know if semen, or any DNA evidence for that matter, was found in or on Natalie or at the scene. I asked, but the cops weren't giving out information. They were immutable and inscrutable."

"That's a mouthful."

"The cops made it clear to us they were there to ask the questions, not to answer ours."

"Nice," Langdon said. "Okay, let's return to the timeline. Natalie must know when she was dropped off because her mother was waiting for her. It's likely her girlfriend also knows. That gives the cops a beginning time. The rape must have occurred within minutes of Natalie's drop off, wouldn't you think? I mean, I can't see a rapist grabbing someone and fooling around for fifteen minutes before doing it."

"No, I can't either," Ray said. "Mike told us Betty expected Natalie around six-thirty. You left before me, and it was already dark outside. Do you remember what time it was?" Ray's anxiety permeated the air like a toxic mist.

"Sometime between six-thirty and six-forty-five, I think, although I can't be certain. Natalie wasn't there yet. I stopped to talk to Rolando in the parking lot before getting into my car, and I didn't hear anything unusual. When did you leave?"

"Several minutes after you," Ray said. "I didn't see you or Rolando in the parking lot, and I don't recall the exact time. Cathy was working late. I wasn't concerned about getting home at a specific time."

Langdon's brain burned with the effort of piecing the information together. The harder he tried to sort things out, the more jumbled everything became. "Do we know when Betty left? What about Mike?"

"Not to the minute. The cops woke us up and wanted to question Mike right away. I haven't had a second alone with him to ask much of anything. The first I knew about the rape was when the cops came to our door. They questioned Mike a little, took him to the station, and I called you. Things happened fast." Ray took a deep breath.

"I was home when Mike came in at eight o'clock though," Ray continued. "If you figure forty minutes to get from the office to our place, he must have left around seven-fifteen, give or take a few minutes. Assuming Natalie's drop off was six-thirty, the time Betty expected her, the cops must suspect a window of opportunity from then until Mike left around seven-fifteen. To the best of my recollection, Mike was in the office when I was there. You think you left between six-thirty and six-forty-five, and since I left after you, between six-forty-five and seven, the amount of time Mike was alone is whittled down to fifteen minutes, give or take a few."

"Yes, but only if we assume Betty left right after you," Langdon said. "We aren't even sure when we left. Our timeline is shaky at best, Ray, and full of holes. For example, maybe Natalie's friend dropped her off closer to seven o'clock than six-thirty after everyone, except Mike and Betty, had left. So many variables."

Langdon was stuck on the timeline. "Let's go back to what we know. First, Mike was in the office when Betty phoned him from her house, and he left immediately after her call. Second, Betty lives ten minutes from the office, and Mike is forty minutes from home. Third, Mike arrived home at eight o'clock. We can conclude, then, that Betty must have left close to seven. Correct?"

"Correct. Wait," Ray said, "if our calculations are right and the cops suspect Mike for the rape, he had to do it in the ten minutes after Betty's departure and before her phone call to him at the office or in the five minutes after her phone call, and before he left for home."

"That's right," Langdon concurred.

"Either way," Ray said, "it's not a lot of time to get the job done. I hope the police will come to the same conclusion. Nevertheless, we're basing our timeline on assumptions. Without knowing the facts, we can't be certain of anything."

Langdon clenched his fist, sighed, and continued. "We have other unknowns as well, such as how fast Mike drove home. You know when he got there, and you assume he was driving the speed limit. Since the cops don't know him like we do, they'll question him about that. What if the rape occurred before any of us left? The rapist and poor Natalie might have been in the alley at the same time we were in the parking lot. Face it, Ray, we're groping in the dark. My God, what a mess." He shook his head.

"Yeah," Ray said, "we're running on pure speculation and an excess of anxiety. I wish we had more information."

"I wonder why neither of us heard any noise coming from the alley."

"I've wondered about that also," Ray said, "and there's something else to think about. We know Natalie was in the alley at some point; we don't know the actual place where the rape occurred. Another mystery until we learn the facts." He took out a handkerchief, wiped his brow, and lowered his chin to his chest.

Langdon glanced at Ray, who was slumped in his seat. Langdon understood his anguish. Mike was incapable of committing a violent act like rape. He told himself innocence would prevail.

"Listen, Ray, Everett will get the facts when he talks to the police and to Mike. The truth is, Mike didn't rape Natalie. He'll be off the hook soon." His little pep talk sounded long on hope and short on conviction. He and Ray would both worry until they had good reason not to.

Chapter 33 - Police Station and Pelican View, Naples, Florida

Langdon and Ray arrived at the police station in time to see Mike, flanked by two burly policemen—one in uniform, the other in street clothes—Cathy, and Jim Everett shuffling down a dimly lit corridor. Mike's back was turned, making it impossible for Ray and Langdon to read his face, but Mike's hanging head and dragging gait told the story. Ray and Langdon exchanged concerned glances.

"Cathy," Ray called down the hallway to his wife.

Cathy spun around, whispered to Everett, and made her way back to Langdon and Ray. Mike, Everett, and the two police officers disappeared through one of the doors off the corridor.

The expression of fear on Cathy's face, made Langdon's heart ache. Her hazel eyes, darkened by dilated pupils, reminded him of a startled deer running for its life. When she looked up at him, however, he saw strength, not timidity, and the determination of a mother bear, ready to defend her cub from harm no matter the risk to her life.

"Langdon, thank you for getting in touch with Jim Everett," Cathy said. "We are grateful Mike doesn't have to go it alone." Before Langdon could reply, Cathy turned to her husband. "Ray, we have to talk. Langdon, will you excuse us for a moment, please?"

Cathy and Ray withdrew to the other side of the room, leaving Langdon by himself near the door of the station. He was familiar with the building and its layout because he had been there on several occasions to consult with Chief of Police Earl Atwood on matters related to policing The Village. As usual, the station smelled of burned coffee and doughnuts, food Atwood called fuel for the force. The hustle and bustle of the ordinary workday was absent. Only the duty officer, engrossed in paperwork, sat behind the black metal desk located opposite the waiting area. Except for the buzz of an overhead fluorescent light, the station was as quiet as the sleeping city.

Langdon crossed the room to the newly decorated waiting area, a reluctant concession to consumer friendliness, and plopped into one of the upholstered chairs. From his vantage point, he could observe the interaction between Ray and Cathy. Ray had his arm around Cathy, and she leaned into him as if without his support she might collapse.

With little else to do, Langdon reflected on the events of the evening and the awful crime that had brought him to the police station in the middle of the night. *For the love of God, innocent Natalie had endured a brutal rape.* Langdon hoped the trauma would not leave her with an emotional scar. He also worried about Betty, a single mom, and a valuable employee. He wondered if she had someone on whom to lean for emotional support.

How such a profane incident could happen to Natalie, let alone embroil the Velez family in tawdriness, was beyond Langdon's grasp. His friends were good, hard-working people. They spent their lives improving the condition of others, Cathy as a nurse and Ray as an activist for farm workers, not to mention Mike's contributions to the community of Immokalee. The ugliness visited on them was unfair, Langdon thought, but he knew better than most not to depend on life to be just.

As he watched Cathy and Ray, supporting each other and whispering forehead to forehead, sorrow gripped him. Their intimacy brought back memories of Ava. In a flash, the despair he battled every day came rushing back, flowing from his heart to his mind and into every pore of his body. The weight of his despair made him feel one hundred pounds heavier.

Without Ava, Langdon struggled to maintain a positive attitude. Cynicism had replaced his former optimism. Life was little more than an agony of memories for him. Again and again, his mind replayed what had been and what might have been. He could not erase the past to get on with the future, a weakness he despised in himself. Frustrated over his inability to pull himself up by the bootstraps, he had given up trying to right his emotional state. He was close to his familiar waltz down self-pity lane when Ray and Cathy rejoined him. Langdon rose to face them.

"Langdon, thanks for calling Everett," Cathy said, her face drained of its usual color. "We didn't know whom to call. I've learned minors in Florida can be questioned without the presence of a parent. The thought of having Mike interrogated without an attorney or a parent in the room frightened me. I panicked when the police wanted to take him to the station. Not for one second do I believe he is guilty of anything, but it was unnerving to think he might say something the police could construe as incriminating."

Langdon patted her shoulder. "I'm happy to help. Everett will protect Mike by doing most of the talking. Try not to worry."

"Well, isn't that easier said than done?" Ray huffed, blowing off steam like an overheated boiler. "I wish we knew what the devil is going on in there." He glared down the empty hallway at the closed doors.

Langdon said, "Everett will fill us in on the salient points when they finish. Don't worry; they won't hold Mike. There's no evidence on which to base an arrest. They'll release him after talking to him."

"I hope you're right," Cathy said. "What do we do about school? I mean, he's been up half the night."

"He doesn't have to go," Ray responded. "Let him stay home and sleep."

"If he stays home, will others think him guilty?" Before either man could answer her question, she was on to another. "Will the papers get wind of it?"

"I think the *Naples Dispatch* assigns someone to check the police blotter every day," Langdon said. "I don't know if the results are reported in the paper. I believe it's legal as long as the paper doesn't mention Natalie's name. I have no idea if the paper can name suspects or even if Mike is a suspect." He made a mental note to see the editor when the *Dispatch* offices opened.

"It's not a bad idea to mention the rape in the papers, honey," Ray said. "It could flush out the real culprit."

Cathy managed a weak smile at her husband's attempt to reassure her. "I know. I just don't want Mike's name bandied about in the papers or anywhere else as a possible rapist. Imagine what his friends and the soccer kids will think, and how Mike will react to being labeled a rapist. You know how people jump to conclusions." She sighed and rested her head on Ray's shoulder.

"Let's not worry about what hasn't happened," Ray soothed. He put his arm around Cathy's waist. "Honey, we can get through this if we stick to the facts and avoid bombarding ourselves with unknowns. We'll make ourselves sick. We must be strong for Mike."

"I know," Cathy murmured.

Minutes later, Langdon heard a door open and men's voices. The police, Everett, and Mike emerged from the interrogation room. Cathy and Ray stiffened. Langdon stepped to one side to allow them time with their son. He watched in silence as Mike and the men walked toward him. At the end of the hallway, the policemen turned down another corridor. Mike and Everett negotiated the remaining steps to the waiting room and the grim trio impatient for news.

The suspense was overwhelming. Langdon scanned Mike's face, wishing he could read his mind. Cathy and Ray gathered around him. Everett stood to one side, studied the strained faces surrounding him, and covered a yawn.

"How'd it go?" Ray asked, addressing Everett with a sideward glance at Mike.

"Why don't we sit down," Langdon suggested, gesturing toward the sofa and chairs clustered together at the far end of the station.

When everyone was seated, Everett said, "There is nothing to be alarmed about. The police don't consider Mike an official suspect. They started with him because the girl's mother said he stayed behind, at her request, to wait for her daughter. Tomorrow or rather this morning, the police will begin checking out the customers who were in or near the Crazy Monkey, when the incident took place. Maybe someone will know something."

"Is Mike free to come home with us and go to school?" Cathy asked.

"Absolutely," Everett replied. Turning to Mike, he said, "Keep a low profile and don't talk to anyone about Natalie, okay? We don't want to stoke the fire."

"Yes, sir," Mike said. His face pale, he raised his glassy eyes to meet Everett's.

Ray leaned toward Everett. "What happens next?"

"Aside from questioning everyone in the area and gathering evidence from the scene they might have missed, the police will wait for the rape kit to come back from the lab, unless they have enough evidence to arrest a particular suspect without it. If DNA is recovered from the rape kit or any other evidence at the scene, the usual procedure is to run the lab results against local and national databases of known rapists and other felons for a match."

Langdon felt Ray's anguish. "What happens if there is no match?"

Everett sighed. "Then we're back to square one, and the cops will examine those in or near the Crazy Monkey at the time of the rape more closely."

A muscle twitched in Ray's jaw.

"Are you saying this awful thing will be hanging over our heads for a week, maybe more?" Cathy asked.

"Yes, and frankly, probably longer. I'm sorry. Many rape cases are unsolved, and there's a tremendous backlog of rape kits waiting to be analyzed." Everett cracked his knuckles.

"Why?" Cathy pressed. "I mean, the backlog."

"There are lots of reasons: a lack of departmental funds, shortage of crime labs and personnel, priority of cases. You get the picture," Everett said.

As Everett ticked off the reasons for the pileup of unanalyzed rape kits, Langdon studied Ray's face. He had the strong impression that Ray wanted to leap out of his seat and spring into action, but what could Ray do? Langdon thought of Ava then, and he understood his friend's feelings of helplessness.

"Sounds as if this won't go away soon," Ray groaned.

Mike shook his head. Tears brimmed in Cathy's eyes.

"Let's not put the cart before the horse," Everett cautioned. "First, there may be no DNA recovered from the scene or on Natalie to test. We don't know yet. Second, someone without an alibi may turn out to be a better suspect than Mike. Third, some person might confess out of guilt. Fourth, a bystander may have heard or seen something suspicious. It's too early to jump to conclusions. Let's wait for the evidence, the facts, and the investigation to unfold, and then we'll see."

Langdon found little comfort in Everett's words, and the uncharacteristic look of defeat on Ray's face said he was equally dubious.

Everett looked at the long faces around him. "Remember, I'll be by Mike's side each step of the way. I'll keep you apprised of the details. You can call me anytime. I know you're worried, and I do understand. Mike, trust me, you are going to be fine." Everett stood.

Langdon stood as well. "Jim, thank you again for handling everything. I'll be in touch." They shook hands.

Everett offered words of encouragement to Mike, Cathy, and Ray as he shook hands with each of them before making his way to the door. In his wake, two parents and a teenage boy huddled like sheep united against an assault. Disturbed by the expressions of fear on their faces, Langdon vowed to use every resource he could muster to help them.

Chapter 34 – Offices of the *Naples Dispatch,* Naples Police Headquarters, and Pelican View, Naples, Florida

When Langdon knocked on Ian Blakely's door after a mere three hours of intermittent sleep, he felt dog-tired and worn around the edges like an old shoe. Despite his attempts to block out the events of the early morning, sleep was a poor match for his restless mind. Every half hour or so, he was startled awake by images of Natalie fighting her rapist, Mike shambling down a long, dark corridor, Betty crying at Natalie's bedside, and Ray and Cathy holding each other with fear in their eyes.

Until the rapist was found and put behind bars, Langdon knew a good night's rest was a thing of the past. By visiting the editor of the *Naples Dispatch,* he hoped to speed up the investigation. The sooner the police caught the real rapist and exonerated Mike, the better. There was no telling how long the boy could withstand the pressure.

To keep circulation high, the *Naples Dispatch* pandered to interests of the majority and underreported the news about the poor in Immokalee. Langdon, hoping an informed public might generate leads for the police, wanted Blakely to run the story of Natalie's rape. His other reason for visiting Blakely was to extract a promise from him not to mention Mike's name in the story, should he agree to run it.

Langdon had known Blakely since grade school. They became fast friends after Langdon interceded to keep at bay a much larger kid, who was inclined to be aggressive. Saved from the school's most obnoxious and feared bully, Blakely developed an intense case of hero worship. He had not forgotten the incident, and reminded Langdon of his hero status each time they met.

Langdon, jittery from pumping himself up with too much coffee, knocked on Blakely's door and then jumped when Blakely's voice boomed, "Come in."

When Langdon entered the editor's office, short, pot-bellied, and graying Blakely was clearing away piles of paper from a chair next to his desk. With a handful of papers clutched in his fist and his face red from the exertion of bending over, Blakely stood erect, as if called to attention.

"I'll be damned if it isn't you, Langdon," Blakely said. "I haven't seen you since, well, since Ava died. Where've you been keeping yourself?" He transferred the wad of papers from his right hand to his left, stuck out his chubby paw, and pumped Langdon's hand up and down.

"Hello, Ian. Good to see you again. Yes, I'm like the old song, 'Don't Get Around Much Anymore.'" Langdon chuckled. Side by side, the two men looked like Mutt and Jeff, Langdon close to a foot taller than Blakely.

"Have a seat, Langdon, or I'll get a stiff neck looking up at you. Bad joke, I know. So what brings you to my door? It must be important."

"It is. I'll be blunt. I came to ask for a favor."

"And it is?" Blakely prompted without hesitation as if he had already granted the favor.

"The daughter of one of my employees was raped out at The Village behind the Crazy Monkey. Do you know the place?"

"Nope, can't say as I do."

"Do you know about the rape?"

"No, we are a little shorthanded." Blakely looked apologetic.

"I guess you'll hear about it on the afternoon news. Anyway, the police questioned the son of a close friend of mine early this morning. The boy's name is Mike Velez. He's a senior in high school, great kid, headed for Harvard next year, accepted by early admission and all. He didn't do it. I've known him since he was an infant. I'm his godfather." Langdon swallowed against the ire rising in his throat.

Blakely sat up straighter in his chair. "You want me to do what?" He drummed his fingers on the desk.

"I want Mike's name kept out of the story, please," Langdon said. "It kills me to think a false accusation could ruin his life." He raked his fingers through his hair.

"First, it doesn't sound like a story we'd run," Blakely said. "Sometimes we report the police blotter, little more than a list of events. We wouldn't run a piece on rape at The Village, not enough interest to warrant using the space, if you know what I mean."

Langdon did know what he meant, and his hackles rose. They were back to the subject of the poor—especially Hispanics and immigrants—and the media that omitted their news.

"I understand more than you think I do, Ian, and that's the problem. I want you to run the story. The more people who know about the rape, the more leads the police might get. I want the rapist caught."

"To get your friend's son exonerated, you mean."

"Yes, because he didn't do it."

Blakely took a deep breath before he responded. "Langdon, you and I go way back, and I get your point. I also sympathize with the boy's dilemma. To run a story, there needs to be something bigger in it than the rape of a Village employee's daughter. I'm sorry, Langdon, that won't draw anyone's attention."

Langdon's acid stomach rebelled. "Okay, how about this? Florida's crime labs are sitting on evidence from more than one thousand, four hundred rape, murder, and assault-and-battery cases waiting for DNA testing. Would that be enough to grab the public's interest?" He leaned back in his chair and crossed his legs.

Blakely's eyelids popped open. "How do you know?"

"Talk to Everett, Jim Everett, the defense attorney. He'll update you."

"Sounds like a hook that will pique the public's interest. We'll run the story and keep your boy's name out of it." Blakely smiled. "Anything else I can do for you?"

"No, that's all. Thanks, Ian, I knew I could count on you."

Mission accomplished, Langdon thought, leaving Blakely's office and heading for the first of two local TV stations to repeat the process. He disliked using his influence and connections to pull strings, but he would do anything for his godson. Mike's involvement made Langdon's mission as personal as it was urgent. He wanted to see Natalie's rapist brought to justice, and Mike, the boy who was as close to a son as he would ever have, was counting on him. *By God, I'm not going to fail!*

The sun shone like a rare yellow diamond high overhead in the March sky when Langdon left the second TV station and made his way back to the police station. Weary from lack of sleep and emotional upheaval, he wanted to finish his errand, go home and put his feet up, reflect by the pool, and recover his energy.

The most uncomfortable task was ahead: visiting Betty to express his sincere concern about Natalie and to see what he could do to help both mother and daughter. He was fond of Betty, who had been with the firm since she was pregnant with Natalie. Her competency and diligence had earned her a quick rise through the ranks. She was indispensable. Langdon could not bear to think about what she must be going through. He would go to the hospital after dinner. First he had a few more errands to complete.

Twenty minutes later, Langdon was back at the police station. The sergeant behind the black metal desk directed him to Earl Atwood's office. Atwood was another old friend, a bright man who as a college student, became interested in criminology, a career choice Langdon found surprising. Atwood had never deviated from his goal to be the chief of police in Naples. His title, spelled out in black block letters on his office door, was a testament to his foresight and stick-to-itiveness.

Atwood was a piece of work as a kid. Langdon smiled at the memory of the ace pitcher who brought their ball team to victory four years in a row. Nowadays, he and Atwood moved in different social circles, but over the years, they had played a fair amount of squash. Their mutual respect was evident to any observer.

Atwood began the conversation. "What's your batting average these days, Skinner?"

"Pretty much zero. Golf game's better."

"You always were good at swinging things." Atwood chuckled. "Remember the time you banged out a homer with bases loaded to rub Sarasota's nose in it? What a victory."

The day was one Langdon would not soon forget, because it was his first taste of being a hero. The team had lifted him to their shoulders and paraded him in front of the Sarasota bench, only to lose their grip and drop him to the ground.

"Yeah, I got lucky."

"Bullcrap, luck. You were the man that day."

"A once-in-a-lifetime event, I assure you," Langdon replied. The praise embarrassed him.

"I'm sorry about your employee's daughter. I got the report this morning. Nasty business."

"Yes, it is, and it's why I've come. Do you have any new leads in the case?"

"Have a chair." Atwood shoved a straight-backed chair toward Langdon.

Langdon sat.

"My men are canvassing the neighborhood and interviewing people as we speak."

"The Crazy Monkey must have been packed," Langdon said. "Happy hour either was underway or near the end. Someone saw something."

"We're working that angle. People are hesitant to come forward. We'll have to dig up each piece of information ourselves," Atwood said. "No one will hand it to us on a platter. The good news is, we've already questioned one person, a Mike Velez."

The pleased expression on Atwood's face irked Langdon. "No," he said, a prickly edge to his voice, "it's not good news, at least not from my point of view."

Atwood tensed as if awaiting a blow. "Why is it not good news?" He got up from his desk and walked to the widow.

"Look, Earl, I don't want to offend you or your men. You do an excellent job, but this kid, Mike, is my godson and a good person. You don't have to take my word for it. Check him out."

"We're doing that now. If your he's not our man, we'll keep looking. He has nothing to fear if he's innocent."

"He *is* innocent, except it's not that simple," Langdon said. "A cloud of suspicion that could damage his reputation and his standing at school with his peers and his teachers is hanging over his head. His parents are upset, and I am worried about them. Everyone who knows Natalie loves her. She is a wonderful girl. When she was a baby, Betty would bring her to work ..." Langdon stopped to catch his breath, rein in his memories, and get back on track.

"You're a good judge of character," Atwood said, "and I accept your belief. I have rules I have to follow, however. You know, pro forma stuff, by the book, blah, blah. I can't bend the procedures on this one, because there are bigwigs involved. If I screw up and don't do the dance, people will accuse the department of favoritism, and a label like that could put the kibosh on our effectiveness. You understand."

"What bigwigs are you talking about?" Langdon asked. He hoped another suspect would wipe Mike off the bad-guy board.

Atwood cleared his throat. "Well, you for one."

Langdon stopped short of tumbling out of his seat. "Me? You have to be kidding."

"I wish I were, my friend. Of course, I don't have any doubt you are not involved, but since you were there around the time of the incident, you are on our list of people we want to question.

Maybe you saw or heard something that can help us."

The chief's comment did not mollify Langdon. "Seems a big waste of time to question me while the bad guy gets away," he growled and glared at Atwood's ice-blue eyes.

"The kid's father, Ray Velez, will also be questioned. I understand he's a friend of yours. Don't take it personally, Langdon. It has everything to do with going by the book." Atwood returned Langdon's stare long enough to emphasize that he meant business.

"I get it, Earl, I mean, your responsibilities and all. I don't have to like it, though," Langdon grumbled. "You wouldn't either in my shoes. Let's get it over with. What do you want to ask me?"

"My men will visit you and Mr. Velez sometime in the afternoon. I don't know the exact time. Again, I'm sorry, but the investigation must run its course."

Langdon thought Atwood's apology sounded sincere. "Earl, please put the damned investigation on full throttle. I'm concerned about the Velezes. They are taking the situation hard, and they are terrific people. I don't know how long they can tolerate the misplaced suspicion. And by God, keep our names under wraps. I don't want to read about myself in the papers or hear our names on the six o'clock news. You know how people jump to conclusions." He rose to leave.

Atwood swung away from the window. "That I can do. You have my word."

Atwood's attempts to reassure Langdon were unsuccessful. He left the police station feeling disheartened; he had not cleared Mike. At least he had succeeded in getting Blakely's and Atwood's promises not to name names. The full force of being questioned as a rape suspect struck Langdon then. Good God, it was hard to comprehend. When he got home, he would call Ray to let him know he was also on the suspect list.

The phone rang the second Langdon closed the front door at Pelican View. Sunny was on the line. She said she was calling to chitchat. Langdon knew better. She was checking up on him, worried about his moodiness.

Sunny opened the conversation by asking how he was, had Rosa had her ears checked, and what did he think of Elizabeth's fiancé? When she wondered if Mike was excited about his forthcoming graduation, he told her about the rape, the morning at the police station, and the visit he expected from the police. Sunny offered him words of reassurance, but her tone was sharp and angry.

"What about a lie detector test? If you, Mike, and Ray each passed one, you'd be off the most-wanted list, wouldn't you?"

"Good question," he said. "I didn't think to offer it. Next time I see Earl, I'll ask him. I'm going to give him some space for a couple of weeks, and then I'll mention it. I want to talk to Ray and Mike, first, to see what they want to do."

For a moment, Sunny was silent. Langdon assumed she was thinking through the bad news.

"Will you retain an attorney?" she asked.

"For what?"

"For when they question you."

"No, not for being questioned. I have nothing to hide. We retained Everett for Mike because he needed representation in case he said something that could be twisted or taken out of context."

"It was smart to get an attorney for Mike. The poor kid. What about DNA evidence? Did they find anything to test?"

"Another question I haven't asked. Good thing I have a smart friend." He envisioned her toothy smile. "I'll call Everett. He'll know the answer."

Langdon's next phone call was to Everett's office. After several minutes of holding, a secretary with a sonorous voice put him through.

"Langdon, sorry about the wait. I had someone in my office."

"I'll be short and sweet, Jim. Did you find out about DNA at the scene?"

"My assistant's connection in the police department said there was. What kind, we don't yet know. Remember what I said though: crime labs have more DNA than they can process. I wouldn't count on a result any time soon."

"Thanks, Jim. That's what I wanted to know. Oh, by the way, the police will be questioning Ray and me this afternoon."

"You don't have anything to worry about. This is all preliminary stuff. It will go away soon."

"I hope you're right. Thanks, Jim"

Langdon had one more call to make. He dialed the number. Ray answered.

"How's Mike doing?"

"He's buried in his room," Ray said, "but I don't think he's sleeping. He's upset about Natalie and wants to go see her. Everett told us it wasn't a good idea. He said to write a letter instead. I guess the best way to describe Mike is distraught."

Langdon thought Ray sounded tense. "Rotten luck," Langdon mumbled. He paced as he talked.

"Yeah, worse than rotten, I would say, if there is such a thing," Ray said.

"Ray, I went to see Earl Atwood this morning," Langdon said, "and he advised me to expect to be questioned, cops at the house and everything. You, too." Langdon heard Ray swear under his breath. "According to Atwood, it's standard operating procedure and not a big deal."

"Now we're suspects," Ray scoffed.

"I don't think we are," Landon said. The police are covering their bases, that's all. I'm going to grab a nap before they come. Phone me after your interview, and I will you. We'll compare notes."

"Sure. Thanks for the alert. Talk to you later."

Langdon hung up and readied himself for bed. The minute his head hit the pillow, he thought of Ava, always his last thought before falling asleep. He imagined her as an angel in a white gossamer gown with her dark-brown, luscious hair spread out around her head like strands of silk floating in water. As he closed his eyes, he asked her to give him the strength and grace he needed to get through the newest hurdle in his life and to watch over Mike.

Chapter 35 – Pelican View, Naples, FL

Two weeks had elapsed since Natalie's rape. Langdon did not have to look at his appointment book to know what headed his to-do list: Call Atwood for an update and accept no excuses.

In the last fourteen days, he and Ray had been questioned by the police—in his mind a colossal waste of precious time—and Rolando said the police had interrogated him about what he and Langdon were doing in the parking lot the night of Natalie's rape. No further contact between Mike and the police had occurred since Mike's questioning at the station. Langdon suspected Atwood had everything to do with keeping the police at bay.

Langdon visited Natalie in the hospital where he learned she could not identify her attacker. Betty told him the rapist grabbed Natalie from behind and dragged her into the alley. Natalie said when she screamed, the man clamped his hand over her mouth. She bit it, and he slugged her hard across the face. She kicked and scratched, and the next thing she knew, woke up in the alley. The man was gone. Natalie thought the man must have knocked her out. Betty confided she was grateful Natalie was unconscious during the rape.

While Langdon maintained his hands-off stance with Atwood, Mike went back to school. Despite Atwood's assurances of anonymity, someone leaked Mike's name to The Village Free Press, and soon the word was out. The paper mentioned Mike as the primary suspect and him and Ray as persons of interest.

Smoldering like a volcano and infuriated to the point of wanting to rip Atwood's face off, Langdon thought it best to wait until he was calmer to confront the chief about the leak. In the meantime, Atwood heard the rumors and called to apologize. He said someone's head would roll when he discovered the blabbermouth.

Langdon had to be satisfied with Atwood's expressed regret because it was too late to rectify the wrong; the damage was done. After the item appeared in the paper, Langdon called Mike to see how he was doing.

Mike said, "My soccer kids are showing up for practice, but they act distant and wary. I think they are afraid of me."

Langdon's heart ached for the boy. If Langdon could convince Atwood to speed up the DNA testing, Mike could get on with his life. Atwood's time had run out along with Langdon's patience. Since the chief owed him big time, Langdon decided to call in his marker. He picked up the phone and punched in Atwood's direct number.

"No leads, only suspects, and we don't want to discuss that issue again," Atwood reported. "Everyone at the Crazy Monkey on the night in question has an alibi. They were with drinking buddies or wives or girlfriends. There were a couple of unknowns at the bar. Too bad for us no one paid them enough attention to provide a description or get their names. One guy told the bartender he was on his way to Georgia, city unannounced, and he left within our window of opportunity. Unfortunately, he paid in cash, and no one knew what he was driving. Dead end."

Atwood took a deep breath and continued. "I checked with neighboring town police—Fort Myers, Bonita Springs, Estero, Marco—nothing resembling what happened at the Monkey. No eyewitnesses have come forward—surprise, surprise. We questioned the various business owners on the street and turned up nothing, zero, zip, zilch. Crime scene guys recovered DNA from the scene; it isn't back from the lab. I asked to have a rush put on it. It's anyone's guess as to when we'll obtain the results. Did I leave anything out?"

Langdon thought Atwood sounded satisfied with himself. "Yeah, Earl, you did. What happens next?"

Next?"

"Yes, next. You can't close the case. The rapist is still out there. The press has demonized Mike, Ray, and me, and rumors are flying. You don't expect us to get on with our lives with the word rapist branded across our foreheads, do you? I'm not worried about myself. My life is already lousy. I'm concerned about Mike. For his sake, you can't leave it this way." He wanted Atwood to feel his desperation.

After a long silence, Atwood remarked, "I don't know what to say. You three were the only men in the area at the time of the rape without ironclad alibis. Mrs. Garcia denies knowing when either of you left, and no one saw you or Velez get into your cars and leave." Atwood sucked in his breath. "And that's not the worst of it. Your boy Mike, well, he was on the street in front of your office a few minutes before six-thirty. He said he was waiting for Natalie. Even if he is innocent, it places him at the scene. That's opportunity. Motive: a crush on the girl. Maybe she refused his advances."

Langdon could not believe what he was hearing. "Listen, Atwood, and listen good," he snarled. "None of us did that horrible thing. We are not going to live with guilt for all eternity because your men can't find the bad guy. And I don't apologize for sounding angry, because, by God, I am."

"Langdon, listen, I—"

"No, you listen, Earl. I have an idea. Get the damned DNA tested, and while you're at it, do Mike's, mine, and Ray's. Then we'll be finished with this nightmare of police incompetence." His breath came in rapid gasps.

"You're taking it much too personally," Atwood said.

"Damn right I am. It *is* personal!"

"I guess it can seem that way. The problem is, there's a backlog of DNA samples waiting for testing. I don't wave a magic wand. I can't wish away the line. Cases much older than yours are waiting for results."

Langdon's mind raced. There had to be a solution to the dilemma. With the palm of his hand, he smacked the side of his head. "There is an answer," he said.

"An answer for what, DNA backlogs?"

"Yes. Can DNA testing be done in a private lab?" Langdon asked.

"Sure. It's done in other states. We don't do it here in Florida. Police samples go to the police lab in Tallahassee."

"Let me get it straight. You say a private lab could test the DNA in a case like ours. It doesn't have to be a police crime lab?"

"Technically, yes." Atwood said. "The thing is, I don't know if we can send police samples to a private lab. The only police crime lab in Florida that tests for DNA is in Tallahassee. Let me give them a call and see what they say. I'll get back to you."

"Today, Earl. I'm sure I don't have to remind you it was one of your people who leaked the suspect list to the *Village Press*, making all this necessary."

"Yeah, yeah, I know. I'm on it." Atwood disconnected.

Two hours later, Atwood called back. "Done," he said.

"Are you saying we can send the DNA to a private lab, and they will do the testing? Will the results hold up in court if necessary?" Langdon hoped it would not come to that. Still, he wanted to leave nothing to chance.

"Yes, except there's a hitch," Atwood said. "Tallahassee wants us to use one particular lab. Turns out the state, thinking it might be wise to hire out some of the testing to unclog the logjam, recently decided to evaluate private labs by police standards. Genius conclusion, don't you think?" His tone oozed sarcasm. "To date, only one private lab has received clearance. Lucky for us it was last week; not enough time for the word to get around."

"That's great. It's a break we'll take." Delirious with relief, Langdon felt as if he could fly. "When can we get started?"

Allison hesitated a moment before he added a caveat. "Uh, Langdon, there's still a small problem."

The comment landed like a punch in the gut. "What?" he barked back, ready to do battle.

"Calm down. We can figure it out together. Here's the deal. The department doesn't have a line on the books to pay for DNA testing in a private lab. In other words, I can't authorize the expenditure."

"Oh, give me a break, Earl. Don't tell me you would withhold DNA testing and ruin three lives because there's no line on the books. You're pulling my chain, right?" He jerked at his shirt collar as his heart rate climbed.

"No, I'm serious. It's the same with the other police departments across the state. They can't jump into the private lab's DNA line for the same reason. But, listen, I have an idea. If you contribute a donation to the department specifying the funds are for DNA testing only in a private lab, I could authorize the expense under the miscellaneous line. Nobody in their right mind is going to look a gift horse in the mouth, and if the donation is large enough, who's going to complain?"

Langdon let go a long, cathartic laugh that brought tears to his eyes.

Atwood waited.

When Langdon found his voice, he wiped away his tears and said, "The chief of police is blackmailing me. Ironic don't you think?"

Atwood let out a hiss. "Don't be ridiculous. I want the damn DNA tested ASAP, that's all. Isn't that what you want? You and your friends will be out from under suspicion, and I'll have the DNA results I need to run down the real criminal. It's that simple."

"Sure," Langdon agreed with a hint of disdain, "a real win-win."

Chapter 36 – Pelican View, Naples, Florida

Langdon awoke to the light of a full moon illuminating his bedroom. He thought it was daybreak until he looked at his bedside alarm, four o'clock. Unable to go back to sleep, he pulled on a pair of shorts and stepped out onto the balcony adjoining the master suite. Years earlier, Millie and Buck had decided to locate the suite of rooms on the southern end of the mansion to afford an unobstructed view of the eastern and western horizons. The arrangement made the balcony the perfect spot from which to greet the sun in the morning or watch it slide silently into the silvery water of the Gulf at day's end.

In season, Naples's beautiful weather provided sunsets and sunrises unobscured by rain or fog, for the most part. Delighted tourists and residents gathered like worshippers at the town pier or elsewhere on the beach to enjoy nature's miracles. The sunsets, especially, rarely failed to draw enthusiastic applause.

Langdon surveyed his sleeping estate from the balcony. The nighttime air was a cool sixty-four degrees, and the soft breeze blowing from the northwest promised southwestern Florida another rain-free day with low humidity.

The best weather in the world, Langdon thought, with a keen awareness he was not alone in his opinion. Thousands of snowbirds from the

Northeast and the Midwest, a large number of Canadians, a goodly number of Brits, and a sprinkling of French, Germans, and Italians agreed. Each winter, Langdon's city came alive with visitors bent on escaping the bitter cold at home to indulge in Florida's luxurious weather. They gave his beloved Naples a rhythm of excitement and a seasonal change to which he looked forward.

Langdon calculated it would be several hours before the sun rose. Since he was wide awake, he decided there was no point in returning to bed and plodded to the kitchen to brew a pot of coffee. Ten minutes later, he shuffled back to the balcony, a steaming mug of Kona coffee in hand, and settled into a lounge chair.

As he sipped the hot coffee with care, he allowed his mind to wander. As usual, it reverted to thoughts of Ava and the last time he wheeled her out to their private balcony. He wanted to share the sunset with her, hoping the experience would elicit a hint of her former self. She was in the final stage of Huntington's, mentally lost, and unable to converse, except for that gibberish phrase, *fein ah abie*, which she repeated nonstop.

He still wondered if the phrase had meaning or was nonsense. Whether real words or syllables, they were significant to Ava, for as soon as she uttered them, she reacted as if the devil himself had entered the room. Gone was the calm Ava, who stared into space and writhed gracefully. In her place, a new Ava jerked her arms and legs like a hyperactive marionette and screamed *fein ah abie* at the top of her lungs. She clutched or grabbed anything within reach: the bedclothes, the attendant's arm, his shirtfront, or his hand.

The nurses and caregivers, who tended to Ava around the clock, told him to pay Ava's strange behavior no mind. They said her gibberish was a manifestation of Huntington's. Langdon was not convinced. It seemed to him Ava was desperate to tell him something. With her death, the meaning of her words would remain a mystery forever.

As Langdon sipped his coffee, he looked out over the moonlit-drenched grounds, remembering how Ava had loved to wander the gardens in the early stage of her illness. It was a harmless diversion until her disease progressed and her mind became less dependable. One night while he was sleeping, she came close to wandering off the property. He intercepted her at the end of the driveway, where the gates opened onto Gulf Shore Drive. Dressed in her nightgown with her head twisting and writhing on her neck and the right side of her mouth drawn up as if she were smiling at him, she was an apparition in the moonlight.

Half out of his mind with panic, he looked into her eyes and realized with crystal-clear certainty she was not looking back at him. He could find no hint of recognition behind her glassy stare. The moment was one he would never forget. He wanted to reach beyond the impenetrable walls of her mind and jerk her back to life, but she was lost, gone from his world. He led the shell of his beloved Ava back to the house. Tucking her body into bed, he climbed in beside her, and grieving for her absence, cried like a baby.

She paid him no heed. She was in a foreign place where he could not go.

The next morning Ava returned to her body as if she were never absent. The incident marked the beginning of a painful new phase in her illness warranting around-the-clock caregivers. Langdon could not trust himself to watch her each minute of the day and night.

A shriek by one of the peafowl pierced his consciousness, and he awoke confused. He scanned his surroundings to orient himself; he had fallen asleep on the balcony. The moonlight had vanished, and from the looks of the sunrise, he figured he had slept at least an hour, an old man dozing off in mid-sentence. The analogy made him grumpy.

Langdon left the balcony and took the back stairs to the kitchen, where he greeted Rosa. He helped her off with her sweater, poured himself a second cup of coffee, and with the *Dispatch* tucked under his arm, walked out to the lanai. Langdon, antsy and unsettled, wondered when Atwood would call. Two weeks had passed since Langdon's so-called donation to the police department, and the results of his, Ray's, Mike's, and the rapist's DNA remained unreported.

The wait was pure agony. Langdon, nearing the end of his forbearance, reminded himself to be patient. In a matter of hours, he, Mike, and Ray would be free of suspicion, no longer persons of interest in Natalie's rape. They could get on with their lives, and the police could get down to the business of finding the real rapist. Langdon hoped the police would catch the culprit soon. Poor Betty and Natalie were living their own nightmares.

In anticipation of a return to normalcy, Langdon sighed. He might even get a good night's sleep for a change. When the phone rang at eight o'clock on the dot, he picked it up on the first ring. Atwood was calling, as he had promised.

"Langdon, good morning, I'm sorry to call so early. I hope you slept well."

"Good morning, Earl. I was thinking about you. I've been up for hours trying to hasten the time. I'm ready to get this mess over with."

"Can't say as I blame you, Langdon; however, I'm sorry to say, there's been a snag."

"A snag?" Langdon swallowed hard. *Not again. Something was wrong. He could hear it in Atwood's voice.* His good mood evaporated in an instant.

"Yeah, looks as if the lab screwed up one of the results. Can you give me one more day to straighten it out? That's all I want, one more day. And don't panic, everything's cool."

"You're not giving me the runaround, are you, Earl?"

"No, I'm not screwing around. Don't worry."

"Okay, Earl. It doesn't sound as if I have a say in this anyway. Then you'll call me in the morning, right?"

Langdon slammed down the phone with more vigor than he intended. He had a bad feeling he was going to be surprised and in an unpleasant way.

Chapter 37 – Police Station and Pelican View, Naples, Florida

At eight-thirty sharp, Ray stood in front of the police station. Atwood had called him. The DNA results were back and Atwood wanted Ray to come to his office to discuss them. Ray thought it odd that Atwood did not divulge the results over the phone. Ray complied because he wanted nothing more than to look into Atwood's face and say *I told you so* when Mike was exonerated. Ray also wanted an apology for the emotional distress the police had visited on him, his family, and Langdon.

Ray understood Atwood had a job to do, but after what Mike had been through, words such as *suspects, perps, vics,* and *persons of interest* brought a bitter taste to his mouth. Forced to watch from the sidelines while his son suffered an unjust accusation, Ray's powerlessness had provoked his anger. Although he not a violent man, Ray's dealings with the police had stretched his self-control to the breaking point.

With an uncharacteristic sharpness, Ray knocked on Atwood's closed door and then, without waiting for permission to enter, barged in. Ray saw no point in being polite to the man who had villainized his son. When his business was finished, he never wanted to see Atwood again.

"Mr. Velez," Atwood greeted him. "Have a seat."

"No, thanks, I'll stand," Ray said stiffly. "I don't plan to be around long."

"You might change your mind when you hear what I have to say. Please, Mr. Velez, take a seat."

Ray remained on his feet.

Atwood shrugged. "Have it your way, Velez."

The noticeable switch from "Mr. Velez" to "Velez," a less respectful form of address, gave Ray pause. For Mike's sake, he was disinclined to appear uncooperative. He sat. "Sorry, Atwood," Ray muttered, fidgeting in his chair and twisting his wedding ring. "I find it disingenuous to be cordial when a leak from your office damaged three reputations with nasty, unfounded suspicions."

Atwood looked uncomfortable. "Yeah, I'm sorry about that. The culprit was a minor clerk whose boyfriend thought he could make a quick buck by passing along the information. She's no longer on our payroll."

"It's too late for my son, Atwood."

The chief stood and paced a tired-looking rut in the carpet.

Ray had an unsettling premonition something serious was eating the chief. "I gather you have the results of the DNA tests," Ray said.

"I do. None of you are a match for the Garcia rape."

"Gee, why am I not surprised?" Ray said. He knew he sounded like a smart ass, but he didn't care. "Are we finished then? Are we exonerated, the three of us?"

Atwood returned to his desk, sat down with a thump, and chewed on his index finger.

Ray found the chief's nervous bearing puzzling.

"With the rape, yes," Atwood said. "But something else turned up in the results you should know. To be honest, I don't know how to proceed."

Ray's breathing became shallow. "Spit it out, Atwood," Ray demanded gruffly. "Nothing could be worse than what we've already been through." He felt as though he were on the edge of a cliff waiting for a push.

"It's delicate, Velez. I don't want to butt into your business. That being said, I think you have a right to know."

"Know what?"

"Your son, Mike, he's adopted, isn't he?"

"What difference does it make? He knows it, and he's fine with it. Cathy and I don't pretend to be his biological parents."

"Do you know who your son's biological father is?"

"No, I ... we—" Ray trailed off, sensing he was approaching quicksand, afraid to take another step. "What gives you the right to pry into our private business anyway?"

Atwood lowered his head, mopped his brow, and sucked in a deep breath before answering. "According to the lab—and I talked to the director himself—two results match to such a degree the findings are indisputable. Your son's biological father is Langdon Skinner."

With a belly full of fear, Ray left Atwood's office and raced to Pelican View as fast as the speed limit allowed. He had a vital, life-and-death message for Langdon.

In the courtyard at Pelican View, Ray took a moment to regroup. His emotions were in an uproar, his mental acuity in chaos. He had no recollection of driving to Langdon's house. Ray rang the door chimes, and Langdon opened the door instead of Rosa.

"Hey, Ray, come in." Langdon offered Ray a broad smile. Have you come to sit out the next twenty-four hours of suspense with me?"

"What do you mean?" Ray said.

"Didn't Atwood call you and beg for another twenty-four hours before revealing the DNA results?" Langdon asked.

"Uh, actually, no," Ray said. He followed Langdon across the foyer past an interior courtyard and out to the lanai. "We've been cleared," Ray said. "Our DNA doesn't match the rapist. I'm glad this mess is over." He delivered the information in a monotone as if it were yesterday's news. Compared to what he had to say to Langdon, it was.

Langdon pivoted to face Ray. "What? By God, that's great," Langdon said. "Why did Atwood tell me he needed an additional twenty-four hours to get the results? Atwood said he had something to straighten out."

Before Ray could answer, Sunny came into his line of vision. Ray screeched to a standstill. "Oh hi, Sunny, I didn't see your car outside." Taken aback, he was discombobulated for a moment.

"Hi, yourself, stranger. Is Cathy with you?" Sunny got up from her chair and gave him a warm hug.

"No," Ray replied without elaboration. He wanted to avoid the entanglement of a three-way conversation. He could think only of what he had to say to Langdon. Even though Ray's message was urgent, he had yet to figure out how to present it. Knowing he could not wait for the correct or polite moment, he cleared his throat. "Langdon, I'm sorry to interrupt. May I speak to you alone? I have to tell you something right away."

"Whatever it is, Ray, if you don't mind, I have no secrets from Sunny," Langdon said. "She's been my safe harbor through thick and thin." Langdon smiled at Sunny. "Why don't we sit down? Want some iced tea, Ray?"

Thrown into confusion by Langdon's response, Ray mumbled, "I'll get it, thanks." He went to the lanai refrigerator and removed the pitcher Rosa kept filled. Working to steady his trembling hands, Ray put several cubes of ice into a nearby glass and splashed the sweet tea over them.

Langdon positioned a chair for him.

Ray's mind was in turmoil; he forced himself to sit down. Since Langdon had said in Sunny's presence that he had no secrets from her, Ray could not figure out how to extricate Langdon from Sunny without being rude. Unwilling to affront either friend, he elected to bide his time. Maybe Sunny's visit would be short.

"Did Atwood eat crow when he told you we were exonerated?" Langdon asked. "By God, I wish I'd been there. What were his exact words?"

Sunny or no Sunny, Ray did not want to lie. He weighed his options and concluded his news was too critical to postpone. Langdon would tell her anyway. With a measured look at Sunny, Ray said, "Langdon, I have some important information you should know. The DNA results have uncovered Mike's biological father." Feeling too restless to stay in his seat, Ray got up from his chair and perched on its arm.

Langdon's eyebrows shot up. "What? Mike's biological father is the rapist?" Disbelief darkened his face. "You can't be serious. Someone has screwed up. You haven't told him, have you?"

"That's not it, Langdon. Listen to me," Ray said. "The results are not a mistake. Allison had the tests done twice. There is no error. You are Mike's biological father."

A silence heavy with emotion enveloped the three friends. Ray held his breath. Sunny's jaw hung open like a trap door, and Langdon froze in place. For many minutes, no one moved or said anything. Ray felt as if he were having an out-of-body experience. Remembering what he had to say, he cut through the silence first.

"Langdon," Ray said, "Langdon." There was no response from his friend. "Langdon, my reaction was the same. Digesting such a fantastic revelation takes some doing."

"Impossible," Langdon mumbled, shaking his head. Regret filled his eyes. "Ava was never pregnant. She couldn't have had a baby. We tried a long time to have children and—" His voice cracked, the words caught in his throat.

As Ray focused on Langdon's face, Sunny took Langdon's hands in hers and leaning in close, peered into his face, her squinty, bright blue eyes as soft as Ray had ever seen them. Langdon did not react. "Langdon, Ava *did* have a pregnancy."

Langdon jerked back to life. "What?" He stared at Sunny as if she had lost her mind.

Ray waited.

"Yes," Sunny continued, "she found out she was pregnant before she left for Maracaibo."

Langdon scrambled up from his chair and paced in front of it. "Ava was pregnant when she went to Maracaibo, and I didn't know?" His face reflected incredulity. "Preposterous. If Ava was pregnant, why didn't you tell me, Sunny? Why didn't Ava tell me?"

"Because I didn't know until I went to Maracaibo," Sunny answered. "Ava told me the baby was stillborn. I had no reason to doubt her. I thought it was inappropriate to tell you about a dead baby when you were already upset."

Langdon's head swiveled toward Ray. "That can't be right. Mike was born in Miami, wasn't he, Ray? And, Ava was in Maracaibo." Denial spread across his face.

As Ray listened to Sunny, the pieces of the puzzle were coming together for him.

"Langdon," Sunny said softly, "it's conceivable Ava would go to Miami for her baby's delivery. Doesn't it make sense she would want her child born here? Ava must have planned the adoption from the beginning. She didn't want you or me to know the baby was alive. She told me a fabricated story, saying she wanted to die because the baby was stillborn."

The word *lie* came to Ray's mind. He buried the thought. When he opened his mouth to speak, Sunny had more to say.

"After the baby's birth, I have no idea what Ava thought she would do or if she had a plan at all," Sunny said.

Langdon lowered himself into a chair. "I don't understand," he whispered. "Ava returned home with me. If she had a baby, why didn't she tell me when I was in Maracaibo?" He thrust his head between his hands.

"My guess is she was afraid you would no longer love her, for doing what she did," Sunny answered. "Think about it, Langdon. How could Ava tell you she gave away your baby? And don't forget, she was extremely depressed at the time."

Langdon raised his head and turned to Ray. "Come on, Ray," Langdon said, "what are the chances of your adopting Ava's baby? She couldn't have known in advance who the baby's parents would be. I don't believe it, any of it. How can you be sure?"

As Sunny was filling in the blanks for Langdon, Ray listened in silence, understanding Langdon's turmoil and his feelings of betrayal. Ray still had another convincing piece to add to the puzzle, however. He spoke up. "Langdon, DNA doesn't lie."

"Oh my God," Langdon said, looking at Ray. "I remember now. I told Ava that you and Cathy were planning to adopt a child, and I mentioned the attorney's name at the same time." Langdon got up from his chair and started to pace again.

"That explains it," Ray said. "Ava also went to Feingold. After that, sheer happenstance put Mike in our arms."

When Ray spoke, Langdon and Sunny looked at him as if seeing him for the first time. Ray realized they were so engrossed in getting the facts straight they had not considered the impact of the DNA findings on him. As his dilemma dawned on them, their faces softened with concern.

Langdon interrupted his pacing. He stood before his dearest friend. "Oh God, Ray, forgive my insensitivity. If Mike is my biological son, I can't imagine what you must be feeling. I'm sorry for everything, especially for Ava's deception. You know I love Mike and Elizabeth, but Mike is your son, Ray, in every sense of the word. I don't want that changed. Maybe you shouldn't tell him."

Ray rose from the arm of his chair to face Langdon. They looked at each other through tear-filled eyes—two old friends who shared one son—and embraced. Over Langdon's shoulder, Ray saw Sunny wipe tears from her face.

"Isn't there a saying about there not being a dry eye in the house?" Sunny remarked, using her Irish humor to put some comfort back into the situation.

Ray said, "Langdon, I should tell Mike. He has a right to know. I have never lied to him, and you are already his favorite uncle and his godfather. I think he can handle it. Honestly, he might be relieved. Most adopted children wonder who their biological parents are. I'm sure there are times when he fears the worst."

"Thanks," Langdon said, "we don't have to decide right away. Why don't you and Cathy think it over for a couple of days?" His face pale, he sank back into his chair.

"We could," Ray said, "and I appreciate the latitude, Langdon, but we have a problem we can't postpone." Ray shot Sunny a questioning look, wondering if what he was poised to say had occurred to her.

Sunny read the expression on Ray's face. "Oh no," she gasped.

"What?" Langdon demanded, alarm widening his eyes. He grasped the arms of his chair, started to stand, and then fell back into it.

Since there was no easy way to present what he had come to say, Ray gathered his courage and said, "Langdon, Mike might have inherited Ava's Huntington's."

The remaining color drained from Langdon's face. "Find a son, lose a son," he groaned. "Is this really happening, or is it another sick joke life is playing on me? Ava's illness was horrendous and now Mike? Oh, my God. I am sorry, sorry, sorry."

As Ray stepped toward Langdon to comfort him, Langdon leaned forward in his chair and clutched Ray's hand in an icy grip. Ray's heart beat faster at the sight of Langdon's gray face and the beads of perspiration gathered on his forehead.

"Langdon, are you all right?" Ray asked.

Langdon did not answer.

Before Ray could ask his question again, Langdon bolted upward from his chair. Gasping for air, he clutched his chest, doubled over, and collapsed. Sunny jumped up to help him. Ray dialed 911.

Chapter 38 – Naples Community Hospital and Pelican View, Naples, Florida

At the Naples Community Hospital, Ray poked his head around the door to Langdon's room.

"Hey, Ray. Come on in," Langdon called out. Dressed for the first time in days, he smiled at Ray from a chair by the window.

Ray glanced around the room. "Are you packed?"

"Are you kidding? I've been packed for a week."

"Everything is set for your discharge," Ray said. "The hospital has freed you, but we have to wait for an escort, some rule about delivering you to your car in a wheelchair. My car is parked out front. Where's your suitcase?"

Langdon pointed to a duffle bag at the end of his bed. "Thanks for picking me up, Ray. You don't know how happy I am to leave the hospital, even though the staff has treated me like the Grand Poohbah. I've never been off my feet this long. Lying around makes me feel elderly. I could have gone home last week if they'd let me." He smiled and patted his shirt over his heart.

Ray chuckled. "Impatient, as usual. I see the old Langdon is back. You gotta take it easy, my friend. A triple bypass isn't minor surgery. Don't go getting all wild on me when they release you, or you'll be back sooner than later."

"Don't worry. I can't afford another episode. I'll go easy. The doctor said I could resume most of my normal activities, except for our squash games. No matter, after I build up my strength, I'll beat the devil out of you, when I get the okay for competitive play."

Ray laughed. "You wish."

"How's Mike?" Langdon asked. "I've had plenty of time to worry."

"Holding his head high again," Ray said. "Oh, by the way, Atwood called me. The DNA from the rape kit matches a known sexual predator. Some creep a month out of jail. They shouldn't let those guys loose on the public."

"I've read about repeat sexual offenders," Langdon said. "Counseling, probation, the sexual-offender registry, monitoring, medication to eliminate urges—none of it's foolproof," Langdon said. "It makes me sick to think my tax dollars feed and clothe the bastards in jail and then babysit them when they are released. Sometimes I wonder if we should castrate rapists when the proof against them is undeniable, a possibility with DNA testing. If we did, the monsters wouldn't need babysitters; they could work like the rest of us, and our kids and wives would be safe."

Ray nodded. "After our experience, your wanting a solution to predatory behavior is an understandable reaction. Some time back, I think lawmakers investigated the option of castration and decided against it—something to do with individual rights." He shrugged. "Besides, Cathy told me rape is more an expression of rage toward women than a sexual act. Castrating rapists wouldn't stop them. They'd find some other way to commit violence against women."

"That's interesting," Langdon said. "Then I guess it would be more effective to treat the underlying issue—if that's even possible—than castrate them." He got up from his chair, pulled the zipper on his duffle bag closed, and sat down again.

"Ray, let's change the subject for a second," Langdon said. "How's Mike doing? Has it occurred to him he might have inherited Ava's Huntington's?"

"No, not yet; at least he hasn't mentioned it to me," Ray said. "I thought he should get used to having two dads before I say anything."

"No, Ray, one dad and a Super Godfather." Langdon laughed and flexed his biceps.

Ray chuckled at his friend. "You're a good man, Langdon. We are blessed to have you in *any* capacity."

"Aw shucks, don't go getting all mushy on me," Langdon mumbled. "Kidding aside, how and when will you tell Mike he's at risk for Huntington's? The thought makes my stomach turn."

"I talked to Carlson Rogers about Mike. Roger's the head of neurology here at Community Hospital. He thinks we should have a neurologist and an HD counselor present when we break the news to Mike. Rogers offered the name of an experienced counselor who will work with us if we want him, and suggested a comfortable, familiar environment for the first meeting. After that, we'll see how it goes. What do you think?"

"I think you're handling it the smart way," Langdon said. "We could have the meeting at Pelican View if you want."

"Sounds good. Should I set it up?" Ray asked.

"You're the boss, Dad." Langdon smiled.

"Okay, I'll make the arrangements." Ray faked a playful punch at Langdon's shoulder.

A week later, the day of the dreaded meeting arrived. Langdon, a bundle of nerves, started the day with Sunny over breakfast at Pelican View.

"Nice to have breakfast with someone besides myself for a change," Sunny said.

"I'm glad you could come. I need moral support," Langdon said. "I'm not looking forward to jerking the rug out from under Mike."

"How do you mean?" Sunny prodded.

"For starters, Sunny, imagine telling a happy kid he's at risk for HD. Picture explaining the disease to him and following up with, 'Mike, if you have the HD gene, you can count on an appearance by Huntington's in the prime of your life, and oh, by the way, kid, it'll kill you because there's no cure. You could even pass the gene along to your children.'"

"Tragic, I agree," Sunny said. She put her napkin down and looked at Langdon, who was toying with his food. "Why don't we go out to the lanai? We can both use the fresh air." Sunny settled herself in a lounge chair, and Langdon stalked the lanai like a lion prowling the Serengeti.

"Oh, Sunny," Langdon groaned, "I wish we could spare Mike the ugliness we will unleash. How can we explain the inexplicable to him? Of course, the HD counselor will present the information in as gentle and optimistic a manner as possible, but that's like sugarcoating arsenic." He touched a finger to the inside of his cheek where it bled from his chewing.

"For once, I am speechless." Sunny said, shaking her head.

"Kinda takes the wind out of your sails, doesn't it?" Langdon asked. "I dread this so-called full-disclosure meeting."

Finding her words again, Sunny said, "I don't envy you your task, and my heart breaks for Mike. Learning he's at risk for Huntington's will be a terrible blow. He's barely eighteen, for Pete's sake. He has a right to expect a full life, not an amputated one."

Langdon stopped pacing to face Sunny. "Even if Mike emerges emotionally intact from the shock of learning he's at risk for Huntington's, he'll have another challenge to face. He'll have to decide between *living at risk* for HD, a constant unknown, or finding out, beyond any doubt, that he will or will not get the disease."

For most of the week, Langdon had imagined himself eighteen again and facing Mike's life-altering decision. *What would I do if I knew I was at risk for HD?* When Langdon considered the options, knowing or not knowing, he concluded he would want to find out the truth, good or bad.

Sunny interrupted his train of thought. "Sit down, Langdon," she demanded, patting the cushion on the chair next to hers. "Your heart still needs a bit of looking after."

Langdon followed her direction. "Can't keep my thoughts straight, Sunny—too much to consider. Let's say Mike chooses the truth, and he tests positive for HD. How will he face the future? Will he make plans and get on with living if he knows Huntington's could strike at any time?"

Sunny cocked her head at him. "Isn't living day-to-day in the at-risk state—not knowing the truth and constantly wondering what the future holds—more or less the same thing?" she asked.

"I suppose." Langdon sighed. "The goblin would be ever-present. I guess some people would prefer to live in suspense than face the monster."

Sunny shifted in her seat and glanced over at Langdon. "I wonder what Mike's decision will be," she said.

"No one in his right mind would want to make the choice we're asking of Mike," Langdon said. "You know, I've thought about Mike's alternatives for days. If I were an eighteen-year-boy, I would want to know, and I would get the blood test done."

"That's you, Langdon. Mike might not feel the same way," Sunny said. "There are also practical matters he'll have to consider when he makes his decision. For example, if Mike elects to have the test performed and it's positive for Huntington's, will he continue his education and build his life with enthusiasm? Will he shy away from falling in love? There are also financial considerations."

"Well, Mike doesn't have to worry about money. If he's positive for HD and his health insurers refuse to cover him, I will."

"That's good of you, Langdon, except Mike and Ray may find your offer hard to accept. What about future employers? If Mike knows for sure he'll succumb to Huntington's, must he alert prospective employers? If his health care company covers him, will his information be kept private? And who knows if a health care company will even cover him with HD as a preexisting condition. He's on Ray's policy now, but soon he will have to apply for his own insurance. Maybe he should wait until he is insured to have the test. Can an insurance company demand the test before deciding to insure him? The ramifications on both sides of the issue are limitless," Sunny said with a sigh.

After Sunny's departure, Langdon was left alone with his thoughts. He continued to stew over how Mike would react at the full-disclosure meeting. As far as Langdon could tell, the proper safeguards were in place. As promised, the neurologist contacted the HD counselor, John Forbes, a veteran in the management of HD cases. In turn, Forbes sent information on the process of counseling HD individuals to him, Ray, Cathy. After allowing them time to digest the material, Forbes called them together to discuss the salient points of a full-disclosure meeting, the first meeting with an individual at risk for HD.

During the session, Ray asked, "Do you think Mike will feel waylaid or embarrassed when so many of us show up for the meeting?"

"He might feel set up at first," Forbes replied. "It's a common reaction I'm prepared to diffuse. His initial self-consciousness or wariness will dissipate when I tell him the neurologist is there to answer his questions and the rest of you to provide support. No matter Mike's reaction," Forbes advised, "be careful not to express your own surprise or fear."

"Then what reaction should we expect from Mike?" Cathy asked.

"If I knew Mike," Forbes said, "it would be easier to predict his reaction than going in cold, but there isn't a typical pattern of behavior. Mike might say little at the first meeting. As you can imagine, coming to grips with the possibility of having an incurable disease takes time."

"And when reality sinks in?" Langdon prompted.

"When reality sinks in, Mike will want to broaden his knowledge of Huntington's," Forbes said. "We'll guide him as he learns about it, and when he's ready, he'll decide if he wants to be tested. Our first meeting will touch on the highlights. The number and pace of the follow-up sessions are up to Mike."

"Is there a cut-off on the number of sessions?" Ray asked.

"Our sessions are tailored to meet the unique needs of each client. We have a general timeline in mind, of course, however, we provide each person with the latitude he or she requires," Forbes explained. "We offer guidance on an as-needed basis, and if issues arise between sessions, Mike or you should contact the center and come see us."

Impressed by Forbes's knowledge, earnestness, and candor, Langdon told himself Mike was in good hands. Still, Langdon would sooner cut off his arm than have Mike go through the trauma of a first-disclosure meeting. All the safeguards in the world would not keep the boy from being shocked and scared.

When Langdon considered he might repeat with Mike what he had been through with Ava, his pulse throbbed in his temples. He could not conceive of losing the son he had just found to that ungodly disease. Overwhelmed by the possibility, Langdon groped for the nearest chair. *Damn Huntington's it's a never-ending nightmare.*

Chapter 39 – The Velez Home, Naples, Florida

As Cathy was fond of saying, even perfect weather can be boring. Very true, Ray thought, as he listened to the heavy rain pinging off the metal roof of their Key-West-style home in Old Naples. Although it was not one of those perfect days, it was an ideal one for lingering over a morning cup of coffee on the screened porch, sharing the paper with Cathy, and watching the May storm blow through.

Ray appreciated an occasional storm. The gurgling of rain-filled gutters, the splat-splattering of drops meeting the pavement, the sound of water dripping from thirst-quenched vegetation, and the drumming of thunder in the distance created a symphony as good or better as any offered at The Phil, the preeminent venue for the arts in Naples.

Several weeks had dragged by since the Huntington's bomb exploded in Mike's face. Ray and Cathy, concerned about their son's emotional state, watched Mike for signs of depression: sleeplessness, lethargy, withdrawal from activities, and risk-taking behaviors. Mike exhibited none of the symptoms Forbes mentioned. *So far, so good*, Ray sighed. *The kid deserves a break.*

In Ray's opinion, Mike was functioning better than those who loved him; at least he appeared to be. Except for being quieter than usual, Mike's behavior was much the same.

His grades were excellent, he was coaching the boys' soccer team on weekends as usual, and he practiced with his band on a regular basis. Mike talked about graduation—most notably the all-night party afterward—and said he was looking forward to having an entire summer free to coach his soccer team and sharpen his beach volleyball skills at Lowdermilk Park.

Ray's anxiety was at an all-time high. Even though Mike seemed fine, Ray thought it odd that Mike had not uttered a word about Huntington's. Ray wondered if his son was exhibiting false bravado or experiencing denial.

Ray took his concern to Forbes who said, "Mike is meeting the challenge of Huntington's head-on." Ray nodded his head, humbled by his son's courage.

Ray and Cathy went with Mike to his first few counseling sessions. Each time they left after fifteen minutes to wait in the outer office where they armed themselves with informational brochures on Huntington's. Although they had lived through Ava's illness with Langdon, they were unfamiliar with some of the newer advances. As difficult as it was for them to accept what was happening to their son, they could only imagine what was on Mike's mind.

Throughout the sessions at the center, a thorough neurological exam, a battery of psychological tests, and a meeting with a geneticist, Mike had not raised the subject of Huntington's to the family. Ray and Cathy had no inkling of how he felt about his frightful new burden. They were steadfast in holding to Forbes's advice not to bring up the subject themselves, but it was as hard as ignoring a snake with two heads.

"Mike needs time to think, unimpeded by the well-meaning advice or opinions of others," Forbes said. "He has a great deal to process."

An understatement, Ray thought. Coaxed from his musings by Cathy who had asked him a question, he looked up at her from his chair and said, "I'm sorry, honey, what did you say?"

"I asked if you wanted another cup of coffee." She smiled and reached out for his cup.

"Sure would, thanks. Coffee's especially good, must be the rain." He handed Cathy his empty cup, and as she walked across the room, he looked after her thinking how lucky he was to have her support and love. They had their troubles like most couples, but none as bad as the curveballs thrown at them the last few months: the rape, finding out Langdon was Mike's biological father, Langdon's collapse, and the possibility of Huntington's. Through all the upheavals and disruptions, Cathy kept him from being a raving lunatic.

While he waited for Cathy to return with his second cup of coffee, Ray ambled across the house to Mike's bedroom. When he peered around the open door, Mike was on the phone. Not wanting to interrupt, Ray waved an acknowledgment and returned to the porch.

A few minutes later Mike found his parents on the porch, engrossed in their papers. "Hey, Dad," he said, "did you want me for something?"

"No, son, just wanted to say good morning."

"Well, good morning to you, too, Dad, and Mom." His tone was cheerful.

Ray thought Mike more animated than usual. Suppressing the urge to ask why, Ray said, "Son, don't you have an appointment around noon with Forbes at the center?"

"Yeah, Dad, it's at eleven."

Following Forbes's instructions to encourage Mike to take someone along to each session for moral support, Ray asked, "Want one or both of us to go with you?"

"No thanks, Dad, Natalie's going with me."

Cathy's paper came crashing down from in front of her face.

"Natalie?" Astonishment raised her eyebrows.

"Isn't that a little weird for a first date?" Ray asked. The reason for his son's uncharacteristic animation was clear.

"I guess it is, Dad, but Mrs. Garcia is worried about Natalie because she won't go out with her friends anymore. I thought if I took her to the center and she learned about Huntington's—you know, how people with HD don't have long lives and stuff—maybe she'd appreciate hers more and get back to living it. She sees a rapist around every corner. Locking herself in the house is a big waste."

Touched by his son's sensitivity, Ray stood, stuck out his hand, and shook Mike's. Tongue-tied with admiration and impressed by his son's ability to focus on someone else's problems when he had plenty of his own, Ray managed to say,

"Good for you, son." And then it dawned on him: Mike had mentioned HD for the first time. Ray gulped around the lump in his throat.

"Look at me, Mike," Cathy said.

Mike turned to face his mother.

"I am proud of you," she said. Her eyes moist, she stood to kiss her son's cheek. "The shame of rape isn't easy for any woman to bear. And you're right; Natalie's a beautiful and bright young lady who deserves to have the world at her feet. What happened to her wasn't her fault, and yet she's unconsciously punishing herself by withdrawing from the things she loves to do. She's lucky to have you as a friend."

Mike fell silent. His face turned red. After a long pause, he raised his downcast eyes. "So, Dad, may I borrow the car?"

Ray nodded. "Some things never change." He and Cathy looked at each other and laughed.

When Mike returned home from his unusual date at the center, Ray and Cathy were preparing dinner. The storm had dissolved as quickly as it appeared, and the sun, refusing to take a day off, was back in the sky. Cathy pulled apart lettuce leaves for a salad, and since it was a lovely evening for grilling outside, Ray worked off an excess of anxiety by slamming burgers together. Cathy's posture appeared stiff to him. He guessed she was also tense and thinking about what he was: When would Mike share his thoughts about HD with them?

When Mike wandered into the kitchen looking for a drink of water, Ray, wondering how the session at the center had gone, scanned his son's serious-looking face for clues. It was unreadable. Ray was poised to start the conversation by asking how the car was running, when Mike usurped the moment.

"Mom, Dad, do you have time to talk?" He plucked a carrot from the salad bowl and popped it into his mouth.

"Sure, son, the burgers aren't going anywhere." Ray, his nerves stretched to fraying, glanced at Cathy for reassurance.

"Why don't we sit down?" Cathy said. She dried her hands on a towel and moved toward the kitchen table. "I need to get off my feet for a minute anyway."

His face a mask of neutrality, Ray felt his heart freeze, even as his stomach felt on fire. He followed Cathy to the table. Weeks of suppressed emotions galloped through his mind. He struggled to corral them, sank into a chair, and folded his hands together on the tabletop. He was afraid to hear what Mike might say. In that moment of weakness, Ray examined his manhood. Would he be strong enough to bear the worst, a son who might have Huntington's disease in the future? Overwhelmed, he stared at the tabletop, not daring to look at his wife or son, not wanting them to see the terror coursing through his body.

Mike turned his chair around backward and straddled it to face his parents. "Well, Parentals," he began, using the nickname he had given them some years back, "I've made a decision. Before I tell you what it is, I have a few things to run by you first, to be sure I understand everything. Okay?"

Ray and Cathy nodded in unison.

Ray felt the room close in; something had sucked all the oxygen from it. He looked around, saw the open doors to the terrace, and realized he was holding his breath. Exhaling, he drew in a deep breath and waited for Mike to begin. Ray noticed Cathy biting her lower lip, a sign of edginess. For his comfort and hers, Ray wanted to put his arm around her. He settled instead for holding her hand under the table. He did not want to give Mike the impression he was causing his mother distress. The suspense was suffocating.

Mike cupped his chin in his hands and leaned toward them. "Here's what I know," he began. "Huntington's is an autosomal dominant disease passed from parent to child by a gene with a mutated allele. Each person who receives an HD gene has two copies, but only people with an allele mutated at the end will inherit Huntington's. Am I right?"

"Yes, son," Ray responded, "and it's important to remember HD symptoms manifest themselves in different people at varying ages. There have been reports of people living as long as seventy years before experiencing symptoms," he added. He knew such cases were rare; he wanted to offer his son a shred of hope.

"Yeah, Dad, I know. Some researchers think the number of CAG repeats—I can't remember what CAG stands for—on the mutated allele has something to do with the age and severity of symptom manifestation. I don't know enough about it yet, except I do know the number of CAG repeats determines whether or not a person will develop Huntington's."

"True," Ray said. He was unable to find a bright side to Mike's gloomy accuracy.

"I also know there's a fifty-fifty chance of passing along the HD gene with the mutated allele to each child I have. Forbes told me scientists are working on a prenatal test to determine if an unborn child has the HD allele."

Cathy interrupted. "Yes, Mike, like other prenatal tests, the HD one will most likely be performed by amniocentesis while the fetus is in the uterus. An amniocentesis has significant emotional and physiological implications. Experts insist on parental counseling before going forward with the test. The emotional issues—"

Ray shot Cathy a look meant to remind her not to influence Mike's decision. "I think Mike wants to tell us what he knows about Huntington's, honey. Let's let him finish."

"Right, I'm sorry. The nurse in me got carried away. Go ahead, Mike," Cathy said in a soft voice.

Sidetracked for the moment, Mike said, "Uh, yeah, thanks. Anyway, when I was with Natalie at the center, a simple realization made it easy for me to decide about taking the test. Here's the way I look at it. First, people die every day from accidents, illnesses, murder, suicide, and most of us take living for granted. We rarely stop to think about what we have or remember to say thank you. Some people even see life as a burden. Natalie showed me living with the bogeyman lurking around the corner is not the way to go. Crippled by fear, she's giving up her life and wasting emotional energy on something that will probably never happen to her again. Not knowing if I will get Huntington's won't work for me. I'd be like Natalie—always living in fear—unless I find out what to expect. I've decided to have the blood test." He sat back and looked at his parents.

Ray and Cathy exchanged glances. Neither spoke.

Breathing hard, Ray swallowed, straightened his shoulders, and said, "You know we support any decision you make, son." His comment sounded bland after Mike's courageous remarks.

A long, tortuous pause followed. Ray and Cathy waited in silence as Mike gathered his thoughts.

"Moving on to my second point," Mike said, "the blood test will determine if I have the HD mutated allele. We aren't worried about a negative result; it's the positive one we don't want. I've also thought about that."

Ray and Cathy moved to the edge of their seats.

Ray, unprepared for life as he knew it to end, feared for his son. Mike had his full attention.

"The way I look at it," Mike said, "a positive result will be bad news. At least I'll know to expect a shortened life. If it turns out that way, I'll have to live the days I have as best I can. You know, make them count, say thanks more often, stop and smell the roses, and all. I bet I can squeeze more top-notch days into the time I have left, say twenty years or more, than most people do in a lifetime."

Cathy brushed away a tear. "When will you get the test done?"

"I've scheduled it for this Thursday after school."

"Are you sure, Mike?" Ray asked.

"I am, Dad."

Ray felt more pride than he believed possible. He stood, walked around the table, and pulled Mike out of his chair, wanting to look at him eyeball-to-eyeball. "Son, I am in awe of your courage. You have more guts than anyone I have ever known. Your mom and I will be with you through the entire process and afterward, for as long as you need us. We love you, son." He gave Mike the biggest bear hug of his life.

Mike grinned. The smile started on his lips and spread to his eyes. Flushing, he looked away from the pride-filled faces of his parents. "Thanks, Dad," he mumbled, and as he turned to leave the room, he said over his shoulder, "Hey, Dad, before I fall out of your good graces, may I take the car to school on Monday and to the clinic afterward?"

Cathy laughed despite her tears. Relief flooded her heart.

Ray, stunned by Mike's unruffled countenance in the midst of his untenable situation, consented with a bob of his head. *Thank God for predictability.*

Chapter 40 – Pelican View, Naples, Florida

Langdon finished his coffee and the morning paper in the breakfast room as Rosa cleaned the stove in the kitchen.

"I'm expecting Sunny this morning, Rosa," he announced. "When she arrives, I'll be on the lanai under the portico." Rosa's new hearing aid meant he no longer had to answer the door himself, the justification he used to convince her to let him pay for her appliance. The best part was he could speak to her without having to shout or repeat himself, and Rosa smiled each time she heard the doorbell as if the sound came from heaven itself. He wished Mike's situation were as simple to resolve.

Thinking the day promised to be warm, Langdon arranged two chairs and a table under a shady, vine-covered portico and turned his mind to Mike. As he had each hour of each day for the previous several weeks, he imagined himself an eighteen-year-old boy facing the same decisions as Mike.

Would Mike choose to live in the at-risk state or have the blood test? Given his limited life experiences, Langdon feared Mike's choice might be unwise. Although there was no right or wrong decision, Langdon was concerned Mike's selection in the present might be an incorrect choice for his future.

Langdon spent most of his waking hours agonizing over Mike's reaction to a positive result. Would he go off the deep end? Would it be better for Mike to have a few more years of maturity under his belt before making the life-and-death decision to be tested? After combing through Mike's alternatives, Langdon found it impossible to select the best course of action, not that it mattered one iota what he thought. The decision was Mike's. Langdon could do nothing, except keep his nerves under control and wait.

"A penny for your thoughts," Sunny said with a grin as she rounded the corner of the lanai accompanied by Rosa. "You look like The Thinker, with your elbow on your knee and your forehead resting on your fist. What's up?"

"Just thinking about Mike." He stood to greet her.

"Hard not to, isn't it?"

"You bet. I can't focus on anything else. I hope you don't mind helping me with the annual kickoff dinner for the board of the HD Foundation."

"We'll have it done in no time. This stuff's my forte, as you know." She grinned, her small eyes crinkling into the edges of her crow's feet.

Langdon and Sunny worked at a steady pace for an hour. Langdon suggested a break, and Rosa appeared with a pitcher of frosty lemonade, two glasses, and an assortment of pastries on a tray.

Sunny selected an éclair. "Has Mike decided whether or not to have the blood test?"

"No, we're waiting for him to complete his counseling, and then he'll decide." Langdon sighed. "Oh, Sunny, I blame myself for all this misery. Poor Mike is facing the biggest challenge of his life, thanks to Ava's deceit, and between the guilt I feel for the part I played and my fear for him, I sometimes wonder if it's worth getting up in the morning."

"Why do you feel responsible, Langdon?"

"Because I made a wonderful baby who grew up to be a great young man with the worst possible curse hanging over his head. How could Ava not tell me? Why didn't she trust me?"

Sunny pleated her napkin between her fingers. "Listen, Langdon, the simple truth is none of what has happened is your fault. In Ava's defense, I think she feared her baby would also have Huntington's. Remember, the gene—or the mutated allele on the HD gene, whatever you want to call it—wasn't known to be the cause of HD when she was alive. She based her choices on a tragic family legacy, her grandfather, her mother, and herself: all victims of HD. And don't forget Miguel. Ava saw him in the advanced throes of the disease. To see him that way had to be terrifying for her. She didn't want to put you through the heartache of caring for her or her baby, especially if it developed HD."

Langdon poured himself another glass of lemonade before responding. "Maybe, but she must have known there was a possibility the child could be HD-free."

Sunny nodded her agreement. "Yes, and I think it was one of the reasons she went through with the pregnancy and arranged the adoption.

Ava was also a good Catholic daughter. Abortion was out of the question. She wouldn't have terminated the pregnancy even if the baby had HD. And you know the importance Ava placed on two parents and a 'real home,' as they referred to it at the orphanage."

"That's true," Langdon concurred. He put his head in his hands.

"Ava couldn't care for her baby," Sunny continued, "and she wanted her child to have an all-American family. Adoption was a step in the right direction."

"I could have managed with the baby. I'm not helpless when it comes to children, you know," Langdon asserted.

"I believe you, Langdon, but if Ava had kept the baby, she would have wanted to care for it. Can you imagine anything sadder than a child watching its mother die a long, slow death for the first ten or twenty years of its life? Ava didn't want that for her child."

"I'll guess we'll never know precisely what she was thinking, will we?"

"No, Langdon, we never will."

"I'm very grateful you rescued her," Langdon said. "Thank God for your snooping, or should I say sleuthing?" He managed a wink. "Ava and I had three or four good years together before her disabilities became severe. Without you, we would have missed out on those precious years.

"And she had time to see the HD Foundation started," Sunny reminded him. "I find it ironic Mike is benefiting from the center's services."

Langdon nodded. "Yes, the foundation gave Ava a reason to struggle on. Her contribution— showing up for fundraisers—furthered the public's awareness of HD. A picture is worth a thousand words, as they say."

"Langdon," Sunny said, "I don't mean to be rude, but I'm going to be blunt. You must stop rehashing the past. We have discussed this issue a million times. There is nothing new to be learned," she said firmly and with a hint of impatience.

"I know, Sunny," Langdon said, "and I apologize for dragging you back to the past with me. I'm such a bore," he said and sighed. "I'll try to do better, really."

The old friends lapsed into silence, each wrapped up in his own thoughts. When Mike stepped out on the lanai, neither Langdon nor Ava noticed him.

"My wife had guts," Langdon said. "She ... oh!" he shouted, leaping to his feet and startling Sunny who came close to falling out of her seat.

"Sunny, I know what Ava was trying to say at the end," he exclaimed. His face was full of excitement. "Do you know the board game called Whatsit? I heard it advertised on TV, and I got to thinking. The object of the game is to guess phrases from syllables. Last night I went to bed repeating Ava's phrase, *fein ah abie*. Just now, Sunny, at this very moment, I know what she was saying: Find our baby! She *did* want me to know, Sunny. Even at the end, she didn't forget our baby."

"And isn't it miraculous, you found him!" Sunny sniffed. "Now Ava can rest in peace, and you no longer have to torment yourself."

In an instant, Langdon's expression turned grave. "I will be tormented forever if Mike has HD, but it's a load off my mind to understand Ava's message. To know she cared about our baby and didn't want to shut me out is comforting."

Langdon's elation dissipated as quickly as it had surfaced, pushed aside by the perpetual sadness with which he lived.

Sunny's eagle eye noticed his mood shift and no longer able to restrain herself, locked her piercing stare on Langdon's face. "Langdon," she said, "I want you to listen to me. I have something I've wanted to say to you for a long time. You've been depressed for eighteen years. Enough is enough. Permit yourself to get on with living, and I mean truly living, not simply going through the motions. Get a shrink if need be. I want the old Langdon back."

"If Mike's HD test is negative, I will be the happiest man in the world, with everything to live for," Langdon said. "You'll grow tired of seeing me smile. I can't believe I have a son, and what a great kid he is, even though I can't take any credit for the way he's turned out. I'm afraid to close my eyes, sometimes, for fear I will wake up and find I was dreaming." He wrung his hands.

At that moment, Mike stepped from behind the column and made himself known. "Okay, Dad Number Two, I heard that, and I'll hold you to it. You can start living right away. The test was negative. By the way, do you think you could make room for me on the board of the foundation? I may even be overqualified, having learned my HD lessons the hard way. Like father like son, as they say." With an ear-to-ear-grin, Mike looked at Langdon and Sunny. "No more doom and gloom," he said, making a victory sign with his hands.

Mike's unexpected announcement of the negative test results rendered Langdon speechless. Having no words, he used his rarely seen smile— buried most of his adult life by Ava's suffering—to communicate his feelings. His reawakened smile arose from deep within and spread tentatively—as if traveling an unfamiliar path—from the corners of his mouth upward to his eyes until his entire face radiated pure joy.

As Langdon smiled at his son, Isabella's extreme sacrifice and Ava's heartfelt wish to have her child reared by a real family came to his mind. His gratitude for each woman's determination and courage was unbounded. Without their bravery, he would not be standing in front of the magnificent young man who filled his heart to overflowing, especially when his child called him Dad Number Two.

Discussion Questions

1. If you were an orphan, would you want to know why your parents gave you away? Would you want to know who your parents are?

2. If you were adopted as an infant and years later, you could obtain the social and medical histories of your biological parents, would you want them?

3. Did Ava make the right choice by hiding her pregnancy and HD from her husband? What would you do in her shoes?

4. Do you think Ava had an obligation to tell Langdon she was pregnant?

5. Which is most important, the best interests of parents or the best interest of a child.

6. Do you think Ava should have put her child up for adoption knowing there was a fifty percent chance it could develop HD later in life?

7. Do you think Ava's decision to end her life was selfish or unselfish?

8. Did Sunny do the right thing by keeping Ava's pregnancy from Langdon?

9. When did you realize who Mike's biological father was? What tipped you off?

10. If you were *at risk* for HD, would you want to know if you would or would not get HD or would you prefer to live in the at-risk state?

11. What are the ethical issues HD individuals face if they want to have their own biological children?
12. How can the further transmission of HD be prevented?
13. How do you feel about legislation that would require individuals who are living at-risk for HD to take the direct gene test? Would such legislation be discriminatory?
14. Should an incurable hereditary disease be diagnosed before symptoms appear? Is there an ethical justification for informing a person he or she will later develop a lethal disease for which no therapy is available?
15. Does HD present a clash between individual rights and the rights of society as a whole?

For more information about HD visit:
www.pbrunn-perkins.com or
www.Twisting Legacy.com

About The Author

Patricia Brunn-Perkins received an A.A. from Stephens College in Columbia, MO, and a B.S., R.N. from Cornell University-New York Hospital School of Nursing. At Central CT State University, she completed the coursework for an M.A. in Community Psychology. Employed in the past as a nurse, a Realtor, and an employment counselor for individuals with chronic mental illnesses, she is a freelance writer who contributes articles to magazines, designs and writes newsletters, and creates content for websites. The mother of three daughters, she lives between Naples, FL, and Southington, CT, with her dog, Daisy.

CPSIA information can be obtained
at www.ICGtesting.com
Printed in the USA
BVHW071925180419
545907BV00001B/18/P